Paul

The

TRUST

COMPANY

ISBN: 0984817409
ISBN 13: 9780984817405

Library of Congress Control Number: 2011943155
CreateSpace, North Charleston, SC

*To Michael Kramer: living proof that
great teachers can change students' lives.*

Acknowledgements

I'd like to thank the many friends and family who assisted in this effort by reading various drafts of the manuscript, offering advice on characterization, plot details, and serious editing. Particular thanks to Nick Altieri, Demetri Andrikos, and Audra Lalley for detailed editing of the manuscript. Thanks also to Todd and Julie McBride, Michael and Melissa Friedl, Marcina Kreta, Kevin Segrell, Karin Zolnick, Wendy Rianda, and my wife, Valerie Stam, for their thoughts on plot and character, as well as support. Thanks to my former law partner Paul McBride (whose life experience somewhat reflects the background of the main character, Nick Sanders) for details on the U.S. Marines. Many thanks to Maria Murnane, who provided guidance to a new author. Finally, the publication of this novel would not have been possible without the hard work of my publicist, Janine Schunk, who spent many hours researching the Byzantine and (unfortunately) depressing world that is the current state of publishing. I hope readers enjoy this novel, but to the extent they find errors or are disappointed, the blame lies with me alone and none of the above or others who offered their time, review, suggestions, and support.

Prologue

Zambezi River, Border of Zimbabwe and Zambia; May 2005.

Marcus Vanderhoff gazed over the edge of the platform that sprouted from the middle of the bridge spanning the Zambezi River. His toes, crossed by the straps of his Teva sandals, stuck out slightly into the abyss. He had accessed the bridge from the Zambian side. A friendly American he had met in the hotel bar the night before told him more tourists used to enter from the Zimbabwean side, but given that country's economic and political turmoil, most people came in from Zambia now. The man had even given Marcus his prepaid coupon for a bungee jump, as, the man had explained, he was quite squeamish about heights, and the jump came with his tour package. Someone braver might as well use it, he said. For $50 U.S., which was a relative bargain, those who had to pay could bungee jump from the bridge. Then again, all of Africa was a relative bargain to Americans, and most of the world was a relative bargain to a young man like Marcus.

Marcus Vanderhoff had been, back in the day, a nerd, a geek, a science guy, whatever you want to call him. He held a PhD in electrical engineering from MIT, which he received in 1995 at age twenty-six. Timing being everything, Marcus came out of MIT just before the dot-com boom. He and a colleague began a start-up with minimal capital, but that was no worry. Back then his name was Mark. That's what his parents and friends all called him. But "Mark" didn't sound sophisticated enough when trying to raise venture capital. So he changed it to Marcus. The service they provided—better, faster, more stable credit card payments through Internet servers—was a tool every online company needed at the time. By 1997 their company, which had begun with just themselves and two temporary employees, had burgeoned to 150 employees (all with stock options, of course) and gone through three venture capital funding rounds. In 1998, the company went public, and despite all the options and funding rounds and resultant dilution of their ownership, Marcus and his partner were rich. Three years out of graduate school.

This wasn't just any rich. It was *really* rich. The kind of rich that even if you lost 90 percent of your wealth, you still wouldn't have to work for the rest of your life. Marcus's position was further reinforced when their now-public company was acquired by another public technology company that was diversified and stable. When the Internet bubble burst, Marcus was already retired (six years out of school), traveling around the world and leaving his money and investments spread among several money managers, including Goldman Sachs, Morgan Stanley, Credit Suisse, and American Standard Bank & Trust (ASBT). His portfolio went up and down, but he would never go broke. His private banker at ASBT prepared monthly consolidated reports for him, which the banker dutifully e-mailed to an account Marcus accessed from whatever hotel room or Internet café happened to be convenient. Most of the time, Marcus simply logged on to confirm he was still rich, then signed off. He was too busy to worry about the details of how his money was being managed. There was little else to do except start another company (if he one day developed the desire again), or travel about the world seeking various thrills.

Marcus noticed the moment he became wealthy, it was easy to find women. In fact, they seemed to find him. He thought at first that he was going to have to do quite a bit of work. Eye surgery allowed him to ditch his glasses. He cut his shaggy hair and started working out with a personal trainer. But even before he began doing so, he was finding it much easier to get dates, as the expensive gyms, hotels, restaurants, and bars he started to frequent hinted at his newfound wealth. He was careful not to get too entangled in relationships. He had married once and that didn't go well. He discovered soon after he and his ex were married, she really wasn't that interested in traveling the world with him and sharing his experiences. She seemed content to stay at their mansion in Atherton and spend his money in various imaginative ways. Two years later that was over, and he promised himself it would never happen again. Thank God he had listened to his private banker and gotten a prenup.

Daily life wasn't difficult. It never was on his budget. New countries, new thrills. Sailing on the French Riviera. Parasailing in the Caribbean. Rock climbing in India. Trekking in Nepal. Snowmobiling. Skydiving. Scuba diving. Eating exotic foods everywhere he went (yesterday's appetizer was Mopawni worms). If he liked a place, he'd stay a while until he got bored, learning in the process a bit of the culture and a bit of the language.

Which is why, fourteen years out of graduate school, six years into his world travels, numerous ex-girlfriends and one ex-wife later, Marcus found himself gazing into the abyss below his feet. He could see the white water below him, but from this distance it appeared only as a dark blue and white ribbon meandering between the cleft of rocks that marched away from the bridge. He could hear the roar of Victoria Falls behind him to his right, and even from this distance felt a bit of the overspray carried on the wind. His ankles were firmly secured in a harness connected to the bungee cord—really just a very thick rope made of several cords intertwined together and wrapped in a stretchy sleeve. The cord was attached to the platform's superstructure via a large steel eye at the end of the bungee, which in turn hooked into an industrial-sized carabiner on the platform. He had used less professional, more wariness-inducing bungee setups in the States and had survived.

So, when he dove off the platform, Marcus had no reason for concern. In fact, he had bungee jumped so many times that he practiced different dive techniques. No screaming, no having to be pushed. Today, he did a simple swan dive, intending to throw in a couple of forward flips when the cord's inevitable resistance yanked his body back up.

As he dove out, Marcus could see the canyon of the Zambezi stretching out before him. Then his gaze dropped down and the river rushed up at him, getting bigger and bigger like the view from a telephoto lens. It was a long fall, but then he felt the familiar tug on his ankles and then ... nothing. His forward motion slowed slightly but didn't stop, and he began falling again as if untethered. His first instinct was to look up, but that was physically impossible to do. Statistically, when someone is in the position of knowing they are about to die, "damn" is the most common word uttered. The second most common is "shit." Marcus had no time for any of that. There was a moment of pure terror in which his brain could process no thought other than "oh no." His arms instinctively, but uselessly, crossed in front of his face as he smashed into the river and rocks below.

Back on the platform, the attendants couldn't believe what had happened. The carabiner had simply broken away from the platform. There was nothing to be done. All above had heard a loud *clunk*, followed by nothing. The bungee disappeared from view. Everyone, tourists and attendants alike, continued to gaze over the edge of the bridge, even though there was nothing to see at that distance. One man, however, had watched the bungee break away and glanced over now to ensure Marcus had not sprouted wings or that some other miracle had not saved him. Assured, he walked off the bridge to the Zambian side and back to the hotel where he had met Marcus the night before.

There would be an investigation (by Zambian authorities, since the tourist had come from the Zambian side of the bridge). It would be concluded that a stress fracture had developed in the overused carabiner, and the device should have been replaced months earlier. The tour operator, a Mr. Morgan, insisted that he replaced it monthly, and he pursued the Chinese manufacturer of the device to no end. Morgan paid a fine to the Zambian authorizes, which was nothing compared to the bribes he had to pay to the tourism commissioner and his lieutenants. Two weeks after the incident, he was back in business. It had been the only death in the history of the attraction.

Chapter 1

Jaco, Costa Rica; March 2008.

Most shit is really simple. People try to make it complicated. They develop complex reasons, usually involving childhood experiences, as to why they made poor life choices. Or better said, why they were preprogrammed to make those bad decisions. Can't quit smoking? "Genetically addicted" to alcohol, food, sex? Mom and Dad were functioning alcoholics and passed on that gene to you? Verbally abused as a child? Lost your virginity to the first boy or girl who said they loved you and were lying and now can't have a fulfilling relationship?

Shut it. You're basically lazy and lack willpower. I'm not crying any tears for you, because the answer is simple: stop. Can't lose that weight? Exercise more, eat less. Can't lay off the sauce? Drink soda water. Simple answers. People just don't want to hear them, preferring to blame their problems on a troubled childhood or growing up poor or genetics. All excuses. The answer is simple. It's the work to implement the answer that's hard.

That same penchant for making the simple complex applies to most criminals, and their enablers. The U.S. justice system is designed to assist defendants in coming up with elaborate excuses as to why they did what they did. A con man who steals retirement money from little old ladies can wax poetic about how he wasn't doing anything wrong, how his Ponzi scheme wasn't really a Ponzi scheme, despite the complete lack of any realistic investment returning the 15 percent he promised his investors. He could tell you how he really intended the best, and that he was going to make good and pay back every last dime. From prison. At thirty cents an hour. And the funny thing is, sometimes he believes it, or makes himself believe it. But his motivations ultimately are not complex. It's always about the money.

Ponzi schemes work because Wall Street operates on a simple principle: trust. You trust the bank to be there in the morning. You trust your broker not to abscond with your wealth. You trust your money manager to give you sound advice. Ponzi schemers play on this implicit trust. They are charismatic confidence men in the original meaning of the term.

Now, I could have been mulling all of this over that particular afternoon in Jaco, but my mind was turned to more important matters. I was trying to synchronize the gentle sway of the hammock I was in with the placement of my Imperial Cerveza so that as I put it on the patio beneath me, it wouldn't continue its motion and fall over. This is a more difficult maneuver than you would think. You have to time it so that you place the end of the bottle flat on the concrete at the very apex of the swing, and remove your hand from the neck before you start swinging back the other way. I had succeeded in doing this many times over many beers over many afternoons at this particular motel, but every attempt seemed new and different; in fact, I had spilled several Imperials over the past few days. It could be that I'm not very coordinated, or it could just be that the more beer you drank, the harder this particular motor skill became. I'm going with the latter. It's the simple explanation, and the simple explanation is usually the correct one.

I was halfway through a spy novel when I heard footsteps coming up behind me. By the sound of the footfalls, there were two of them. Man in dress shoes with worn leather soles, a woman in flats. Side by side, the woman's steps were quicker to keep up with the wider gait of the tall man. Picturing the shoes, I figured the guy was likely wearing a suit in accompaniment, which would make him look extremely out of place not only at this motel but in all of Jaco, a small surfing paradise on the western coast of Costa Rica. I also knew from the sounds of his stride that the man was African American and fifty-six years old. So, two people: one African American man, one woman of unknown ethnicity; man wearing a suit, woman in flats; guy likely carrying seventeen dollars and forty-five cents. I just made that last part up.

I craned my neck up to the left and looked over my shoulder. I knew who the man was before I saw him because I recognized the sound of his walk, having worked with him for years. He was indeed wearing a completely out-of-place suit—Brooks Brothers. I had never seen the woman before.

"Hola, Jimmy. *Cómo está?*" I said to my old boss.

"Sanders." JJ hated to be called Jimmy, but he took it in stride.

I looked at the woman. Early thirties, nice figure, athletic. Light brown, nearly blond hair pulled back in a neat ponytail to create a professional look. Jeans, blouse with a T-shirt underneath. What is it with these government types and dressing inappropriately for the setting? I was wearing board shorts and a tank top. My flip-flops and ball cap were under the hammock. I had four days of beard going.

The woman carried a backpack, the kind you see students draping over one shoulder on their way to school. Better than a briefcase, I guess. I tried to appear calm, but the fact was, no one was supposed to know I was there. I was trying to check out over burritos and beer in Central America while I nursed my injured shoulder back to health.

"Jesus, Sanders, with the money you make, you couldn't afford a nicer place?" JJ asked, looking around.

"I'm divorced, remember? I have alimony to pay."

"Lynn's remarried. No alimony."

"Heard about that, huh? What, you a lawyer now too?" The fact was that JJ, like many in the bureau, *was* a lawyer. "Can I offer you an Imperial? It's the national beer of Costa Rica, you know," I said to the woman.

"I figured. I don't see any other beer advertised," she answered. "But I'm on the job."

"Too bad. Maybe you could get off?"

JJ jumped in. "Sanders, we need to talk. We have a situation we'd like your opinion on."

"JJ, I don't mean to be a jerk, but I'm recovering from a gunshot wound. I'm on vacation, and I don't work for you anymore."

JJ looked around quickly. Feds get all jumpy when you say things like "gun" or "gunshot" in public. "Bomb" doesn't go over very well either.

"Not here," he said. "Let's go somewhere at least semi-private so we can talk."

Curiouser. He had my interest, at the very least. He had to have gotten on a plane with his new underling, flown into San Jose in the center of the country, then gotten out to the west coast and somehow located me in a hammock outside my room in the courtyard of a run-down (but serviceable) motel. This was costing the U.S. taxpayer a pretty penny. And all for little old me. And little old me wasn't really in a position to say no, and all three of us knew it. "You guys hungry? I know the perfect spot."

I got up, slipped on my flip-flops, put on my baseball cap, and lead them out of the motel courtyard down Jaco's only thoroughfare, beer in hand. About two blocks north, we crossed the street and went into a little open-air café on the beach side of the street. Since I had been there every day for two weeks, I knew the owner-cook-bartender very well. Gloria was married with four children, two of whom worked at the café. Her husband was in San Jose working a construction job.

"Hola, Señor Nick. Cerveza?" Same greeting every time since my first day. She knew me so well.

I held up my beer, now only about one-third full. "Sí, gracias," I said, "and dos Coke Lights for mi amigos. And some chips and salsa." Everyone speaks English down there, but you always want to throw in some Spanglish when you can, just to pretend you're trying. "Can we use the room in the back?"

"Sí, claro," she said. "I bring you your drinks and chips."

"Muchas gracias."

We passed the kitchen and went to the "room in the back," which was a bar area with no walls that opened onto the beach. This wasn't exactly the "private" JJ had in mind, but there was no one else in the bar that early in the afternoon in the off-season, and no one within earshot on the beach.

The very cool thing about Gloria's place was that when it filled up, you could stand in the sand at a long, narrow plank set at elbow height that marked the end of the building and have a smoke, drink your beer, and talk to a colorful array of students, workers, prostitutes, fishing-boat hands, boat captains, and men and women from the States just hanging out. Or hiding out, rather. Hiding out from the law. Hiding out from life. Almost everyone in the place was American. Except the prostitutes. And almost all of them were hiding out from something back home. Except the prostitutes.

"How's Engler doing?" I asked.

"Gonna make a full recovery. One in the vest, one in the leg. It broke a bone on the way in, but he should be back in about two more months."

A member of JJ's raid team, Chuck Engler, and I had both been shot a month ago in an airplane hangar at Westchester County Airport, where we had cornered a shitbag Ponzi schemer named Jonathan Huntington III. The "III" was completely made up to give Jon Huntington East Coast patrician street cred. Huntington had made the surveillance truck or been otherwise tipped off to the fact that the FBI's Financial Crimes Division was raiding his shop in Greenwich, Connecticut. He made a run for a private plane he had a fractional interest in, without telling his wife and young son, or even making arrangements for them. While JJ and another agent, Lisa Velasquez, stopped the plane before he had a chance to board it, Engler and I located Huntington and ran him down to a mechanic's hangar. Routine apprehension of a white-collar criminal, we thought. We were wrong. Unlike most such con men, Huntington carried a gun and wanted to use it. As we breached the hangar, Engler went down. I continued the chase into an interior work room. Huntington wildly emptied his weapon through the door, and as I kicked it open I took a slug in the shoulder. My gun clattered to the floor between us. Huntington leapt for it and I grabbed the only weapon I could find, a mechanic's wrench, and threw it at the top of the con man's head. He went down in a heap, and I went on injury leave.

"That's good."

"How's the shoulder?" he asked.

"My range of motion is almost all back, but the strength isn't there yet." I got lucky. The bullet lodged in muscle and didn't hit bone. I was exercising every morning. I saved the afternoons for beer and spy novels.

"You were lucky Huntington was using a .22 and couldn't aim for shit through a door."

"Yeah, that too. So, before we get into this 'situation,' tell me how you were so easily able to locate a guy paying cash everywhere he's been since San Jose?"

"We knew you arrived in San Jose. Pretty easy to track you on the bus system to this hole. So we took the bus here, which let us off at the first Jaco stop at the south end of town. Alex here wanted to take a cab, but I convinced her that you weren't going to spend the time or money to take a cab to the Marriot north of here. We just started walking up the street. Small town. I figured you were at one of the motels near the bus stop. You were at the second place we checked." Gloria arrived with the drinks, chips and salsa. After putting everything down, she turned and went back to the kitchen.

"You would have made a good field agent, JJ."

"I was a good field agent, fuckhead, until they put me in charge of your unit." He was kidding. Sort of.

"Since when are you working outside U.S. borders?"

"National security," the woman named Alex said. First thing she said since the motel.

I turned to the woman. "So, Alex, is it?" I offered my hand.

She shook it with a firm grip and two quick pumps, what my father would have called a businessman's shake. "Alexandra Conrad. Everyone just calls me Alex."

"Nick Sanders. Everyone calls me Nick, except JJ. He calls me fuckhead. Sometimes."

"That's not how he tells it."

"Don't make me blush. So," I said, turning to JJ, "national security still doesn't explain what two FBI agents are doing in Costa Rica."

"Alex is with," JJ responded, "another agency."

The "another agency" bull was obviously meant to convey CIA while maintaining some aura of mystery. Frankly, I didn't have time for that. I had some serious beer to drink.

"Guys," I said (Alex didn't seem offended), "I'm just a consultant. Mostly that means I have enough money to lie around and do the work I want to do, and not get shot again."

"I thought you were already a consultant when you got shot?" Alex asked. She had either gotten that information from JJ or my personnel file. The way she said it made me believe she had not only read my file, but memorized it.

"Consulting's more dangerous than people think. Consultants don't get enough credit—"

JJ interrupted again. "Look, Sanders, we had an overlap with an investigation Alex is working on. We think we've got a fraud case, but there may be some murders connected."

Now I was getting interested. Financial crimes, at least the kind I investigated, usually didn't involve murder.

So, two bureaucrats (I mean that in the nicest way) fly down from Washington to locate me to assist in a fraud and possible murder investigation requiring interagency cooperation. I was curious. Or at least flattered, I guess. JJ had other resources available to him.

"Why me?"

"I would have gone with Spassky, or Dillard, but they're doing al-Qaida asset investigations. Frankly, Nick, I've got no one else. You're it, assuming you want it." Good answer, and the one I expected. Since 9/11, almost 80 percent of the bureau's resources were devoted to domestic terrorism investigations of some sort: surveillance of suspected Islamic militants, or investigation of money laundering from shady "charitable" groups, outright terrorism funders (usually offshore, who move money onshore to be used in operations in the U.S.), or terrorism cells themselves. I did some of this before I quit. There was little time left for pure economic fraud investigations—Ponzi schemes, the Nigerian Defense Department con, and the like. In fact, the bureau had to let the SEC and FINRA do a lot of the fraud stuff that was connected to the public markets. If you were a con man, you had a decent chance of getting away clean on a small, purely economic fraud like a short-term Ponzi scheme. It wouldn't show up until someone complained, and by then the con men were usually long gone. Huntington was an exception.

My mind wandered a bit thinking about this and I said, "You know how many con men retire to Costa Rica?"

"What?"

"Con men. Lots of them take off and land here. No extradition. Everyone speaks English. Dollar goes a long way. I could write a history of U.S. con men living in Costa Rica."

JJ leaned toward Alex. "Sanders' mind works in weird ways. He's a closet historian of financial crimes. Some of them he even investigated. Ed Lawson. Bergner. Harrington."

"Vito Marcase," I added. "Remember him?"

JJ started laughing. Alex shook her head.

"Tried to fake his death," JJ said, still chucking. "What an idiot!"

"Tried to fake his death," I repeated. Alex rolled her eyes. She knew what everyone in law enforcement knew. Faking your death only works in the movies. In real life, the guys who try to fake their deaths are already wanted for something, so law enforcement never believes they're dead until they have a body with matching DNA. Plus, faking your death is hard to do. You have to arrange for a bunch of witnesses to watch you die in a way that seems impossible to survive *and* there has to be a reasonable explanation for why your body cannot be retrieved. Consequently, death at sea tends to be a popular attempt. That's what Marcase tried, and he ended up in a federal pound-you-in-the-ass prison.

"Alan Sterling," I said.

JJ looked quizzical for a second, then his face brightened with recognition.

"No shit?" he said.

"I shit you not. Well, I shit you sort of. He had places all over the Caribbean, but spent a lot of time at his mansion outside Tamarindo. He got Costa Rican citizenship."

Alex asked, "Who's Alan Sterling?"

I realized I had maybe ten years on her. "I guess you're a bit young. You may have been in high school when he made a name for himself. Alan Sterling was the Charles Keating of his time. Or the Richard Whitney. Or Rollo Tomasi."

"He's the guy who got away with it?" she asked. I smiled. "*L.A. Confidential* is one of my favorite movies," she explained.

"Mine too. Yeah, Sterling got away with it. He ran a huge, industrial-sized fraud in the late '80s with his Florida bank, Sterling Trust. It had onshore assets and offshore branches in Bermuda, the Cayman Islands, Nevis, the Cook Islands, and Costa Rica. He attracted a lot of deposits because his CDs were paying higher than competitors'. He had some elaborate offshore investment schemes, before hedge funds came along and popularized them. Some of them were real. He had high-end hotel and condo developments. It wasn't a pure Ponzi scheme. He was actually making the returns he said he was claiming."

"In my experience," Alex said, "the reason frauds are frauds is because they are too good to be true."

JJ answered her. "Oh, he was making his returns. His bank was laundering Miami drug-dealer money."

I continued, "Sterling wasn't stupid. He could recognize when it was time to pull up stakes. One day, he got on a boat and disappeared. The Feds raided all his domestic operations, and had other authorities raid his offshore ones. All the money was gone. And it was gone in paper currency, because there was no trace of any wire transfers of it anywhere. Sterling popped up two years later in Argentina, then moved around a bunch. He finagled Costa Rican citizenship, probably by making generous donations to politicians' reelection funds."

"No extradition," Alex said.

"Nope," I said. "He was a free and rich man when he died here."

"Well, nothing we can do about Mr. Sterling. But we may be able to stop the next one," JJ said, pointing to the backpack. "The bureau will pay you your usual hourly consulting fee, monthly."

Alex picked her backpack off the floor and placed it on the table. She unzipped it and took out a five-inch stack of files. "All of this is, of course, top secret." She knew I still had top secret clearance. She had read my file.

"I'm not sure whether to be impressed you're hiding top secret material in a book bag where no one would look for it or to remind you of bureau policy regarding top secret material."

"I don't work for the bureau," she reminded me. That certainly didn't instill any confidence in the CIA.

There were five separate files, each with a name I had never heard of: Allen, Y.; Jeffries, V.; Morrison, J.; Vanderhoff, M.; and Matsuzaka, M. I didn't touch them.

"What's your theory?" I asked.

Chapter 2

New York, New York; June 2005.

"What exactly is it that you do?" asked Alfred Vanderhoff.

Ernst Klatten, Marcus Vanderhoff's private banker at American Standard Bank & Trust, was not insulted by the question. He had been asked that many times, in situations exactly like this. He sat in a small conference room in ASBT's New York offices after having arranged for Alfred and Henrietta Vanderhoff, Marcus's parents, to travel there from their home in Ohio. They looked downright uncomfortable in ASBT's posh offices when Ernst greeted them in the reception area. Alfred was seventy years old and wearing deck shoes, a pair of tan cotton slacks, a plaid shirt, and a rather faded windbreaker. His eyesight was not what it once was, and he wore thick eyeglasses. Henrietta was a few years younger. She had dressed up for the meeting in what was likely her best Sunday attire, some nice low-heeled shoes, and just the right amount of makeup. She still showed her age, just not all of it. Both sported graying hair and the events of the past month could not have helped the aging process.

"ASBT is a diversified financial services ..." Klatten stopped, smiled, and started again: "We do many things. Let me start with my job, and then we'll work from there. I'm a private banker and trust officer. That means I do two distinct things. When clients deposit their money with the firm, I, along with many other professionals, manage that money. We invest it for clients who don't have the time to do so themselves, like Marcus when he was with us. Think of me as a glorified bank teller who comes out from behind the counter and opens bank accounts, manages investments, lends money, helps to arrange travel, security, tickets to events, and other services for clients." He decided to leave out that he also acted as a "personal bail bondsman" from time to time. "So, that's one function.

"The other is as a trust officer. A trust officer not only manages money, but also distributes that money to the beneficiaries of clients who have passed away. You are the primary beneficiaries of Marcus—Mark's—trust. Mark wanted to make sure that if something happened to him, you would be taken care of, could pay off your home, purchase a new car, maybe even take an extended vacation. If something were to happen to the two of you, then Mark made sure that your remaining son and daughter, and any children they have, would also have their needs attended to. I, with other trust officers in the firm who make up the distribution committee, make decisions on whether and how to distribute funds from deceased clients' trusts to their named beneficiaries. Is that clear?"

"Yes, but we don't really need anything," Alfred said. "Henrietta and I both have social security and pensions from our jobs, and a little savings on top of that. We think it's great that Mark made—"

There was a short knock. Klatten turned to the door. "Come in."

It opened and Jeremy Winfield walked in, impeccably dressed in a starched white shirt with a spread collar and French cuffs with tasteful, understated links, a perfectly tied gold and red tie, and a charcoal gray suit with subtle pinstripes. He wore it quite comfortably, not stiff and formal. He belonged in the suit, as if he were born to it. Winfield was tall, about six feet one. His black hair was speckled with some gray; his graying temples bookended his moderately lined, aged face. He was very fit, but despite that, one would assume he was in his mid-fifties. In fact, he was forty-five.

"Mr. and Mrs. Vanderhoff? Hello, I'm Jeremy Winfield, the president and CEO of American Standard. I trust Mr. Klatten has been taking good care of you?"

They rose to shake his hand. "Yes, yes, he has," said Henrietta.

"May I join you for a bit?" he asked them.

"Please," Mr. Vanderhoff said.

Winfield settled in to the remaining chair next to Klatten. "Well, let me start with my condolences. I can't imagine the pain you must feel at losing Marcus. I lost my parents a few years ago, and it was quite trying. But I don't think that compares to losing a child."

"Thank you," they said in unison.

"Given what you're going through, I am sure this is all quite overwhelming. It is Mr. Klatten's and my job to keep it as simple as possible for you. Can I answer any questions for you?"

"Well, Mr. Klatten was explaining to us about how you handle Mark's money. But like I was telling him, we really don't need much. We may want to give Mark's money to charity."

"I understand. Let's cover a couple of things. First, Mark's accounts are held in the name of his trust, which became irrevocable upon his death. That means that we as the trustee have to follow the instructions Mark laid out in the document for how the money is to be managed and distributed. It was Mark's clear intent that the money be held in trust so that you, your remaining children, and their children could enjoy it and use it as needed, but that it be professionally managed and not spent on outlandish items. For instance, while he would want you to be able to purchase a new car, I am certain he would not want us to distribute funds for you to buy a Ferrari."

They seemed befuddled and looked at each other. Alfred looked back at Winfield. "I'm sorry, Mr. Winfield. This is all a bit confusing. We really have no idea how much money Mark made during his life, so we don't really understand what we're dealing with."

"Oh, sorry. I understand," Winfield responded. "Since you are both beneficiaries, by law you are entitled to a copy of Mark's trust and monthly, quarterly, and annual consolidated account statements. At this point I think Mark's holdings are just a shade under two."

They looked at each other, then back at Winfield. They seemed shocked. "Two million dollars?" asked Alfred, eyes wide, as if his son had won the state lottery.

Winfield looked at Klatten, who subtly shrugged back at Winfield. Winfield spoke. "I'm sorry. This may come as somewhat of a shock to you. Not two million. Two *billion*. With a *b*."

Henrietta took in her breath in a gasp. Alfred just kept staring at Winfield as if he did not comprehend. "Billion?"

"Billion. Can we get you some water?" he asked Henrietta.

She did not respond and Klatten jumped up and got them both a bottle of water.

Winfield smiled. "Mark picked ASBT to manage his money and distribute it pursuant to his instructions because that is what we do, day in and day out. Mr. Klatten, I, and numerous other professionals deal with sums lesser and much greater than this on a daily basis. Now, under state law you can petition the court for a change of trustee, if you wish. You are certainly not married to us. However, I have a suggestion which I think you might find helpful. Currently, Mark has his two billion dollars split up among various money managers, such as Goldman Sachs, Morgan Stanley, Credit Suisse, and us.

"What that means is that the trust is paying numerous money managers a fee, usually about one-half to one percent of the annual value of the funds with each manager, to have that money managed. Since we are the trustee, we can keep all of the investments in one convenient place. To the extent we need to use outside money managers to invest in areas in which we are not experts, then we can still do that. For instance, we might hire an offshore hedge-fund manger to manage some of the funds. We might make direct investments in emerging markets, such as Brazil or Vietnam. But, because of the size of the account and the firm's reputation, we can likely do this while still saving a significant amount in fees.

"My suggestion is that we gather the funds here, then after developing an appropriate investment plan, we begin parceling some those assets out to various managers around the world. We would of course maintain the bulk of them here, invested in cash, stocks, and bonds in the U.S."

The Vanderhoffs were still processing the fact that the word *billion* started with a *b*.

"So," Winfield continued, "the bottom line is it will be cheaper and more efficient for the funds to be collected here, and we can discount the trustee fee due to the size of the account. Sound good?"

Alfred and Henrietta Vanderhoff nodded, quite numbly.

"Excellent. Tell you what, could I entice you to join Mr. Klatten and me for dinner tonight? Nothing too fancy, maybe some steaks if you are up for something like that? We can fill you in on our other services, and what allocation we would recommend for Mark's money. In the meantime, I will leave it to Mr. Klatten to finish up here and will see you all later this evening." He got up. "Mr. Klatten, please let me know what time our clients would like to eat. It was a pleasure to meet you both and I look forward to seeing you tonight."

Within a year of Mark Vanderhoff's death, ASBT had fired all the other money managers and consolidated his investments onto their brokerage platform. This saved the family fees, as ASBT reduced the overall money management and standard trustee fees since the account was quite large. It also ensured ASBT made more money than they had during Marcus Vanderhoff's life, since they were now collecting their management fee and a fiduciary fee on a larger base of money. Thus, even though the Vanderhoffs paid less overall, ASBT made more.

As Klatten and Winfield told Mark's still-dazed parents over dinner, it was unlikely they would utilize the two billion dollars during the lives of the three generations of the family already in existence. In fact, given the way the trust was drafted, it was impossible without court intervention. Ernst made a mental note to send a thank-you gift to the trust's drafting attorney.

Chapter 3

Jaco, Costa Rica; March 2008.

"That's your theory?" I asked. They looked at me and nodded together. I still had not looked at any of the files. I just wanted to hear the story.

"Ever hear of American Standard Bank and Trust?" asked JJ.

"Yeah, sure," I responded. "ASBT. Started by a guy named Jeremy Winfield. You'd like him, JJ. He hates to be called Jerry. After his father died, Winfield left a position as number two at a large bank to start his own shop. He's well-respected. ASBT only caters to extremely wealthy clients. So, it's a boutique shop, but they make a ton of money. It's privately held, so tough to confirm, but he has no problem maintaining his reserves. Less clients, more money. A banker's wet dream." I stopped and thought a second. "So, these five folks, who were relatively young, unmarried, all but one with no children, who had trusts naming ASBT as their corporate successor trustee, have all died in the past three years?"

"Yes," said Alex, with a tone of affirmation.

"And your theory is someone at ASBT is killing them off so ... What? So ASBT can become successor trustee?"

"Yes," she repeated.

"Wow. That's a lot of work to go to for half a percent," I said.

They both looked at me as if they had never considered it. "What do you mean for *half a percent?*" Alex asked.

High-end private banks and trust companies make money the usual way: making the difference between what they pay depositors and what they are paid by their borrowers. But another important revenue stream is the fees they charge (living) clients for money management and the fees they charge (dead) clients to manage that money as a trustee for their ingrate children and trophy wives after they've died. Management fees on very large accounts could be as little as one-half of one percent for an all-bond portfolio. (Once you go under a percent, the fees become known as "basis points" or "bps" or, colloquially in the industry, "bips.") Throw in some stocks and exotic "alternative" investments, and you could theoretically make three quarters of one percent (75 bips) or even a full percent (100 bips) on, say, a one billion dollar account, per year. If your investment performance is poor, you'll be fired, so the annual income stream isn't certain.

Now, let's assume your client dies and you take over as trustee. Being a trustee is no picnic. You have regular accountings you have to perform and annual tax filings for all the trusts you oversee. In large estates, the tax work alone can take months, and that's just the one client. You also have to deal with the surviving family. They could sue you at the drop of a hat. When a bank becomes a trustee, they charge an additional fee for this service to offset the additional work and liability. That fee, on a very large account, might be only 25 bips (one quarter of a percent), up to 50 bips. So, all in, on a billion dollar account with some exotic investments and where the bank acts as trustee, the bank may make fifteen million dollars per year. Admittedly, this isn't chump change. But before the client died, the bank was already earning ten million a year on the account.

"You think it's worth the time, money, trouble, and risk of prison for a respected bank to kill a client for an additional five million dollars a year?" I asked.

Silence.

I assumed they agreed the initial theory was weak. Still, all five of the dead people were single, only one had children (who were minors), and all had trusts that were designed to last multiple generations. I had to admit that the statistical chances of five people with that demographic, who were all clients of the same boutique bank, all dying within three years of each other was pretty small. And, since they all had different beneficiaries, the heirs benefitted only from their own relative's death, not any of the other deaths. I thought some more about this. It looked like Alex was going to say something, but JJ gently put a hand on her arm. He wanted to let me mull it over some more.

"And the money is still at ASBT?" I asked.

"Yes and no. They allocate about fifty percent in domestic investments, and the rest in alternative and offshore investments," JJ answered. There was nothing unusual about this. In very large estates, it's difficult to generate a significant return with your average stock and bond portfolio, so you have to diversify the account into a lot of pieces. Some of those pieces are held offshore.

"At best, they are firing other money managers and collecting all the assets. But we're still only talking about an incremental increase in fees. I know people have killed for less, but it doesn't make sense that a highly profitable bank would do so. They're already making a bunch of money. Plus, how would they know they are named as successor trustee? I mean, you could kill a guy and then find out he changed his will or trust without telling you. There has to be something else going on, *if* these deaths are really connected," I said.

I thought a bit more. I looked at Alex, then at JJ. "Maybe I'm looking at this wrong. How did you two hook up? What was the overlap in the cases? What's the CIA want with a domestic-based murder case?"

"I'm not with the agency," Alex said. "I used to be. A couple of years ago, I got seconded to the director of Homeland Security's office. I work for the director." Finally, a revelation.

"Alex was investigating arms sales in South America," said JJ.

Alex continued, "There's an offshore hedge fund, DP Partners, based in the Caymans that has large movements of cash out of their accounts. The movements correlate to arms shipments moving through Venezuela and Ecuador. Problem is, we don't know how the fund is generating the investment returns to the U.S. investors. I mean, they appear to be *buying* arms but not selling them, or at least not getting any money from the people that are receiving the weapons."

"And ASBT is investing some of their clients' money in this hedge fund?" I asked.

She nodded. A lot of what she just told me sounded like sheer guesswork. The problem was that hedge funds are private investment vehicles. They are unregulated and don't have to report anything but raw earnings to the investors. They never like to discuss their investment strategy, because someone else could either copy it or, worse, engage in an opposing strategy that would destroy the fund's returns.

"So, we got ASBT investing in an offshore hedge fund," I continued, "and some of that money may go into arms purchases. ASBT clients may or may not get killed so that ASBT can collect all their assets, charge more fees, and move more money offshore to engage in illegal arms deals. And apparently, these arms deals suck for the investors because they don't appear to make any money. That about sum it up?"

"Well, ..." JJ began.

"Yes," said Alex. She was looking a little uncomfortable but was sticking with her gut-developed theory.

"How did you find the connection between the dead clients?"

"Echelon," said JJ.

"JJ, Echelon is a communications listening program," I said.

He looked at Alex, who said, "Echelon is best known as a communications monitoring program. In truth, since 9/11 it has many arms. One of the subprograms run out of Echelon is information collection and analysis. The software looks for connections in a diverse array of information that passes through governmental agencies, and does it a whole lot faster than humans can. So, you've got death certificates filed around the country on five dead people, all entered into the Homeland Security Directorate system. They have accounts at the same money manager. Without Echelon, it's unlikely any single agency would have made the connection."

I had to agree. Since there was no single law-enforcement agency that would have seen information on all five deaths, none would have seen that all five, or even two, had the same money manager and trustee.

JJ continued: "When Echelon spit this out, the case was assigned to us. All files we open are copied to the DHS office where Alex works. She was already investigating the arms deals and the hedge fund in the Caymans connected with ASBT."

"Jesus. That's a little Big-Brotherish for my taste. Can you guys tell me how many guys my ex-wife was sleeping with before we got divorced, 'cause I—"

"Nick, let's focus on the case," JJ said. Alex laughed. A little.

She was actually very attractive when she smiled, but since that was the first time I'd seen her smile, I hadn't realized it. She had a very athletic figure and perfectly round breasts that came in on the larger side of the size scale. OK, Sanders, focus on the case. I closed my eyes to get my attention off the hot Homeland Security agent.

"Let's think this through," I said. "If I'm a bank and I want to profit by killing off my clients who have named me as their successor trustee, I have to know a couple of things. I have to know what and where *all* their assets are. I have to know that they've named me as a successor trustee. I have to know their will or trust is valid and enforceable, and that they haven't replaced me with some other trustee."

Alex smiled. Damn, that was a winning smile. Wait, why was she smiling? Oh. She had left something out. And she knew exactly where I was going next.

"There's only one person besides the client that would know all of that information," I said.

Alex and JJ nodded in unison.

"Are you going to tell me that all five victims shared the same attorney?"

They both nodded.

"Son of a bitch!"

I breathed.

"That's where we have to start," I said.

Chapter 4

Papagayo, Costa Rica; July 2005.

The old man closed his laptop as the waitress approached.

"Can I get you anything else, Señor de Plata?" she asked.

"No, muchas gracias, Rosa." He was always kind and considerate to the help, which she appreciated. She didn't much appreciate the tips he left. For a man of obvious (as well as rumored) wealth, he was cheap. He was a little more generous when he required extra service, something all the female waitstaff understood they may have to supply from time to time. The pay was good as long as you were willing to allow the groping, fondling, and from time to time, the trip to the "Presidential Suite" for something more. Even though he was the owner of the hotel, he was too cheap to use the real Presidential Suite for anything other than paying customers, so he used a small standard room at the end of one wing of the hotel for his trysts. He was not unattractive, even for his age, and he was not physically abusive during sex, but you still tried to imagine someone else while you were doing it, which was difficult. There were a lot of attractive women employed at the hotel, and as he aged he required less and less "servicing," so Rosa only had to put up with it once about every other month.

She put his coffee down and walked away.

De Plata reopened his laptop and reviewed his holdings around the world. He really didn't need to look. He instinctively knew every moment of every day exactly how much money he had to the penny. At some level, he understood it had become pathological—his need for wealth and the continual reinforcement that it was still where he thought it was. He was not the type to engage in introspection, but if he were, he would likely trace his craving for money back to growing up in the shadow of the Great Depression. Prior to the crash, his family had been quite well-off. While he had never partaken of that wealth during his youth, he had experienced the bitterness of his parents, who had tasted the good life and then lost it. While he was growing up in a one-bedroom apartment in Chicago, his parents never let de Plata or his siblings forget that they had once been prominent. As a boy, de Plata would help his mother in the kitchen, there learning her ingenious frugality: reusing coffee grounds for three days; developing recipes to use the skin and rinds of fruits and vegetables; reusing the bones of the Thanksgiving turkey for a week's worth of thin soup; carefully opening presents so that the wrapping paper could be reused for later presents. Everything was saved and used again. While his mother tried to make this seem fun, his father was ashamed at what had befallen the family.

While learning lessons of survival during this upheaval, Alejandro de Plata also promised himself that he would do what was necessary to return his family to greatness. He would work. He would save. He would learn business, and he would become one of those prominent Chicago businessmen he saw wearing thick wool suits and starched, French-cuffed shirts. He worked his way through college and got his first real job as a runner on the floor of the options exchange, taking order tickets to the traders in the pits and back to the specialists. As he moved up, his father passed away—before he'd had a chance to purchase a house for his parents. He promised his mother he would do so, but she told him to save his money and not spend it on anything so lavish as a house.

His sister married and moved to New York. His older brother dropped out of school and went to work for the City of Chicago. The brother became a gambler and a drinker, and eventually faded away from the family. When de Plata's mother died, he continued her legacy of frugality, saving every penny, spending only when absolutely necessary. At some point he became so parsimonious, he was called a miser by those who knew him. Many of his coworkers at the brokerage firm he rose through spent lavishly and exuded a pretense of power. But what he knew, and they did not, was that the mere possession of wealth *was* power. He noticed that friends in need always came to him. That City aldermen sought out his advice (and contributions).

The word of his wealth became a self-fulfilling prophecy. Because he had wealth, he was offered opportunities to make more of it. At some point, beyond security, money just begot him more money. But in his deepest fiber, he knew that if he lost any of it, his ability to control his own destiny would be lost. Any opportunity, legal or not, that would increase his monetary position was taken. He would never enter a deal if he thought he would lose money, and in every deal he always built in guarantees of a minimum return. If those returns did not materialize, the guilty party would be convinced to make good on their promise.

De Plata never had to have such ugly conversations with those who attempted to cheat him: along with security and power, money supplied hands for the dirty work. Which meant that a man in de Plata's position could keep himself clean, and still make money. It bothered him that on occasion he had to part with valued treasure just to enforce a contract, but sometimes this was the cost of doing business. And as long as that cost was factored into the deal to begin with, then the calculation of his percentage gain would not be disturbed.

De Plata had never married. He'd had, instead, a series of women. But he learned early on, ironically from his frugal mother, that women were expensive. If he had ever met a woman of his mother's quality and caliber, then he might have considered marriage. Now, however, in the twilight of his life, it seemed irrelevant. He could simply pay for what he needed. And in this part of the world, those kinds of pleasures came cheap.

De Plata switched screens to his encrypted email. He began a new missive to a business associate.

Señor R: Despite your recent setbacks, I can offer a further 5 container shipments for re-supply. Payment to be t.o.d., but due to increased cost of shipment of supply to you and reimbursement from end user, payment will need to be increased 25%.

He hit send. Despite the government-quality encryption program he had obtained, it was good to keep these things short, to the point, and more or less vague. De Plata was certain his terms would be accepted. Reyes was having trouble finding anyone who could supply the needed materials. Despite promises from the administration of Reyes's neighboring country (which allegedly shared his revolutionary vision), de Plata was the only one who never changed the terms of a deal at the last minute, and he always delivered. This was good business practice, and de Plata never missed an opportunity to point it out to those with whom he did business.

He created a new mail window and entered another email address in the "To:" space. All of the contact information for de Plata's business associates was memorized, never written down. Despite his advanced age, his memory was as sharp as it had ever been. Passwords, codes, phone numbers, email addresses, all were memorized once and locked away, never to be forgotten. He began his new email:

L, please make arrangements for a new product shipment to R, 5 containers. Please also arrange for payment processing per usual avenues, plus 25%. Please handle delivery vs. payment in normal method. I realize this will involve some travel, but your pro rata increase should alleviate inconvenience. Please reply ASAP your ability to complete by end of month. Also, thank you for your efforts in completing the African transaction. It should pay off in another 6 to 9 months. Meanwhile, we will continue to utilize revenue from last transaction.

And so his day continued, on the veranda of the hotel he owned. Deals were made, debtors dunned, deposits confirmed. And every hour or so, a continually updated spreadsheet confirming he was ridiculously wealthy, and allowing him to relax a bit for the next hour, was reviewed. Later, he thought, he might take Rosa to the Presidential Suite.

Chapter 5

Jaco, Costa Rica; March 2008.

I went back to my motel, showered and shaved. I put on a pair of jeans, a T-shirt, socks and shoes, and stuffed everything else in the single duffel bag I had brought. I talked to the owner about arranging a driver back to San Jose. He had an itinerant brother who fit the bill. JJ sat in front and I sat in back with Ms. Homeland Security Information Clearinghouse. She asked me about my background, since the file she had read didn't have the complete Nick Sanders history.

"What I don't get is," she said, "you're making a bunch of money as a tax lawyer at a big firm in New York. And one day you up and quit. And join the Marines?"

"Yeah, well, I'm a patriotic guy. Make sure you put that in your report at Homeland."

She gave me a smirk.

"OK, truth is," I said, "I had gotten divorced the year before, and was doing nothing but working. The partners all told me I was on the fast track. But during that year after my divorce, I looked around and saw all of them working the same hours I was. They all had second or third spouses and lots of kids, and they never saw them. I decided I didn't want to live that way. That and the fact I was totally bored out of my skull doing the tax work. I would have killed myself if I'd stayed."

"OK. But ... the Marines?" she asked.

The cool thing about the Marine Corps is that your first year in, everyone is equal. Everyone goes through the same training, everyone learns to shoot, crawl through the mud, carry fifty pounds of weight for twenty miles and blow crap up. Now, I can understand how some might think this really wouldn't appeal to someone who graduated from an Ivy League law school. But this is exactly what appealed to me at the time. I would be learning something new, which at the same time was completely mindless. All you had to do was follow directions and not piss off your drill instructor, which I was surprisingly good at. After your first year, you specialize. In my case, since I was already a licensed attorney, I was not surprisingly made a judge advocate, or military attorney.

This was something completely foreign to my prior experience as well. As a judge advocate, you prosecute or defend all kinds of cases. I was put in the prosecutor's office, where there is very little of the hierarchy of a normal county prosecutor's office. You could jump from a barroom brawl one day to a murder case the next. I met JJ through an overlapping military/civilian case involving a contract administrator who was shaking down government suppliers for kickbacks.

JJ and I worked the investigation together. We got to like and respect each other, and JJ offered me a job. This is the history that I relayed to Alex Conrad, hopefully in an entertaining fashion.

"So," I concluded, "JJ got himself a guy that understood financial crimes, banking regulations, tax laws, and could shoot. Basically, that's what they're looking for at the FBI. Smart people that can shoot."

"Sanders can't shoot that well," JJ put in.

The car continued past the public terminal to a private plane terminal.

We got our bags and walked out onto the tarmac, where a private jet was waiting. The pilot and copilot were standing by the stairs, and when they saw us immediately went up the steps and into the cockpit. A ground crewman took our bags and put them in the belly hold. Alex was first into the plane. I was about to follow, when JJ grabbed my arm.

"Hey, I can't talk about this in front of the Homeland babe, but I have some other work for you on Huntington."

"OK. It'll be late when we land, so why don't we carve out some time tomorrow morning at the office?" I offered.

"Sounds good."

The jet was a Bombardier Challenger 605. You learn a lot about private jets when you investigate financial crimes, because all the big criminals seem to have access to them. Despite my knowledge of them, I had yet to fly in one. This particular model was new, and the interior was quite plush. "Homeland Security is stepping up," I said.

"Seized from an executive who couldn't pay back taxes after his stock tanked," Alex said. I wasn't sure if she was kidding or not, but chances were that a private plane like that was seized from someone. "All the Homeland babes get one," she said, looking hard at JJ.

JJ turned beet red, which is somewhat difficult for a black man. "I'm sorry, Ms. Conrad," he said. "I didn't mean anything by it."

She smiled. "I've been called worse, trust me. And please, it's Alex."

"Damn, your hearing's good" was all I could say.

"Thanks," she said. After a beat, "That was a compliment, right?"

"Actually, I think I was just reminding myself to keep my voice down."

After takeoff, I asked Conrad how she had gotten to the DHS.

"I was a math major at MIT. The CIA was recruiting code makers and breakers, and since I could computer program, I was on a team that was assigned to try to break private encryption algorithms that terrorist groups were using to try to mask their communications. We were successful and that got noticed, and they moved me to Homeland Security and introduced me to the connect-the-dots project that's part of Echelon. Because the program is written by humans, it's obviously not foolproof, so sometimes it connects things that you or I looking at would think are not related. Most of the time it's pretty simplistic. Voiceprints match communications. Names on wire transfers are the same. Or names on death certificates match records at a single bank in a statistically unlikely time period."

"So you've never done fieldwork?"

"You mean like spy stuff? Ha! I've been through both the Farm and Quantico training, but that's it. I don't even carry a gun."

"So what do you do with all the information?"

"Well, I try to organize it, make sense of it, or call bullshit if I think Echelon's wrong. If I think there's something to look at, I contact the appropriate agency. In this case, JJ contacted us before I could refer the case. We're pretty inundated."

"Since you have all the files and materials, it might be useful to have you around for a few days. You know, go talk to the attorney, Winfield, stuff like that. If you're interested."

She thought for a minute. "I would *love* that," she said.

I looked at JJ, who simply shrugged at me.

"Oh, I'm gonna like this case," she said.

"Better clear it with your boss, Conrad," JJ said.

I noticed he dropped the "Ms." He was treating her like one of the team. "Tell me about the attorney," I said.

She reached into the magic backpack and took out a file. She handed it to me.

"Edward S. Lazeris," I read aloud. There was a picture on the inside flap, apparently taken from a website, probably a bar association's or his own firm's site. Solo practitioner, midtown Manhattan. Wills, trusts, complex estate planning for the wealthy. But not always. Judging from his bank accounts (how do they get this stuff?), Ed Lazeris had only recently hit it big. He represented all five of the decedents. "Settling just those five estates alone would keep him busy for years, and there would be follow-up work from the families," I said. "How does this guy do it without any attorneys working for him?"

"He has an assistant and several paralegals who do a lot of the grunt work. From what I can tell, his biggest crime is billing his paralegals' hours out as his own."

JJ and I both laughed. "What?" she asked.

JJ spoke. "If they prosecuted every lawyer who did that, there would be a whole lot less lawyers."

"It wasn't uncommon at my old firm," I added. Nor was padding the bill, or partners billing associates' time as their own at a much higher rate. "I don't see a travel schedule," I said.

"He travels six times a year, always to the same resort on the Caymans. Lives and works in the city. He's not under surveillance, but we flagged his passport so we'd know if he left the country. He never does anything other than his six trips per year."

"And his fees are all paid and deposited into his domestic bank accounts. Nothing overseas?"

"Not that we can see. But it can be hard to tell, 'cause he could have an overseas account in the name of an offshore entity and have clients deposit the money directly. It would be difficult to trace. And since we don't know who his other clients are, we can only look at the money paid by the five clients we do know about—the dead ones. They appear to have simply written him checks as bills came due and those checks were deposited into his domestic account. These clients have money transfers all over the world, so it would be tough to tell if one of the entities they paid overseas has any connection to Lazeris."

"So he's not doing the killing, maybe just supplying privileged client information to the killer." I read the file some more. "Young guy to have such a rich clientele. What, ten years out of school, and it looks like he might have gotten fired from his first firm?"

"He left to open his own practice."

I shook my head. "He would have been fired if he hadn't left. He was there five years. Long enough to know if he was going to make partner. He probably saw the writing on the wall. He's not married, no kids, so if he was any good, he would have devoted all his waking hours to the firm and made partner pretty early, say, seven years. If he left after five years, he was shown the door or was made aware he wasn't going to make partner. He might have screwed up a case."

"For a guy who told me my theory was bullshit," Conrad said, "you jump to a lot of conclusions. You haven't even talked to anyone at his old firm."

I shrugged. "I'd like to think I'm making an educated guess based on prior experience. So, we need to talk to Lazeris and Winfield."

"Winfield?" Alex sounded surprised. "You sure you want to let him know he's being investigated?"

"I'm doubtful that Winfield is in on it. He's already rich. He's got a great clientele without the need to kill them. I just don't see it. But there's no question that his company has benefited from their deaths. I need to size the guy up. We can tell him we're investigating one of the dead clients for something they did while they were alive, say, insider trading. We note, without overstressing it, that we're not investigating the bank. I'm sure under those circumstances he would give us some of his time."

"Might take a few days to get a meeting with him."

"I'm an optimist. By the way, do we know Winfield's travel schedule?"

"Yes. He travels all over, all the time. But there's no apparent correlation with his schedule and the client deaths."

"Yeah. Guy like that won't do the dirty work. He'd hire it out." That gave me another thought. "Let's take a look at the manner of deaths again."

She retrieved the other files and handed them to me. I was about to open them when she began from memory. "Vincent Jeffries—he was the first one—died of a heart attack at his home in Chicago, the only one not an accident."

"Heart attacks can be drug induced," I threw in.

"Hmm" was all she said. "Yamika Allen, car accident in upstate New York—," she began.

"Isn't that a city in Washington?" I interrupted.

"*Yakima*, Washington, *Yamika* Allen," she retorted.

"Oh. Sorry," I said.

She turned to JJ. "You actively recruited this guy?"

"He's better when he hasn't been drinking," JJ explained. "I think."

She continued: "Joanne Morrison, drowned while scuba diving off Bermuda. Marcus Vanderhoff, bungee jumping accident in Africa."

"Ouch."

"Yeah. And Matsui Matsuzaka, killed in September last year in the crossfire of two Yakuza gangs' pitched drug battle in a nightclub in Tokyo."

"Well, it could be one guy, but it's probably multiple unrelated contractors," I said, thinking aloud.

"I agree. If it were one guy, he'd have to have enough knowledge of car mechanics, scuba equipment, bungee equipment, and medicine to make the first four look like an accident. Also, he'd have to have some 'in' with the Yakuza to arrange the fifth death, if it was arranged," she added.

"Yep. Only people I know that could be trained for this are CIA," I said. She smirked, as if I were kidding. "Hey, they tried to kill Castro with an exploding cigar, remember? Only difference is with the CIA it's not a single hit man, it's the resources and people of the whole agency, so even then it's not one guy." What we all knew was that the lone, well-educated, well-equipped, highly paid assassin was an invention of spy thriller novels and movies. "Hit men," as most people think of them, really don't exist. Practically speaking, there are two types of killers for hire: low-paid but well-trained government agents who sometimes have to kill in their line of work; or thugs—hired by the mafia, gangs, or governments without the resources of developed countries—who kill indiscriminately and don't really care if it looks like an accident. The fact that the five deaths we were dealing with were all of different types, took place all over the world, and involved a need for diverse knowledge and contacts seemed to argue against a single-assassin theory.

And we couldn't forget that this might all really be a coincidence, and these unfortunate folks had all died just as advertised, with no foul play involved. We could just be letting our imaginations get the best of us.

Chapter 6

Tokyo, Japan; August 2006.

"This will be quite difficult, Lester-san. There will be many questions. This is not good business for us. Perhaps we can arrange for an accident instead?"

"I understand your reluctance, Hikiro-san. However, this is quite important to my client. It is vital that there be many witnesses and no question as to the manner of death. The fact is, your police would just as vigorously investigate an accident, especially one involving such a prominent citizen, which could be traced back to your business associates in any event. Given the target's predilections, there will be pressure to resolve the matter quickly with little public disclosure." *And I've arranged too many accidents already*, he did not add.

John Lester took a sip of $500 per bottle sake from a tiny cup. He sat across a small nightclub table from Kenji Hikiro, his contact in the Tokyo mafia. He had negotiated with Hikiro many times over the past eight years, since the day they met in a Laotian prison. Hikiro was pointing out the reality of the situation: staging a shootout in a Japanese nightclub was dangerous.

First, such violence in Japan was almost unheard of. Officially, only the police had guns. Everyone knew that the Yakuza also had guns, but they rarely used them in a public venue, and it was exceedingly rare for innocent civilians to be killed. There would be a significant investigation. However, the Yakuza would make a back channel contact to the police, advise them that the hit was not authorized, and arrange for the authorities to "find" the perpetrators and all the evidence that would link them to the shooting. While the Yakuza was an organized crime syndicate, they recognized that they could not offend Japanese sensibilities. The "shooters" who would be given up would be Yakuza members who had crossed the gang or were suspected informants.

There was one other factor that would truncate the police investigation of the shooting. One of the victims would be quite prominent, and if word leaked out that the club he was in (which would remain unnamed in all reports) was known by the authorities and the underworld as the mercantile center for illegal drugs and underage prostitutes, it would be socially devastating to the man's family. And in Japan that would simply not do.

What Lester knew was that you had to use a mark's own weaknesses against him. In Matsui Matsuzaka's case, that was his penchant for girls aged ten to thirteen. While Japan was quite forgiving about their men keeping mistresses or employing the services of a prostitute, certain things were simply not done. A man's wife and mistress could never meet in public. And men did not engage in sex with girls too young to consent. A man of Matsuzaka's means could have simply avoided the whole problem by visiting Bangkok as often as he liked. In fact, he did visit Bangkok at least once a month on "business." But his constant need for the touch and feel of prepubescent girls was so strong that he could regularly be found in the shadier districts of Tokyo. Indeed, Matsui Matsuzaka was quite well-known in the Japanese underworld, even if he was not *of* it.

It was this defect in character that would ultimately lead to Matsuzaka's death. But only if Kenji Hikiro agreed.

"I would never tell you no, Lester-san. But this is quite unorthodox. It will be costly in money and lives."

"As always, the money is of no concern. The lives at stake are simply the requirement of the transaction. Unfortunately, there is nothing I can do about that part." Lester was always brutally honest with Hikiro. He smiled slightly at the irony that when dealing with ruthless killers, honesty was truly the best policy.

"Shall we say 150 million?" Hikiro asked, bringing Lester back to reality.

"Yen, I presume?"

"Of course. No offense to your fine currency, John, but the American dollar isn't what it used to be."

Lester didn't need a calculator to figure it out. Basically, every ten million yen was just over one hundred thousand U.S. dollars. Hikiro's offer would be a bit over $1.5 million. "Half now, half upon completion?"

"Certainly. Payable in the usual fashion," Hikiro confirmed. The usual fashion was a wire transfer from the Cayman account to a Singapore account used by the clan.

Lester hesitated. "Would you take one-third of the payment in kind?"

Hikiro turned his head slightly, both in mild surprise and thinking about the offer. "I suppose it depends on what the item you wish to barter is?"

"Pure white lady, from Colombia via Central America. It is quite difficult to get it across the U.S. border lately, what with the Mexican gangs at each other's throats and the increased U.S. border enforcement. I would consider it a personal favor," Lester added.

"Aren't they all personal favors?" *Good point,* Lester thought, nodding in agreement. "All right, John, but the price of cocaine fluctuates more than the yen–dollar exchange rate. Make it an even two hundred million, payable one-half in yen and the rest at the spot price of powder on the date of exchange."

Lester knew that was coming. By paying Hikiro in cocaine, he would transfer his sales problem to Hikiro. Hikiro would probably make more in the end, but he still had to sell the drugs. The hitch was the add-on: the spot price on the date of exchange. This put Lester in a position of having to arrange for more drugs to be at the exchange than a predetermined amount; otherwise, as the price fluctuated he could be short on the payment, which simply wouldn't do if Lester wished to continue his business relationship with Hikiro. It was Hikiro's way of sweetening the deal even further. Lester would arrange for the delivery of more cocaine than was necessary to assure that full payment was available. His delivery agents would not want to keep any excess (they were being paid for delivery only), so Hikiro would get that too. At the end of the day, Hikiro would likely make two and a quarter million dollars on the deal, rather than just two.

"Fair enough, Kenji."

"Excellent, Lester-san. Now, let's drink."

When Lester finally left, it was early morning. He took a cab back to his hotel room at the Four Seasons and emailed his client the terms of the deal. After he was finished, he poured himself a Diet Coke (fifteen dollars for 11.2 ounces out of the hotel mini-bar) and sat in a plush chair looking out over the morning Tokyo skyline.

It had not always been this luxurious a life for John Lester. He grew up on a farm in a small town in Nebraska where every day was school and work, unless you excelled at basketball, in which case every day was school, basketball practice, then work. John Lester excelled at basketball and most other sports. He was a whip-smart student as well. Lester didn't mind hard work, but it was obvious that if he didn't go to college or use some other path out of town, he would spend the rest of his life there. His

English teacher in high school thought this would be a shame, and took it as his personal mission to ensure that John submitted college applications and attempted to secure a sports or academic scholarship, or both. The following year Lester left Nebraska, returning only for the usual holidays when he was available and to thank his English teacher for what he had done for him.

Lester attended Columbia University on a combination of academic scholarships and work-study programs. He enjoyed college and did well, but could not figure out what he really wanted to do with his life. He couldn't be behind a desk. He seriously considered getting a PhD in some field that would allow him to get outside, but when he explored this, he decided archaeology or geology were not for him. Then, two serendipitous things occurred in his senior year that made his mind up for him: A man named Saddam Hussein invaded a little-known country to the south of Iraq called Kuwait, and the CIA came recruiting at a Columbia University job fair. Lester crossed a picket line of student demonstrators to go into the hall and express some interest.

Initially, the entire interaction was business-like and mundane, as if he were applying for a job at a bank. Fill out this application. We need three references. Ever been convicted of a crime? He did what he was told. He also visited some of the other employers with booths at the job fair. In a couple of weeks, he heard back from several potential employers that were interested in hiring John after his senior year for various entry-level positions. He was not that interested in those jobs, and was seriously considering the army or Marine Corps so he could see some action before the Persian Gulf War was all over. Such was the mind of a patriotic twenty-one-year-old.

He went to a local armed forces recruiting office and discovered he was not the only one expressing interest. Many kids his age wanted to go to Iraq. He filled out an "interest card" and talked to a recruiting officer, a marine. The officer told him that it would be better for John if he finished college, as there would be many more opportunities in the service open to him. However, he could join immediately and the military would pay for him to finish his senior year later. John told the officer he would think about it and left.

Two days later he was visited at his off-campus apartment (which he shared with two other students) by a guy in a suit. That was what his roommate told him: "a guy in a suit."

"Black or white?"

"Don't really recall."

"Name?"

"Oh, yeah, dude, he gave me a card. Let's see, it's here somewhere ... yeah, here."

"You spill something on this?"

"What? I dunno. Maybe."

The card read "Central Intelligence Agency" and described the card's owner, a man named Paul Blattman, as a Human Resources Officer. Lester called and made an appointment to meet at a coffee shop on the edge of campus.

Blattman was not particularly impressive. Rumpled suit, fortyish, thinning hair.

"So, you want to join the military, John?" Blattman began.

"What? Oh, I dunno, maybe," he said. "How did you know that?"

"You're kidding, right, John? We're the CIA."

John looked around. No one seemed to be paying too much attention. Blattman wasn't being particularly loud, but he wasn't speaking in hushed tones either.

"Look, John, the military is a good background for an agent, but we can give you that same training. In fact, you'll have to go through some pretty tough military training. Our attrition rate is seventy-five percent. That means only twenty-five percent—"

"I know what it means," John said.

"Good. Good. John, you are a very bright kid. And you're quite an athlete. Kinda picked the wrong school to excel at sports, though, huh? I mean, not exactly an NCAA powerhouse, right?"

"The competition is weak, makes me look better," John said, smiling.

"That what you're looking for, poor competition?"

"What? Uh, no." *Crap. This guy was playing mind games*, John thought. "It was a joke. My parents and my teacher thought a quality education should come first," he said. "Where did you go to college?" he asked, changing the subject.

"U.S. Military Academy at West Point," Blattman said. He held up his right hand, which had a large class ring.

"So you joined the agency from the army?"

"I'm supposed to be interviewing you."

"Is that what this is, a job interview?"

"Let's say we're interested and want to know more. For instance, what makes a Nebraska farm boy want to join the CIA? Action? Adventure?"

"I get the feeling you're mocking me. You're going to tell me it's all drudge work, right?"

Blattman leaned back in his chair and looked at John for a long time. "You're very confident for a twenty-one-year-old, John. See, I don't really care what your answers are. And I don't really care why you want to join the agency or the military, unless you're some sleeper terrorist, in which case we'd tell you no thanks. Then kill you. What I want to assess is how you carry yourself. And you carry yourself well. And yes, it is a lot of drudge work. But I can also tell you that depending on the job you do, it can be very exciting, and dangerous. What you don't want to be is some techie analyst back at Langley, which unfortunately is the wave of the future. The whole cloak-and-dagger cold war thing is over. But there is no replacement for direct human intelligence, John. I don't care how many billions they spend on satellites and listening outposts and robot planes. Humint is real intelligence. The guy on the ground who's getting dirty, he's the guy who's gonna decide if we win in Iraq. He's the guy who's gonna tell us where the next big threat to this country is coming from. And he's the guy in the agency who sees the most action."

"You get kinda worked up when you talk about your job, huh?" asked John.

"Don't be a smart-ass. A recruit like you, a lot of different departments are going to want to get their hands on you. Don't let them. You have field agent written all over you. If you want it, you can work for my team. Pay's shitty, work is hard, but it won't matter. You'll be going all over the world on the taxpayers' dime. You'll learn stuff you never knew existed, and I think you'll love it. But that's just one man's opinion."

"Why did you join?"

"Action, adventure … and I was right. Because twenty years ago I was sitting where you are, and a guy in a crappy suit who didn't look like much gave me the field operative speech. And he was right. And I'm right. About the job and about you."

"Let's say I want to do this, Mr. Blattman. What's next?"

"Well, first of all you'll stop calling me Mr. Blattman. Second, you'll not see me for several years, and you'll become the bitch of every trainer in the military and the agency we assign you to. And you will bleed, and hurt, and be intimidated and broken down and built back up, all in the name of protecting your country. I want you to go back to that armed forces recruiter. You tell him we spoke, and that you want to join the army."

"He was a marine …"

"Yeah, I know. You tell him we spoke and you want to join the army."

"When?"

"Tomorrow would be good."

"Uh, I have a test …"

"You passed." He reached into his coat pocket and pulled out a piece of thick paper folded into thirds. It was a diploma. It showed John Lester had graduated from Columbia University with a BA in history, minor in chemistry, cum laude. "You graduated."

"Is this—"

"Yes, it's real. But only if you go to the recruiter tomorrow and tell him what I told you. You don't, then you finish your senior year like every other schmo out there. Wear a suit and tie. Go to work for Citibank. And trudge along in your daily existence thinking about what you could have been."

"Are they going to send me to Kuwait?"

"Kid, you won't be done with basic before that thing is over. But don't worry, there will be other wars. Wars most people will never hear about."

"You're very good at your job, Mr. ... Paul."

"Yeah, I know," Blattman said as he got up. "Don't try to suck up to me, son, it doesn't become you. Recruiter, tomorrow. I might see you again in a few years if you're still alive. Thanks for the coffee." Blattman turned and walked out, sticking college student John Lester with the bill. But he did leave the diploma.

Lester returned to the recruiter. He said what he was supposed to say, signed some paperwork, and was given two days to pack up his things, tell his parents they should be so proud he had graduated early and saved them a year of tuition not covered by his scholarships, and that he was joining the military. Funny thing was, his parents were quite proud, even though this wasn't the path they had anticipated. His father had fought in Vietnam, was proud of his service, and was glad to see his son following in his footsteps.

If Dad knew what I was doing now, Lester reflected as he looked out at the Tokyo skyline, *he'd be appalled.*

Chapter 7

Queens, New York; March 2008.

The morning after our return from Costa Rica, I got up and did exercises for my shoulder. There was still some pain when I tried to fully extend my arm, so pull-ups or anything else that made me raise my hand above my head was trying. But I noticed improvement every day. Pain, but improvement.

I was in by 6:30 a.m., and the office was half-full. I got some coffee and walked over to Chris Winkler's cubicle. Chris was our tech specialist, and his cube was adorned with all sorts of Trekkie crap. And *Star Wars* crap. And *Battlestar Galactica* crap. He was somehow able to squeeze two CPUs and three flat-screens in there too. Chris was immersed in something that was no doubt enthralling to him, but everything on his screens looked like the code from *The Matrix* to me.

"Chris, we got a meeting with JJ," I said.

Without turning around, he waved his hand above his head like he were shooing a fly away. "I'll be there in a sec. I'm printing some stuff out in the conference room. I'll meet you guys there."

I walked down the hall to the conference room. A printer on a credenza was spitting out pages. There was a PowerPoint projector on, shining blank blue wallpaper onto the screen. JJ walked in behind me.

"Get enough sleep?" he asked.

"Yeah, fine. Winkler's on his way. So what's happened with Huntington since I left?"

"Huntington lawyered up. He's not talking. No bank codes, passwords, nothing. We can't locate any little black book, so Winkler is working on his hard drives to see if he had reminders in there. They're encrypted, but Winkler hopes he can break it given enough time. We've traced wire transfers and payments to offshore bank accounts in Bermuda, the Caymans, and Antigua. Most are to Antigua. Their government may cooperate in pressuring the banks there to help us get back the money. But no guarantees."

We would probably get most of what was left, eventually. Our first line of attack would normally be Huntington himself. He had the account numbers and passwords, and he could try to negotiate a better sentence if he assisted in recovering the money, but there were problems with that. Next, we could locate his account numbers and passwords, and then pose as Huntington online and try to get some money wired back. This had worked in the past but depended on the criminal recording the password information in some manner. Some criminals are smart enough to recognize that they should memorize the information and never write it down. Huntington was one of them.

Last, we could launch a proceeding in Antigua and the other jurisdictions to recover the ill-gotten gains. Some jurisdictions were easier than others. But, one way or another, most of the time we could get a lot back.

"Think Huntington will talk?" I asked JJ as Winkler entered the room.

"I don't know. He's an avaricious fuck." JJ had a way with words. "The problem is that he used a gun."

"Can't he negotiate a better sentence in exchange for the money?" asked Chris.

"U.S. attorney won't go for that," I said.

"Fuckin' A bubba he won't," JJ said. "No way is the U.S. attorney going to let a guy go to Club Fed when he shot two federal agents. He's going to a max or super-max. He's got no incentive to cooperate. He knows he's going away to date-rape central."

"How's the code-breaking going, Chris?" I asked.

"This guy had a significant program. We're talking 1024-bit polymorphic encryption ..."

"English, please," JJ said.

"English? It's really fucking hard to break! We may never get it without the encryption key."

"That's not why we're here," JJ said, turning to me. "You remember on the day of the raid you told me Huntington got tipped off?"

"Yeah. He could have guessed, though. Made the surveillance truck. Whatever."

"The very morning of the raid? And only two hours before? Right after we asked the U.S. attorney to start freezing assets? Bullshit. He was tipped off," JJ said, turning to Winkler. "Show him."

Winkler pulled the pages from the printer and brought them to the table. There were about ten sheets of paper. I read the top one. It took a second for it to sink in.

"Where did this come from?" I asked.

Winkler spoke. "Huntington's personal email account. It was sent from a cybercafe in Chevy Chase, Maryland."

The date and time stamp on the email read February 20, 2008, 7:54 a.m., the morning of the raid. The email read: *Huntington: Jordan's team to raid your offices this morning. Get out. CCS.*

"We got a leak," I said quietly.

"Yup" was all JJ said.

"It couldn't have been anyone on the advance team. You, Chris, Sanderson, Velasquez, Engler, or me. We were planning it for a week. Any of us could have given the guy five days' notice, in a way that couldn't be traced. And it couldn't be anyone else on the raid. They were all in Greenwich when this was sent."

"I agree. We've looked at everyone's communications, and there's nothing to indicate they ever spoke, emailed, or wrote Huntington or anyone at his firm." Everyone on the team had at least confidential clearance, and most had top secret. Their lives were an open book. The government got to look into every nook and cranny of their lives at any time, without ever telling them they were doing it. Problem was, there weren't enough people to do the looking, which is how guys like Aldrich Ames and Robert Hanssen were able to get away with their crimes for so long. Basically, you had to do something that brought you to the attention of the investigators before they started looking. An event such as the Huntington leak, however, meant everyone connected with the investigation was under suspicion.

"We got any video from the cybercafe?"

Winkler pointed to other pages. There were screenshots from video footage of a cash register counter. "The cybercafe is open twenty-four-seven. There's a surveillance camera at the checkout counter. It wasn't too busy that morning. Several people came in and out during the hour before and hour after. The video's not very good, and a few of them are wearing hats. Facial recognition software didn't get any hits, but that doesn't mean much given the shitty tape."

Unlike what you see in television and movies about government surveillance tools, facial recognition software is far from perfect. The software makes guesses based on facial features, comparing it to a database, but cannot positively identify most subjects. First, the subject has to be in the database to begin with. If you have high-quality source material, like a digital-camera drive, this enhances the ability to make an identification. Even then, facial hair, glasses, and hats can obscure the subject.

Chris punched some buttons on his laptop, and the projector displayed the raw camera footage. Chris sped it up. It was terrible quality. The camera was mounted above the clerk, looking down over his shoulder, making a baseball cap as good as a mask.

"How about going in and out of the café?"

"There's a bank ATM across the street," Chris noted, "but you can't see the door to the café from the surveillance camera. We matched a couple of these people by clothing passing by on the sidewalk, but that's it. Too far away, not much good."

I took a look at the printouts of the ten or so photos. Gang couture didn't help. Almost everyone wore a baseball hat, and the brims obscured their faces. You could tell there were a couple of girls or women, one with a particularly hot body. A glitzy ball cap obscured her face, and you could just make out a watch on her left wrist, but nothing that would help you to identify the person. It was cold on that February morning, so everyone wore long sleeves. No tattoos or other body markings were visible.

"This person couldn't have been stupid enough to pay with a credit card, I guess?" They both stared at me like I was an idiot. "Forget it. So at 7:54 a.m.," I continued, "someone walks into a cybercafe in Chevy Chase, Maryland, and sends an email using Huntington's personal email address. They had to use an email account of their own, right?"

"Which they created on the spot one minute beforehand with the username 'a1b2c3d4'."

"OK, so they walk in and send Huntington an extremely short and to the point email. Indicates they understood the urgency of the situation, and seems to indicate that they had just found out about it themselves. Maybe indicates they think the communication could have been traced, so kept it short so they could get out quick. We know this person wasn't on the team, but could have been communicating with someone on the team."

"We've looked at everyone's communications for the week before, and there's nothing that jumps out," JJ said.

I thought some more. "Either our internal communications are compromised, or we've got a bad seed in the chain somewhere who is very good at covering their tracks."

JJ nodded. "We're going to need to check everyone in and outside the bureau who could have possibly known about this and review all their movements and communications. Everyone on the team will have to take a polygraph."

"Maybe we're looking at this backward. Instead of trying to trace how the emailer found out about the raid, maybe we should work from their position back. Put yourself in their shoes. You have some reason to want to help Huntington. You've just found out about a raid on his offices, and you have to get word to him. You presumably have communicated with him in the past, using the 1024 polyglot ... the really fucking hard encryption software, but you don't have time to get to a computer that has that. You can't use any means of communications that would lead back to you, so that leaves public phones, a one-time-use cell phone, or a cybercafe. Phone's a non-starter because of voice recognition. Best communication is email. But you have to let Huntington know you are for real. Otherwise, he might think it's just a crank. So, you add two things: JJ's name and a code at the end that somehow is meaningful to Huntington. JJ's name seems to indicate that the two have communicated before, and about this particular division. Gives the email credibility. Huntington and the emailer both already know who JJ is. *How* is another question. And presumably 'CCS' would mean something to Huntington. Does that correspond to anything we know about him?"

"Nothing we've found so far," Chris replied. "We need to break his encryption."

"Keep working on it. JJ, see if the U.S. attorney can set up an interview with Huntington and his attorney. We should at least pretend to deal if we're going to shut down the leak. Meantime, Conrad's due in and we have to go see Winfield and Lazeris."

The phone in the conference room buzzed. The voice of JJ's assistant, Barry Serveilles, came through. "JJ?"

"Go ahead," JJ said.

"Alexandra Conrad from DHS is in the lobby for you and Mr. Sanders."

The lady's timing was spooky. "She really is in the intelligence business," I said.

Chapter 8

Western Colombia; March 2008.

"These damn jungle revolutionaries. They will be the death of me," Major Fernando Pinchao thought as he swatted a mosquito away from his neck. He was being realistic—they probably *would* be the death of him. No one hunted these terrorists with as high a profile as Major Pinchao and expected to live long. If they didn't assassinate him, then he would contract some horrid jungle disease and die from that. But if he could trade his life for that of Raul Reyes or "Tirofijo" Marulanda or Alfonso Cano, that was a trade he was willing to make. Because the death of just one of them would likely drive a stake into the heart of the ailing FARC.

Pinchao discovered his life's goal seven years ago, when his wife was killed in a FARC bombing in a shopping district in Bogota. In a strange way, the FARC had redeemed Major Fernando Pinchao. Prior to his wife's death, Pinchao was a corrupt army officer on the take like so many in his homeland. If he wasn't seizing wads of cash from drug busts, he was shaking down the cartels for protection money. In turn, he would use some of this money to entertain his bosses in the army and the political class, which further assured Pinchao's steady, inexorable rise from lieutenant to major. And had nothing changed, he would likely have been a general by now.

But things had changed, quite drastically. Pinchao adored his wife, Maralina. They had two children, both in schools away from home now for safety. Maralina had doted on the children, and ensured they did well in their studies.

When Pinchao was assigned to the Anti-Cartel Task Force in Bogota, they would often meet for lunch at a café near his office. One afternoon, they walked together from the café to the front door of the "barracks" (really an office building), where they kissed. She told him she would be doing some shopping, and off she walked. A half an hour later, he heard the explosion. The sound was incredible. It could never be mistaken, even ten blocks away, for the *pop pop pop* of fireworks, the way arms fire is sometimes heard. It sounded like a gigantic sonic boom, and Pinchao's windows rattled in their frames. He knew right away it was a bomb, and a very large one. He opened his window and looked out across the city square. Blocks away, he could see smoke rising from the general vicinity of the Unicentro shopping center. It was a modern, air-conditioned, upscale place his wife favored. And Pinchao immediately had a sick feeling in his stomach.

He was not able to identify Maralina's body until the following day, as it took rescue crews all night to reinforce the area so it was safe enough to retrieve the dead and wounded. Even then, Pinchao would have had trouble identifying her without looking at the ring on her finger. Her clothes were burnt and torn, her shoes gone, her handbag not recovered. Her face was unrecognizable, and Pinchao believed she must have been close to the source of the blast. When he touched her, and saw the ring, he knew it was her.

The FARC took responsibility for bombing the decadent capitalist center. And it was that day that Pinchao dedicated himself to destroying the group. It was also the day that Fernando Pinchao went straight. Because he was a prominent victim, Pinchao received a personal visit from Presidente Alvaro Uribe. It was during this audience that Pinchao confessed his prior crimes, identified other corrupt officials, and rededicated himself to the personal service of the president. Within days, the management of the armed forces was purged, with Major Pinchao overseeing appointments and handpicking replacements for the corrupt officials he had identified. The president offered to make him a general in order to solidify his authority, but Pinchao demurred. He had no desire to take a management position. Rather, he asked to oversee the anti-FARC effort, and this request was granted.

Pinchao was slowly but determinedly closing in on the FARC's jungle havens. By using arms, helicopters, and listening devices provided by the U.S., he was able to monitor their communications, triangulate their sources, and pick off one cell at a time, pushing the FARC to the western-most provinces, limiting their movement, and more importantly, their ability to produce drugs and kidnap targets, working from outside the jungle inward like a slowly closing bag. Pinchao was definitely one of those targets of the FARC. He may not have had long, but he was determined to strike a severe blow while he could.

Recently, his job had been made more difficult, as the top echelons of FARC leadership had gone radio silent. Garbled communications could be heard, but not triangulated. They seemed to have obtained some technology that prevented this. While the group was experiencing defections and cells were being sold out, not being able to monitor their planning was still troubling. He needed the help of his American advisers, who had proven quite valuable at training his men for jungle warfare.

The American liaisons were quite interesting. At the start, he had wished he could bottle their dedication and energy and hand it out to his men. The Americans did not participate in the graft or corruption that was common in Colombia. Once they began training his men, and his men recognized that they were becoming a professional force rather than a corrupt third-world army on the take, something strange happened: They began to take pride in themselves and their units. Their uniforms were kept cleaner and worn more trimly. They saluted smartly, and when they should. Moreover, they also took pride in their leader, Major Pinchao. And as he developed a reputation for honesty and dedication, they emulated him. Corruption in his units almost disappeared, and those who offered bribes to his troops were arrested.

Ironically, the FARC had cleaned up the Colombian Army (or at least a significant part of it), the last thing they wanted to do. And they had redeemed the life of a corrupt army officer, and given him a goal: to completely stamp out this brutal and anachronistic group, a radical revolutionary leftover from the 1960s and 70s. He would see that it was done. And to do so, he had to find out how they were communicating, and where they were. For the time being, this minor jungle camp would have to suffice.

"Major, you may wish to look here," his second-in-command, Arturo Jaramillo, called softly.

Pinchao crawled on his belly across the jungle floor. They occupied a richly forested high ground looking down into a valley. Although well camouflaged, the village huts below could be seen by a trained eye. Jaramillo handed Pinchao his field glasses. It was 06:30. His platoon had been up since 04:30, working their way in the darkness to this point. They suspected a rebel camp sat in the village below, and could not take the chance of traveling by day. The night-vision goggles supplied by the Americans solved the problem of traveling by night. However, the fidelity was not good enough from this distance to make out all the village structures. They had to take up a concealed position above and wait for daylight. Now that they were here, they could reconnoiter.

Pinchao smiled and reached back behind him. He waved his American adviser forward. Lt. Colonel Armin Smith crawled forward slowly and silently on his elbows, his powerful arms visible even under his camouflage tunic. Pinchao marveled at the man, who was gray at fifty-two years of age but incredibly fit. He could outrun any of the young men in Pinchao's unit. Smith was a widower as well. He and Pinchao had become close friends.

Smith slid up to them, took the offered binoculars, and looked through. "Mmph," he grunted. "It's there, claro." Smith had become so adept at switching back and forth between English and Spanish he didn't even realize he was mixing his languages in the same sentence. He handed the glasses back to Pinchao, who handed them back to Jaramillo. Smith said, "We have to wait for darkness if we are going to take it all at once."

Jaramillo looked confused. "Major, I could lead four or five men back over the mountain, around the perimeter, and then back in the other side. Once there, we could coordinate an attack from both sides of the camp. You could flush them to us and rescue the hostages while we take the rebels running out."

Both Smith and Pinchao had already considered this and both had rejected it. Pinchao explained: "Lieutenant, it would take you at least six hours to make it all the way around, and in daylight there is too great a chance of discovery. If we wait for nightfall, we don't have to backtrack. We can go straight down and split our force at this end of the village. Your team can work their way around the perimeter and take up that same position on the other side, and still be far less likely to be discovered until we attack."

Smith nodded.

Jaramillo saw the wisdom of the plan and nodded as well. They would wait for darkness and use their night-vision advantage.

Pinchao tapped Jaramillo on his shoulder to get his attention. In this dense forest, he could have been within inches of Jaramillo's face and never seen him without night vision. Using a series of hand motions, he indicated that Jaramillo should get B Team going. They headed off, while Pinchao, Smith, and their remaining team waited. It was a good time to reconnoiter the camp again. Maybe ten structures. A generator with cans of gasoline next to it. Pinchao shook his head. These terrorists needed to see a few Stallone or Schwarzenegger movies. If they had, they'd know that the first thing an attacker would do is throw grenades into the fuel depot to create confusion and fear. By placing them next to the generator, the rebels risked creating their own explosion if the generator created too much heat, or sparked. Not bright, these men.

The generator was running quietly, and a few weak lights were on in a handful of cabins about the camp. Twelve men in dirty camis were gathered in a *cabina*, a wall-less platform with a corrugated roof. They sat at two tables, AK-47s either on the ground next to them or leaned up against their chairs. One of the two groups appeared to be playing cards, the other talking and laughing. All were drinking beer, which they retrieved periodically from a top-entry refrigeration unit to the side of the cabina. The refrigerator was likely sucking most of the generator's power, which explained the dim lighting.

Click-click, Pinchao heard in his earpiece. He looked at his watch. Forty-five minutes had elapsed since Jaramillo's team left. They had made good time. Through a series of prearranged clicks, Pinchao told Jaramillo to remove the night-vision goggles and allow his team's eyes to adjust. Soon, the camp would be lit up with fire, and no one wanted to be night blind. He advised Jaramillo that A Team was proceeding.

They approached on a narrow, single-track path. The next part had to happen as quickly and as silently as possible. Quickly was no problem. Silently was. The FARC didn't have the resources to set a lot of booby traps or alarms. Their primary defense was secrecy—they hid their camps deep in the jungle, so it was rare for a camp to actually be located and invaded. The rebels were still at their two tables. Pinchao clicked his comm to let Jaramillo know A Team was approaching the cabina. After A Team removed their goggles, Pinchao whispered, "Let's go."

In an operation of this nature, it was the small things that had to be done right. Surprise was critical, and had it not been for a seemingly insignificant element, Pinchao and his men would have maintained it. When a flashlight is attached to the M16 barrel, the shaft of the torch must be insulated from the heat of the barrel, and it has to be set so that the on/off switch can only be turned on by reaching over the top of the barrel with the non-trigger hand, rather than on the same side as the free hand. This is to prevent what happened next. As one of Pinchao's men walked slowly and silently down the hill, he reached back with his right hand to pull his M16 forward to his hip. The flashlight's "on" switch brushed against his leg, and the light blinked on. The man turned it off immediately, which only made the situation worse, because it was the blink that drew the attention of one of the soldiers in the cabina.

The lighting in the forest helped Pinchao and his men. The FARC soldier was in a bright area looking into a dark area, and the Colombian Army soldiers were well-camouflaged for night operations. But despite being unable to see an actual threat, the soldier stood up, called everyone's attention to the fact that he had seen the light, and picked up his gun. Smith understood that there were two things to be done in this situation: find cover and hide, hoping they would look, see nothing and return to what they were doing; or attack immediately. Smith knew which he preferred. He ran forward, lifting his gun to his shoulder, and shot the rebel in the head. The entire platoon broke into a run at the cabina. The rebels scattered, knocking over tables and chairs as they struggled for their weapons.

Smith broke right, firing a constant stream to suppress a counterattack and to allow Pinchao's men to spread out and surround the cabina. As he moved down the main path, firing at the cabina on his left, his peripheral vision caught movement. He tucked in next to the wall of a hut and heard a bullet whiz by over his head. "I've got fire coming from the huts on the right," he said into his mic.

Once Smith cleared their field of fire, Pinchao's men spread out and advanced on the cabina, firing methodically. Their targets were well-lit until an errant bullet hit the overhead light and plunged the area into darkness. It would be lit again soon enough. The man bringing up the rear on Pinchao's team threw a grenade into the cluster of gasoline cans next to the generator and then ran forward. The explosion, unlike those involving shrapnel bombs, was essentially a bright, Hollywood-like incendiary one. A huge fireball burst upward into the air and smaller secondary explosions followed. The initial fireball lit up the whole camp before imploding into itself. Its primary brightness created a shadow of the gunman Smith couldn't originally see. The shadow allowed him to gauge the approximate location of the rebel, and without poking his head out, he turned the M16 around the corner of the hut and fired, moving the barrel slightly up and down, left and right. As he continued to fire, he stood up and turned the corner. A rebel, whom Smith took to be a short man, lay on the ground, frantically working the slide on his AK-47. Smith continued to fire and hit the man in the head and shoulders. He fell back and stopped moving. Rather than continue forward, Smith moved back to assess the situation and wait for backup before he moved in among the sleeping quarters.

At that moment he heard a fusillade from his left, the direction of B Team. Some of the rebels had clearly run away from the danger posed by A Team, only to be caught in the automatic-fire buzz saw of Jaramillo's B Team.

Pinchao was still at the cabina and saw Smith come from between two huts on the other side of the camp's main path.

"I need a team to clear the huts," Smith said.

Pinchao called to one of his men, then clicked his mic. "Corrivas and Smith clearing sleeping quarters. Do not fire into the huts. I repeat, do not fire into the huts to the north of the main path. B team, report contacts."

Jaramillo's voice came over the comm: "Multiple contacts, unknown number, no friendly casualties. Continuing suppression."

"Montes, pull two men back and guard eastern egress, ensure no rebels escape."

"Copy," came Luis Montes's voice.

Manuel Corrivas, Smith, and Pinchao took a triangle formation, with Corrivas taking the lead point and Smith and Pinchao behind him to the right and left. There were seven huts, three on the right and four on the left of the tributary path leading away from the camp center. Pinchao looked over. "Stop," he hissed. Smith and Corrivas froze.

He looked to the now-useless generator and saw the lead power cable running from it and then splitting off into a few branches. One led to the cabina lights and refrigerator. Another traveled overhead on a series of poles down the path they were now on and split between two cabins, both at the end of the row. Damn. He wanted to rush those first, before anything of value—like papers or a computer hard drive—could be destroyed.

He motioned toward the last cabin on the right using prearranged hand signals and began running. Corrivas and Smith followed. They stayed low, and as they passed the first two cabins, nothing happened. But as they passed the next one, a popping sound burst out. Corrivas broke left while Smith stopped short of the hut and took cover behind its outer wall. Smith pulled a grenade from his belt, popped the pin, and threw the grenade into the hut through the window opening. "Fire in the hole!" He dove to the ground and covered his head. Corrivas covered, holding his position across the path. Pinchao, on the other side of the lane, didn't bother to cover and instead pulled his M16 up to the ready position.

The door to the hut flew open and Pinchao fired immediately, without waiting to see anyone fill the doorway. He heard cries, then *bam!* Smoke came wafting out the hut window. All went silent. Pinchao ran to the last cabin, tugging at Corrivas as he ran by.

"Come on!"

Smith was up and behind him, turning his back to Pinchao to provide cover fire if necessary. The major stepped to the side of the door and, using the butt of his rifle as a battering ram, hit just inside the knob. The door flew open and gunfire erupted out of the cabin. Smith, to the right of the door, felt rounds go by him. He jumped further to his left, spinning. He fired into the open doorway of the cabin and methodically advanced. It was an incredibly brave and stupid thing to do. Anyone not in Smith's field of fire could fire back, either through a window or through the thin walls. No one did fire back. Smith's first five rounds hit the rebel who had been shooting, center chest. Later, Pinchao would marvel at the pentacle pattern that resulted, a nice grouping in near-complete darkness and into a doorway in which the only gauge Smith had as to the location of the rebel was the muzzle flash from his weapon, and that only seen from his peripheral vision.

Pinchao followed Smith in. The rebel was an older man, at least fifty-five, probably past sixty. Pinchao's eyes immediately passed over his face and onto a computer CPU tower, a satellite phone, and some paper files. "We need to secure this." He hit his mic button.

"B Team, report."

"We had multiple contacts, but they have ceased."

"OK, proceed into the camp and clear every building you come to. Gather all prisoners in the cabina. Montes, report."

"No contacts this direction."

"OK, do the same. Proceed in and clear buildings."

"Yes, sir," came the response. Pinchao turned to where he thought Smith would be, but he was gone. He turned completely around, concerned that he may have been hit, but Smith was not in the hut. He was out in the pathway, checking on the rebel he had initially taken out. The short man turned out not to be a man at all, but a boy of about age twelve.

"Fuck" was all that came to Smith's mind. Pinchao exited the cabin and readied his weapon.

"Armin, we're not done," he called. Smith came back and they reentered the last hut. "Ivan Marquez," Pinchao said, pointing to the body on the floor. "Number four in the FARC."

There was a computer monitor, a CPU, and a printer on a desk, and a file cabinet. Smith was about to sit down at the computer but Pinchao stopped him. "Could be wired," he explained. He turned to Corrivas, who was certified in demolition disposal.

"Manuel, I want you to check for possible booby traps. We need to retrieve the hard drive."

"Yes, sir." Corrivas directed Smith and Pinchao out of the hut while he set to work. They decided to rejoin everyone else at the cabina. His men had the survivors and noncombatant camp population secured there.

"Those of you willing to lay down your arms and return to your families may do so," Pinchao began. "No further questions will be asked, and the government of Colombia will require no prison stay or penalty from you. However, in exchange, we require your assistance in locating other camps and tracking down the leadership of your 'People's Army.'" It was the same speech he gave at all the camps they had raided. It was quite effective, since the majority of the FARC rank and file were quite demoralized. Some had been in the jungle all their lives and had never known living outside. But most had come from the cities and at some level yearned for the comforts of city life.

Pinchao and Smith began walking back to the computer hut. As they approached, they heard Corrivas yell, "Stay back!"

They stopped in their tracks.

"Manuel, what is it?"

"It's wired," he called. "The keyboard, the monitor and the CPU. I'm going to try to slide the hard drive—"

BAM!

"Shit!" Corrivas came running out of the cabin with a rectangular box in his hand. "Down!" he yelled. They all hit the dirt. An explosion blew out the window of the hut. They all looked at each other. Manuel held the hard drive up in a charred right hand, smiling broadly.

"Two incendiaries, designed to destroy the computer rather than do much damage. When I slid this out, the first one blew but didn't damage the drive much. It did set off the other one wired to the keyboard and monitor, though."

Pinchao clapped him on the shoulder. "Nice job, Manuel."

All in all, a good day for the Colombian Armed Forces. No casualties of significance. A FARC leader killed. Potentially significant information recovered from the CPU and cell phone memory of Marquez's equipment. Another FARC safe haven eliminated. Before departing, Pinchao ordered the camp burned to the ground. As always.

Chapter 9

Midtown Manhattan; March 2008.

"Winkler," JJ said, "get as many people from IT to help you as possible. We need to break the code."

"OK," said Chris. He gathered his materials and all the papers and left.

Alex Conrad was escorted to the conference room. Both JJ and I stood up and exchanged handshakes with her. She had a Starbucks cup in her hand, so we left out the "coffee?" pleasantries and all sat down.

"So, what'd the boss say?" I asked.

"He wasn't real pleased with the whole field agent aspect of this, but he also recognizes that ASBT could be an arms-dealer funding source. So, I've got a few days to hang around with you guys to prove my theory, and hopefully help you with your side of the case too."

"Great. Let's go make an appointment to see Winfield, then we'll try out Lazeris."

"How's it going on the Huntington case?" she asked

JJ and I looked at each other. JJ spoke, "Conrad, we can't really discuss that with you."

"It's going to cross my desk eventually," she pointed out.

"JJ," I said, "we need all the help we can get." I turned to her. "You used to be a tech geek, right?"

"Thanks for the title. Yes."

"Encryption?"

"Yeah." I looked at JJ.

"I'll need to talk to her boss again," he sighed, rolling his eyes.

"I think we gotta do it. If he approves, she can help Chris on the 1024 polynumeric—"

"1024-bit polymorphic encryption?" she asked.

"What you said," I replied.

"You've got your work cut out for you," she said. "I've never heard of it being broken without the cipher key. But I may be able to harness some assets at Langley to take a look—"

"First things first," JJ interrupted. "Let me talk to Borenstein,"—he meant Conrad's boss—"then we can cross that bridge if we ever get there."

"Cool. Let's go see Winfield," I said.

Chapter 10

Valle del Cauca, Colombia; March 2008.

Raul Reyes shut off his computer. He could hear the hum of the generator diminish now that he was drawing less power from it. The lights in the camp, which had dimmed slightly when he turned on the computer and plugged in several mobile communications devices to recharge, now returned to normal. To be sure, "normal" was not exactly bright, just less dim than they had been. Raul still found it difficult to read in this light, more so as he aged. "Damn my aging eyes," he thought. He took off his normal glasses and put on his reading glasses.

"Let me see the schedule for this week, Tirofijo."

"Tirofijo" (Sureshot) was a term of respect, a compliment bestowed when Raul and his lifelong friend, Manuel Marulanda, began in the Revolutionary Armed Forces of Colombia, known colloquially as the FARC. Technically, it was the FARC-EP, or Revolutionary Armed Forces of Colombia–People's Army, which reflected a long-ago adoption of a title during the heady days when Leonid Brehznev, then the Premier of the Soviet Union, had suggested the group would receive more support if they moved from a guerrilla movement to a conventional military force. They obliged, and for a while the FARC-EP looked to be on the verge of attaining its goal of creating a Marxist-Leninist society in Colombia. It looked that way until a man named Mikhail Gorbachev took power in the Soviet Union and engaged in a series of cutbacks to try to right the faltering economy of his nation and bring it into parity with the U.S. Then, all aid disintegrated when the Soviet Union collapsed. The FARC had to root about for other sources of income to keep its revolutionary dreams alive.

That's when Manuel "Tirofijo" Marulanda, Raul Reyes, and their third in command, Alfonso Cano, hit upon a very un-Marxist-Leninist plan. With all of the arms they had at their disposal, and considering they occupied the same territory as the cartels (of which they had been a beneficiary client), Raul and Manuel realized they could become the cartels rather than kowtow to them, begging for scraps from their table. After calling a summit meeting of the cartel bosses at which Tirofijo arranged for a mass execution, the FARC became the largest cocaine producer in the world, holding the Colombian monopoly and bringing all the diverse cartel family employees under their control. For the past ten years, the FARC's primary funding source had been the sale of cocaine in exchange for arms, food, medical supplies, and other materials needed for the revolution. Raul never perceived the irony that as head of one of the last remaining Marxist revolutionary groups in the world, he was the biggest capitalist of all. To him, this was simply a means to an end, and once the revolution was achieved, he and Tirofijo would eliminate the drug trade altogether using means that the democratically elected governments lacked the will or desire to use.

Reyes recognized that many of his rank-and-file followers had lost their revolutionary fervor. However, he also understood that their dream of a better, more just world could not be achieved without assets and materials. And the only way to obtain those materials was through the sale of drugs to a decadent and unjust North America, although he had been told that Asia had recently become a larger market for his product. Besides, in effect he was engaged in barter: he was simply trading his product for arms. And what could be more Marxist than that? To each according to his needs, after all.

Tirofijo handed the Microsoft Outlook printout to Reyes. Reyes, a big fan of technology, had dragged his friend into the twenty-first century. Before they adopted computers and encrypted phones, all communications had been by hand, or rather, by messenger. If the messenger was caught or killed, the message never got through. Organizing the drug trade forced the FARC to adopt modern conveniences, since this was the way the cartels had done business. Once Reyes had seen the efficiency, and relative safety, of doing business this way, he urged the FARC to use the same methods for all their work. It had not been an easy discussion, and Tirofijo had objected fiercely. But when Reyes pointed out that the Cartel lost just ten people a year to intercepted communications, whereas the FARC lost hundreds, Tirofijo relented. Reyes hired the son of a soldier from Cartagena who had just come out of technical college to set up their network.

It was difficult, since the FARC cells were dispersed over the wide mountainous and jungle region of western Colombia (and eastern Ecuador and Venezuela as well). But the boy had been more than up to the challenge, setting up wireless, networked communication that linked all the cells together and allowed Reyes and Tirofijo to coordinate attacks, shipments, and arms transfers. Moreover, once they had met Alejandro de Plata, and his encryption specialist at the Cayman bank, their communications became unbreakable. De Plata showed them the magic of encryption and diversified cipher keys with different access rights—more access for higher-level members, less for lower-level ones. Moreover, Comrade de Plata was the key to the barter system. He had the connections that allowed them to bring arms in and to ship drugs out. He kept the profit, which Reyes was certain was large, but with the technology at his fingertips, Reyes could ensure he wasn't getting completely screwed on the deals. He (roughly) knew what the average price of his raw powder was at any given moment.

What these recent events showed was that the power was shifting from the titular head of the FARC, Tirofijo, to the operational head, Reyes. While all decisions had to be cleared through Tirofijo, it was Reyes who made the decisions and suggested a course of action to his aging and ill friend. And everyone including Tirofijo understood this. If something happened to Tirofijo, Reyes would take over in any event, so it was logical to start shifting power now. The decision regarding their impending Bogota operation was one example.

"So, did our shipment arrive from next door?"

"Next door," as Tirofijo and Reyes referred to it, was Venezuela, through which most of their arms shipments were routed.

"Yes. Almara is bringing it in on horseback convoy." Horseback was about the only transportation method the FARC had at its disposal, given the terrain. "With this shipment, we should be able to strike at Uribe and his fascist government directly."

Both men had made grand statements about their ability to bring the Colombian government to its knees, and every time they meant it. But they knew this time was their best chance, and perhaps their last best chance, to do so. Although neither would admit it to the other, or any of their soldiers, they were in trouble. They had been living in the jungle for decades, pursuing their revolutionary dream and in the process becoming drug dealers and kidnappers. But they had yet to strike a decisive blow against the fascists in Bogota. And now with Uribe in office, the army had become much more aggressive. The FARC had had to move their base of operations across the border to Ecuador. Venezuela was also willing to assist. Those governments shared their socialist vision and turned a blind eye to their presence.

This time, their ability to strike was different. With their secret communications, they had been able to develop and coordinate a plan that would hit directly at Uribe, as well as his party's leaders in the Congress. And the last of a series of arms shipments was making its way to them. With the cache they had amassed, they would be well-armed for a final push into Bogota immediately following the thrilling first strike. The people would realize the FARC had taken control and would take to streets to support them. Reyes and Tirofijo knew this would happen. Their moment had finally arrived.

"Oh, one other thing, Reyes. We had an offer for the French woman. It appears the new French president is willing to pay for her. And we could probably get an additional payment for her child."

"Not the child, Tirofijo. Just her. What is he offering?"

"Two million U.S."

"Take it. But the child is off limits. He stays with us."

"Raul, the child will be a burden without the mother."

"We will find a wet nurse. The child will forget about his capitalist mother in time. She was a means to an end, that's all. The boy stays."

Tirofijo had never seen Reyes so adamant about a child before. Neither man had any children of their own, at least not that they knew of. There had been many women, but it was only the comradely thing to do to share those women, so knowing who was the father of any given child within the FARC was difficult. Children were reared by the cell. Tirofijo wondered if Reyes somehow knew he was the child's father. It was possible. He had interrogated the woman many times when she first arrived. And Reyes had made special arrangements for her, especially after the woman was obviously pregnant.

"I will accept the money for the woman. They don't know about her *hijo* anyway, and she won't be able to tell them until she is gone."

"Good. Let's do it. Now, about the attack. We need our contacts in the army to do some reconnaissance work, and perhaps some logistics."

Chapter 11

Midtown Manhattan; March 2008.

At ten in the morning, Conrad and I popped into the main corporate offices of ASBT. They were on a couple of floors halfway up a midtown highrise. I had been given a badge and a gun by JJ, which I had to sign for. While the badge was a close replica of a bureau special agent badge, the credentials with it, if examined closely, indicated I was a contractor for the government, not a direct employee. No one ever looked closely. Conrad's DHS badge was a bit more impressive, which could give a guy an inferiority complex if he cared about that sort of thing.

"Hi, I'm Nick Sanders with the FBI," I said as I showed the receptionist, whose nameplate indicated her name was Sylvia DeStefano. "This is agent Conrad. We don't have an appointment, but we were hoping to get about five minutes of Mr. Winfield's time."

Sylvia looked appropriately startled at first, but then quickly regained composure. She handed my credentials back without looking past the badge and said, "I'll see if Mr. Winfield is available. If you'll have a seat right over there, I'd be happy to bring you some coffee, water, or any other beverage you'd like." Damn, she was good. We were just like any other client, except we didn't have any money.

"Thank you. Could I get some coffee with cream, no sugar?" I asked. I looked over at Alex and tilted my head.

"Nothing for me, thanks." Apparently she was not as impressed with Ms. DeStefano's reception skills as I was.

We sat down and I could hear her dial the phone and speak softly into it. "Hello, this is Sylvia at reception. I have a Mr. Sanders and a Ms. Conrad from the FBI to see Mr. Winfield. They don't have an appointment but hoped to get just a few minutes."

There was a pause, some more hushed conversation, and then, "Mr. Winfield will be down to collect you in a moment, Mr. Sanders. In the meantime—" *DING*, the elevator rang and a young man in a suit came out with a china cup and saucer on a tray with cream and sugar on the side. He deposited it on the table, turned and left. "—enjoy your coffee," she finished. I hadn't even heard her order it.

Now you should know that I am a coffee connoisseur. I've been all over the world and had all sorts—Parisian Espresso, Italian Espresso, Greek coffee, Turkish coffee (same as Greek but don't tell the Turks), South American coffee, Vietnamese coffee (with a thick, sweet condensed milk)—and I've splurged on "varietals," select beans from a particular farm. Starbucks? Dunkin' Donuts? Peet's? Seattle's Best? Been there, done all of that. Even had to settle for Folgers Crystals when I was stuck on a boat for a week. I know what I like. And I liked this coffee. I don't know what ASBT was pouring, but there had to be some heroin in there, because once I tasted it, I drank the entire cup down. I was about to ask for more when *DING*, the elevator opened and a stately gentleman who appeared to be in his mid-fifties exited the elevator, looked at Sylvia and turned toward us. Impeccable suit, not a strand out of place on a full head of black hair, speckled with gray, and gray at the temples, white textured shirt with French cuffs and masculine, understated links. I noticed his tie had a half-Windsor knot.

He put out his hand to Conrad first. "Ms. Conrad? I'm Jeremy Winfield." He shook her hand then turned to me. "Mr. Sanders, I presume?" I nodded. "I see Ms. DeStefano has gotten you some coffee. Why don't we go into a conference room?"

He led the way down a hall and past a very large conference room and into a second one, not as large but still bigger than we needed. He indicated two seats near the end of a conference table with the flat of his hand, saying, "Please." We sat. He took the chair at the head of the table.

"So, Ms. DeStefano tells me you are with the FBI. May I see your identification, please?"

We both pulled our creds and showed them to him. He looked closely at them and then said, "Mr. Sanders, it indicates here you are a contractor with the bureau, not an agent?" Damn, he actually read them. I had to make a note of this for the future Nick Sanders autobiography under the chapter headed "Shit I Never Thought I'd See Suspects Do."

"That's correct. I left the bureau about eight months ago and opened a consulting practice. I still work for the bureau from time to time, and have virtually the same authority as a special agent."

"I see. And Ms. Conrad, you're not with the bureau at all?"

"No," Alex responded, "I'm with the Homeland Security Director's office. The information gathered by the bureau and other law enforcement agencies feeds up to us."

"All right. What can I do for you?"

"First you can get me some of that kick-ass coffee you guys are serving," I said. OK, I made that up. I didn't really say that. Instead, I said, "Mr. Winfield, we're investigating an insider-trading allegation against one of your clients, or rather one of your deceased clients. But I think you still handle his money. Marcus Vanderhoff?"

He seemed quite surprised. "Marcus? Really? I'd be quite surprised since after he sold his company, Mr. Vanderhoff hired professional money managers to handle his funds. That would mean that one of the managers was trading illegally, since Marcus never really took an interest in the day-to-day purchases of securities."

Wow. Damn. Shit. All this went through my head. This guy knew what was going on in his firm, which is actually quite surprising for a CEO. Most CEOs have a vague notion of day-to-day operations but are too busy organizing strategy, moving the boxes around on the org chart and golfing to notice.

"You seem to know Mr. Vanderhoff's account very well," Alex said.

"Indeed," he said. Did he really say indeed? Made him sound like Mr. Spock. "I know most of our clients and their beneficiaries very well. We're a boutique bank. We cater only to accounts of twenty-five million dollars or more, and Mr. Vanderhoff's account, or rather his trust account for the benefit of his family, is two *billion* dollars. You tend not to lose sight of an account like that. Anyway, what stock is at issue?"

Now, we weren't complete idiots, and we were actually prepared for this question. We picked a post-Internet bubble stock that was pumped up by the CEO and then took a huge dump, perfect for an insider-trading accusation against those who got out just before the fall. "HCD," we said in unison.

What we were doing was actually a bit dangerous. We knew Vanderhoff was not trading, and we didn't know of any accusation against his money managers at the time. The only reason we were here was to feel out Winfield, to check Conrad's theory against gut instinct. If it turned out in the future we had to come back to investigate further, then we would have to admit to Winfield that we had lied to him about the reason for this first meeting. That tended to tick people off.

"Oh, I see. Yes, I could see how that might look if Marcus or a manager had sold it before it went under. Well, while I am familiar with our clients, I don't know all of their holdings. Perhaps," he said, writing down the ticker on a notepad, "I can get Mr. Klatten, Marcus's private banker, to dig up the files for the years in question. We prepared consolidated statements for Marcus from all his money managers prior to his death. Of course, before I do so I'll need to see a warrant."

Stomp. Well, he just about brought the conversation to an end. Not that a warrant was a problem. We could certainly get one, though not for the reason we asserted. But we would be quickly finished with Mr. Winfield for today.

"No problem," I said. "We're happy to go get one and return Monday, if that's all right?"

"Certainly."

"Just a couple of other questions," I continued. "You said you prepared statements consolidating information from his other money managers prior to his death. What about after his death?"

"Marcus's trust gave us full authority to manage his money. For cost efficiency, we had all the other funds transferred here. We saved his beneficiaries quite a bit of money."

"You do well here, don't you?" Alex asked. A little too harsh, but he seemed unfazed.

"Yes, we do, Ms. Conrad. But we never forget what our mission is."

"What's that?" I asked.

"We take care of our client's money during their life, and after their passing we take care of their beneficiaries pursuant to their wishes."

"And collect all the money here."

"Sometimes. Many times, however, the funds get reallocated to outside money managers with whom we have contractual relationships for management at reduced fees."

"I thought you managed the money," Alex asked.

"Ms. Conrad, we cannot be experts at all strategies. For instance, while we manage several portfolios of publically traded

U.S. stocks and bonds, we typically outsource the management of international securities, hedge funds, private equity and other alternative investments. We sometimes commit a minimum investment amount through exclusivity agreements with a particular manager or strategy in exchange for a significantly reduced fee."

"It must be tempting . . ." I said, looking about the wood-paneled room, my voice trailing off.

"I'm sorry?"

"Oh, I mean it must be tempting to just move numbers from one side of the ledger to the other. Then you could take private planes everywhere, golf at Augusta, helicopter ski in Austria, just like your clients."

He seemed only mildly perturbed, as if he were dealing with a child he caught taking one cookie too many. "First, I would point out that we are not just a bank, we are a trust company. While the word carries obvious meaning, most people don't appreciate what holding such a title entails. It is much more than our clients trusting us to hold and manage their money. We have a fiduciary responsibility to our clients. That is, we have to put their interests ahead of our own. That's what being a trust company is all about.

"As to your question, Mr. Sanders, I've been in banking my entire adult life. I have never once coveted any life other than the one I lead. But you're right, it is quite tempting to those who don't understand the important function we serve. I always tell our young bankers and trainees that we are permitted to move through our clients' world, but we don't live in it. It's not our money to do with as we please, and the client can fire us at any time. So, we'd better be answerable to them." Good answer, and obviously well-practiced. Nevertheless, he seemed sincere.

"Mr. Winfield, what was your background before banking? I mean, where'd you grow up, what'd your folks do for living?" I always like to ask this question because it puts people at ease.

They like to talk about their background, and it gives me insights into their character. Also, although I had no right to the information, it was not objectionable to most people.

"Well, I grew up in New Jersey. My father owned a gas station. My mother was a schoolteacher. My father made sure all his children went to college, something he was unable to do himself." He stood. "And we all did." The meeting was over.

I was starting to like this guy. "OK, well, we'll check into the warrant and be back. Thanks for your cooperation and time," I said as Conrad and I got up. "You know, I would have taken you for a full-Windsor man."

"It's casual Friday. I like to let loose a little," he said with a wink. He led us to the elevator bank.

"Thanks for your time."

"No problem at all. Please call in advance next time and we can be ready to assist you with the material for your warrant."

We got in the elevator and rode it down. "Smooth," Alex said.

"Very. He didn't show any fear that we were with law enforcement. No sweat on his brow, no nervous movements of the hand. Kept his hands in sight the whole time, and used them for normal conversational gestures. He's either a sociopath or he's not in on it."

"I'm starting to agree," Alex said. "Let's go talk to the lawyer."

Chapter 12

Midtown Manhattan; March 2008.

Five years ago, Ed Lazeris was in danger of becoming the attorney he feared the most: working out of a storefront, taking any case that came along, frayed coat, bad tie, those shineable shoes that looked like sneakers, living hand to mouth. His mother would not have been proud. It had all started off so differently.

Lazeris graduated near the top of his class at the University of Miami School of Law and moved back to his home state of New York to take a job at a powerhouse law firm. He was making $125,000 a year right out of school, a monstrous sum for someone who knew nothing about the actual practice of law. He was placed in the tax, trust and estate planning department of Clausen & Kemp, an international firm with over one thousand attorneys on staff. Lazeris soon discovered that despite how smart he felt he was, and despite the fact that he had graduated number five in his class, everyone else at the firm was just as smart, and many more so. He also discovered that the practice of law involved, at least for a junior associate at Clausen & Kemp, six and a half days per week of work in order to accumulate forty hours of time that would actually be billed to the client, taking into account hours the supervising junior partner would write off and other time the senior partner on the account would simply bill as his own, despite the fact that while Lazeris was toiling away in the office, the senior partner was chipping in for a birdie on the eighteenth green.

By his second year, Lazeris discovered that he had accumulated fifty thousand dollars in savings, since he had no time to spend his money. By his third year, he understood the business model at Clausen & Kemp: hire young, eager associates, don't let them have any client contact, keep them billing with ridiculously high billable hour requirements, and when the firm runs out of work or the associate begins to think he or she should meet with clients, make more money or have some recognition, gently advise them they are not on the partner track, give them a poor annual review with little or no raise, and ease them out the door; hire a new young, eager associate, and repeat.

So the typical associate track was try to get some client contact without the partner knowing and get hired directly by the client as in-house counsel, or leave for a smaller firm, or leave for another big firm that would pay more, or leave and open your own shop. By his fourth year at Clausen & Kemp, Lazeris knew what was coming. His last review had been average, no one spoke about partnership, and his senior partner barely spoke to him at all. He began leaving early, taking longer smoking breaks and lunches, and began drinking at lunch. He didn't really care, and was completely disillusioned with the practice of law. Not that he wasn't good. If he found a case that piqued his interest, he could do extremely good work. There just weren't many of those, and he had already mastered all the work necessary to assist wealthy clients in avoiding income and estate taxes.

It continually amazed Lazeris how these clients, who were little different than Ed, had gotten wealthy. Some were just lucky. Some were, by accident of birth, handed advantages others didn't have and simply held on without fumbling. Some were genuinely good at what they did, but couldn't tie their shoes without assistance. And many were just crooks who screwed over business partners and associates and had better attorneys than those partners and associates. The fact that these people got driven to and from work every day, flew in private planes, were given citizenship awards at black-tie galas, and feted as if they were royalty disgusted Lazeris. The things he knew about them because of attorney-client communications could land many in jail, or ostracize them in the New York social scene. There was no difference between them and him, but Lazeris saw himself as a far superior person than most of his clients. They had been lazy and lucky. He had worked hard his whole life and been handed the short end.

Lazeris figured he had about one more year before he was shown the door. Then an amazing thing happened. Or rather, an amazing *person* happened. Ed Lazeris met Jeremy Winfield of ASBT. One of Ed's clients had insisted that ASBT be named as his successor trustee. The client died soon after the drafting of the trust, and Lazeris was assigned to handle the estate settlement in conjunction with ASBT. Lazeris made numerous trips to ASBT, where he met initially with Ernst Klatten, a young but smart, energetic banker and trust officer. Eventually, Klatten introduced Lazeris to Winfield.

One day, Winfield called Lazeris at his office and asked him to lunch. They met at Del Frisco's, and over steaks and wine, Winfield got around to asking Lazeris about his plans for the future. At first, Lazeris was hoping Winfield would offer him a job. But as the conversation progressed, Winfield suggested that if Lazeris would go out on his own (he could sublet space in the office of a friend of Winfield's), ASBT would keep Lazeris busy with plenty of referred work. "You see, Ed," Winfield told him, "we get complaints from our clients about the outrageous fees they're paying to attorneys for what seems like boilerplate trust work. The way I see it, if we referred those clients to a solo practitioner with low overhead, but who had good support staff and big-firm experience, you could likely double your income while charging the clients less, and we would have happier clients."

Lazeris had thought about going out on his own but was nervous about trying to market himself. "Ed," said Winfield, "I'll get you a year's free rent, and I promise you at least ten solid referrals the first year. Now, that may not seem like much, but you have to remember that our clientele is quite large"—there was an understatement, thought Lazeris—"and just a couple of those clients a year could cover your overhead. The rest would be profit."

It didn't take much cajoling to help Edward S. Lazeris decide. Within three months he had quit his firm, opened his already furnished space a few blocks away from ASBT's headquarters, and opened the doors. Within six months, he had doubled his income and had more work than he could handle. He hired two paralegals for the overflow. And that's when things moved up for Ed Lazeris. Or went sideways, depending on how one viewed it.

A few months after opening his firm, Lazeris's secretary added an appointment to his electronic calendar. Mr. Jerry Logan. Lazeris had never heard of him.

"Who's this on my calendar for tomorrow?" he asked "Legs" O'Brien. He didn't really call her "Legs," not to her face anyway, or to her mammoth breasts either. Her name was Jessica. He often forgot her name because he was too busy getting lost in the "I'm banging my secretary on my desk" fantasy while his eyes traveled from her perfectly shaped ankles, up her calves, to her slightly rounded thighs, perfectly firm rear, athletically flat stomach and unnatural and medically enhanced bosom. She had some experience as a legal secretary, was OK with clients and scheduling, but was a complete waste at any paperwork. Which is why he had to hire a third paralegal, which he blamed on overflow. The paralegals didn't share his assessment, complaining to each other in the lunch room that they were always doing "Legs'" work.

Jessica bent over his desk to look at his computer screen. Lazeris closed his eyes and took in the scent of her hair. As she leaned back he opened his eyes. "Jerry Logan," she said.

"I can see that, Le ... Jessica. How did he get on my calendar if I've never spoken to him?"

"Oh, you were out at lunch when he called. He said Mr. Winfield referred him to you."

"Well, I guess I'm going to meet with Mr. Logan."

The next morning, John Lester arrived at Lazeris's office and introduced himself as Jerry Logan. He was shown in to Lazeris's office. Ed came from around the desk, adjusting his waistband to hide his expanding gut, then reached out and took Logan's hand. It was big and strong, and Logan gave a firm shake. Logan was six foot two at least, and built like an anvil, huge in the shoulders tapering down to a firm, slim waist on what appeared to be powerful legs.

"Thanks for taking my meeting on such short notice, Mr. Lazeris."

"Call me Ed, please. And it's no problem at all. I am always happy to take a referral from Mr. Winfield. Sit," he said, pointing to the conference table in his office. "Can we get you some coffee, water, anything?"

"Thanks, no." The two sat down. "Well, let me start with a confession. Jeremy Winfield didn't refer me to you. He doesn't even know who I am," which, in the greater context of things, was in fact true. Lazeris looked at Logan quizzically. "I am here to make you a business proposal."

"Look, Mr. Logan—" Logan put up his incredibly large hand. Lazeris stopped immediately.

"Listen to my proposal. If after we have spoken you are uninterested, you'll never see me again. I promise."

Lazeris considered Logan for a moment, then said simply, "OK, go ahead." Five years later, Lazeris would come to regret he ever said, "OK, go ahead."

In the meantime, however, he would enjoy himself immensely. The deal was so simple. And in practice, it worked so well for everyone involved. For a while. And Lazeris made quite a bit of money. He moved to Larchmont, joined the yacht club, and bought a house in Orange County for his parents. On weekends, he drove a Porsche which he stored there. Now Lazeris could look clients in the eye and not flinch. He was their equal, and could talk golf at Sawgrass, high-performance cars, and who he saw at the last black-tie gala. Clients began inviting Lazeris to their homes in the Hamptons for the weekend. "Here, Ed, just take the key. We'll be in Paris for a couple of weeks." And pretty soon, after quitting smoking, some personal trainer work and a few lavish gifts, he was able to play out his long-held fantasies about Legs O'Brien.

Ed Lazeris was living the life, when one day he called Legs into his office. "What's this meeting on my calendar?" he asked. She leaned over his desk. He didn't need to close his eyes and smell her anymore. He had tasted every bit of her many times.

"Oh, that's Nicholas Sanders and Alexandra Conrad."

"I can see that, Legs." He started calling her that as his "pet name" for her after they started sleeping together. She seemed to like it, as long as no one else was around. "Who are they?"

"They said they were with the FBI. They're investigating an insider-trading allegation against one of our clients. Marcus, I think."

Lazeris was startled at first when Jessica said FBI, but calmed down when she mentioned they were investigating Marcus. Still, odd that the FBI would be investigating an insider-trading charge two years after the suspect had died. "Well, I guess I'll be meeting with Mr. Sanders and Ms. Conrad," said Lazeris.

In the basement of the midtown building in which Lazeris & Associates maintained offices, a computer in a utility closet forwarded five minutes of recording on either side of "FBI". The flash drive on the computer recorded everything spoken in the office and over the phone, and everything written in electronic communications in the offices of the firm. When key words were spoken, such as FBI, CIA, police, state bar, investigation, and the like, the computer dutifully forwarded the conversations in an encrypted audio file to designated recipients. One opened the file immediately, as he was already on his laptop and a pop-up message made him aware of the recording. He plugged in his headphones and listened, raising an eyebrow. About four thousand miles away, another recipient got a message on his Blackberry about the file. He did not rush home or to his office, as many such files were sent every week, since the trigger words were vague and could be used often outside of any context he was worried about. About two hours after receiving his Blackberry notification, the man plugged into his computer and listened. "Shit" was all he said. Then he clicked on the encryption software for voice communication on his computer, picked up the phone, and hit a speed dial button.

Chapter 13

Midtown Manhattan; March 2008.

If Jeremy Winfield was the essence of calm and reserved, Ed Lazeris and his office were the furthest things from it. His receptionist/assistant, Jessica "Stripper" O'Brien, was overdone in every way. Her makeup was put on with a spackle knife; her breasts were purchased from the Michelin Man (and she made sure you could see the logo); her heels were three inches too high; and her clothes were far too tight and revealing. She looked to be two layoffs away from pole dancing her way to retirement.

Lazeris himself was presentable. He wore an expensive suit, a custom shirt, and a colorful tie. But unlike Winfield, who looked like he was born to the role, Lazeris seemed like a kid whose mother had dressed him in a suit for the first time. He was constantly fidgeting with his waistband or tie. There was a line of sweat above his lip as he spoke.

The office itself was quite lavish. The furniture and wall paneling were matching blond wood, and a credenza with a hutch doubled as a liquor cabinet. We sat in guest chairs in front of Lazeris's desk.

"So, what can I do for the FBI?" Lazeris had only glanced at our creds, and assumed we were both special agents. "I understand from Le ... Jessica this is about Marcus Vanderhoff?"

This part was going to get dicey. We had to ask about the freak deaths and see how he reacted. The problem was that if Winfield was in on it, Lazeris would immediately call him. But until we started asking questions, there was no way to learn anything, and we were going to have to tip our hand at some point. I always preferred later, but I couldn't see any way around this.

Conrad began. "We're investigating the deaths of several of your clients. Let me stress that this is preliminary, that we don't know that any crime has been committed, and we are just fact gathering." Strangely, this seemed to put the fidgety Mr. Lazeris at ease. This made me think he had something to hide, but it wasn't the murders of clients.

"Well, I'm an estate planning attorney. I plan for my clients' demise, unfortunately. Nature of the beast. Which clients are we talking about?"

Conrad looked at her notepad. "Allen, Jeffries, Morrison, Vanderhoff, and Matsuzaka."

Lazeris seemed surprised. "You think all five deaths are connected?"

"We don't really know. As I said, we're just fact gathering."

"Well, first of all I can't really tell you if they were my clients or not. That's part of the attorney-client privilege."

Oy. "Mr. Lazeris," I said, "I am an attorney. The fact of employment of you by a client is not privileged. Any content of their communications with you would be, except that they're dead."

Lazeris thought about this a moment and said, "Let's assume for a moment they were all my clients. Can I ask how you found out I was their attorney?"

"You can ask," I said. There was an awkward, elongated silence, which Lazeris finally broke.

"Mr. Sanders, I am going to agree with you that the fact of employment is not privileged. However, their communications with me still are despite their death. Remember that the privilege runs two ways: the client can waive it, but the attorney is not required to reveal communications despite the waiver. Now, I want to help you out, so I'll do what I can to negotiate our way around communications. For instance, I can tell you that I knew of no connection between any of these clients other than the fact that I represented all of them. By the way, I have a lot of clients who are still living, so I have to say I think your theory's a little weird." While he was saying this, he seemed a bit distracted. His eyes wandered up and to the left. Normally, I would take this as an indication that a suspect were lying, as if they were trying to think of a lie. In this case, Lazeris seemed to be considering something he hadn't thought of before.

"Did any of your clients indicate that they felt threatened by anyone, or that imminent bodily harm was going to come to them?" I asked.

An attorney has a duty to report if a client has communicated that they are going to injure or kill another. It is one of the few times the attorney can ignore the privilege. In this case, I was turning that exception on its head, hoping Lazeris would see a way to assist while justifying the waiver.

He thought about this carefully and smiled a bit. "That's a good way to go," he said, looking at me. "Let me put it this way: In the entire time I represented these five individuals, I had no reason to think they were in any danger. Moreover, the way they died doesn't seem to indicate foul play, although I am certainly no criminal investigator. I mean, unlucky, sure. But murdered? Marcus died bungee jumping. Not exactly the safest activity. And as I understand it, Mr. Matsuzaka was in the wrong place at the wrong time. I really have to say this is a stretch. Is there anything else these clients had in common?"

"Nothing you wouldn't already know about," Conrad said. She wasn't exactly the subtle type, but a lot of times you need this in an interview to see if you can throw the subject off. I tried to hide a smile. Lazeris didn't seem to take offense, and actually thought about it.

"Well, I suppose so. They were all rich, but you knew that. They had no or limited families, but you knew that too. None had the same beneficiaries, of course. I just don't see it."

Conrad leaned forward. "Well, they all had the same attorney, who stood to make money from their deaths by settling the estates." Shit. We were going to have to get her some interrogation technique lessons.

Lazeris looked shocked and sat bolt upright. "Now, wait a minute! If I'm a suspect, you need to Mirandize—"

"Mr. Lazeris," I jumped in, "you are *not* a suspect in their murders." While this was true on its face, he could have been an aider and abettor. "Ms. Conrad is speaking hypothetically and we have to look at all possibilities. We know you were nowhere near these folks when they met their demise." He calmed down. Just a bit.

"No, I wasn't. And the fact is I have plenty of work and make a good living *without* killing my clients. They were all young. Had they had families, which presumably at least a few of them would, I would have made even more amending their existing documents and creating new ones. So, Ms. Conrad, you better get your facts straight."

"You're right, Mr. Lazeris," Alex said. She seemed to have recognized that she overstepped. "I apologize. As Mr. Sanders indicated, you are not a suspect in their murders. We don't even know if there were any murders. By the way, is your sole source of income your clients' fees?" I again had to hide a smile. Just when I thought she was a newbie, she pulls out a key question that could connect Lazeris to the killers. If there were any killers. I had a newfound respect for Alexandra Conrad.

Lazeris immediately said, "Yes. Of course." Sweaty, fidgeting, his collar was suddenly too tight again. She had hit on something here. Problem was, we didn't really know anything about his finances, since we didn't have a warrant and never sought one for that information.

"It's just that you've been filing an FBAR and a 5471, reporting transfers from offshore accounts to your personal account." Correction: *I* didn't know anything about his finances. Conrad had pulled all public records on Lazeris and (maybe) hit some pay dirt.

"Of course. Mr. Matsuzaka was a Japanese resident. Moreover, I have some investments in an offshore hedge fund in the Cayman Islands. Both those transfers had to be reported." This was a perfectly legitimate response, and Lazeris could have sold it if he hadn't been so fidgety. He was hiding something, but we'd have to get a warrant for more.

"Of course," Alex repeated, which really meant *of course you're a lying sack and I don't believe you.*

"This whole theory of yours is just silly." He looked over at me for some help. "I had nothing to gain from these clients' deaths. Now, I think we're done."

"Here's my card, in case you think of anything else that could help us." I left it on the edge of his desk.

Back out on the street, I said: "Mighta been nice if you'd told me about the offshore transfers."

"Well, you know now," she said. "I didn't think to look until just before we left the office. I signed onto the Treasury Department website and pulled the form he filed."

"If he were trying to hide it, he wouldn't have reported it."

"He had to. His bank would have reported it. Besides, criminals who are smart dot all their i's and cross all their t's. Otherwise, they become the next Al Capone." She had a point. Lazeris might have been filing so he could make the very statement he made: *I*

*have nothing to hide. These were fees and investments, and do you think
I'd be stupid enough to report it if there was something illegal going on?*

"Yeah. Listen, can we trace that money back?" I asked.

"I confirmed the Matsuzaka thing. The other transfer was
from a numbered account, which doesn't necessarily mean he's
lying."

"We need to get into the bank's records and see who owns
that account."

"There may not be a way to do that," she said, "legally."

We regrouped back at the office. JJ, Conrad, Winkler, Lisa
Velasquez, Evan Sanderson, and I were in the conference room.
Velasquez and Sanderson had been on the Huntington raid team,
and they were tactical specialists as well as investigators.

Sanderson was a bureau lifer. He had done time all over the
country in the last twenty years and was incredibly well-respected
as an investigator and raid tactician. This was not a natural ability.
It had been learned, crafted, and honed as a marine in various
hotspots around the world. When he got married, he left the
Marine Corps for something more stable. What that meant was
that instead of being posted all over the world, he was now posted
all over the country. Two years ago, his loyalty was rewarded with
a posting in the midtown Manhattan field office. He, his wife and
two kids lived in Jersey. Sanderson loved the field work and his
enthusiasm was infectious. At fifty-four years old, he was getting
to be one of the older members of the raid team, but other than
the graying hair, his body betrayed not an ounce of his age. If he
had dyed his hair, you'd have thought he was thirty-five.

Velasquez was a team leader. I had worked on various cases
with her during my six years at the bureau, but had no idea how
old she was, whether she had kids, or what she did in her free
time. I think she may have been divorced. The job tended to be
transitory, and it was unusual for the same group to work together
so long, especially after 9/11. But since most other FBI assets
were allocated to the war on terror, the few of us with expertise

in financial crimes had gotten stuck together, and lately business was good. Velasquez had risen pretty fast. She was smart and absolutely deadly with any number of small and large arms. While she preferred the Glock 17, I had seen her shoot incredibly well with sniper rifles, automatics, you name it. She was a walking encyclopedia of munitions. I decided she probably wasn't married. A girl like that tends to scare men off, despite what appeared to be a killer body. Or maybe because of it.

"Look," I said, "we need to start writing all this down. There are a lot of different ways to take this investigation, and we're going to need more manpower. Let's start with a list of what we need to look into."

"Circs of each death, for one," Sanderson said. Great point. We assumed because of the connections that there was foul play involved. But it could all just be coincidence. The problem was, of course, that looking into deaths that were as old as three years left a pretty cold trail, and the fact that some occurred overseas meant we may get no information on them at all. Nevertheless, we had to investigate all leads.

"Transfers between offshore accounts and the decedents' accounts at ASBT," I said.

"And Lazeris's personal accounts. And Winfield's," Conrad added.

"Travel schedules of all employees of ASBT, and all of Lazeris's employees," Velasquez piped up. "Need to see if there is any overlap with the locations of the deaths."

"JJ," I said, "what are our chances of getting a warrant for each dead client's account, and a wiretap on ASBT, in particular Winfield's phone and email?"

"Well, here's what we got," he began. "Your Honor, there were five folks that died in accidental or natural ways in the last three years. They all named ASBT as their trustee. They all had the same attorney. And some of their money went, before and after their deaths, to offshore hedge funds which might have, in turn, funded illegal arms sales in Latin America, maybe. But we can't see a return money trail for the arms sales, and we think the bank's been killing the clients, collecting the money and the fees, funding the arms purchases, and golly gee, we'd just like to look all over the bank records to prove our theory."

Everyone looked around the table for a moment. "Man, that's pretty fucking thin," Sanderson said. "I don't even think you'd get a warrant out of our preferred judges."

OK, it did suck. I started doubting the theory, but my gut was telling me that there were too many connections to ignore. My cell phone began vibrating in my pocket. "Look, there has to be some other avenue we can look at without a warrant. Can we get a national security wiretap?" I asked Alex as I reached for the phone.

"What, a FISA court tap on Winfield? Well, I suppose we could, but I'd have to run it past Borenstein, and I'm having trouble selling this as it is."

I opened my phone. "Nick Sanders," I answered.

"Mr. Sanders?" I snapped my fingers several times at everyone. It was Lazeris.

"Mr. Lazeris?" I could hear street traffic in the background. He was calling from a pay phone.

"Yes. Listen, I think we should meet." He sounded nervous.

"OK. Do you have a time and place in mind?"

"Yes. Astor's Deli on Fifty-fourth. Eleven tomorrow morning. You and Ms. Conrad. OK?"

"We'll be there." I hung up.

I sat there for a moment, stunned. "He wants to meet tomorrow, in a public place. He was calling from a pay phone."

"He thinks his office is bugged," Sanderson said.

"Or his staff can't be trusted," I added.

"Where?" asked Alex.

"Astor's on Fifty-fourth. Tomorrow at eleven."

"OK, I guess we're onto something after all," said JJ.

Just what we were onto was anyone's guess. Lazeris might have been trying to cut an amnesty deal for unpaid taxes.

"We better set up at nine," I said.

"What? Why?" asked Conrad.

I looked at Velasquez. "Velasquez, a suspect calls you to meet at a certain hour at a certain place. What do you do?"

"Get there at least an hour prior, usually more, and set up surveillance from all angles, assess lines of sight, exits from the meet, geography of the area which would make movement and surveillance difficult, travel time to and from the meet for the suspect, and review civilian population in the area. Then sit and wait to see if the suspect arrives, and if so, if they're followed. Who's the newbie?"

"Alexandra Conrad, meet Lisa Velasquez." They shook hands, somewhat coldly. I got the impression they weren't going to double-date anytime soon. "Velasquez is an encyclopedia of tactical support and the best backup a guy shot in the arm could have." Velasquez blew me a kiss.

"I guess if tactical support got there sooner you might not have been shot," Alex retorted.

"OK," JJ jumped in before it got heated. "Let's get a map of the area and plan this meet, then we can work out logistics in the morning."

"Am I going?" asked Alex.

"He asked for both of us. We shouldn't disappoint him. He might get squirrely."

"I'll have to call Borenstein and let him know." She got up and left the room, giving Velasquez a quick glance on her way out.

"Is it just me or does she not like me?" Velasquez asked.

"It's just you," I said.

Chapter 14

Hoboken, New Jersey; March 2008.

Prep time was going to be tight. Worst case, he would have to knock on Lazeris's door that night and shoot him in the head, which he preferred not to do.

Lester explained all this to his client, who assented to the plan and price (although there was always some negotiation on this point), then hung up the phone. He thought for a moment. Public spot. No way to avoid collateral deaths. But the client didn't want any federal agents harmed. In this way, the client was "old school." He had no problem if civilians were killed, but he did not want cops or government agents on a vendetta. Plenty of murders remained unsolved, but rarely murders of law enforcement agents. The client saw it as bad for business, since no law enforcement agent death file ever got dropped into a cold-case drawer.

Lester ruminated over his choices. When in doubt, he always liked to go with what worked in the past, unless there was some compelling reason to get creative, which in this case he simply didn't have time for. There was no time to identify a character defect that would play into an accident. He wasn't a bungee jumper. Car accident? Lazeris didn't drive while in the city, and wouldn't be leaving until the weekend. A shot to the head was starting to look good.

Wrong place, wrong time? Lester mulled this over. A Matsuzaka-style shootout couldn't really be set up in this time frame to ensure all the principals got away. Plus, there would already be police present. But ... Lester turned to his computer and brought up Google. He typed in the name of the deli, then checked out the map of its location and the deli's website. Astor's Deli on Fifty-fourth had a long and storied history, starting as a central meeting place for the New York Jewish community and evolving into a must-eat location for tourists. The tourism industry had died down with 9/11, and Astor's was going back to its roots by reaching out to the local Jewish temples and billing itself as a meeting place after services, priding itself on its all-kosher menu (which, Lester noted, in New York really wasn't a point of distinction, but whatever). Lester recalled having eaten there. *Corned beef on rye with mustard and a Diet Coke. Damn good sandwich.*

He pictured the place in his mind. Close to the curb, wide storefront, but not deep, which was unusual for New York. As he recalled, the kitchen took up the entire back of the shop, leaving all the patrons in the front. That was good. And Fifty-fourth was wider than normal. You could double-park there, run into a store, grab something, and run out without severely screwing up traffic. OK. That settles the method. Just need materials.

Lester clicked on his encrypted email icon, and a window opened. He wrote to an address.

R: Need transaction contact for NYC ASAP. Must have service van deliver materials tonight if possible. Payment per usual method or increased shipment to be negotiated directly with client. -L

Lester sent and waited. If this didn't pan out, he'd have to figure out something else. As he was reviewing other possibilities, a response came back. Lester marveled that everyone seemed to have a Blackberry, even terrorists living in jungles.

L: Contact my NYC franchisee (Lester had to laugh. Despite the fact that the email was encrypted, everyone in the network discussed everything they did in business terms) *Javier at 212.764.8989, his office line* (Reyes meant the line was secure). *He can arrange for delivery. Will discuss payment options with Sr. P.*

Lester sent back a note of thanks and clicked off his email. He waited about two minutes to allow Reyes to email Javier to let him know he would be calling, then dialed the number.

"Señor L?" a Latino voice asked.

"Yes, this is L. Who am I speaking with?"

"Señor L, my name is Javier, and I am Señor R's New York representative. I have some noise on this end, can we switch to another line?"

"Already switched over," Lester said, indicating his software was scrambling their communication.

"You are John Lester, no?" the man called Javier said.

"Yes, this is John Lester."

"Señor Lester, it is an honor to assist you in this transaction. I have heard so much about your past work." Reyes apparently told Javier of other deals Lester had completed. He probably was trying to instill in Javier a semblance of respect for Lester, and convey the importance of coming through for him. *Whatever,* Lester thought. *Javier better learn to keep his mouth shut, or he wouldn't live long.*

"Javier, we need to meet. I have a shopping list."

"Sure, sure. We should meet at the store."

It was approaching 11:00 p.m. when Lester pulled down an alley in Harlem. The darkness accentuated the roll-up steel door that had an overhead light. He pulled alongside it. He was about to get out of his car when the service door next to the roll-up began opening. A thin Latino man in sweats and a hoodie came out. His hands were in the single center pocket across the stomach of the shirt. Lester's hand shot out the window and he pointed his index finger at the man. Lester's foot was on the brake and the car was in gear so he could take off if he needed to.

"Stop right there. Let me see your hands, now!"

The man slowly removed his hands, saying, "Señor Lester, take it eas—"

"Keep your mouth shut for a second, OK? Just nod or shake your head when I ask you questions." The guy just stood there, five feet from Lester's window. "You Javier?"

He nodded.

"Anyone else inside?"

He shook his head.

"Is there room for my car inside?"

Nod.

Lester backed up while Javier opened the roll-up door, then pulled his car into the building. He got out. "Close the door," he told Javier. While Javier was going to the door controller, Lester looked around. There was a beat-up white van with no side windows. Bad stenciling indicated "Nora's Mail Delivery" on the sliding door panel. It wasn't the best option, but it would do. Lester looked at Javier, then nodded his head toward the van.

"Best I could do on short notice, Señor. I borrowed it from the storage yard. *Mi amigo* delivers for them." Borrowed. Lester's mouth turned up in a one-sided, cynical smile. You only borrow something if you're going to give it back. This van would not go back to its owners. But that's what insurance was for.

Lester would have preferred a U.S. Postal Service truck, which could double park just about anywhere in the city and be left alone. Mail delivery services were different. They were private companies hired by other private companies to pick up a business's metered mail and take it to the post office, as well as deliver the mail to that business, which the local post office collected in plastic bins. The postal service required large companies to drop off and pick up their mail at their assigned post office. A mail delivery service saved businesses the time of having an employee drop off and pick up mail. The van could double-park for very short periods, but then cops and parking enforcement would have it towed. That shortened the window and made the whole thing a bit more complicated. Still, it was doable.

Lester looked around the remainder of the warehouse. Boxes were stacked everywhere along the walls. A wooden loft with a stairway leading up from the ground floor had more boxes stacked to the rafters.

Store, indeed. Lester was looking at the Costco of Death. M16s. AK-47s. MP5s. Grenades. Rocket launchers. A box of stinger missiles over here. A few boxes of RPGs over there. A work bench on one side with a soldering iron, electrical wire, timers, and other electronic-device construction material. Whoever had amassed this stockpile was ready for the next revolution. In the meantime, it appeared they were willing to do business.

This was incredibly ironic. Here was Mr. P, selling arms to Reyes that Reyes was desperate for. Yet Reyes had contacts in New York who had plenty of materiel Reyes would need to fuel his revolution. Since 9/11, he couldn't get to it, nor could he ship it to himself because of ICE X-ray machines. It had to be smuggled in small amounts, which was too slow for Reyes's needs. So, Reyes apparently sold his stockpile in the U.S. to fund additional purchases in South America. This actually made sense. He could get top dollar in the U.S. and pay half the price for the same arms in South America. In fact, this stockpile represented *two* such warehouses in Colombia or Venezuela or Brazil.

"The van will do. Semtex?"

"You don't want C-4?"

Lester shook his head. "Not good for my purposes." The chemical composition of Semtex made it more volatile, delivering a bigger bang for the same amount of material, and also had a slightly better chain-reaction assurance. That is, when placed close together, if one or more detonators failed (which had been known to happen), the explosion of one brick had a better chance of setting off all the other bricks.

"Yeah, we got Semtex, up in the loft. How much?"

"Six bricks."

Javier whistled. "Señor, they already blew up the World Trade Center ..."

Lester wheeled around and looked hard at Javier. "Look, Javier. I like you. You're a funny guy. But I don't trust you because I don't know you. Mr. R trusts you, so I'm willing to overlook my misgivings. But here's how this works: I tell you what I want, and you either have it or you don't, or can get it or you can't. Everything else is just wasting my time. So let's keep the 'get to know you' chat for another time over some cervezas. Now, open the van."

Javier went to the van side panel and slid the door open. It was an empty cargo space, corrugated floor, somewhat rusted. Lester looked it over and nodded. "I'll need about fifteen square feet of steel paneling to reinforce the interior, an air compressor, air hammer, an acetlyne torch, one hundred sixteenth-inch blind rivets, PL construction glue and a dispenser, and three disposable cell phones. And four bungee cords, about twelve to eighteen inches long each."

"The fuck you need—?" Javier started to say before Lester's head snapped around with a hard stare. "Look, this isn't Home Depot."

"Can you get it or not?"

Javier thought a moment. "Sí, I can get it. But the rivets may not be to your exact specifications."

"That's OK, just don't go over eighth-inch. More than that, they'll be too big. Close it up." Javier closed the van. Lester asked him: "Ball bearings?"

"Of course."

"Detonators?"

"Over here." Javier waved him over to a small cardboard box and opened it up. Lester looked inside and saw a pile of the sorriest-looking detonators he had seen since an operation he did in Guatemala.

"Jesus. You ever seen these work?"

"We've never had any complaints, Señor."

That's because the guy who would have complained blew his own ass up. "OK, but you're putting your money where your mouth is. Once I get the van set up and the charges properly arranged, *you* are inserting the detonators." Javier tried to put a brave face on, but as he nodded Lester could tell he was worried.

"Cell phones for ignition?" Javier asked, changing the subject.

"I'll rig that myself. OK, Javier, I can't do anything until we get going on the steel paneling."

"I know a construction supply site about fifteen blocks from here. They'll have it, but I need some cash to pay off the guard. Also, I gotta wake up my friend who works at a mechanic's shop and get the air compressor, gun, and torch."

Lester reached into his pocket and handed Javier a wad of cash. "Take the van, go pick up the stuff, and bring us one of those large cardboard coffee pots from a Dunkin' Donuts. Get some donuts, too, OK?"

Javier nodded.

"Javier, I'm working with you only because Mr. R trusts you. You run out on me, I will find you, and I will rip your spine out through your asshole." *What little you have.*

Javier nodded nervously and got in the van. Lester opened the door for him and he drove out. Lester closed the door and went upstairs to the Semtex. He picked up two boxes and brought them down. Then he gathered what materials he could and set them in the order he thought he would need them.

At 3:00 a.m., Javier returned. The van had a stack of steel panels in the cargo area, atop of which was an air compressor, air gun, four bungee cords, rivets and a welding torch. In the front passenger seat were the cell phones, coffee urn, cups, and a dozen donuts. Javier even remembered to get cream and sugar. Lester didn't take anything in his coffee, but he appreciated the attention to detail. He knew details mattered.

"First things first," Lester said as he took the coffee and donuts over to a workbench. He poured some coffee and opened the box of donuts. "Next time, more chocolate crullers, OK?"

"OK, Señor."

Time was of the essence, but Lester wanted to do this right and he didn't want to be worried about his stomach while he was working. So, after five minutes of eating and drinking, the two men set to work.

As they were finishing up, Lester saw he had two steel panels left. He looked at the floor of the van. He thought about the focus of the blast and made a decision, which in hindsight would be the best one he made all day. He had Javier help him place one of the leftover panels on the floor of the cargo area. He didn't bother to weld or rivet it, because he knew that during primary detonation the blast would keep it in place. He couldn't place a panel on the ceiling of the cargo hold because he didn't have time, and he needed to be able to hang the shrapnel container from the supports. Some of the explosive force would diminish because it would blow up through the roof, but that couldn't be helped.

He looked at his watch. 7:00 a.m. "OK, time to roll," he said. He had three hours to get his car back to his apartment, then take the subway and meet Javier at the staging point. He normally wouldn't leave until the operation was done, but he couldn't leave his car in the city. If something went wrong, it was another loose end that had fingerprints on it. While he doubted the police would find this place, he could not take that chance. He pulled the map out and showed Javier where to drive the van and park.

"I'll meet you here at 10:30. It's an open parking lot. Pay the attendant on your way in, and don't move. Stay in the van. Understand? You get there, you don't get out for coffee, a piss, a blow job from your boyfriend, anything. You don't move."

Javier nodded. Lester got in his car and left. Javier got in the van, pulled into the alley, closed the warehouse door, locked it and left.

Lester got to his apartment building and parked in the underground parking. He locked his car and ran up to his unit. He sent an email and almost immediately received the answer he was hoping for. Lester changed into clothes more befitting a delivery man: khaki pants, golf shirt, windbreaker jacket, and brown work shoes.

On his way to the train, he stopped by the loading dock of a local business. He had noticed that there were always plastic mail-delivery tubs stacked to the side of the dock, and he grabbed three of them on his way by. By 9:45 a.m., he was on the PATH train to Thirty-third Street, ready to meet Javier.

Chapter 15

Midtown Manhattan; March 2008.

"I still don't see how we're connecting the arms sales in South America with all this white collar stuff."

We met at the office at 7:00 a.m., same conference room, same parties, with one addition. Adolph "call me Al" Borenstein, director of Homeland Security, had joined us. He was expressing his enthusiastic support for our meeting with Lazeris later that morning, and advising Conrad she was in for a promotion. I just made that up.

Conrad answered him: "The money movements from ASBT to the offshore hedge funds correspond in amounts and times with the money moving to known arms dealers and subsequent shipments to Venezuela."

"Oh, come on, Alex, I could point to thousands of transactions in the same time period and in similar amounts that could be the source of the funds," said Borenstein.

Alex was ready for this. She pulled out a spreadsheet from a file on the table and unfolded it.

"Here. Every time one of the victims died, six to nine months later their funds are collected at ASBT. That's the second column.

Within two months of collection, about one-half of the account is sent to several offshore hedge funds. That's the amount in the third column. The fourth column shows the five largest transfers out of the hedge funds' bank accounts within the week following receipt of funds from ASBT." I wondered to myself how she got that information. "We can't trace where those funds go because they are taken out in cash, but we do know that within three weeks of the withdrawals, significant shipments of arms arrive in Venezuela, and from there, go to numerous left-wing, socialist or communist terrorist groups—FARC, Shining Path, what have you. You can see that the estimated cost of the arms is roughly equivalent to the withdrawals from the hedge funds, which is roughly equivalent to the amounts received from ASBT."

"Roughly equivalent?" asked Borenstein. "JJ, do you buy this?"

"Al," JJ started. Adolph hated to be called Adolph, and who could blame him? "All I know is that we think the deaths are connected. Alex brought us the arms purchase angle. I can't speak to that, and it's out of my jurisdiction anyway. But, if the attorney gives us some evidence so we can get a warrant, we will be able to trace the funds and prove it one way or the other."

"No offense, Alex, but you're not field personnel. You're an analyst." Borenstein turned back to JJ. "I'm not sure I appreciate you guys putting one of my best and brightest in harms way."

"We'll take good care of her, Al," I said. It was completely inappropriate for me to address him that way, or speak when I hadn't been spoken to, but sometimes I just can't help myself. I could see Sanderson cover his mouth to keep from showing a smirk. Velasquez smiled.

"Who are you again?" Borenstein asked. There is no better comeback to a smart-ass underling than to question who they are. In this case, it was the actual truth, because we had never met, and in normal circumstances never would have.

"One of *my* best and brightest," JJ said before I could speak. "He and Alex will be meeting the lawyer at eleven today."

Borenstein assessed me for a bit, then said: "OK. If the lawyer gives us something, we'll pursue a warrant and see if we can connect these. If he doesn't give us anything, Alex, you are back in the office in the morning. If it doesn't pan out, I wish your team luck with the five murders, if that's what they are, JJ."

"Thank you, Al. One other thing. We recovered a computer from a Ponzi schemer a couple months back. He has some pretty impressive encryption software on it, and we'd like to enlist your help in breaking it. Since Alex is already here, we were hoping to get your approval to let her take a crack at it."

Borenstein seemed only annoyed at the addition to the shopping list. "Whatever. But if it's going to take more than a few hours, I'll want to know and approve."

"Thank you, sir," JJ said.

Borenstein got up and left. Normally at this point in the meeting, someone like me would say "asshole" under their breath, but the fact was Borenstein had made some good points. He didn't want to waste his resources, and JJ never would have put up with us showing that kind of disrespect. So, everyone kept their opinions to themselves and turned to the marquee event of the day.

"Sanderson?" JJ said.

Evan stood up. "Sir, I'm having Velasquez plan this one and lead the tactical discussion." Everyone looked to Lisa Velasquez. She was wearing military boots, navy blue pants, and a standard-issue short-sleeved white polo shirt with the FBI crest on it. Her black hair, pulled back in a no-nonsense ponytail, contrasted sharply with the shirt. Before the surveillance, over this shirt would go a thin, long-sleeved fleece top (also navy blue), a vest and an FBI ball cap.

She wasn't surprised that Sanderson had given the lead to her. They seemed to have discussed it beforehand. I wondered if Sanderson, given his age, was starting to see the end of his active career and was preparing Lisa to take over his position. It was a good choice. Velasquez was a good tactician in her own right. Moreover, Sanderson would make an excellent instructor at Quantico, which was where guys like him went when their active duty career in the bureau was over.

Velasquez approached the front of the room. A PowerPoint projector shot a Google map of Fifty-fourth Street on the screen. The deli was highlighted.

"OK, our suspect picked a very public area within which to meet. We can draw a couple of conclusions from this. He feels safe in a crowd, and while he may think his communications are monitored, he probably doesn't think whoever is monitoring will be following him. Otherwise, they'd be wondering who the hell he was meeting with and ask him about it.

"The deli itself is wide and shallow. The kitchen takes up the back area. This makes surveillance easy. We can see the entire dining area from the street. Plus, the view isn't obstructed. We don't have to be looking straight on. We can set up west and east of the deli and still get a good view."

Velasquez didn't have to mention the importance of this to anyone in the room.

"Why is that important?" a voice to my right asked. Guess I was wrong. It was Conrad. I gave her points for not being afraid to ask.

"We can leave the area directly in front of the deli open. If anyone is following this guy, we'll be unobtrusive, but the guy following will be out in the open and easily identifiable. If something goes down, we're close enough to move in and leave him wondering where all the cops came from," Velasquez answered.

"Plus we get to see what Lazeris orders, so we'll know what's good there," I added. Conrad kicked my shin under the table, smirking. Velasquez ignored me. She did that a lot.

"We'll need a plainclothes guy in the back alley, but accessing that from the front is difficult and doesn't lend itself to a quick exit. You have to go back through the kitchen and there are some turns in the hallway. It's unlikely the attorney, if he gets nervous, would run out the back.

"Sanders and Conrad will want to be west of the deli. Lazeris will probably be coming from that direction. Sanderson and I will set up east of the deli in a van. We will watch the western approach and likely see Lazeris first. Sanders, until you get out of your vehicle, you're point for your team, God help them. I'll be point for me and Sanderson. With Engler still out, we're short-handed a little, but this shouldn't be a big deal. We got one attorney looking to spill his guts. I think we can handle it. Tony Scala will be in the back of your car, Sanders. He'll take point after you exit to the meet."

"Point" meant I would be the only one speaking into the mic from our position. We would give Conrad an earpiece and a mic, but those would be removed before we met with Lazeris. If he saw we were wired, it was unlikely he would give us any useful information. After we left the surveillance car, Scala would take over the microphone.

"JJ, we were planning on putting Nick Sebastien in the alley, if that's OK, Velasquez asked."

JJ shrugged, "Fine."

"We'll set up at 0900, keep the entire area in view. Subject shows at 1100, Conrad and Sanders exit the car and enter the deli, have their meeting. No plans to take the subject into custody?"

I spoke up. "Not right now. Need to see what he says. Even if he cops to a crime, we will probably need him free to help expose who he's working with. No way Lazeris is the mastermind."

"OK, so, you leave the meet, Lazeris leaves the meet, and after another half-hour, we wrap it up. You want anyone ready to follow him afterwards?"

I thought about it. It wasn't a bad idea. But until I knew what he was going to say, I couldn't justify it. "Not sure. We can pick him up"—I meant institute surveillance—"after the meeting if he says anything that warrants it."

"Fair enough. OK, so total team is six, five in front in two cars, one in the alley. Oh, one other thing: If anything does go down, you two"—she waved over at me and Conrad—"are to do nothing except get yourselves safe. You will not be vested, you'll be wearing civilian clothes, and you are not to engage in any activity that could get you injured or killed. Clear?" she asked, looking directly at Conrad.

"Crystal," Conrad responded coolly.

JJ stepped up to the front of the room. "Folks, this is our only lead in the five murders, and it may prove DHS's theory on the arms dealing as well. I will be monitoring communications from here. Once this thing is over, get back here ASAP and report what we've got. Let's go."

On the way out, Velasquez pulled me aside. "Take care of Snow White," she said under her breath. "A techie like that could get people hurt 'cause they don't know what they're doing." I wanted to warn Velasquez about the parabolic microphones Conrad had in place of ears, but it was too late.

"Snow White had black hair," Conrad said as she brushed past us and out the door, "like you."

"Jesus!" Velasquez exclaimed. "How the fuck she hear that?"

"Tell me about it. Look, I'll prep her in the car, but this guy isn't Lex Luthor. He's gotten in over his head and is scared."

"Like Huntington, right?" she smirked.

"That hurts, Velasquez."

"Just keeping you safe. That's my job, Sanders. Besides, you're fun to have around here."

"Yeah, I notice you laughing at all my jokes."

"Just watch her."

"OK."

The teams suited up and we headed out of the underground garage from the midtown office. The meet was only eight blocks away, but it still took us awhile because of morning traffic. Tony Scala was in the back seat. I drove and Conrad rode shotgun.

"What's up with Velasquez? She doesn't like me very much. I'd say she was jealous."

I checked to ensure I wasn't inadvertently pressing my mic button. Many a private-life secret intended only for a partner had gone out over the airwaves during operations, and I didn't want to be the guy who made the hall of shame. "She's a professional. JJ's never lost an agent in the line of duty, and he makes sure his tactical leaders know it. Plus, Sanderson's letting her run it and she doesn't want to blow it. She could ease into his position one day, but not if things go bad. And I doubt she's jealous."

Conrad turned to look at Scala. "I dunno, what do you think, Tony? Think Velasquez has something for Sanders here?"

Scala laughed. He'd been with the team for about three years after coming over from Treasury. "The only thing Velasquez has any 'thing' for is her MP5 and the last issue of *Jane's Weapons Weekly*. If she had a date, it would be burgers at the firing range."

"You guys go ahead and make fun," I said. "If I had to pick someone to back me in a firefight, it would be Sanderson and Velasquez. She's serious about it because it's her job to be." What I didn't tell them was why she was serious about it. I frankly didn't know why because I didn't know Velasquez that well. She kept to herself. The most affection I ever saw her show was hugging Sanderson after a nasty operation two years before in which the suspect ended up dead.

I hit my mic button. "B Team approaching deli." Fifty-fourth Street was one-way, west to east. We pulled up about twenty-five yards short of the deli and parked on the opposite side of the street. This gave us a good view of the eastern approach and the front of the deli. It was packed at nine in the morning, as one would expect. "B team in place."

"A Team approaching deli." We saw the black van Velasquez and Sanderson were in pass us, drive by the deli, and attempt to park just past it. No luck there, no parking on either side of the street, another reason why you always set up well in advance. "A Team going 'round." This meant they would circle the block again and keep doing so until a spot opened up an acceptable distance from the deli storefront. It took two more passes but they got situated. "A team in place."

"C team in place." This was Nick Sebastien. He was in the alley posing as a homeless guy with a shopping cart. This was always a good cover. There were plenty of homeless people who never got a second look. Also, the shopping cart allowed the agent to conceal all manner of weapons and equipment without anyone knowing about it. Homeless folks tended to talk to themselves, so a homeless guy mumbling would be ignored, which made talking into your mic in plain sight acceptable. And Nick dirtied up better than anybody. For some reason, he simply looked the part of a homeless man, and he had mastered the body language, vacant stares, and clothing so well we always used him for the cover when we had the need.

"You guys anywhere on Huntington?" Conrad asked.

"Not yet. Winkler is pulling apart the hard drive. We have boxes of documents to go through from his house and office, and his secretary is going to help. After this meet we'll start looking. You should go back and get together with Winkler after this."

"OK. But 1024 polymorphic can't be cracked."

"I remember a cyber-security instructor at Quantico telling us no lock is unpickable."

She thought about that a little and said: "Imagine you're a thief, and I told you the exact model and specifications of the safe at the bank you were planning to rob. You gather the right equipment and practice on a mock up. You break in, but when you get there, the bank has changed out the safe. What do you do?"

"Leave and come back another day with the right tools."

"And when you get back to the bank, they've changed the safe *again*. That's what 1024 polymorphic encryption does. It doesn't just require the right key, it requires the right key at the exact moment you insert it, because the lock is always changing. It's virtually unbreakable. You could have one hundred super-computers trying combinations constantly for one hundred years and not get the right code."

"We don't have that long."

Chapter 16

Midtown Manhattan; March 2008

Lester sat behind the wheel of the van, pretending to look at a clipboard. In fact, he was running through the sequencing over and over. He had dispatched Javier a few minutes before. Timing was critical. Too early and the van would be discovered before Lazeris arrived. Too late, and he could end up killing the agents who were supposed to meet Lazeris, which the boss had forbidden. Lester wasn't keen on killing people he viewed as fellow professionals either. He knew they would arrive early, scope out the area and let the lawyer get situated before they went in. They would want to make sure he wasn't being followed. This had to be timed right. He needed some intervention, but not too much. The whole thing was dicey, but he had thrown together more complicated operations in less time and succeeded.

He thought about his first real job while still officially in the army. He had done well in basic training, then multiple specialist trainings: sniper school, demolition, artillery, tactical warfare, jump school, language classes, and more. It was three years before he saw any action, and it was in one of the last places he expected—an allied country.

After he was deemed worthy to go into the field, he was sent to Langley to meet with Paul Blattman again. Blattman seemed slightly older, but the suit hadn't changed a bit. Blattman sat at a conference desk in his large office in the operations wing. He smoked a cigar, which Lester was certain was forbidden, but no one seemed to be telling Paul Blattman what to do. Lester drank stale coffee with bad powdered creamer from a Styrofoam cup.

"Told you I was right about you, John."

"Yes, sir." Blattman pulled the cigar out of his mouth and gave him a severe look. "Paul," Lester corrected.

"Better. Look, we've got a job for you to bust your cherry on. Well, you and a team, but you're going to lead the tactical end of it." Blattman slid a file across the table. "Know this guy?"

Lester opened the file. Inside was a grainy eight-by-ten surveillance photo of a fit white man in a well-tailored navy blue suit with tie and matching kerchief. "No. Should I?" Lester asked.

"I hope not. If you did that might mean you're planning on selling nuclear weapon technology to North Korea. His name is Henri Phillipe Bruel, a French scientist and executive of an energy company that builds nuclear power plants. Henri's got a nice side business. He likes to sell excess or obsolete fissile material, centrifuges, plans, and spent core material to folks willing to pay him a lot of money for it. He's been on the payroll of the North Korean government for about two years. He's being paid in counterfeit U.S. currency, by the way. They've got a cottage industry in counterfeiting over there. Did you know that?"

"Yeah, I actually did know that."

"Really? Shit, we gotta be more careful who we're telling these things to."

"I read it in *Jane's*. So, what, you want me to kidnap this guy while he's en route somewhere?"

"Kidnap him? Fuck no, kid. We need you to kill him, and fast."

Lester half-expected that was coming, but he had never been given a kill order before. Hell, he'd never been given an assignment before other than follow, observe, and assist when asked. Despite the fact that he knew he was being trained for this, it still hit him like a bucket of cold water. He recovered fairly quickly.

"We have his travel schedule?" he asked.

"Page two." Lester leafed through it. Blattman studied him while he did so, and Lester knew he was judging him for a reaction. Bruel had apparently been under surveillance for some time, as his daily schedule for at least a year was in the file.

"Timeline?"

"Tomorrow. In France."

Damn, that is tight. "Character flaws?"

Blattman leaned back and beamed at his protégé. "That's my boy," he said.

It was a tight timeline, but Lester planned and implemented the entire mission himself, quite successfully, poisoning Bruel by adding a tasteless poison to his sugar at the café where he took his regular morning coffee.

"Great job, John," Blattman said upon his return. "So, I was right about field ops, wasn't I? You enjoy it, don't you?"

Lester thought about it then, and thought about it again behind the wheel of the mail delivery van in which he now sat. The answer was the same both times. God help him, he did love it. From planning to execution, he loved the entire job. And he was good at it.

Lester checked his watch. He put down the clipboard and started up the van.

Chapter 17

Midtown Manhattan; March 2008

"Got him. Shyster approaching, your five o'clock," we all heard Velasquez say in our earpieces. Lazeris was apparently walking down the sidewalk from behind our position toward the deli in front of us. Conrad instinctively started to turn to her right to look over her shoulder behind us.

"Don't do that," I said immediately. "Just sit here and look forward. Velasquez and Sanderson will tell us what's going on."

"OK. Sorry," she said as she turned back.

Within thirty seconds, Lazeris passed to our right and continued on the sidewalk to the front door of the deli. It was 10:55 a.m. He stood at the front door and looked down the sidewalk in both directions. He didn't appear to see anyone he recognized, and pulled the glass door open and walked in. He took a seat at a table in the middle of the restaurant, facing out toward the windows. From this seat, he could see everyone approaching from the east or the west once they came into the frame of the plate glass windows.

Alex put her hand on the door handle.

"What are you doing?" I asked.

"What do you mean? Lazeris is there, let's go talk to him."

I shook my head. "We need to wait and see if he's being followed by anyone."

As Lester turned onto Fifty-fourth, he saw Lazeris entering the deli. He slowed and put on his emergency flashers. As he approached, he saw a black Chevy Suburban to his left that screamed FBI. The back windows were blacked out, so he couldn't tell how many people were in it. He also couldn't take the risk of glancing through the front passenger window as he passed, as this would draw too much attention and expose his face. He continued on slowly and marveled at an amazing piece of luck: a car directly in front of the deli was pulling away from the curb. He would not have to double-park and risk that the explosion would be shielded by a parked car against the curb. He pulled into the spot and stopped, turning off his flashers since he was now legally parked.

"Hmmm," I said and heard Velasquez echo the same thing in my ear as a mail delivery truck pulled up in front of the deli and parked. The driver exited, wearing pants, a windbreaker, and a hat. He was tall and white, but his face was difficult to make out as it was somewhat obscured by the cap. He moved quickly to the back of the van, opened one of the two rear doors and pulled out an empty plastic bin. I couldn't make anything out in the back of the van other than a couple more plastic bins. There appeared to be a divider shielding the rest of the cargo area from view. He crossed the street in front of us and entered an office building opposite the deli, disappearing from our line of sight.

"Can't see anything from here. More mail bins, cargo area not visible," I said into my microphone.

"Is that a problem?" Conrad asked.

"Not really. These trucks are all over the city. Just the same,"—I hit my mic button—"Velasquez, we should call in the plate just to make sure."

"Already done, waiting to hear back," Lisa said.

"Scala, you got a cell?"

"Yeah."

"411 Nora's Mail Delivery, see if their truck number"—I read the number on the back door of the van—"C453 does this route. Tell them you're NYPD and he's double-parked."

Scala got to work as I heard Velasquez reply: "Van is registered to Nora's Mail Delivery, not reported stolen."

"OK. I think we're good here." I turned to Conrad. "OK, let's dump the walkie-talkies, mics and earpieces." We both took them off, laid them on the seat, and got out of the car.

Lester stood behind a support pillar in the office building across the street. He pretended to be taking a call on his cell phone so that he would not be bothered by building security. His position was not ideal. When he got out of the van, he had glanced over and seen Lazeris in the deli and no one was with him yet. The deli's morning crowd had emptied out and there were only two other patrons inside, which was good. Not too much collateral damage. The problem with his position now was that his line of sight was blocked by his own weapon, the van. However, he could see the Suburban, and a black van east of the deli which he presumed was another observation post for the feds. Ideally, he would have been on the second floor, able to see the entire scene from above. But he wasn't really a mail delivery person, so wouldn't get past security in the building, where he would need to sign in, show ID, and identify the company he was visiting. He was stuck here, hoping that the feds did everything they were supposed to. He needed them for this to work.

I joined Conrad at the front corner of the Suburban, and we began to walk toward the deli. We were just coming into view of the front windows when I heard Scala yell to me. I turned, grabbing Conrad's arm.

Scala waved us back.

"Come on," I said to Conrad. When we got back to the Suburban, Scala pushed his mic button so all could hear and said, "Nora's Mail Delivery says the van wasn't supposed to be out today. Until I called them, they thought it was still in the yard. The guy I talked to is checking the sign-out log and comparing it to the vans that are in the yard. He's gonna call me back in about one minute."

I thought about this and said, "OK, let's get back in the car for now." We piled back in and I held the earpiece to my ear and clipped the mic to my shirt. "Suggest someone check the van," I said. *Someone wearing a vest*, I didn't need to say.

Lester saw two people, a man and a woman, exit the Suburban and approach the deli. They weren't going toward the van, which was a problem. *Damn,* he muttered. They hadn't called the company to check on the van. *What kind of investigators were these?* Just then, he saw them turn around and look back over their shoulders. A third agent had stepped out of the Suburban. He waved them back and they returned. *Good.* He couldn't see Lazeris but hoped he hadn't seen them approach and then turn back, as it might spook him.

Ed Lazeris sat down in the deli. He ordered a cup of decaf, and when it came, didn't touch it. His eyes passed over the other two customers in the deli. They didn't look familiar or suspicious. He was sweating, and soaked a paper napkin by constantly wiping his upper lip and the palms of his hands. He kept looking out at the street, hoping to see Sanders and that lady agent approach. A mail delivery van parked in front of the deli, but Ed didn't think much of it. He used a mail delivery service too. Those things were all over the city.

"I'll go," Velasquez said into the mic, but then I heard Sanderson overrule her.

"No, this one's mine. Velasquez, you're running tactical. You need to stay in observation and coordinate unless something significant happens." Sanderson was absolutely right, but I also understood the dynamic of what had just occurred. Velasquez was so used to working for Sanderson, and not the other way around, she instinctively undermined her own authority by taking on a task she had always performed in the past. Sanderson took the opportunity to give some instruction.

I saw the back of the van open and Sanderson get out, approaching the delivery van. He walked to the front of it, then to the passenger side against the curb. I watched as he tried the front passenger door, which apparently was locked, because he moved to the sliding cargo door.

Lester watched as the back door of the FBI van opened and a man who appeared to be in his late forties, but quite fit, stepped out and closed the door. He was wearing military boots, black pants, black shirt, a protective vest and had a wire traveling from an earpiece to a walkie-talkie clipped to the front of the vest.

"Here we go," Lester breathed. He watched the agent approach the front of the van, stand at the front passenger door, then move to the rear door. Lester's view was blocked, but he could see the agent's boots and shadow under the van body. He pulled the phone away from his ear, and hit a speed dial code, holding his thumb over the "Send" button.

Lazeris saw a man who looked like a SWAT guy approach the mail van. At first he was confused, then nervous. He stood up to get out from behind the table. His positioning, while perfect to view the approach of anyone in front of the deli, was poor from the standpoint of needing to escape quickly.

Sanderson grasped the handle of the sliding door and pulled it toward him. It gave a bit of resistance but a familiar *thunk*. "Unlocked. Opening the door," he said into his mic. He slid the door back and was momentarily stunned.

Lester saw the shadow move in a familiar motion that made it appear that he opened the sliding cargo door. Lester had been counting on this, so that the shrapnel would have a clear exit into the deli. "Now just don't be a hero," Lester said as he counted silently to himself. "One-one thousand, two-one thousand ..."

Sanderson was looking at a cardboard coffee urn suspended at eye level, and behind it, steel sheet metal with C-4 or something similar glued to it with two cell phones attached, and wires between the plastic bricks. His eyes moved down to the floor of the cargo hold, where he saw the body of a Latino man, eyes wide open, obviously dead, a large piece of paper pinned to his chest with black felt-tip writing on it: YOU HAVE THREE SECONDS. Sanderson's instincts took over.

"Instincts" for Evan Sanderson and instincts for normal people were two different things. Twenty-five years in military and paramilitary jobs trained you not to freeze in place, or waste time saying statistically common last words like "oh shit." Sanderson saw the paneling and knew he was looking at a homemade cannon designed to direct shrapnel into the deli. He knew the safest place was not to the left or right but actually *under* the van. He immediately dropped to the ground, rolled off the curb and under the truck body, yelling "BOMB" into the mic. At that moment, John Lester hit "Send."

When you hear someone yell "bomb" and you're nearby, your instinct is to fall to the ground and cover up, or take cover behind a large object. When you're further away, your instinct is to run to your teammate who found the bomb to see if you can help. You are taught to fight that instinct, because all that does, obviously, is expose you to danger. Scala and I dropped down in our seats, but Conrad grabbed the door handle and was moving to get out. I grabbed her arm and pulled her down.

With everything happening at once, Sanderson was incredibly observant of details. As he rolled under the van, he saw blood dripping at the outside edge of the undercarriage, apparently from the body of the man inside. That was bad, as it meant that the sheeting job on the inside left some openings, and the shrapnel could tear through. He stayed directly underneath the van and was moving to cover his ears with his hands and get into a fetal position on his right side when the explosion drowned out everything.

Ed Lazeris was frantically pushing the table away from him, trying to extricate himself from his observation position. He got out from behind the table, and somewhere in the reptile-base of his brain, his instincts told him not to go out the front door, but to run to the back of the restaurant. Having been to the deli before, he turned to his right and got two steps down a hallway leading to the bathrooms in the rear behind the kitchen when a gigantic boom sounded and the glass of the deli's front wall blew in. Edward S. Lazeris never had a chance.

In hindsight, John Lester would realize that the ball bearings were just overkill. The glass shattered into millions of micro-scopic knives, ripping apart anything made of skin, fabric, cloth, or foam. Just behind them, the ball bearings tore into metal and bone. Between the two types of fragments, all material in the deli was torn into small pieces, including the two patrons in the dining area, the hostess at the cash register, a waitress, and the head of one cook visible above the tall meal-delivery counter. A second cook, who had been bending down to get a bottle of milk from the refrigerator, would survive, but would have several bro-ken bones from the fridge falling on him. None of the deceased victims would be identified by sight. The body of the dead man in the van was vaporized by the blast.

Immediately after hitting "Send," Lester walked away from the windows, which rattled from the sound of the explosion, but didn't blow in. Everyone around him screamed and fell to the ground, including the security guards. Lester did not. No one was paying attention to him. He walked out of the doors, turned left, and ran with the rest of the panicked crowd past the FBI van and down the street, his arms over his head to guard against falling ball bearings and to shield his face from surveillance cameras. When he turned the corner at the end of the block, only ten seconds had elapsed from the time he set off the bomb. He kept his face pointed down, took off his jacket and hat, and threw them in a nearby trash can.

Sanderson felt the force of the explosion push him down, but didn't feel much heat since he was sheltered by the sheet metal in the bottom of the van. The blast force initially pushed the van down on its shocks and out toward the street. After the primary blast, the van recoiled up and off the street. He felt the van lift into the air and knew he had to move. Maintaining his fetal position, he rolled into the street away from the van and kept rolling toward the opposite curb, hoping the van would not fall over on its side and on top of him.

Velasquez had fought the urge to run to her teammate when he yelled bomb, but only temporarily. The back door of the van sprang open and Velasquez was out in the street before the blast wave had stopped reverberating. She noticed in her subconsciously that the van was in the air, but she was focused on Sanderson, who was rolling across the street in front of her and into cars parked on the other side. Out of the corner of his eye, Lester saw her as they were running in opposite directions. He marveled at her bravery, if not her intelligence.

Velasquez got to Sanderson and thought it had started hailing. She suddenly realized the shrapnel from the bomb was raining down. She fell over the top of Sanderson's legs and covered her head with her hands as the initial group of ball bearings rained down. They were bouncing everywhere but had lost the primary force caused by the explosion and were merely falling back to earth. Just the same, looking up at the sky at that moment, an instinctive thing to do for most people, could cause serious eye damage or, in a particularly unlucky event, be fatal. Neither Velasquez nor Sanderson looked up until the pitter-patter of metal hail had stopped.

There are two basic kinds of explosive devices: incendiary and fragmentation. Both have a blast force, but incendiary devices are mostly used for structural damage, whereas fragmentation devices are typically used to kill people. Consequently, when a fragmentation bomb explodes, there is a loud boom, a shock wave, and, carried with that shock wave, multiple small fragments of metal designed to enter a person's body and destroy it instantly. Landmines are typical, if somewhat small, fragmentation devices.

During the actual explosion, a fragmentation device has some (but compared to an incendiary bomb, not much) heat. In movies, the types of pyrotechnics used for bombs are almost exclusively incendiary. This leads most civilians to believe they will see a huge fireball whenever a bomb goes off. In most terrorist bombings, this is not the case. Terrorists, by definition, try to kill as many people as possible. To do this, they need a fragmentation device. Consequently, victims and witnesses to terrorist bombings see almost no fireball at all and wonder how such a loud sound but no fire could cause all that damage.

While I didn't witness the explosion, having ducked down behind the dash of the car, I felt it as the Suburban moved a few inches backward, and I could picture the shock wave in my mind. What I pictured, as it turned out, was completely inaccurate. I saw a 360-degree wave flashing out from the van. In fact, as I learned later, the van was designed like a ship's cannon shooting grapeshot. The blast was directed in two directions: up and out toward the deli storefront.

When the sounds of falling shrapnel ceased, Conrad, Scala, and I slowly rose from behind the dash to see the van still on its tires, but obviously deformed, and two bodies in the street. There was smoke and haze around the van and the deli. Scala and I knew this wasn't smoke from the bomb, but rather microscopic remnants of materials destroyed by the blast which hung in the air or were falling from the sky. As such, it was actually more dangerous to your lungs than smoke.

I got out of the car and ran to Velasquez and Sanderson. Velasquez's clothing was torn and she had numerous small cuts, but she was clearly going to live. Sanderson I wasn't so sure about. He was bleeding from his ears, his face was blackened, his clothing torn. I knew he would be unable to hear a thing for at least a day, and only if his eardrums had not been completely destroyed. He appeared conscious, but otherwise confused and unaware of his situation. I was going to turn to Conrad and tell her to call 911 when I realized the ringing in my ears wasn't a remnant of the explosion, but rather sirens approaching.

I turned and Conrad was gone. I realized she probably went to look for Lazeris in the deli, a ludicrous proposition absent intervention by the hand of God. "Velasquez," I said as I rolled her over. No response. She was looking around wildly, as if she were ready to pull her weapon on anything. I put my hand to her cheek. "Lisa," I said slowly and calmly. No one called anyone by their first names in the bureau (at least not on the job), and this coupled with the manner in which it was said seemed to cause her eyes to suddenly lock, focus, and then slowly turn up at me.

"Can you hear me?" I said in a normal tone of voice. She nodded at me. "Are you hurt?" I asked. Then, realizing what a dumb question this was, added, "Badly?" She shook her head, then suddenly grabbed around my chest powerfully. I held her back and she was shaking, a sign the adrenaline was falling off and her body was letting itself realize it had survived a near-death experience. A paramedic van pulled up next to the Suburban and stopped. Two paramedics got out, retrieved equipment from the side storage units, and ran toward us. "Lisa, the paramedics are here. They'll take care of you." Still shaking, she nodded, and I slowly let go of her.

One paramedic looked at me. "Sir, you're injured," he said.

I looked down at the front of my shirt, which was now speckled with Velasquez's and Sanderson's blood. "Not my blood," I said as I stepped past him and walked toward the deli. I passed the remains of the van. The sidewalk in front of the deli was a war zone. You couldn't get into the restaurant since the storefront was obliterated, and pieces of chairs, tables, furniture and human remains lay strewn everywhere. Also, as law enforcement, I knew not to walk through the crime scene unless I was pursuing a suspect or there was hope someone was still alive. There didn't appear to be any such hope. Conrad was crouched down on the balls of her feet, her hands on her head.

"Jesus Christ, Nick. What's going on? Who the hell would do this to kill one lawyer?"

"I don't know," I said. What I was about to say, but didn't because it sounded too cold and detached at the time, was that I was pretty sure we were now going to get the warrant we needed.

Chapter 18

Midtown Manhattan; March 2008

The bombing occurred at 11:04 a.m. By 12:30 p.m.,
the entire New York contingent of the FBI Bomb
Investigation Squad was on scene. They cordoned off
an area reaching across the street to the other building and
one hundred yards west and east of the deli, and then scoured,
tagged, and photographed nearly every square inch. The entire
scene was videotaped as well. No bodies of any patrons in the deli
were immediately identifiable, but one cook, trapped beneath a
refrigerator, was found alive and rescued. One other body in the
kitchen was headless.

One hour after the bombing, a phone call was made to CNN
and the *New York Times*. A previously unknown al-Qaida splin-
ter group was claiming responsibility for the bombing. The lead
story on the news nationwide was that at least fifteen were dead
in a Middle Eastern style bombing at a "predominantly Jewish"
deli in midtown Manhattan, and were any of us truly safe, etc.,
etc. I didn't really know what a "predominantly Jewish deli" was.
I knew Jewish delis. I knew Greek delis. I knew Middle Eastern
and Persian delis. But "predominantly Jewish" was a new one on

me. The press was clamoring for more information: Was it a suicide bombing? How many were dead? (We left the dead guy in
the van out of our count, as no one but us knew he even existed.)
What kind of device was used? How was it obtained? Obviously,
this was being planned for a while, so how could law enforcement
agencies have missed it? And the implied but unspoken, What,
you guys still can't connect the dots? which was the issue editorials
began to raise the next day.

We were oblivious to all of this at the time because we were
seizing Lazeris's files on the five victims and the hard drives from
his office. All other cabinets were sealed with FBI crime evidence
tape. I hadn't considered the volume of paper a rich client's case
required, and I should have known better from my own experience in the practice. The five files in question occupied about one
lateral file drawer each. The secretary, Jessica O'Brien, was helpful in locating the files, but beyond that, we had to talk to one of
three paralegals Lazeris had doing his grunt work. We obtained
every employee's personal data and would do background checks
on all of them, but from our brief discussions, I could tell every
one of them was genuinely shocked by Lazeris's death and didn't
appear to be involved in whatever it was Lazeris had got himself
caught up in. All of them appeared to be as helpful as possible.
As helpful as you can be when you realize that your sole source of
income just got blown up in a terrorist bombing.

Melissa Dumond was typical of the paralegal triumvirate. She
completed responsibilities as assigned, but never had client contact and never spoke with anyone at ASBT.

"Ed referred them a lot of clients because he liked them.
They're really good at what they do. Client statements are on
time, and accurate to the last penny. If we had a question, Ed
would get the answer from them right away," she told us.

"Did they refer Ed clients?" Conrad asked.

"Sure, all the time. Ed was a trust and estates specialist, and
he was very good at what he did. He was a technician. He went

over the client documents with a fine-tooth comb. From what I could tell, it was two good professionals referring business to each other."

"What kind of work did you handle, if he was drafting the docs?"

"Title transfers, distribution requests, probate petitions, typical boilerplate filings."

"Did you ever meet any of these clients?" I showed Melissa a list of the five clients we were interested in.

"I wasn't here until after these two"—she pointed to the first two names on the list—"passed away, and I never met the others."

After more conversations like that, we moved all the files into a van and back to our midtown offices. We had Winkler transport Lazeris's and O'Brien's hard drives to the office as well.

At 6:00 p.m., we all met back in the conference room, and Al Borenstein was back. I wasn't looking forward to this conversation, but as it turned out, Borenstein was smarter and more professional than I gave the political appointee credit for.

"I presume no one in this room believes this is an al-Qaida bombing?"

This was the first we had heard of al-Qaida involvement. "Sorry, sir, we've been a little busy. Where'd that come from?" I asked.

"About an hour after the explosion, an al-Qaida cell took responsibility on their website and with a call to some media outlets."

"Well that's bullshit," I blurted out. "Sir."

Borenstein smiled. "Yeah. I think we all agree. It's a doubled-edged story. On the one hand it's convenient, since it keeps the media occupied on it and out of this investigation. On the other, it also appears to be the first terrorist attack on U.S. soil since 9/11, which isn't so convenient. At some point, we are going to need the truth to come out, and quickly, otherwise we'll look like we can't do our job."

So it's better that a domestic criminal organization bomb a Jewish deli, rather than a Middle Eastern terrorist organization? I didn't ask. I had to mull that one over. But Borenstein had said wrong place, wrong time, and that made me remember something.

"This is actually consistent with their MO," I said. I turned to Conrad and said, "Matzusaka?"

"Sir, he may be right," Conrad said. Maybe? My ego was bruised. "In 2006, an ASBT client named Matsui Matzusaka was killed in the crossfire of a Yakuza shootout in Tokyo."

Borenstein asked: "You think whoever bombed the deli arranged for the Yakuza to kill Matzusaka?"

"We can't prove it at this point, sir, but that's the working theory," she said.

JJ spoke. "Let's not get ahead of ourselves. We need to figure out what happened today. Whoever we are dealing with found out about the meeting with Lazeris, and with enough time to arrange the theft of the van and construct the bomb. Sir, for the time being we have to presume our communications are compromised. Only the people in this room and Sanderson knew about the meet far enough in advance to warn anyone. We'll review all their communications, but based on previous audits, I'm fairly confident no one in this group is communicating with anyone outside. And I presume you can vouch for Ms. Conrad?"

"Of course. Alex, we'll have to audit your communications as well."

"Yes, sir," she said.

Borenstein thought for a moment. "OK, right now all communications regarding the two cases we think are connected are now limited to the people in this room: Me, JJ, Conrad, Sanders,"—hey, Al, you remembered my name—"Velasquez, your tech analyst, what's his name?"

"Chris Winkler" JJ said.

"Winkler," Borenstein repeated, "and Sanderson, if he recovers to active duty status. We have an update on him, by the way?"

JJ spoke: "He probably has permanent hearing damage, extent unknown, but he is otherwise not significantly injured, which is just about a miracle. The guy was directly underneath the van when the bomb went off. He said that when he opened the door of the van, he saw steel panels on the back, sides and floor of the cargo area. He figured the safest place was under the truck."

"That's some good news, anyway," Borenstein said. "Let's assume for now he will not be back on active duty for the duration of this investigation. So, six of us. Here's the hard part: everyone here will give up all mobile personal communications devices—their cell phones, Blackberries, email devices, and allow the bureau to monitor their home landlines and computers. You will be issued a cell and text device directly from the bureau, which will be monitored by us until the investigation closes or we decide otherwise. You can use the landlines here to call friends and family and advise them of your new contact numbers. JJ, please collect all such devices and put them in the evidence locker. Only you and I jointly are authorized to release them. Anyone here goes out and buys a new phone or other mobile device, or borrows their spouse's or significant other's phone, you just put yourself on the suspect list. Everyone understand?"

Everyone hated it, but understood. There were about a million ways around what Borenstein was doing, such as going to an Internet café, buying a disposable phone, etc., but it was a good start and we all knew it. Somehow, some way, the guys who killed Lazeris had found out about the meeting, and it was unlikely they had tapped every pay phone in New York City. It was far more likely the leak came from one of us, a tap on the office, or someone Lazeris had told. Judging by Lazeris's fear, it was doubtful he told anyone.

"That's it for me," said Borenstein. "JJ, keep me updated. Let's plan on speaking every morning and afternoon, regardless of events. Alex, I'm going to let JJ second you for the time being. You folks were right about there being something bigger going on. Let's find out what, and fast. We need to nip this al-Qaida thing in the bud."

"Thank you, sir," JJ said as Borenstein left. "OK, everyone lay your cells, Blackberries, everything on the table." He reached for the phone and dialed an extension. "Barry, can you bring an evidence box in here? And have Winkler join us ASAP. Thanks."

"I'll get you all new phones within the hour. In the mean-time, we've got a long list: review the lawyer's files on the dead folks, analyze all his bank statements, review the explosion today, review banking transfers to and from the lawyer's office to abso-lutely everyone, get the bomb fragments analyzed, what else?"

"Need to view any payments going from ASBT to the lawyer or vice versa. Any chance of getting a warrant for ASBT's com-munications?" I asked.

"So far, ASBT isn't involved except that some of their clients were also shared by Lazeris. No judge is going to give us a war-rant yet. Let's see if we can use the client files from the lawyer to make some kind of case against ASBT."

"Don't forget the encryption. Chris and Conrad still need to work on that," I reminded JJ.

"That's Huntington. This case takes precedent. We're going to have to back-burner that for now. Best avenues right now are trying to find the bomb maker and review the lawyer's files. Let's get to it."

Velasquez and JJ went to collect video of the bombing from surveillance cameras in the area. Winkler, Conrad, and I reviewed the client files, particularly the funds passing in and out of their accounts. We also had all Lazeris's firm's billings and bank state-ments, which the paralegals gave us. One of the paralegals had the online banking login and password, so we could verify the ledger against those records as well. What we didn't have were Lazeris's personal accounts, and we would have to wait on a warrant for that. Most likely, we wouldn't see them until the morning.

Conrad and I took the paper statements and highlighted anything that appeared to be an extremely large payment or receipt, or a payment to a nontraditional vendor.

"This is stupid," Conrad said. "He's not going to run payments to or from criminals through his law firm. He'd keep them in a personal account no one knows about, or offshore."

I shook my head. "If there is one thing criminals fear more than the FBI, it's the IRS. A lot of financial crimes are discovered because of an IRS audit. A tax evasion charge becomes the easiest to prove so the first to be prosecuted. Al Capone, right?"

Conrad shook her head.

We reviewed billings against bank statements going back four years. Other than the fact that Ed Lazeris charged quite a bit, nothing appeared out of the ordinary. Every bill matched with every deposit. He never had a client not pay the full bill, which was somewhat surprising, but since he only represented wealthy clients, I suppose explainable. We needed to see his personal accounts and match his draws from the law firm account to his funds in his personal account. That would have to wait for the warrant.

At about 11:00 p.m., JJ and Velasquez came back in with a laptop, which they hooked up to the PowerPoint projector. "OK," JJ said. "We have lots of video, but not much on the driver of the van. There are three sources of video: our van, external of the street from an ATM, and the internal camera at the security desk in the building across from the deli."

JJ punched a few buttons and the wall screen showed a view down Fifty-fourth Street from the van. You could see our Suburban against the curb to the right, and some cars parked in front of the deli to the left. It was five minutes before the explosion, and we all looked for anything out of the ordinary. Other than seeing Lazeris walk toward the camera, then turn into the deli, it looked like a normal, busy weekday street in New York. The mail delivery truck turned onto Fifty-fourth, and JJ slowed the playback down. We all watched the van approach. The driver had a cap pulled down low, and the windshield was dirty. Other than a white male who appeared to be in his thirties, there was nothing distinctive about him. As he was approaching the deli, a car pulled away from the curb.

"Lucky there. Didn't have to double-park," Velasquez said.

"Yeah," I agreed. "Did we check that car out?"

"We checked it out," JJ offered. "Car belongs to a housewife in New Brunswick. Her husband loves the corned beef from the deli, so she was picking him up a sandwich to surprise him at work. She actually called NYPD to tell them she had been there and wasn't she lucky and was there anything she could do. We'll follow up, but I doubt she's involved. Bomber just lucked out."

JJ backed up the recording, and we watched the van approach again and move into the spot vacated by the car. The driver got out. He never gave our van a glance. He opened the driver's door, got out, turning to his left. His windbreaker collar was pulled up and his cap was down. His eyes were always looking down at the street. He moved to the back of the van and was obscured by its body. He never opened the back door enough to even see any portion of it around the corner of the van. He walked across the street, a fast walk but not a run, a delivery guy in a hurry, but not in a panic. He disappeared inside the building across from the deli and could not be seen again.

"He's a pro," I said. JJ and Velasquez nodded.

"Of course he is. He built a cannon out of a van in less than twenty hours," Conrad said.

"You're assuming he built it. I don't mean he's a demolitions expert—he is if he built the bomb—I mean he's had surveillance and infiltration training. Can you identify him? Would you know him if you bumped into him on the street?"

"I guess not."

"JJ, back it up to when he gets out of the van." JJ did so. "Check it out. He never looks up. The cap is always pulled down. Collar on the jacket is always up. He never draws attention to himself in any way. And he's wearing gloves, even though it's not quite cold enough. I assume it's the same inside the building?" I asked JJ and Velasquez.

Velasquez nodded. "Never looks up, no clear view of his face, and the surveillance camera was mounted about twelve feet off the ground, looking down. He knew that."

The film continued. Conrad and I get out of the Suburban, walk toward the camera, then Scala gets out and calls us back. We go back and Sanderson's back enters the frame as he exits the surveillance van and walks toward the delivery truck. He looks in the windshield, the passenger window, then opens the cargo door. Until he dives under the van, there is no clue anything is wrong. Sanderson didn't recoil, he just suddenly dove under the van. You could see his shadow from the front end, and then the van rocking down and right, then coming up off the street and back down on its tires while Sanderson rolled across the street to the right. JJ backed up the recording and slowed it down so that you could see the ball bearings fly out and up like a swarm of black flies, and smoke blow up and out of the van. The deli storefront collapsed in and then out as the blast force pushed all the fixtures in. The ball bearings tore them apart, and the debris flew back out toward the curb.

"Oh, God, was that an arm?" I had forgotten Winkler was in the room until he spoke. This wasn't his usual gig, so I was sure there was some excitement to it until the point where it became stomach churning.

"Looks like," JJ said.

The other two angles were just the same and of no help. They did provide further evidence that the driver was indeed well-trained. The camera inside the building never caught a glimpse of his face from anywhere other than the side, and he never looked up. Moreover, he kept moving even as the bystanders were trying to dig foxholes in the lobby floor with their bodies. The ATM camera showed him move down the street and then turn at the block, running with everyone else, arms over his face and head.

"Cameras on the next block?" I asked.

"Nothing for two more blocks until a surveillance camera at a loading driveway, and he never passes it, or at least no one wearing the same clothes passes it. This guy reminds me of the Unabomber. How's it coming with the bank records?"

"Nothing jumps out, but we need Lazeris's personal records. Someone's getting a warrant, right?" I asked.

"Yeah, should have it in another hour," JJ explained. "We can go to Lazeris's personal bank in the morning with it and get his records."

"When can we talk to B about the bomb?"

"Give him until tomorrow," JJ said. "They're still out there processing the scene. Probably will be for a couple of days, but he should have the major fragments tonight. I'll email him and let him know you're coming."

Chapter 19

Hoboken, New Jersey; March 2008

"Well done."

Two words, in encrypted email, from his client. That was all. John Lester leaned back in his desk chair, feet up on the edge of the desk, nursing two fingers of Johnnie Walker Blue Label. De Plata wasn't one for excessive or fawning compliments. Lester thought back to the morning and marveled at the quick thinking of the agent who had the unlucky job of sliding open the cargo door. In less than two seconds, the guy had taken in the entire scene and hit on the one place in the immediate vicinity he would absolutely be shielded from the shrapnel. The press had not reported on any law enforcement deaths, so Lester presumed he had succeeded in limiting the fallout. Moreover, his attempt to disguise a murder as a religiously motivated terrorist attack appeared to be working for the time being. He knew the bureau wouldn't buy it, but it gave them convenient cover when they were unable to solve the crime, and they could claim it was a suicide bombing, since Lester had given them an unidentifiable body inside the van.

Lester actually did like Javier. He was efficient and got Lester everything he needed on short notice. But the kid was too talkative and the only link to Lester. Reyes would have known that the moment he offered Javier's assistance. Reyes's immediate assent to John's emailed request after the bomb construction was proof of that. It was tough for guys like Javier to survive long in this business, to reach the upper echelons without getting killed or imprisoned.

Lester understood he was lucky: he was essentially given an entry ticket to elite crime due to his extensive training. He was just too valuable to kill, and too good to be captured. And Lester was smart enough to know when to get out. He had no interest in becoming some sort of kingpin. He was a hired gun who was well-paid and saved his money. He paid his taxes as part of his "consulting" business. And he maintained large accounts offshore, ready for the day when he would simply disappear. That day was coming, and soon. Lester could feel it. He had more than enough to live on the rest of his life, or three of his lives. It was time to get out, and leave guys like de Plata to find other efficient problem solvers.

Lester thought about the day he decided to freelance. The day he realized his country and his mentor had betrayed him. A job gone wrong, and Lester rotting in a jail cell in Southeast Asia. The humidity in the concrete box unbearable, the scars from the beatings still visible to this day. He realized after several weeks he had been disavowed. It was then he began plotting his escape (successful), his freelance career (very successful), and how he was going to beat the living shit out of Paul Blattman (still pending).

With the contacts he had made in his career in the CIA, John Lester set up shop as a security consultant, worked for himself, and made a lot of money. One day, this kind of work had to end. Lester was pragmatic enough to realize that early on. So he saved his money and kept his lifestyle Spartan. This assisted him in two regards: it allowed him to accumulate his "fuck you" money (as he liked to call it) offshore, and it also kept him further away from tripwires by limiting transactions that would be viewed by the government.

The last few years his work had been performed almost exclusively for Mr. de Plata, or one of his business associates, such as Reyes. Lester liked de Plata because he was careful. He had met him face-to-face less than ten times. All communications were secure. It was de Plata who had introduced him to the security consultant who provided the encryption software. De Plata's entire network used it, but each had their own cipher key, so no one in the network could hack another's system or listen in on another's communications without express permission. The additional security didn't come cheap but was well-worth the money.

Lester was tired now. He could not keep doing what he was doing and avoid arrest or death. He had killed five innocents to silence one man and preserve the security of the network. It was by far the worst job he had performed in his eight years as a "security contractor." He would have to start making arrangements for his retirement. He would miss the life: the planning, the execution, the action. But he had to get out before he got caught or killed.

Five innocent people. Jesus Christ. John Lester was not a man who cried. But if he had been, at that moment he might have. In this way, he differed greatly from Alejandro de Plata. To de Plata, five people translated to dollars preserved on a ledger, but Lester could remember a time when each life had mattered. He wished they still did.

Well done, indeed.

Chapter 20

Midtown Manhattan; March 2008

"So this guy is Russian?" Conrad asked, as she, Velasquez, and I stood in the elevator headed to the basement to see Maximilian Andreyevich Bodorofsky, our unit's ballistics expert.

"Parents are Russian. He was born here. His dad might have been CIA, protected double agent, whatever. There's a lot of myth around that, and B likes to maintain the aura."

"'B?'" she asked.

"Easier than Bodorofsky, no? This guy knows more about munitions and explosives than anybody, even Velasquez."

"That's true," Velasquez agreed, "and that's saying something coming from me."

"He can be a bit pretentious about it, but he is the resident brain trust on bombs and ballistics. You can learn a lot from him." I paused. "Don't tell him I said that, OK?"

Ballistics and bomb analysis were performed in the basement, which always struck me as somewhat dangerous. If a material the buereau was analyzing exploded, the whole building could come down. I had been assured the basement was specially designed for such an event. I hoped so.

Bodorofsky was tall, gangly, and balding. He wore thick glasses and a lab coat over his jeans and short-sleeved collared shirt. When we walked in, he was looking through a microscope on the other side of the lab. We stepped in but B didn't do anything, just kept looking in his microscope. Conrad gave me a "what's up?" look and I motioned for her to wait and keep quiet. Meanwhile, we looked around the worktables at a collection of weapons, all in the process of analysis. Conrad was looking at a K-5 35 mm assault rifle, one of the largest portable guns on the market. It also came with a grenade launcher on the bottom of the barrel. She reached out to touch it.

"You muck up my case, I'll shoot you with that, young lady."

Conrad snatched back her hand. Bodorofsky hadn't looked up from his microscope.

Finally, he leaned back from the scope and pushed his glasses up while simultaneously rubbing the bridge of his nose. "Well, Nicky, you surely stuck your nose in a big case, didn't you?"

B was the only one who ever called me Nicky, at least since my mom stopped calling me that when I was nine. It didn't bother me. Much. "Looks that way. Middle East terrorists and all."

"That what you're telling the press?" B asked as he turned on his stool to face us. "That's bull. Ah, Lisa Velasquez, my favorite gun aficionado. How's that MP5 I lent you holding up?"

"I thought the sighting was off until I found the defect in the barrel you could have let me in on."

"Now that wouldn't have been any fun, Special Agent Velasquez. I always like to see how good you are. How long did it take you? Honestly."

"Ten minutes of firing and adjusting the sight until I broke it down and vented the barrel. Felt it when I pushed the brush through."

"Very good. Took me less, but I had the benefit of studying each bullet I fired. Anyway, I can't let you take the K-5, but if there's another around here you're interested in, let me know. I so enjoy hearing your opinions on these things."

"You guys dating?" Conrad asked Velasquez, who only rolled her eyes. While they hadn't exactly warmed to each other, they appeared resigned to working together. Velasquez still saw her as an inexperienced agent who had no business in the field, but since we had all been through the bombing, Valasquez was less overt about her feelings.

"B, before you get all mushy and propose to her, can we discuss the deli bomb?" I asked.

"Perhaps. Who's the lady with the wandering hands?"

"B, this is Alexandra Conrad from DHS. She's on loan to us for this case. We had an overlap with their department."

"Everyone calls me Alex," she said as she approached him, hand extended to shake.

B took it with a limp wrist, just touching the ends of his fingers quickly to her palm. "Charmed," he said. "So, Nicky, who do you think made the bomb?"

"How the fuck am I supposed to know, you condescending dipshit? I'm a tax attorney. You're the bomb expert." OK, I didn't really say that, but I thought it. Instead, I said, "Well, I can tell you who didn't—Middle Eastern terrorists."

"On that we agree, but why do you say that? Not based on bomb analysis, since you never looked at it, right?"

Here we go, "the speech." "B, Conrad hasn't heard this part twenty times, so why don't you direct this to her?"

"Oh, very good. Ms. Conrad, when you come on the scene of a murder, and there is no suspect in sight holding a smoking gun or blood-stained knife, how do you identify the killer?"

"You interview witnesses, try to collect evidence from the scene, preferably DNA or fingerprints left behind by the killer, and hope you have that same DNA or the same fingerprints in a database somewhere to match it to."

"Exactly. That's what a bomb is. It's DNA. It's the DNA of the bomb maker."

"How so?"

"Bomb makers tend to be monogamous—they find one design that is effective, they perfect the construction of it, and use it over and over again. Over time, they develop the same method of making a bomb using the same parts and similar construction methods, such as on which side of the device the detonating wire is placed, or how it is tied off, or the color of the wire used. Taking all these facts together, and putting them into a database, we can sometimes identify not just the materials used, but the school of bomb-making the killer attended, or if we're lucky, the very bomb maker."

"Isn't that 'bomb makers are monogamous' thing from *Speed?*" I asked.

"I was using that line before that horrid and unrealistic film ever came out," B said, only slightly incensed that I had stopped his train of thought.

"How do you identify the bomb maker? Fingerprints on the bomb parts?" Conrad asked.

"Fingerprints? Oh, not usually. Leaving a fingerprint behind is a sign of two things: an inexperienced bomb maker who was not using gloves at the time of construction and a bomb that didn't go off."

"I don't follow."

"Ms. Conrad, how are fingerprints left at the scene of crimes? I mean, biomechanically, how does it occur?"

"Oils in the skin are transferred to the object being dusted. The dust adheres to the oil and the print can be lifted."

"Correct. What do you think happens to the oils left on bomb parts when the bomb goes off?"

"I don't know."

"Ah, at least you aren't burdened with the ego of Sanders here to try and bluff. Very good. I'll tell you what happens: they dry up from the blast heat. In most bombs, enough heat is created during ignition that any oils left behind by the bomb maker dry up and are no longer there when we dust for prints. So, the print is the bomb itself."

B got up and walked over to another workbench. "Now, your little device here has all the hallmarks of an Iraqi car bomb."

"I thought you said it wasn't a Middle East bomb," Velasquez said.

B turned and looked at her sadly. "Oh, Lisa, you're turning into Nicky Junior. I wasn't finished yet. It has all the markings of an Iraqi car bomb, except for the detonators. Whoever built this device had some experience with Middle Eastern bombs, enough to try to make it look like a typical Muslim terrorist bombing. But he couldn't overcome one problem—the materials he had to work with. Look here."

B pointed to several pieces of the bomb and a section of steel paneling that looked cut away from a larger piece. "First, the explosive. Residue analysis from the steel panels show it's Semtex. Used all over the world, but second only to pure gunpowder as the explosive of choice in the Middle East, particularly in suicide bombings because of its efficiency—lots of blast power in a small brick. But, by itself, the Semtex really doesn't tell you anything. Anyone can get it anywhere in the world.

"Next, cell phone used as detonator, practically perfected by guerrilla bombers in Iraq. Just dial the phone and the ringer creates an electric charge that sets off the detonator. Lithium ion batteries preferred, but this bomber used single-use cell phones with nickel cadmium. Risky, because if not fully charged, it may not generate enough energy to set off the detonator. So, we know that concealment was important to this bomber, as he wanted to use an untraceable phone at the risk of the bomb not going off, which explains why two phones were used.

"Third, wiring. No help. Electrical wiring is a vanilla commodity used all over the world, and even though Sanderson tried his best to draw what he saw for me,"—he motioned to a piece of eight-by-eleven paper with a sketch of the van interior on it—"he didn't get much of a look as he was diving under the van. Good bit, that, by the way. To take in the entire scene in about one second and realize the safest place is actually closer to the bomb. Overcoming your natural instinct to run. Very impressive."

I picked up the sketch. It showed a cardboard coffee urn hanging from bungee cords in the middle of the van, surrounded by steel panels with plastic explosive bricks on them. Presumably the urn held the shrapnel. There was a lump on the floor, which I took as a representation of the dead man Sanderson had seen.

"Fourth, shrapnel. Ball bearings. Again, pure al-Qaida. They love that shit, pardon me ladies, especially in their suicide bombings.

"Next, overall construction. Now, I don't know much about your case, but I am guessing this bomber was trying to limit damage to one area, and maybe to one specific person."

"Why do you think that?" I asked.

"Well, if you know your target is going to be in a specific area, say, a place that is no more than one hundred feet long, and that he or she won't be more than fifty yards away from your bomb, you want to maximize the killing potential in that area, right? So, instead of doing an Oklahoma City where you just indiscriminately blow up an entire building because you don't care who you kill, you focus the blast like a gun or cannon so that you are sure to direct all of its force and shrapnel at your target. That's what your guy did here."

"B, it doesn't exactly sound like you're onto anything here …" I began to say.

"Ms. Conrad, I beg you, don't take lessons from Nicky here. He's already led Special Agent Velasquez down the path of questioning me before I'm done. Poor manners, you know." Alex and Lisa laughed.

"OK, B, whaddya got?"

"Like I said. The detonators." He held up a charred black object no bigger than an inch and a half across. It had a flat, round back like a coin and a point or cone emerging from the opposite side.

"May I?" I asked as I reached for it. He handed it to me. Until I touched it, I couldn't tell it was made of metal.

"It survived?" I asked.

"Good point. Most detonators, in fact, are destroyed in the explosion they create. However, some are made to withstand pressure and heat."

"Why?"

"Excuse me?"

"Why make a detonator to survive? You can't exactly get the detonator back and reuse it, right? And detonators are a dime a dozen," I pointed out.

"In point of fact, this detonator can be purchased on the Internet for seventy-four cents, plus shipping. You can get a volume discount, or so I understand."

"The Internet? You mean everyone in America can buy a bomb detonator?" Conrad asked.

"Sure. No ID required. Because it's not a detonator."

"What?" we all asked in unison.

"That part my dubious colleague is holding is, in fact, the igniter for a water heater pilot light. Made in Mexico. Go home and open up the little panel at the bottom of your water heater. You will find that part."

"I don't get it," I said.

"Of course you don't. You're not me. This is a multi-use tool. Pilot light igniter. Space heater igniter. Bomb detonator. Not the most trustworthy device, but cheap, freely available, and not traceable to anyone in particular. Used almost exclusively in bomb making by South American terrorist organizations, but most prominently by the FARC."

"You're saying Colombian terrorists built this bomb?" Conrad asked.

"No, I can't say that. I can say that whoever built it used parts commonly used by the FARC."

"Seems to give your theory some credence," I said to Conrad.

"What theory?" B asked.

"That some of the money from a suspect bank is being funneled to purchase weapons for the FARC and others," Conrad explained.

"Hmmm," B mused.

"OK, B, anything else?"

"Just some conclusions I drew. I think the bomb maker was pressed for time, which explains the detonators and the cell phones. He"—B paused—"or she was relegated to using devices that could have failed. But they were smart enough to build in redundancy to assure success. No prints yet, and I don't expect to find any, because anyone who can build this quickly is a professional."

"The meeting we were supposed to have wasn't set until the afternoon, day before yesterday. If the bomb maker knew when we did or soon after, he had less than twenty hours, probably a lot less, to build it."

"Impressive. That means the materials were freely available— I mean the Semtex, the ball bearings, the wiring. You should worry."

"Why?"

"Well, you need to turn a van into a directed-blast bomb. You have less than twenty hours. What materials do you need?"

"The van, explosives, detonators, wiring," I said.

"Oh, not just that. You have to *direct* the blast, so you need thick steel panels to weld inside the van. You need shrapnel, so you have to have a large supply of ball bearings or metal fragments.

You need a welding torch. A rivet gun, an air compressor. It's a long list."

"OK."

"So, if I have to get all that together and build this essentially overnight, all the materials have to be close by, preferably in one place. Like a Walmart of bomb making. A warehouse store. I am suggesting you worry because most likely all of this stuff is probably sitting in one building, ready to make the next device. And it's probably very close, because building it in an outer borough and trying to bring it in subjects the transporter to too much risk of discovery at the bridge or tunnel checkpoints. Nicky, this"—he spread his hands across the worktable—"proves to me that someone's got a bomb-making factory right here in Manhattan."

Chapter 21

Langley, Virginia; March 2008

"What do we have on this deli bombing, Paul? I need to know now if this is a group we were tracking and missed."

Blattman was being called on the carpet, which to him was no big deal. It had happened many times in his career. It was part of a job that was inherently political, and when political appointees lost their nerve because an operation went south, he had to lumber up to the seventh floor at Langley and speak to the DDO, who invariably had just had his ass chewed by the DCI and needed to get answers fast. The new DDO, Al Lopez, was a decent guy, even if he was an overtly political, pompous name-dropper. Blattman had worked for better in his day, but he had also worked for worse.

"Have you talked to the FBI, sir?"

"Not yet."

"Sir, I can unequivocally tell you this was not an operation from a known group. In fact, there's something about this that doesn't ring quite true. Muslim bombing, I mean. I'd be interested to see what the bureau has on the bomb forensics."

"I have to go through Borenstein to get them to liaise with your people. But that could be tough if you don't have anything.

165

Right now we have to treat this as a domestic crime, and primary investigational responsibility will be the bureau's."

"That'd be fine, sir." Blattman turned to leave but hesitated at the door.

"Something else, Paul?"

"Yeah." Blattman wondered how many of his thoughts he should reveal to a political appointee. He had survived in the agency for over thirty years, primarily by not being backstabbed by his superiors. And you prevented being backstabbed by knowing what information to reveal and when to reveal it. "Sir, be careful with Al Borenstein. I've known him a long time. He may have his own agenda on this and try to lock us out."

"Borenstein doesn't have an operations arm, Paul. DHS is an information clearinghouse, that's all. We and the bureau run operations. Borenstein needs us."

Blattman could have given his DDO an education. If he didn't realize that sitting at the crossroads of all domestic and foreign intelligence information made Borenstein the most powerful bureaucrat in Washington, then he would soon be replaced by someone who did. Blattman decided not to educate him. Lopez could learn fast, or he could get his ass fired. And Blattman would answer to the tenth political appointee of his career. It didn't matter to him. He kept doing his job the only way he knew how. It didn't matter what party or administration was in power. Events took their own path and timeline without taking into account the American electoral schedule. The dictator or terrorist group that was a problem when a Republican was in the White House was likely to still be there when a Democrat took over, and vice versa.

Midtown Manhattan

"I understand, Mr. President. We are analyzing the data. We will have something on this within days. Right now, as I said, our operational assumption is that this was not an Islamic or Middle Eastern terrorist organization. The bureau believes a lawyer who may have been involved in financial crimes was the specific target of the bombing, which was made to look like a terrorist attack."

While Paul Blattman was deciding to leave his boss to learn a hard lesson, Al Borenstein was busy getting his ass chewed by his own boss. The whole operation, which had started out so simply, had quickly gotten out of hand. The ass chewing this president gave was low-key. Borenstein could tell he was pissed, but the president always kept his temper in check. That made him a good leader, because despite his emotions, he could always process new information and make informed decisions. Nevertheless, if Borenstein didn't have something to show that this *wasn't* a terrorist bombing on U.S. soil, the entire intelligence management team, including Adolph "call me Al" Borenstein, were in jeopardy of losing their jobs.

"OK, Al," Borenstein heard the President say on the other end of the phone. "You know the stakes. Get your wunderkind to wrap up her end of your investigation. We may be able to defuse this if we can move forward on that front. Seems like we have enough to do it."

"Yes, sir. But, sir, I'm not convinced the bombing is related."

"Even if they're not related, a good outcome on that piece alone would go a long way to showing our intelligence agencies can still tell their ass from a hole in the ground."

"I see your point, sir."

"Good. I'll look forward to hearing from you soon, Al. When you have anything of substance, don't wait on it. Whatever my schedule, I will make time for you when you need to speak to me."

"Yes, sir. Thank you, sir. We are on it."

"Good. Good-bye, Al."

"Good-bye, Mr. President."

Chapter 22

Federal Holding Unit, Downtown Manhattan; March 2008

"You aren't offering me anything. I got nothin' to tell you."

We had left Velasquez back at the office while Conrad and I went to the Federal Holding Unit, which most people would refer to as a jail. But when you're the federal government, "jail" just isn't catchy enough, whereas "FHU" has a certain ring to it. Conrad and I had an appointment to talk to Jonathan Huntington III and his attorney, which we had set up before the bombing. But I figured if we solved the Huntington leak, we (probably) solved the Lazeris leak also.

Sitting in his jumpsuit and in shackles, you would think Huntington would know the jig was up. He was never going to see the outside of prison again, so he was never going to be reunited with his offshore stash of other people's money. But somehow, little Jonnie Huntington didn't see it that way. He was acting as if he controlled the conference, his lawyer a mere afterthought. And we were just keeping him from his important jailhouse activities, whatever those might be.

"You shot two federal agents, Mr. Huntington. Your wife is divorcing you. We are tracing the money you stole, which you're never going to see again—"

His attorney interrupted: "The word is 'allegedly,' Mr. Sanders. My client had been investing his clients' money in various funds around the—"

"Shut up, Bobby." Huntington cut him off. "Really? Tracing my money, Agent Sanders? How's that going for you?"

The motherfucker knew his encryption was unbreakable. He was lording it over us. Huntington's records, his account numbers, his passcodes, all of them were recorded using encrypted software or were in his head, or both. We weren't getting the information unless he gave it to us.

"Where'd you get the encryption software, Jon?" Conrad asked. She was nothing if not direct.

"I don't know a Jon, honey. I know a Mr. Huntington, who might respond if that's the way you addressed him."

"My apologies. Where'd you get the encryption software, *Mr.* Huntington?"

"Better, but not that easy. I need to have something from the U.S. attorney which says something like, we'd just love for Jonathan Huntington III to help us locate his money and return some of it to investors who were too greedy and lost it even though Mr. Huntington advised them they could lose all their money, and gosh, if Mr. Huntington does that, we'll make sure that even if we press bullshit charges against him after threatening his life for which he felt compelled to defend himself, and even if he gets convicted on those trumped-up charges because we have vast resources to fake a bunch of evidence against him, we'll make sure he gets out of jail real soon because he helped us locate some of that investor money. Something like that would be good, sweetie."

Conrad took that pretty well, but I was fuming and could barely contain myself. "Hey, Jon, you like your cell mate?" I asked. "'Cause we can arrange for a new one. One more attending to your womanly needs. By the way, how's your head?"

"Yeah, Agent Sanders, you really screwed the pooch on that one, huh? 'Cause if you hadn't beaten my head with a blunt object, I might not have this blurred vision, blackouts, and memory loss I've been experiencing. I might actually remember useful things like who I got the software from, and the cipher key. You know, shit like that. But, since you and your overzealous agents sought to persecute and torture me, you inadvertently destroyed your only means of getting the information you need. Unless I recover, of course. A deal from the U.S. attorney might help that."

Fuck. Fuck. Fuck. Fuck. I wanted to kill the guy right there, attorney or no. I had to get out of there.

Conrad could see I was about to blow, and she leaned forward. "Well, see, that's funny because the folks at CCS send their regards. They're backing you for now as long as you keep quiet. But we just need to get a local Bahamian court order, and they'll be more than happy to help us out. So we'll get it that way. And you won't be getting any deal."

It was there. A flicker of doubt. Then some confusion. And then his face hardened and he said, "Honey, I don't know what CCS is. If you think you can get help from them, that's great. Are they a counseling agency or something?"

It was a good bluff. We really had no idea who or what CCS was. Or even that it was a Bahamian entity. But Huntington's answer seemed to tell us it was an organization of some kind rather than the initials of a single person. We had to get inside the offshore banks to find out more. But as far as getting any help from Huntington, we were done. He wasn't going to break. He had one goal: get the best deal he could get from the U.S. attorney. And the U.S. attorney wasn't about to give him one. If the case went to trial, and Huntington's defense really was he invested the money offshore, he'd have to prove to the jury that it was still there. There was no way he could defend himself and not produce the money. We exchanged a few more pleasantries with Jonathan "don't call me Jonnie" Huntington, and left.

Chapter 23

Midtown Manhattan; March 2008

Winfield had to start planning much sooner than he had hoped. The Lazeris thing was quite troubling, as was the text message he received on his secure line the night after the bombing.

Need to wrap up my end soon. Days not weeks. Will get pressure on the codes. Need to complete your plans ASAP.

Winfield didn't think he was ready, but it was clear he had to accelerate his timeline. And then he realized the recent events could actually help him, and get him face-to-face with the man he needed to see. But his communication had to have just the right balance of carrot and stick to make it happen.

Dear Senor de Plata,

Due to recent events, we are reconsidering our recommended strategic asset allocation for our clients. While, to date, the majority of client investments have been U.S. domestic equities and fixed income, our investment committee foresees the need to move a greater share of our clients' wealth to foreign markets and to alternative investments, including hedge funds operating in emerging markets. However, before allocating a greater share of our clients' wealth abroad, greater due diligence is required.

Consequently, we request a meeting with your fund's principals and management committee, a review of all holdings, and an analysis of your investment strategy before committing any additional assets to your fund. A positive outcome from our increased due diligence requirement will likely result in a greater share of our clients' assets being allocated to your fund. Conversely, a lack of cooperation will result in a significant decrease or a complete redemption of our assets from your fund and a withdrawal from our exclusivity agreement. We look forward to strengthening our business relationship with you and to your continued professionalism as we seek to immunize our clients from potential increased volatility in the U.S. domestic investment market.

We will be contacting you to arrange a meeting and provide details regarding the scope of our review.

Very truly yours,
Jeremy Winfield
President and CEO

Costa Rica; March 2008

Damn. Alejandro de Plata hated face-to-face meetings. But he also couldn't afford to have investors pull his money (it was *his* money, after all) out of the fund, or even attempt to. The day he got a request for a significant redemption was the day he would have to disappear and start over again. So, they wanted to meet the investment committee. He chuckled. How about an "investment committee" of one? This probably wouldn't impress them. He had to drum up a few empty suits for the meeting. He could include his security consultant for good measure.

De Plata reread the letter attached to the secure email. He considered telling Winfield no, but he got far too many of his funds from ASBT and needed them to continue. Plus, the promise of additional monies was tantalizing.

Fear and greed. He had found the right balance between the two his entire life. The risk didn't seem that significant, and the reward seemed tremendous. Wall Street was in disarray; it looked like Bear Stearns could go under. So Winfield was acting out of fear. But the U.S. turmoil could result in even greater investments in his offshore fund.

Fear and greed. Greed was going to win out, primarily because de Plata couldn't see anything to fear. He had never met Winfield but didn't think much of him. Winfield never asked questions about how de Plata was able to generate his outsized returns. Any competent banker would already have asked to see the books and the strategy. It wouldn't have mattered to de Plata, since they would never see the *real* strategy. He had plenty of fake documents and computer ledgers to show them. And that is what he would show Jeremy Winfield, personally.

Chapter 24

Midtown Manhattan; March 2008

Back in the conference room, JJ, Velasquez, Conrad, Winkler, and I sat around the table. It was brainstorming time. We had to compare notes from our day's work and see where to go next. Conrad, Velasquez, and I filled JJ and Winkler in on our meeting with B and our talk with Huntington. JJ was a little perturbed that I was "wasting" time on an unrelated case, but he let it slide. Mostly. Winkler started in on the Lazeris bank records.

"Someone was paying this guy a lot of money," Chris began.

"Ya think?" I asked. "The guy was attorney to the richest people in the country."

"I don't mean his clients were paying him a lot of money. I mean *someone* was paying him. By my calculation, in the last three years, Lazeris drew about $400,000 pre-tax out of his law firm every year, and paid his taxes on it."

"Good living," JJ said. "Can't believe Sanders left the practice."

"I was never that good," I said.

"We know," Velasquez threw in.

"Yeah, well Lazeris was *spending* $900,000 a year, at least. He paid for his Porsche 911 by wire transfer of cash last year. He paid down the mortgage on his house to next to nothing *and* bought a house in the Hamptons that was twice as expensive as his New York apartment. He paid cash for everything. He also had a membership at the Larchmont Yacht Club and was buying a boat that was being built at a shipyard in the Caymans. He was spending $1,500 a month in greens fees at two different country clubs, one in Westchester, one on Long Island. The equity buy-in at the Westchester club was $200,000, which he paid cash."

I was always amazed at how much money rich people could spend. At some point, spending money becomes work in and of itself. Take Lazeris. Unmarried, no kids, and only five years ago living in a modest apartment on the East Side. How much money did he really need? A couple hundred grand a year would yield a nice lifestyle for someone like that. But for a guy in his position to spend almost a million bucks a year was a second job. "Where was all the money coming from?" I asked.

"It wasn't in his bank account, and not on his tax return either," Chris explained. Oh, now that was disappointing. I had thought that Lazeris was at least a smart crooked lawyer. He should have known better than to risk an audit. "And he took trips to the Caymans five times a year. Every time he came back, within two weeks he'd make a large luxury purchase, or put more money down against his apartment mortgage. So, I am guessing he had an offshore account with a foreign bank and brought back cash."

"How would he get that through security?" Conrad asked.

"He didn't go through normal security. He took a chartered private jet every time. We got those records too. Westchester County Airport to Grand Cayman and back, usually a weekend trip, Thursday to Sunday. Makes it look like a short vacation."

"Oh, come on, he still has to go through customs," Conrad protested.

I answered her. "He had it on his body. He was a heavyset guy to begin with. If he established a regular pattern of going to Grand Cayman on vacation, he'd get to know the customs agents at the return terminal for private planes. They'd x-ray the bags but not him. 'Hey, Mr. Lazeris, how were the islands? Welcome home.' He doesn't fit any profile that would raise suspicion."

"So, someone was depositing a bunch of money in an offshore account for him. Do we know which bank?" JJ asked.

"Yeah," Chris explained, "but only because Lazeris screwed up. He never filed an FBAR for this money." Chris meant a Foreign Bank Account Report disclosure form, aka FBAR, aka a T.D. 90-22.1 Form. All Americans with more than ten thousand dollars offshore had to file the form every year to let the government know they had signature authority over the foreign account. "He needed money to close escrow on his Hamptons house and was short. He had to get an extra seventy-five thousand wired from Atlantic Grand Cayman Bank and Trust. So, we have a source account number and bank routing number." He passed around several photocopy pages of an account ledger.

What Chris said made everyone sit up. Having those numbers could reveal a treasure trove of information, because if we could see the account, we might be able to see who was depositing the money into it. There was one small detail, however.

"What're the chances of getting a local warrant for the bank account info?" asked Velasquez.

"Nil. No way they are going to break their own banking secrecy laws. The second they did that, every American depositor, or non-Cayman for that matter, would pull their money out," I explained. "But, since we have the routing number and account number, we could at least peek at the account."

Conrad turned slowly to me, disbelief on her face. "You mean hack the bank? Even if we found something we could use, it would get excluded."

JJ was a tad more blunt: "Sanders, are you out of your fucking mind?"

"You all need to stop getting lost in the weeds on this case. Look at what we have so far, big picture. We know that someone was paying Lazeris. Potentially millions being paid to an attorney to do nothing more than violate his attorney-client privilege, and the moment the attorney shows that he's nervous and willing to talk, he's killed. And the people that did it have links to arms traffickers and South American terrorists. And the only lead we have is this attorney's offshore account and being able to see who is depositing money in his account. We're beyond U.S. borders. That means we, the FBI, can't enforce U.S. laws against these people anyway. That means Alex, or her counterparts in 'other agencies,' are going to end up taking care of this problem. So worrying about whether we can get a warrant or not is beside the point."

Everyone mulled this over. They were at least considering the idea when JJ turned to Winkler.

"Let's not get ahead of ourselves," JJ said. "Can this even be done?"

"Hell yeah! The bank probably doesn't even know Lazeris is dead yet. If I can find his password, we can just log in as him."

"That doesn't get you the account information on the depositor," Alex pointed out. That was a good point. Seeing a deposit go into Lazeris's account didn't tell you who made the deposit. For that, you would need to hack into the depositor's bank.

"No, but it would give us a routing number, and maybe an account number. If we got lucky, the depositing account would be at the same bank, and that would make it easy. And then we have you," I said to Conrad.

"Me? What are you talking about, Sanders?" she asked.

"Well, you've already hacked a bank in the Bahamas or Antigua or somewhere, right?"

She paused. "I don't know what you're talking about."

"Give it up. How else do you get the trail of money from ASBT to an offshore hedge fund, and then withdrawals from the hedge fund? I'm guessing no judge gave you a warrant based on a theory everyone thought was bullshit when Echelon spit it out, right? So how did you develop your spreadsheet with the matching transfers and withdrawals? There's only one way to know that information, and that's to see the bank's ledger."

"You're right. You'd have to see the account ledger," she said. "But you're wrong about how I got it. We need to leave it at that." Son of a bitch. She had an insider feeding her intel.

"We can't leave it there, Ms. Conrad," JJ interrupted. "If this is a matter of your department revealing further information to us, we can all sign extended confidentiality agreements, and I can talk to Al Borenstein about the issue. But everyone here is in harm's way as a result of this case. If you have a C.I. in an offshore bank, we need to talk to that person." JJ meant a Confidential Informant.

"It wouldn't do you any good. The routing code for the Lazeris account is different, so it's a different bank entirely."

"All right, first things first," JJ said. "There's no problem getting a warrant for domestic accounts. We've already got it. And the fact that Lazeris used the Internet to move money not reported to the IRS shows wire fraud, so we can get a judge to let us pretend to be him and see his offshore account. Do it. In the meantime, I have to call the director, then Al Borenstein, and let them know what's going on."

Chapter 25

Jungles of Eastern Ecuador; March 2008

Marquez had missed his check-in. Reyes wasn't sure whether Marquez was busy or whether the army had somehow located his deep jungle camp. If it was the latter, Reyes had to do something about Major Fernando Pinchao sooner rather than later. His main supply lines and camps were already over the border in Ecuador and Venezuela. Pretty soon the FARC would be an Ecuadorian rebel group rather than a Colombian one. Luckily for them Uribe could not sanction a cross-border incursion, so they were quite safe as long as they stayed in Ecuador to re-arm and regroup. But they had to strike at Uribe soon, or they would lose their ability to travel within Colombia because they would lose control of the jungle.

He picked up his satellite phone and punched in a code on the keypad. The phone on the other end rang several times. Finally, Marulanda picked up.

"Manuel? We may have lost Ivan. We need to move up our schedule. We have to go within days, not weeks."

✳ ✳ ✳

Bogota, Colombia; March 2008

Edgar Joaquin Gomez tapped the keys on his keyboard at the Security Services office in Bogota. He knew he would be there late, again. In fact, he would be there so long as Major Fernando Pinchao decided he wanted to stand behind him, looking over his left shoulder as Edgar analyzed the hard drive recovered from Marquez's camp. Edgar would have to take a bathroom break just to call his wife and let her know she should go to bed without him. Again. When Pinchao wanted something, he wanted it now and would simply wait there until he got it. The situation was made more annoying because standing over his right shoulder was the American adviser, Armin Smith.

Pinchao had much faith in Edgar. He had studied in the United States and gotten his degrees in computer science and electrical engineering from UCLA. Unlike most exchange students, Edgar had returned home to a lower-paying job in his hometown, working for the government to root out the FARC. A review of his personnel file answered the question of why: Edgar's parents had both been murdered by the FARC, his mother raped repeatedly prior to her death. Edgar's motivations were not questioned, and he was the only one in the Security Services office Pinchao would allow to touch the Marquez hard drive.

Pinchao and Armin Smith looked at the screen. To Smith, it looked like the entire screen was filled with unrelated numbers and symbols.He couldn't understand any of it.

"Sirs, this could take a while," Edgar said. "In fact, we may never get anything. It looks like they're using a very sophisticated encryption program. 1024-bit polymorphic encryption."

"How sophisticated?" Pinchao asked.

"Top corporate and government level."

"How would they get it?" Smith asked.

"Well, it's expensive, but assuming they had the right contacts, say inside a large bank or a government, they could have stolen or bought it."

"What about his phone?" Pinchao asked.

"Very sophisticated satellite phone. Can only be used when the correct code is tapped into the nine-digit keypad at the top, and then will only connect to another designated phone, and only if the person on the other end taps in their code. This is military level as well."

"Son of a bitch. These guys are professional," Smith said.

"Yes and no. They have the tools," Pinchao explained. "But they don't have the professional training. There are some soldiers among them, but they have not utilized their knowledge and used them to train their entire force. Also, many of them are sidelined on the drug trade, since that is their primary source of income."

They both looked back to Edgar. "Why don't we let Edgar have at it for a bit without us standing over him. Come on, I'll buy you a beer," Smith said. Beer seemed to be the answer to many problems of American advisers, Pinchao had noticed. Sometimes, however, he had to admit that leaving professionals to do their job and regrouping over drinks cleared the mind and allowed you to see a case differently. He nodded and they both left, much to the relief of Edgar Gomez.

Outside across the plaza from the Security Services building, they sat at a table, each drinking a Pilsen and mulling over the situation. "When did they start using the encrypted communication?" Smith asked.

"We're not sure. Once they realized we started monitoring their communications about five years ago, they went back to the Stone Age—everything by courier. But we could still intercept couriers and find their camps. Their couriers still had to use cell phones, so we could track them. Since this new equipment, I haven't found a single camp through our—well, your—monitoring program. Marquez was dumb luck. We caught a smuggler walking through the jungle with several horses, all packed with arms. He gave us the location of the camp. That is rare, though. You have to be in the right place at the right time."

Smith mulled this over. "Think someone in your government is working with them?"

"Of course. Many are. It is hard to resist the lure of the drug money. But if you mean do I think they got this security software from them? No, I don't. We don't have anything this sophisticated. I think perhaps they bribed a security consultant at a large bank. Banks spend much money on such things."

"You may want to run the hard drive through FBI or Langley. They may be able to crack it," Smith suggested.

Some might have been insulted by such an offer, which essentially implied the Colombian military was not up to the task. But Pinchao was a realist. He knew that if Gomez could not break the cipher, then the next best resource was the Americans.

"Who would I contact about this? Your secretary of state?"

"Fernando, if we took that route, it would be months before all the i's were dotted and t's were crossed. I think we need to back channel this. Let me call someone I know at the agency. He gets things done, the right way. Old school."

"What is this, 'old school'?"

"It's an expression. It means he is old fashioned—does things based on trust and a handshake."

"I would like to talk to this man if possible."

☆ ☆ ☆

Langley, Virginia; March 2008

Paul Blattman sat in his office in Langley, Virginia, looking over a copy of the bureau's preliminary investigation of the Fifty-fourth Street deli bombing. Whoever planned and executed it was quite professional, he had to admit. It also looked as if SAIC Jordan had a leak. That much was clear. Lazeris had called this guy Sanders at 3:30 p.m. and requested the meet. Assuming one of the people in the room was the leaker, or that someone outside the bureau had tapped Sanders' cell line, the soonest the opposition could know about the fact that Lazeris would spill his guts was at the same time, and this was being very generous. In all likelihood it would take one of the people in the room at least ten minutes, and maybe a half hour, to come up with a pretext to leave the building and make a call. So, by 3:30 or 4:00 p.m., whoever doesn't want the shyster to talk knows. Even if they began planning immediately, thatgave the bombmaker and extremely short window in which to construct the bomb.

He looked at the stills from security cameras and the camera in the back of the FBI van. No way to make out the driver clearly. Whoever he was, he was good. Something about him. Familiar. Blattman noodled on it a bit. Ah hell, could be anyone.

Then there was the other thing. The thing Blattman just couldn't get out of his head. Somehow, somebody seemed to think there was a connection between the dying clients of this bank, ASBT, and money transferring to offshore hedge funds and on to the FARC and other groups in arms sales. How the hell do you make that connection? Blattman parsed it out. "OK," he thought. "Separate the two."

Deaths of ASBT clients. How does that get connected? They're all over the place, not related to each other, and nothing suspicious about the deaths. No way one person sees they are all clients of ASBT, so no way anyone makes this connection. Somehow, JJ or one of his investigators did. He put that to the side for a second.

The money. One of Borenstein's geniuses from MIT or Cal Tech or whatever had found connections between funds leaving ASBT, then to hedge funds in a Cayman bank, then matched withdrawals with arms purchases and shipments that eventually ended up in South America. The domestic transfers are easy; they have to be reported. But the offshore transactions. Gotta hack the bank or have someone on the inside to get the information that the money is leaving the bank. If they had a source offshore, Blattman should have known about it. Hell, intelligence or operations should have been running the source. But he didn't know of any source, and that bothered him. It meant Borenstein had an asset reporting directly to DHS.

"Goddammit. Borenstein's running his own operation," Blattman said out loud to no one in particular since his office was empty. He closed the file and leaned back in his chair. The agency had been deliberately bypassed. Paul Blattman wanted to know why.

Hoboken, New Jersey; March 2008

John Lester had never before had a moment's trouble sleeping at night. He had killed many people, but their faces did not haunt his dreams. He did not hear their screams of terror or hatred in his sleep. He could look at himself in the mirror every morning and know that he was doing a job, and doing it well. In most cases, the people he had visited death upon fully deserved it. Lester felt no guilt because that was simply the way John Lester was. It wasn't complicated. Most things weren't.

But this night John Lester had trouble sleeping. He tossed and turned and couldn't get comfortable. As he lay there and analyzed the situation, he realized he was scared. It was an unusual emotion for him.

For the second time in his life (the first time was in college), Lester had no idea what he was going to do. The smart move (and Lester prided himself on always making the smart move, never letting emotion, especially ego, drive him to the wrong choice) was to "retire": to disappear to a faraway island and enjoy his money. In fact, he didn't really have to leave the country for some exotic locale. He could simply disappear into another persona anyplace in the U.S. As long as he was never fingerprinted and his DNA was never analyzed, he had a good chance of living out the rest of his life in peace. And that was the problem. Lester had no desire for a peaceful existence. It was simply anathema to his nature.

Nor, however, did he desire to live out the rest of his life in prison, or have his life cut short by a death penalty administered by any one of a number of countries where he would be wanted if he were ever identified and connected to his many crimes.

Get out. The smart move. Something would come along, right? Lester got up and went into his kitchen, pouring himself two fingers of The McCallan. He noted that his email inbox was flashing, indicating he had a message. He opened the missive. Indeed, something had come along. One last job, although his employer didn't know it would be Lester's last. De Plata needed him for security for a guest who would be visiting, but not in Costa Rica. Since he couldn't sleep anyway, Lester went online and made tentative arrangements for travel to Grand Cayman. When he was done, he noted he was feeling much more relaxed, probably a result of the alcohol mixing with the realization he still had a job to do, a mission to plan, however dull this one sounded. He shut down his computer and went back to bed, this time falling asleep quite quickly, and sleeping without disruption.

Chapter 26

Mel's Corner Tap, Midtown Manhattan; March 2008

“If we come up dry on Lazeris's account, we need to talk to Winfield again. The bombing is the perfect excuse,” I said as I put my beer down. “I'll call in the morning and set it up. So, who runs the hedge fund that's supposed to be buying all these arms?” I asked Conrad. We were down the street from the office grabbing a bite at a local pub. FBI agents hung out there after work, but it was 9:00 p.m. by the time we got there. Back at the office, Chris Winkler had all of Lazeris's computer hardware and was trying to develop a list of potential passwords.

“No idea,” said Conrad. “All I have is the account number and a ledger showing amounts going into the fund. The title on the account isn't helpful: DP Partners V. Could mean there were or are four other hedge funds before this, or it could just be a marketing ploy.”

I nodded. Hedge funds adopted different strategies, or multiple strategies, for managing assets. They typically gathered a certain amount of assets and then closed. Hence, you could get one group of wicked smart investment guys who controlled ten or fifteen or even more separate investment funds of, say, one billion dollars each. So you could get a series of partnerships called, for instance, Greedy Investors I, Greedy Investors II, etc. There were all sorts of strategies being marketed, and some of the guys running them were rocket-scientist smart. Some were charlatans. Others were just lucky and were able to be in the right place at the right time.

One strategy I had never heard of was the buy-arms-for-Latin-American-leftists-and-get-(apparently)-nothing-in-return fund. Basically, what Conrad had was money coming in from ASBT and other banks (more than half from ASBT), going out to buy and smuggle arms (maybe) into Venezuela or Colombia, and then more deposits from unknown sources. These could be returns on the arms sales, but leftist rebels didn't have that kind of money to buy arms with. They had drug sales and hostage ransoms, but typically that money was used to fund current operations. The fact was, however, no one knew how much the FARC and other groups generated from such activities.

"Is this the only fund your insider has turned you onto?" I asked. "Seems a little risky running all of this out of one entity."

"It's the only one we know about, but we suspect there are more at other banks."

"I think I would *own* the bank and fill it with my own people, and take the risk out completely. I just pay off local regulators and I'm forever clean."

Conrad smiled, and her eyes went up and left like she hadn't considered this before. "You have a low opinion of third-world countries, don't you?"

"Nope. I love 'em. The weather's great and the beer's cheap. But I also know from experience that they run on graft. The concept of saving and reinvesting money in a business is a distinctly U.S. and European concept. Most third-world businessmen get the business to a level that will support the lifestyle they want, then suck all the money out of it. They try to avoid paying taxes, and have to invest heavily in bribing regulators and paying for personal security. They try to stay under the radar because being known for wealth is dangerous."

"I'd say you're cynical."

"Cynicism is the result of experience. Only the inexperienced are idealistic. On the other hand, I do have the utmost faith in the U.S. and its institutions. So you can call me naïve on that score."

"You are naïve," she said bluntly, "and that's kind of surprising given that you do nothing but bust corrupt businessmen all day. People in this country make money too easily and for nothing. I mean, look at these dead clients of ASBT. They're all young, and the market paid them billions for ideas it wasn't even sure would pan out. Look how many got rich during the Internet bubble. Once it burst, nothing was there. And all the guys that got their money out first made out, and the investors who were saving and investing for the long term and working hard lost it all. You want to see a Ponzi scheme, I'll show you the entire U.S. stock market."

"Every system has problems, but there hasn't been a better one to come along. Yes, people in the U.S. get rich quick, but that's the exception, not the rule."

"Why are you such a student of history?" she asked.

"What do you mean?"

"JJ says you're an encyclopedia of financial crime, and you asked Winfield about his background. Every time we're analyzing something, it seems like you analogize it to some past event."

I thought about it for a second. I hadn't really focused on it, but I guessed she was correct. "Pattern recognition," I said finally.

"Excuse me?"

"In the case of crime, I'd say my reference to history is just trying to recognize patterns. There is very little that's truly new and original, just variations on a theme. For instance, a Ponzi scheme always operates the same way: new money is used to make payments to older investors. The method of collection differs, but usually the charismatic operator has developed a convincing lie to explain how he or she generates unusually large returns. Embezzlement is just a form of money laundering: you layer transactions and suck some amount out of every one and hope no one notices. Inevitably, someone does. It helps to review past large financial crimes to understand present ones, because there's really nothing new or original about the current ones. In the case of people, personal history is important because it *can* be an indicator of future behavior, although it's not one hundred percent reliable.

"That's partly why I ask suspects like Winfield their background. It's a disarming question because it's not expected. It can build rapport, and it can be a loose indication of whether the suspect is a good candidate for actual criminal activity. And it's why I'm still not convinced Winfield is guilty of anything. He's a guy who has built a reputation over many years. He's run banks, he's well-educated, and he has substance. Not your typical drug dealer, arms merchant, embezzler, or Ponzi schemer—" My new bureau-issued phone began to vibrate. I looked at it. "It's Chris," I told her as I answered it. "What's up?"

"I think I have a password from his keystroke record. I'm going to give it a shot."

"We're on our way." I hung up. "I'll get this," I said as I picked up the check. She looked like she was going to protest, and I said, "Business expense, fully reimbursed under my contract with the bureau." Her mouth closed and she smiled.

"Thanks."

"Just remember this when I stick you with the bill when you take me out to dinner on Saturday night."

"I'm sorry, did we have a date I didn't know about?"

"Not yet," I said. We left and headed back to the office.

"Sanders, you're a fun guy, and you seem nice. But you wouldn't like me. I have issues," she said on our way back. "Besides, I think Velasquez would get a little jealous."

"I keep telling you, the only way I am going to make Velasquez jealous is if I have a bigger gun than she does," I said. "OK, that came out wrong."

Conrad laughed. Damn, she was beautiful when she laughed. We walked into the building and took the elevator up to our floor. Winkler's cube was lit like a beacon in a sea of darkness.

"OK, Chris, let's see what you got," I said as we approached his cube.

Chris was typing away on his keyboard. "I'm already in. There's ten million dollars in this guy's account, and he's already spent about five. So he had a total of fifteen million. Check this out." He pointed to the screen.

Chris had highlighted in yellow all the deposits into the account. There were a set of deposits, all $1.5 million each. "I compared the dates of deposit to the dates he signed up the clients we're investigating. It's about ten business days after each client completed their estate planning documents. Now, this guy had a lot more clients, but these were his biggest ones. I would bet there are two or three more of these that will correspond to other very large clients. Ones that aren't dead."

"Yet," I said. "Shit, look at the description. 'Cash deposit.' That's it?"

"That's it," Chris confirmed.

"So," I concluded, "someone's walking into a bank on Grand Cayman with a briefcase full of U.S. dollars and depositing it directly into Lazeris's account. Completely untraceable. No source."

"Seems that way."

"This case is getting aggravating. Every lead turns into a dead end. We need to rethink this. Winkler, is JJ still here?"

"Yeah, his office."

I turned to Conrad. "Come on."

JJ was behind his desk. "Boss, can we talk a bit?" I asked.

JJ looked up, removed his reading glasses and tossed them on his blotter. "Yeah, sure, why not extend my day even more."

We sat down and I explained where we were in tracing the Lazeris money.

JJ mulled this over a bit and spoke. "The only way this works is if someone gets something out of killing these clients. And the only thing I can see them getting is their money. And the only constant in all of this is that the money is at ASBT."

JJ was right. It was all about the money. It always was. I began thinking out loud. "OK, so we know money is going into ASBT after clients' deaths. We know that a lot of that money is going offshore to hedge funds, and we *think* some of that money is then being used to buy arms. We're not seeing a return on the investment, but no one seems to be complaining. The only way to ensure a consistent stream of money is to kill rich clients every so often, so that's where Lazeris fits in, maybe. Otherwise, the money paid to Lazeris doesn't make sense, unless it's for something else entirely." They were both staring at me. "Sorry, sometimes I just have to think out loud. So we're back to ASBT, unless Winkler can make some other connection with the Cayman bank."

"Yeah, well that's not the only lead we have. The bomb looks like FARC, right?" JJ asked. We both nodded. "The DNA came back on the guy in the van," he said as he opened a file on his desk. "Javier Rolando Guerro. Arrived from Colombia under the name and passport of Jesus Edgar Navarro five years ago, moved to an apartment building on the edge of Harlem, no apparent means of support after he quit the job he said he had to get into the country. ICE made a house call about three years ago—no Javier. Guy just disappeared. Inquiries to Colombian security and Interpol say the guy was FARC and was wanted. So that seems to connect Ms. Conrad's case to Lazeris, and Lazeris connects it all to ASBT."

"Can I make a suggestion?" Conrad asked.

"Please," JJ said.

"There's another person I think we ought to talk to. The man leading the anti-FARC campaign in Colombia is a major in the army named Fernando Pinchao. I know him because we've been working both ends of the arms trading side of the case. A lot of my information on the arrival of arms comes from Colombian Armed Forces. We should fly down to Bogota and see Pinchao. We compare notes, we might be able to open this up. If arms are going to the rebels, something is coming from them, and he might be able to help us. He's been running the FARC ragged raiding all their camps, driving them over the border into Ecuador and Venezuela. He may have intel that might be useful."

"I thought you weren't field personnel," I said. "How you gonna get Borenstein to sign off on that?"

"I have a personal relationship with Major Pinchao. I've never met him, but we've spoken many times. He speaks perfect English. I think it's time we met."

I looked at JJ. "Not sure what that gets us," he said.

"We're never going to know until we talk to him. We should take all our info on the bombing to him, see if it looks like a bomber they know. And stills of the guy delivering the bomb."

JJ considered this. "OK, we got five people dead in what is supposedly a terrorist bombing and a directive to get to the bottom of it as fast as we can. You two go see Winfield, then go down to Bogota and talk to the major. We'll let their attorney general know you're coming so they can set up security. Then come right back. And Sanders, keep all your receipts."

"Yes, sir," I said. "On another topic, I think we ought to have Winkler copy over the Huntington material so Conrad can look at it while we travel. She might come up with something we haven't."

"OK, go tell him I said it's all right."

We walked back to Chris's cube and explained what was going on. "Oh, yeah, on that," he said as he turned to another laptop and started punching buttons. "We're fucked."

"Whaddya mean?" I replied.

"Just that—we're fucked. You aren't getting anywhere without a cipher key or the manufacturer's password."

"Whaddya mean the 'manufacturer's password'?" I asked.

Conrad answered for him: "He means whoever developed the algorithm probably built in a back door without telling anyone. Ever see *War Games?*"

"Yeah, yeah, Matthew Broderick. I get it. So the programmer's got a passcode, and the client's got a passcode. And if you don't have one of those, you can't see what's in the file?"

"It's not that simple," she explained "The password that the client has only encrypts their input, and only allows them to see what the guy on the other end of the conversation wants them to see. It's double-protected. So if we're using the same encryption software, I can encrypt a message to you that only your cipher key will decrypt, or I can give multiple users who all have different cipher keys decryption rights, or any combination in between so that some users can read parts of a message but not others. Basically, if you want to see the entire conversation, you might have to have all participants' passwords. Or you could short-circuit that with the designer's back door password. And of course all of that depends on the client not having someone else do an add-on."

"She's good," Chris said, looking at me.

"That's why we hired her. What do you mean an 'add-on'?" I asked her.

"Let's say the client is tech savvy and untrusting of his or her encryption vendor. He or she could add an additional layer of password protection, so even if you had the programmer's code, or even the source code for the algorithm, you couldn't break it without the client's additional password."

"So basically we're fucked," I concluded.

"Well," Conrad said, "*probably*. But Langley's got some software that we might try to put to work on it. I can get my hands on it if I have a secure server to work from." She looked at Chris.

"You're dreaming," he answered. "I don't care if Einstein's brain is sitting in Langley—no way you break this. But you can hook your laptop into my Ethernet here and I'll get you hooked into the bureau's server. You'll need an assistant director or higher here and one at Langley to approve the download."

"Well, it's 10:00 p.m. No way we get that approval now unless you wake some folks up or interrupt their aperitif," I said.

"Borenstein can bypass all that," Conrad said, slightly annoyed by our sidebar.

Chris and I just looked at her.

"What?" she asked, taken aback by our stares.

I looked at Chris and then to her. "You're telling us that 'don't call me Adolph' can just hook you into the agency's servers?"

"Well," she said. "Yeah. That's why DHS exists, after all."

"No shit?" Chris said.

"To borrow a phrase from Sanders here, I shit you not."

I wasn't sure if this was good news or troubling information. The safeguards existed for a reason. Conrad had just told us something they weren't exactly advertising over at DHS. I was pretty sure that while the Senate Intelligence Subcommittee and the president knew about it, they didn't appreciate the gravity. Apparently, Al Borenstein could hook into both FBI and CIA computers whenever he wanted to. Which was fine as long as everyone trusted Al Borenstein. But it also made him just about the most powerful man in the country after the president.

"Look, don't go around talking about this, OK. I probably shouldn't have said anything," Conrad said. "Chris, if you could give me your cubicle for about a half hour, I can hook up my laptop, get Borenstein on the phone, and get the software downloaded."

"Just like that?" I asked.

She smiled. "Just like that."

I looked at Chris. "Can you give the lady your cube?"

"Yeah, I'm going home anyway. Let me sign off. You have a bureau password?"

"I do, in fact," she said.

"OK, so just hook your Ethernet cable here and ..." Chris trailed off, apparently realizing he really didn't need to tell Alexandra Conrad, PhD, how to hook her computer up to our servers. "Forget it. If you have any problems, here's my cell number." He wrote it down. "I'm going home."

"Me too," I said. "Conrad, I'll see you here about 8:00 a.m. We can go over to see Winfield, then head to the airport."

Chapter 27

Eastside Manhattan; March 2008

Alexandra Conrad let herself into her temporary apartment after midnight and dropped her keys on the side table. The place was a small studio, an extended-stay corporate apartment. But it was all she needed. It was in a quiet neighborhood, and only a few blocks from the park. She could run every day if she could find the time. It was also a damn sight better than her place in Bethesda, which was all she could afford in a relatively decent neighborhood that was driving distance to her office in Washington.

She turned on the lights and poured herself a glass of wine. She was two-thirds into the bottle, which she had opened two days before. While the wine was still good, it had a slightly bitter finish. She thought about Nick Sanders and smiled to herself. He was a good-looking guy, and pretty funny. It is true: women do like a sense of humor in a man. It helped even more if it came in an attractive package, however. She was definitely attracted to him. But she could not afford any complications in her life right now. Of course, later it might not be possible at all.

Her thoughts were interrupted by the low drone of what she referred to as the "bat phone," a secure cell phone networked to Borenstein's cell.

She answered. "Conrad," she said.

"How long?" Borenstein asked immediately without introducing himself.

"How long to what?"

"How long to wrap up our end? We can't afford to help JJ with his dead ASBT clients anymore. I thought I made that clear. I also thought I made it clear that the president supports that view."

"You did, Al."

"Good. This deli bombing. It's just an unbelievable reaction by them."

"I agree. No way we could have seen that coming."

"So, how long?"

"Al, I don't know if you've thought this through, but 'our end' is two parts. The more pressing one is the FARC. I convinced JJ to send us down to Bogota. I'll connect with Pinchao, give him the package, and we can tie off that end. That's a couple of days. Then we can work on DP Partners."

"Us?"

"Yeah, me and Sanders."

"Sanders? What the hell do you need Sanders there for? He can't be involved in your conversation with Pinchao."

"Al, we don't run operations, remember? All we do is gather and analyze information. So if I don't have a bureau or CIA sponsor, how do I explain what I'm doing down there if the Senate Subcommittee looks into our investigation of the deli bombing?"

There was some silence as Borenstein thought this over. "Good point," he finally said. "Actually, it's preferred, because there will certainly be an investigation. So if Sanders can testify to this FARC connection, that's even better. Good work, Alex."

"Thank you, sir. Anything else?"

"Just make sure Sanders doesn't learn the real reason you're going. He's not a stupid guy, and while it might eventually come out, I'd rather control the information release."

It's why you have your job, right, Alex wanted to say but didn't. "I understand, sir."

"Good. Good night, Alex."

"Good night, sir." She hung up. Sometimes a nervous boss was a good thing to have. Borenstein's moving up the timeline made everything easier for Alex. It also made her look like a savior when she could handle everything under a compressed time requirement. He was certainly right about Sanders. His presence in Bogota was necessary for several reasons. And *dumb* was not a word she would use to describe him. She would have to be very careful around him. She sat on the couch, put her wine glass on the coffee table, and looked around. Then she thought about the last two days. The bombing. She started to shake. Then she put her face in her hands and cried.

Jungles of Eastern Ecuador; March 2008

Raul Reyes read and reread the email several times. It gave him explicit instructions on how to handle the guests who would be arriving. He just couldn't understand why. It didn't make any sense to him. It would obviously serve Mr. de Plata's purpose; otherwise, he wouldn't be asking. Reyes just couldn't fathom it. Well, if that was the way his arms source wanted it, that's the way he would get it. Reyes forwarded the encrypted email to his lieutenant in Bogota and instructed him to make arrangements and check back with Reyes when everything was prepared for the final go ahead.

Señor de Plata's request, while odd, was also a blessing, because Reyes could mobilize the assets he needed in Bogota for two purposes at once. Thus, he only had to send his messages once, rather than twice. Moreover, as it appeared the guests would be meeting government officials, his intervention would serve both de Plata's purposes and the FARC's. Since Reyes couldn't go to Bogota himself, of course, he had to send detailed instructions via encryption to Guerra in Bogota.

De Plata had not given him much time, but he was able to mobilize a team and organize the job. In truth, there was little to it: a van, a warehouse away from the city, a video camera, a few medicines, some bindings. All in a day's work and all already on hand or nearby, anyway. It was gathering the materials for the other jobs that would be more difficult.

Tamarindo, Costa Rica; March 2008
De Plata was deciding how much to show to Winfield, and more importantly, where. He owned buildings all over Latin America and the Caribbean. Officially, the hedge fund in question, DP Partners, was headquartered in Hamilton, Bermuda, with an operations center in Grand Cayman. In actual fact, these places were merely mailboxes, and no employees other than clerical personnel actually lived or worked in these locations. When a potentially large investor came calling and wished to see the operation, de Plata used the offices of legitimate hedge funds actually located in buildings he owned in both places. This was easier than it sounded, since as the landlord he could inspect the properties at any time, and maintained an office and conference room in the same buildings, which cost him nothing other than

forgone rent on the unused square footage. If a client or sponsor such as Winfield came to visit, de Plata would fly to the location, meet the client at the office, and then walk them through the trading floor of the hedge fund he did *not* run. He then walked them back to the conference room, where they could speak about the fund's strategy, and sent the inspector on his or her way. De Plata was surprised at how well it worked, but then again, most clients asked few questions when shown the returns of DP Partners. Who could argue with statements showing consistent 15 to 20 percent returns? In actuality, these statements massively *understated* the profits. But showing the real profits would create more questions, and Alejandro de Plata could not have that.

De Plata reviewed the email again. It seemed as if Winfield himself would be coming. Odd, but the man did have a reputation for being involved in day-to-day operations. De Plata had to respect the fact that Winfield was performing the due diligence himself. It's what he would have done, after all.

Then there was getting Lester there in advance to ensure everything was safe before de Plata arrived. This would give Lester at least three full days for surveillance and setup. He had done more with less, as the deli bombing had proved. Lester was the second most expensive line item on de Plata's expense statement, but worth every penny. The most expensive item, his encryption software, was demonstrably valuable, since it prevented the need to use a man like John Lester very often in the first place.

Hoboken, New Jersey; March 2008

Lester opened the *New York Times* to the continuing coverage of the Fifty-fourth Street Deli Bombing, as they were calling it. He was looking for a particular section amidst the four middle pages of coverage. There, a sidebar listed the six dead, their hometowns, immediate family who survived them, and where services, if any, would be held. Lester carefully ripped this page out and went to the computer. He Googled every name and town, and got addresses for most of the families. He even got Lazeris's parents' address.

Chapter 28

Midtown Manhattan; March 2008

Recent events had put us in the position of having to admit we lied to Winfield the first time about our investigation. We had painted ourselves into a corner with the insider trading bullshit. We were going to have to come clean on that and tell Winfield why we were really there. This would no doubt invoke the question about whether he was a suspect and should have his attorney present. Frankly, I wasn't holding out much hope for our interview.

When I got into the office, Conrad was waiting for me in the conference room, sipping from a Starbucks cup. She looked like she could use about three more cups. "You get to bed at a reasonable hour?" I asked.

"More or less," she said.

"Looks like less."

"You really know how to flatter a girl, Sanders."

"My ex thought so too. Sorry. Up late working on the encryption stuff?"

"Yeah, got nowhere. But I got the agency analytical software downloaded to my laptop. I left it at my apartment so it could chew on it. I figure I won't need the laptop for what we're going to be doing. I'll check on it when I get back."

"Good idea. How do you want to handle Winfield?'

She looked at me quizzically. "Sanders, I'm not an investigator. How do *you* want to handle Winfield?"

"Well, I think we have to tell him we weren't completely honest with him. If he's involved, the Lazeris thing has probably shaken him and he'll know why we were there the first time anyway. And if he's not, then he will likely be willing to overlook our initial lie and help us, given the circumstances."

"Sounds reasonable. Should we discuss it with JJ?"

"Probably." We walked down the hall to JJ's office and let him know how we were going to approach Winfield.

"I hate having to admit to a suspect that you lied to him," he said. Tell me about it. "But I agree, you have a better chance with him if you come clean now. OK, go talk to him. Then get to Colombia and back. You're flying commercial. Barry has your tickets and the investigation file on the bombing." Barry was JJ's assistant.

I had Winfield's card and called his office.

"Mr. Winfield's office," the silky voice of his assistant said.

"Hi, this is Nick Sanders with the FBI's midtown office. We met with Mr. Winfield the other day, and given recent events—," I began, but didn't get to finish.

"Yes, Mr. Sanders, Mr. Winfield told me to expect your call." Really? "He is going out of town for annual due diligence meetings, but if you would like some time with him ..." She trailed off.

"Thank you. We would like to meet with him for a few minutes this morning if possible," I said.

"Well, his plane leaves around noon. If you could get here by nine, I think Mr. Winfield could find a few minutes before he has to get to the airport."

"Thank you, that would be great. See you then." I hung up and turned to Conrad. "He's expecting us. Interesting. We need to hustle."

Considering ASBT's offices were walking distance from ours, we didn't have to hustle that much. We arrived by 8:55 and were directed to the elevators. The receptionist came out from behind the counter and, using a special card, swiped a pad on the button board and then pressed the next floor up. "Mr. Winfield's assistant will meet you in the foyer."

"Foyer," I said to Conrad when the door closed. "Any business that has a foyer instead of a lobby is either pretentious or caters to pretentious clientele."

She giggled. "I think we know it's the clients. Ever notice that you get called a client if you're pretentious? Other businesses have customers."

The elevator arrived and we entered an area decorated much like the previous floor, but without a reception desk. Standing in the middle of the "foyer" was an attractive, well-dressed woman in her thirties.

"Mr. Sanders, Ms. Conrad? I'm Mr. Winfield's assistant, Rebecca Porteus. Can I show you to Mr. Winfield's office?" she asked as she motioned to her left. She asked if she could get us something to drink, and we demurred, although I did want a cup of that coffee they served. Rebecca took the lead down the hall. I noted that she was quite a bit different from Ed Lazeris's secretary. For one thing, she was professionally dressed, showed no cleavage, and her skirt went slightly past her knees. It was also tight enough to illustrate she kept in shape, but not so tight that it hugged every curve. A man's mind didn't shoot to "stripper," or thoughts of "tapping that" later in the day. Well, not right away that is. Truth is it's difficult to keep such thoughts out of a male's mind regarding any reasonably attractive woman.

The executive offices actually took up two floors, so the ceilings were twenty rather than the usual ten feet high. We were ushered into an outer office paneled in mahogany with burled wood insets. The tasteful furniture was expertly arranged. We faced double doors, which presumably led to Winfield's office.

Rebecca approached the doors and knocked lightly, then opened them without waiting for a reply. Clearly, Winfield was prepared to meet us. Rebecca showed us into the office, and the moment I entered I involuntarily let out a whistle. The sheer size of it was impressive. It was at least three times as large as most executive offices I had been in. There were not one, but two conference tables: a smaller one to the left that would seat four or five (who could play poker or more likely take tea) and another to the right that was rectangular and could easily seat ten. Left of center in front of us was a desk two small children could play football on, and standing in front of it was Jeremy Winfield, dressed in a suit, no tie.

"Mr. Sanders and Ms. Conrad," he said as he approached. "Good to see you again. Can Ms. Porteus get you anything? Coffee? Water?"

Conrad spoke: "She's been kind enough to already offer. No, thank you."

"Wait. I'll have some of that heroin coffee you have on tap." I didn't really say that, and instead shook my head.

"Well then, please, let's sit at the small conference table."

"No tie today?" I asked as we approached and sat.

"As Ms. Porteus told you, I am traveling out of town today on our annual due diligence meetings. I'm hoping to sneak out without any clients or employees, other than Rebecca, seeing me."

"Due diligence?" Conrad asked.

"Yes. I have to meet with our outside investment advisers annually and review what they are doing. Based on the outcome of those reviews, we might lower or raise our clients' allocation to certain managers."

"These managers are domestic or offshore?" I asked.

"Well, the ones I am going to see over the next week are spread across the Caribbean, South America, and Central America. But we have domestic managers that we visit as well."

"Sounds like a lot of travel. Your family must not like you to be gone so often." I didn't see a ring on his finger, but you never know.

"I'm not married, Mr. Sanders, and have no children. ASBT is my family."

"I'm surprised you're doing the actual investigation. Aren't you supposed to take some young Wharton whiz kids with you to look at the books?"

"I used to do that. But frankly, the onsite meetings are really to judge the offices, the number of employees, the educational level of the stock pickers, the character of the people you're dealing with, all of which I can do myself. The review of the books is done from this office by those whiz kids, as you call them, and more often than annually—usually quarterly. In any event, I presume you would like to give me a subpoena for Mr. Vanderhoff's file?"

Conrad and I glanced at each other, and then I spoke. "Actually, no. Mr. Winfield, we weren't entirely honest with you about why we spoke with you the other day."

He showed very little reaction. "Then why are you here?" he asked.

"Ed Lazeris," I said.

"Yes, a tragedy. Mr. Lazeris was a fabulous attorney and referred us his biggest clients. I cultivated that relationship myself, along with Ernst. I was shocked to hear about his death. I would look into increased security for myself and my employees, but frankly it is hard to imagine what could insulate you from such an event. If restaurants are going to be bombed, and you're in it, I don't see what extra bodyguards will do for you."

"I agree," I said. "The choice is between going out in public and not."

"And I'd rather not live in fear. I trust you good people to find the murderers and keep the rest of us safe. Anyway, before we speak more about Mr. Lazeris, I'd like to know why you lied to me about Mr. Vanderhoff."

Lied. It was such an ugly word. I'd like to be able to say we exaggerated, or stretched the truth a little, but there was really no way around it. We had lied to him, and now he knew it.

Conrad took the lead. "Mr. Winfield, we were trying to judge your reaction to our questions and your level of concern or nervousness, rather than the answers themselves. We needed to determine if we believed you were involved in something larger."

I had to admit after that revelation that I agreed with her: she really wasn't an investigator. She had basically just told a suspect we wanted to see if we thought he was good for a crime. And the implication was that we had failed, since we were admitting it.

"Something larger?" he asked.

"Ed Lazeris sent you all of his large clients," I said. He nodded. "Mr. Winfield, Mr. Lazeris asked to meet with us to give us what we think was important information about those clients. He was killed before we could speak, however." Now, here's a fine point in interrogation. If the subject immediately makes the next connection, that we think he killed the potential witness, chances are he did. That mental leap betrays a guilty mind. But another response, such as "who would do such a thing" or the like, is a good indication that the suspect is not the perpetrator, or that he's a good actor. Sometimes you never know, but if you got lucky with the "and you think I killed him" answer, you focused on the suspect fairly quickly. Winfield did neither. He waited. No one spoke. Both Conrad and I looked levelly at him, trying to judge his reaction to our statement. He looked only momentarily distracted, as if he were lost in thought.

He finally spoke. "You think he wasn't in the wrong place at the wrong time?" We didn't respond. He thought some more, concern on his face. "Mr. Sanders, are you telling me someone killed Mr. Lazeris and five other people just to keep Ed from speaking with the authorities?"

At this point, I really shouldn't have been telling him what our theory of the case was, and I should have tried to waffle with a "we don't know" kind of response. But we had come there to own up to a lie, and I felt I could make some progress with him if I told the truth. "Yes," I said simply.

"And if you knew what the nature of Mr. Lazeris's intended statements to you were, then that might help you find the bomber?"

We both nodded. "It might," I said.

"Well, I'm sorry I can't help you in that regard. But if you can tell me what you initially saw Mr. Lazeris about, I will try to help."

The way this was going, Winfield was going to get more information about our investigation than he was going to give us. So I had to head off this path and move the focus back to what had really brought us here.

"Mr. Winfield, I can't share with you the details of an ongoing investigation. Let me tell you what we think is happening, and you see if you can't think of ways to help us." He nodded. "Five of your richest clients have died in the past three years. After their deaths, all of their liquid wealth was collected here and then reallocated, much of it offshore. That offshore money may be used to fund illegal activity." Now, what I didn't say was just as important. I didn't tell him that we thought the clients' deaths involved foul play. I didn't say who we thought was responsible (and, since we really had no clue on that score, it was better to say nothing anyway). But a guilty person would make those leaps. Again, Winfield said nothing. Cautious, thoughtful, as if something was occurring to him that he hadn't considered before.

"I'm sorry, I don't see how these clients, who unfortunately passed away, relate to what Ed was discussing with you."

Either this guy was the best acting murderer I had ever interviewed, or he was honestly perplexed by what we were getting at. Conrad spoke before I could formulate an answer.

"Mr. Winfield, the only person or organization that would benefit from all those clients' deaths is ASBT," she said. See, now I gotta tell you, I wouldn't have laid it out like that. It was an accusation, and it really wasn't helpful because the very next statement was going to be "perhaps you should be speaking to our attorneys." I had to jump in before the whole thing went sideways.

"Understand, Mr. Winfield, we're not accusing anyone. We think, but don't know, that the deaths might be related. We're looking for connections, nothing more."

Winfield was either the least emotional man I ever met, or was simply calculating his next move. But he also seemed stuck on something. "How would we benefit from our clients dying?" he asked, looking directly at Conrad.

"We—," I started to say before Conrad spoke over me.

"Increased fees, more money in the bank," Alex said.

He turned to me. "Mr. Sanders, you were a tax attorney, weren't you? You worked at Neville and Wright for several years, a very well-respected firm, correct?" I nodded. "And Ms. Conrad," he said, turning toward her, "you were an MIT graduate in mathematics and computer science, correct?" She nodded. He had obviously checked us both out. "So you're able to calculate percentages fairly well, wouldn't you say?" Oh boy, here it comes. "So you two really think ASBT benefits enough from making an incremental amount more on a client account because we can collect the money here? And that's after lowering our fee because the client has met certain break points. That's your theory?" he asked, his voice rising slightly. "That the benefit is enough to justify us murdering our own clients? I'm sorry, but for two very smart people, that theory is simply dumb. I have been in banking my entire professional life. Before that, I worked at my father's gas station business while going to college. Now, I didn't go to the best schools like you two did, but I'd like to think that I can reason fairly well. And none of what you have told me makes much sense, nor do I see how Mr. Lazeris would be involved."

Conrad was about to speak, but I put my hand up to wave her off. She had already laid it out, so we might as well finish it. "Lazeris and ASBT were the only things all five people had in common. Lazeris named ASBT successor trustee for all five clients. After each death, all of their money was collected here. Lazeris knew something, but we don't know what."

"I'm sorry, Mr. Sanders. You seem genuine to me. But Ed wasn't a killer. He was a lawyer, and a good one. And we were happy he thought enough of us to refer business to us, and we to him. That's all there was. Now, I have a plane to catch. If there is anything further on this subject you would like to speak with me about, please call and I will arrange to have our lawyers present at our next meeting. Good day to you both."

He stood. I stood, knowing the meeting was over. Conrad hesitated, but I jerked my head in a "come on" motion. She stood and Winfield showed us out. "Rebecca," he said at the door, "could you please show Mr. Sanders and Ms. Conrad to the elevators?" With that, he closed the door.

On the way down in the elevator, I kept my mouth shut. "I notice he didn't say he thought I was genuine," Conrad said, trying to break the tension. I smirked at the joke. But I was upset. We had shown our hand to a suspect and gotten nothing in return. Moreover, the guy was leaving the country, and we gave him a reason not to return if he was guilty. But I didn't think he was. He seemed honestly puzzled, but not necessarily by what we had told him. He seemed distracted by something else that occurred to him *as a result* of what we had told him.

"It could have gone better," I said, "but what happened in there only reinforces my opinion. I don't think he's involved."

"I agree. Not in the murders, anyway."

But I was bothered by something. Every time someone laid our case out to us as Winfield had just done, it sounded flimsy. It was a weak theory, but there were too many connections and coincidences, and Lazeris's death certainly seemed to lend our beliefs credence. There was something we weren't seeing. I didn't say a word to Conrad the entire way back to the office, lost in my thoughts.

Back at the office, we saw Barry to pick up our travel packs. "JJ says you have to go see B before I give you these."

Curiouser. We went down to the basement and saw Bodorofsky. When we got there, he said, "Ah, my new guinea pigs." He began slipping on a pair of latex gloves, never a good sign.

"What's going on, B?" I asked apprehensively.

"Got a new SOP for international travel to high risk locations—a subcutaneous transponder."

"You're going to implant a transponder on us?" Conrad asked. She seemed shocked.

"That's right." He turned to me, tilting his head. "She's the smart one, eh, Nicky?" he asked out of the side of his mouth. He turned back. "We can locate you to within fifty feet of actual anywhere in the world that we can see with a satellite, which is pretty much everywhere. I don't even need to make a cut, just a small pinprick." He lifted up what looked to me to be a massive hypodermic needle. Small pinprick, hmm?

"So, who goes first?" B asked.

Now, here's a dilemma. As a man, you don't want to show fear, especially in front of a female colleague, particularly one you wouldn't mind going to bed with. On the other, a gentleman could rely on the "ladies first" justification for letting Conrad take the shot first and seeing if she keeled over dead. Of course, this would expose the man as pretty much a wussy. So, my ego won out and I stepped forward. I lifted the sleeve of my pull-over golf shirt, and B said, "Uh huh. Shirt off. Gotta put this in the top of the shoulder."

I took off my shirt and B moved to my right shoulder. I stopped his wrist and said, "Uh huh. Gun shot wound there."

He shrugged and waved me to turn. He said what all doctors say right before they give you a shot: "Just a little pinch here." And then a searing burn went through the meat of my shoulder. I had to consciously try not to grunt.

"That'll hurt some for a few hours. Go outside while I administer to your lovely partner here, since she will need to take her shirt off too. But don't leave, I have to calibrate that little beauty."

I walked out into the hallway until B called me back in. He picked up a small handheld device, tapped the screen a few times, and then reached for the phone. "Winkler? Bodorofsky. I've implanted Conrad and Nicky. I'm sending you the link that will allow you to monitor them." A pause. "There, you got it? OK, click on it. See the 'agents in field' button to the lower left. Click it. Yeah, just like Google Maps. In fact, it is Google Maps. The bureau finally decided to stop reinventing the wheel and— yep, those two dots right there. OK, great." He hung up and turned back toward us.

"OK, don't stand near any industrial electromagnets or get electrocuted, and you two should be just fine. I can take them out when you get back."

"This Big Brother shit is getting out of hand," I said as we took the elevator back up.

"You'd rather go missing in South America?" Conrad asked.

"I'm getting this thing taken out the minute we get back." We retrieved our travel docs from Barry, which left us just a few minutes to leave for the airport. No bags. Everything we needed for a short overnight in Colombia would be at the hotel for us.

Chapter 29

Bogota, Colombia; March 2008

Ignacio Guerra left his "job" at the coffee roasting plant where he "worked" during the day. His phone chirped. He had a text message that was several hours old, but he couldn't hear the alarm above the din of the factory during the workday. He opened the phone and saw he had to get to his laptop and contact the boss. His real boss. For while Ignacio Guerra worked as a manager in a coffee roasting factory, his real job was as a "fixer" for the FARC. In the barrios of Bogota, Ignacio Guerra knew how to get absolutely anything at any time. The coffee factory job was a convenient cover only, and a decent "beer money" paycheck.

As a boy growing up in those barrios, Ignacio had seen his father beaten by a loan shark from whom he had borrowed money for "just a week." A week, then weeks, then months, and his father had been badly injured such that he couldn't work anymore. At twelve years old, Ignacio lost respect for his father, watching him grovel before the shark's enforcers. But despite the fact that he had lost respect, he recognized that his father was still family, and family was to be protected above all. So, at age twelve, Ignacio Guerra traded drugs for a gun and followed the enforcers back to a café. Their boss sat in back and did his work on the books, deciding who would get a beating versus a bone break versus tied to an anchor and thrown in the ocean. When both enforcers and the boss were seated at the table, Ignacio walked back to the table and fired dead center into the forehead of the fat shark. Before the two enforcers had time to realize what was happening, he shot them too. And out the back he went, grabbing all the cash and the shark's ledger recording debts owed off the table on his way out.

His father's debt, as well as those of hundreds of others, was permanently forgiven. His family never knew, but rumors of a boy who had killed the shark circulated around the barrios of Bogota. Ignacio knew better than to take credit, and the stupid ones who did ended up dead. It was enough for Ignacio that Ignacio knew.

The boy grew up to be adopted by another family, one that fought the sharks and others who took advantage of the oppressed. Ignacio was introduced to Manuel Marulanda and passed on to others. He ended up being the fixer for the FARC in the barrios of Bogota under the direct command of Raul Reyes. And this time everyone knew it, even the police. But they didn't dare cross him. Because had anyone touched The Fixer, that person would be dead. Everyone stayed out of his way. Except the women, which Ignacio had to admit was a nice perk of being a well-known revolutionary. He didn't quite understand the attraction, but didn't think about it too much either.

Once he got to his computer, Guerra used the code in the text message (itself encoded using a prearranged cipher) to decrypt the e-mail Shit. He only had the night to plan and execute. What was this? He would need some sort of anesthetic or sleep agent. And a couple of Tasers. Guerra was no pharmacist, but the FARC had plenty of contacts who were. He would be interrupting several dinners to put this operation together, but that was OK. It dovetailed the longer-term operation Reyes had been planning and Guerra would help execute. This immediate one, however, certainly was new. Guerra couldn't really see why Reyes wanted it this way, but he knew enough to take orders and not question his new father. He began calling around on his cell phone, setting up meetings with the appropriate people but never mentioning on the phone what he needed or why. The people on the other end of the calls all assented to meet at the times Ignacio specified. Within eight hours, Ignacio had amassed the equipment and, more importantly, the manpower he needed.

But as he thought through his instructions, he realized Reyes was missing an incredible opportunity. The plan would need to be changed just slightly, and only at the end. Someone would have to be sacrificed, but if Reyes could understand Ignacio's vision, he was certain to agree. He encrypted another message to Reyes.

Jungles of Eastern Ecuador; March 2008

Reyes received Guerra's's message. "My God," he thought, despite the fact that he did not believe in God, "Ignacio is right. This is an incredible opportunity." But it was not without risk, as it would violate de Plata's orders. Reyes pulled up the instructions he had received. He wanted to avoid having to ask de Plata for permission to alter the plan, since this would cause delay and de Plata might say no. But while instructions as to the woman were quite specific, it was clear the man was to be a witness only. Reyes could solve that problem. Yes, in fact, it would work better all the way around. He sent Guerra back a missive with specific instructions on how to proceed.

If Raul Reyes had emailed his benefactor for permission, he would have discovered that Alejandro de Plata had no idea what the hell Reyes was talking about.

Chapter 30

Bogota, Colombia; March 2008

Bogota was hot and humid, and I suspected it was pretty much like that all year-round. We took a cab that I picked at random from the middle of the cab line at the airline terminal. Conrad thought I was paranoid, but in a third-world country you never know who is on the take, who would sell you to kidnappers, who would kill you for the money in your wallet, and who is the honest cab driver. The first three, however, had to have a plan to direct you to them. By picking a cab at random against the normal routine, like the front of the line, you threw these plans into disarray. For instance, the crooked cabbie might have paid the post man or placer—the guy employed by the airport to ostensibly keep the cab line moving by directing each tourist coming out of the terminal to the first cab in line—to direct a particularly wealthy-looking couple to the second or third cab. If you ignored the placer altogether and just acted like you knew what you were doing, you had a better chance of avoiding that scam. It was while I was explaining this to Conrad in the cab that I realized something about the ASBT case. I stopped mid-sentence, gazed off and said:

"It is one guy."

Conrad looked at me quizzically. "And the dog barks at midnight," she said. "Sanders, is that some sort of code?"

"The killer. The person who killed the five clients, if they were all murdered. Remember in Costa Rica one of the reasons I didn't believe your theory was that there's no such thing as the professional, well-paid hit man who is good at everything?" She nodded. "Well, I've changed my mind. The guy exists, if in fact these people were murdered."

"I don't get it. How do you know that?"

"Look, if you're planning to kill multiple people all over the place, and you can't do it yourself, do you hire a different person for every crime?"

She thought. "Well, I could, but that's risky."

"Exactly. Instead of one guy who I need to keep quiet, I have to depend that all five won't go to the cops and report me. No way. Way too risky. So if these are murders, there's just one guy, or small group, involved in *every* murder."

"And you thought of that because ..."

"The cabbie who works for kidnappers. He's got to have a system, and it has to involve the same guy he can depend on to direct the client to him. You change it up, throws his whole plan into disarray."

"Someday I'll figure out how your mind works, Sanders."

"And on that day you will recognize you lost more than a few IQ points," I said.

"When we get to the hotel, let's check in and get some dinner. I am starving," she said.

"Fine with me. When do we meet with your buddy Pinchao?"

"He's going to call my Adolph phone in the morning and let us know when and where to meet. I presume the army office building in the Government Center, but we won't know till the morning." We had all taken to calling the new phones we'd been issued the "Adolph phones," after Borenstein. For me, it wasn't a big deal because not too many friends and family had been calling my old phone anyway. But for some of the others, it had turned into a real pain. They had to call everyone on their contact lists and give them the new number.

We arrived at the hotel, which was much more upscale than the typical Hilton or Marriot, where the government usually put its employees. Pinchao had arranged for us to stay at a historic colonial hotel, and the room—whoa. As I entered and dropped my bags, I noted it was bigger than my apartment. Admittedly, that wasn't tough to accomplish, but this was much bigger—a suite with a living room, sitting area, office, and massive bedroom. Too bad it was just one night.

The phone rang as I was unpacking. It was Conrad.

"Hey, I'm going to take a shower and meet you downstairs in about half an hour. OK?"

"That works. You know, I need a shower too. We should conserv—." *Click.*

I met her downstairs. Her shower had made a significant improvement, as did her attire. I felt refreshed as well. We asked the concierge about late dinner, which was never a problem almost anywhere in South America. Everything was done on a slower pace, and meals were much later than in the States. In fact, the nightlife didn't really get going until 10:30 or 11:00. The concierge recommended a place within walking distance but suggested we take a cab for safety's sake, despite the fact that Bogota was a much safer city than it had been in the past. We took his advice. As we stepped away, I turned back and asked him: "You have customers or clients?" He looked at me like I was from Mars. Conrad slapped my upper arm, then grabbed it and led me out the door.

"You ever been married, Alex?" I asked once we got seated at dinner and had a couple of cervezas in front of us. We were sitting outside in a town square in the Usaquen district, a hip and newer area of the city. There were a lot of bars and restaurants open to the square, and the seating areas were set apart by metal crowd-control barriers painted to match the look of each establishment. Our restaurant, El Campeón, had party lights strung above the seating area, so you could see your food and the person you were talking to.

"It sounds weird, you using my first name. No, Nicky, I've never been married."

"Hey, I let B call me that because if I killed him, I couldn't solve many cases. You have to solve a case before you earn that right."

"OK. Nope, I've never been married, Nick. I know you have. What happened?"

"It's complicated," I lied. She waited. "I was working all the time, and she was sleeping with another guy."

"Yeah. Wow. Complicated."

"So why aren't you married?" I asked.

"Ever notice guys hate talking about failed relationships? They always turn it back on you. Which is weird, 'cause normally guys just love talking all about themselves on the first date."

"This is a business meeting, but if you want to call it a date, that's OK. So, why haven't you been married?"

"It's complicated. I haven't met the right guy," she said with a grin. "Basically, men find smart and successful women intimidating."

"I think that's a myth. I like smart and successful women. More to talk about."

"Yeah, I have to admit, you seem willing to talk about anything."

"Where'd you grow up?" I asked, changing the subject.

"OK, I'll give you the history so we can move on." She seemed exasperated with all the questions. "Roanoke. My dad was in Army Intelligence, which is how I got into cryptology. He was a big influence. He was a math whiz too. He and my mom still live in the house I grew up in. How about you?"

"New York, then Jersey. Went to Catholic school all through grade and high school. Dad was a general practice lawyer, which is kind of a dying breed." In this case it was the actual truth, because Dad had a heart attack and died on the golf course when I was seventeen years old, but I left that part out. "He had a small office and did all sorts of work. I was his file clerk in grade school, got comfortable with law, and it just seemed natural to go from Rutgers to law school. Then the Marines. And here I am, in Bogota. Who woulda thunk."

"Indeed."

"Indeed? Who the hell uses the word indeed in normal conversation? Only Alex Conrad."

She smiled. "It's underused. So what's the deal with you and Velasquez? I can tell she likes you. Or at least respects you."

"We've been through a lot. I respect her too. But I've never seen her as anything but a professional colleague. She has a certain ... edge."

Conrad almost spit her beer out. "No shit? I hadn't noticed." She laughed.

I laughed too. "There might be a soft side there, just haven't found it yet. And I haven't actively been looking for it." I changed the subject. "Heard from Pinchao yet?"

"Yeah, his office called while I was getting ready. Thanks for reminding me. He's going to send a car for us in the morning to take us to his office."

"Gotta appreciate the service, and the hotel. Remind me to thank him tomorrow."

"I will thank him. My room's a football field. Yours?"

I nodded. "Gigantic." I had to raise my voice because a band positioned nearby in the square started up with salsa music. Our food arrived and we talked and ate. If this were a first date, I was doing pretty well. And I was having a great time. She was intelligent, could carry a conversation, had a good sense of humor, and was definitely easy on the eyes. We finished dinner and took a cab back to the hotel.

"So, what are your issues?" I asked as we stepped into the elevator.

"That's a long conversation."

I looked at my watch. "I got time."

"Well," she began as the elevator started up, "I'm always a sucker for gun-toting ex–tax lawyers who joined the Marines so they could blow shit up." I took that as an invitation. I leaned toward her, but not too quickly. I paused to see if she would respond. She did. We both got off on her floor. I never made it back to my room that night. She was right. Her room was gigantic. From what I could tell. I only saw the bedroom.

Chapter 31

Bogota, Colombia; March 2008

"**M**s. Conrad? Two of my men will pick you up in an army van in thirty minutes."

"Sí, gracias."

Ignacio Guerra hit the end button on his cell phone. He turned to the army officer he had paid off. "OK, I will follow behind on the motorcycle. Put them at ease, get them in the van. You'll need to subdue them both at the same time. No hesitation. You hesitate, the guy could take you out in close quarters. Then back here and you're done, OK?"

"Understood, Ignacio. Where's my money?" the officer, Andres Maldonado, asked.

Ignacio removed a wad of bills from his shirt pocket, all U.S. dollars. "Half now, half when they're here."

The officer nodded, took the cash and stuffed it into his pocket. He walked over to the Colombian Army van and talked to his two men sitting in the front. The rear was windowless, and instead of seats facing forward, it had a bench on either sidewall so that passengers would face each other. "Julian, in the back with me. Santiago, you're driving." Maldonado explained the signals they would use. They both got in the back of the van. Guerra opened the warehouse door, and they drove toward downtown Bogota.

Chapter 32

Bogota, Colombia; March 2008

onrad called me and told me that Pinchao's van was thirty minutes away. I had gone back to my room early that morning to shower, shave, and dress in business casual clothing for our meeting. I took off my watch and made sure that while my clothes were clean, they were not nice enough to draw attention. No American labels. Conrad would accuse me of being paranoid, but I liked to think I was just cautious.

I met Alex in the lobby. She had the magic backpack with her. She smiled at me, but we didn't touch each other or show any outward sign of affection. In fact, there was an awkward moment as I approached, since neither of us knew how to act. If there's one thing that will break an awkward silence, it's: "Coffee?"

She smiled, breathed out, and said, "Sure."

The hotel provided coffee in a large urn in the lobby. I poured two cups. There was some milk and sugar, but I took neither. Conrad put some milk in hers, no sugar. As she reached for it, I noticed she was wearing a nice gold watch. "You might want to take that off." She rolled her eyes. "Can't be too careful," I said.

"Will it make you happy?"

"Ecstatic," I said.

She handed me her coffee, took off the watch and put it in the bag, then took her coffee back. "You know, Sanders, we're walking right out of the hotel and into an army van. I doubt anyone will mess with us."

"Probably right, but better safe, right?"

She nodded. Over her shoulder, I saw a man dressed in crisp green fatigues walk through the front doors of the hotel. "Our ride is here."

We walked over. "I am Lieutenant Luis Montes," the man said in English, shaking hands with both of us, "Major Pinchao's administrative officer. Please, come with me." We followed him out the doors of the hotel and to the van waiting under the porte cochere. Montes slid the door of the van open and motioned us inside. The vehicle had wooden benches on either sidewall. If full, the van cargo area could hold eight: two groups of four men would be staring at each other. The driver's cab area was walled off. The whole setup reminded me of a paddy wagon. (Not that I'd ever been in one.) Normally, we would have sat next to each other, but after what had happened the night before, we were trying to appear as professional as possible. So we sat opposite each other. This caused us to be looking at each other. Conrad smiled at me, then glanced down at her feet. My phone rang, again breaking an awkward moment.

"Where the hell are you?" JJ's voice asked as Montes entered and slid the door shut. He sat next to me. Conrad was next to another man in army fatigues.

"Bogota," I said. The van started forward.

"I can see that on my computer screen, but it looks like you're still at the hotel." Damn transponder. "If it's not too much trouble, do you think you and Conrad could actually meet with Major Pinchao?"

"On our way now. It's only 8:00 a.m. here, JJ."

"Your meeting was at 8:30," he said as if he hadn't heard me. "You're a half hour late. Pinchao's office called because they can't raise Conrad. At least I know you aren't dead." It took a second for what he was saying to compute. Then I realized we were in deep shit.

"JJ, I'll have to call you back." I hit end and put my phone in my pocket, smiling a stupid smile at Conrad, horribly overacting the "everything's OK" bit. She looked at me like I'd grown a third arm.

There were only two ways for this to go. I either overpowered my guy immediately, with Conrad freaking out not knowing what the hell was going on, or I'd try to warn her, in which case these guys would clue in and be on us. I decided on a little of both. I turned to Montes and said, "Lieutenant, that was my boss. He says Pinchao doesn't know you." Before he could fully process that, I slammed my forehead into his right eyebrow and my right fist into his stomach. I threw all my weight forward and pushed him off the bench and onto the floor.

"Sanders!" Conrad yelled. But I was already on Montes, or whatever his name really was. I heard a loud buzz, but was too busy with the lieutenant to register what was causing it. I held him down with my left arm and grabbed for his pistol with my right. He was dazed, trying to push me off. I couldn't get the snap cover off his pistol. I slammed my knee into his side, which did not have the desired affect: instead of reducing his resistance, his body instinctively curled up, making the gun less accessible. He reared up, and I pushed his head against the bench. He howled in pain. The snap finally gave and I closed my hand around the butt of the pistol, trying to pull it out. I yanked at it, then discovered I had an extremely tight grip on the thing. My arm stuck straight out, the gun in my hand, and I heard that buzzing again. I began shaking, and pain shot through every muscle. My entire body convulsed. When the buzzing stopped, I fell to the floor, and the gun clattered into the corner under the opposite bench.

I was slack, and found it hard to control my movements. About the only thing I could do was flop over. That's when I saw the second guy holding a Taser. He stuck it to my neck and hit me again. I stiffened, and when he stopped, I went slack again. This time, I couldn't control anything. I could see Conrad on the floor at my feet.

Montes's "assistant" had done the smart thing: Instead of trying to get me off his boss, he immediately tased Conrad to take her out of the equation, creating better odds for them.

He reached back and tased her again. Then he pulled out a pair of handcuffs, flipped me over, and cuffed my hands behind my back. He stepped over me to Montes, who was still down. He had gotten an electrical shock since I was touching him when I was first tased. The current passed through my body and into him. His face was bleeding. His number two fished another set of cuffs from a compartment on the back of Montes's belt, then cuffed Conrad.

I heard the driver yell back: "*Todo* OK?" I had the completely random thought that OK was a universal term.

The guy yelled, "*Sí!*" He helped Montes up to a sitting position, then retrieved duct tape and a black bag from a duffel he had stored on the floor underneath his bench. He taped my mouth, then put the bag over my head. I heard him do the same to Conrad. Then he put the Taser up against my left shoulder and shocked me again.

Chapter 33

Midtown Manhattan; March 2008

A minute after Sanders said he would call back, the transponders stopped sending their signal: first Sanders', then seconds later Conrad's. JJ tried calling Sanders back but only got voicemail. He called Winkler, then Bodorofsky. Neither could explain why the transponders had stopped transmitting the agents' position. He called Borenstein to let him know what was going on, and then Pinchao's office as well.

Major Fernando Pinchao mobilized his entire office, first accounting for every one of his officers, then his enlisted men. They were all accounted for. He called JJ back and advised that his men were all accounted for, and that he had spoken to Conrad the day before. She had told him that she and her colleague would be taking a taxi from the hotel to Pinchao's office. Pinchao set their meeting time for 8:30 a.m., and Conrad had assented.

Within fifteen minutes of the agents going missing, Pinchao sent a bulletin to every army unit, advising of the two agents' descriptions. Within a half hour, he and Armin Smith had arrived at the hotel and interviewed the valets at the door. They described an army van, and at least two men, one an army officer by the name of Montes. Montes was Pinchao's administrative officer, and he was still back at the office when Pinchao and Smith had left. Whoever kidnapped the two had knowledge of Pinchao's staff, and access to uniforms and an army van. The hotel had no surveillance cameras outside, so there was no way to get a plate number. Smith walked out and looked up and down the street. The hotel was not in a commercial district, and he couldn't see any surveillance cameras on nearby buildings.

As Pinchao was well aware, if they had become hostages of the FARC, there was little chance of recovering them en route to their final destination. He couldn't shut the entire city down, and it was probably too late to take such action anyway. Moreover, not only did the FARC have two American FBI agents, they also had Conrad's files, apparently detailing the investigation to date in the recent deli bombing in New York. He called JJ back late in the morning and advised of his findings, which were troublingly sparse. He suspected the FARC had kidnapped JJ's agents, but he would not know for certain until a ransom demand was received, which could be weeks. He would continue to follow all leads and ask confidential informants for assistance. He would also be assisted by Lt. Colonel Smith.

As it would turn out, one of the agents would be recovered much sooner than anyone expected.

Chapter 34

Colombia; March 2008

When I woke up, I was sitting in a chair, my wrists cuffed behind the chair back. Criminals being criminals, they never trusted anything or anyone, so I was also strapped to the chair around my waist and legs with webbing straps similar to those used to secure shipments on pallets. It was dim, but there was some light. As my eyes adjusted, I could tell it was natural light coming in from windows high above our heads. The floor was cement. About fifteen feet away, Conrad was strapped to a chair facing me. She looked significantly better, I suspected, than I did, since she had not had a fight in the van. She was awake and alert.

"Sanders?" she whispered.

"Yeah," I said groggily.

"I think we're still in Bogota, but pretty far from the city center. It was about a half hour to get here. At least it seemed like it."

"No talking, please," came a voice from behind me. Latino. Male. A man walked from behind my left shoulder, turned, and stood in front of me. Early thirties with curly, somewhat unkempt

237

hair. Might have looked cool on a younger guy. "Awake? Good." He was wearing army fatigues, but it was not a crisp uniform like the ones our captors in the van had worn. This was a worn, faded set, as if he had lived in them every day for two years.

"You let us go now, we'll forget about it," I said.

He slapped my face lightly, almost playfully, and smiled. "I said no talking, didn't I?" He held up my wallet. "Let us see. Your name is Nicholas Sanders. And I see here you are a con-tractor with the FBI." He held up my business card. Another guy who read the fine print. "And people complain your capital-ist business executives outsource jobs. Their own government is doing it." He dropped the wallet in my lap. "And your friend here, Miss Conrad, is it? She seems like a spy to me." He walked over to her chair. I heard a crinkle as he stepped toward Conrad, and noticed her chair sat on a large sheet of industrial plastic. That wasn't good. He picked up the backpack that sat next to her. "You know what Stalin said, right? *Smert spionam.*"

"Death to spies," I said. He turned back at me quickly.

"You know your history, Señor Sanders."

"Not really. I saw *The Living Daylights*. I'm a James Bond fan."

He smiled a big smile at me. That's always bad. It meant he was supremely confident he was in control of the situation, which I found hard to argue with except for one thing. The transpon-der was no doubt transmitting our position to Chris and JJ, and they would mobilize the entire Colombian Army. Of course, this was little comfort if the guys who kidnapped us were with the Colombian Army.

"Yes, I have seen this movie too. I too am a James Bond fan, but I must admit, not a Timothy Dalton fan, eh?"

"Look, I'd like to debate who's the best Bond with you, but in about ten minutes, you're going to have the entire Colombian Army busting down these walls." I leaned forward as much as I could and whispered conspiratorially, "So you and your *compadres* had best skedaddle." Skedaddle. There's a word I had to keep alive. Indeed.

He walked toward me and put his hand on my left shoulder. He squeezed. "Ow," I said.

"Your shoulder hurts because I had to cut into it. And, Nicholas, I'm no surgeon, I must confess. But you will heal." He looked past my shoulder and said, "Bring it." There was some clatter behind me, and to my left a man appeared carrying a tripod and small digital video camera. The man, in his twenties and Latino, wearing a T-shirt and jeans, set up the camera pointing at Conrad, then disappeared for a moment. When he returned, he had a large spotlight set up on a second tripod. When he plugged it in, the area of the warehouse around Conrad was illuminated. She was not beaten in any way I could tell. Her blouse showed a bit of blood on her left shoulder. She looked terrified. And for good reason. The whole thing had turned into a shit show. Both men put on masks, then the assistant turned the camera on.

"She's just an assistant. She's worthless. Let her go. Have her be your messenger for the ransom."

"No, Nicholas, I am afraid it is you who are worthless to me, except as a witness. You will bear witness to the crimes this woman has committed. You will hear her confession. *You* will be my messenger."

"Sanders, I fucked up. I'm sorry," Conrad said. Tears began streaming down her face. She looked at our captor. "I don't know anything. I'm just an analyst."

The man waved the backpack in front of her. His voice rose, and he was clearly agitated. "Just an analyst!" he sneered. "Carrying top secret documents? *Analyzing* one of the operations of our revolutionary brothers in New York? Why are you here with this information? Why did you come to see Major Pinchao?"

Sometimes you can learn more from your interrogators by the questions they ask than they can learn from you. As far as I was concerned, the guy had just admitted that the FARC had committed the deli bombing. What he also told me was that they knew we were here to see the major, but not why. I tried to parse this out because what it seemed to indicate was that some of our communications were monitored, but we might not have a *personnel* problem. Had there been a leak directly from the bureau, the people who knew Conrad and I were in Colombia would probably also know why. And yet they knew about the transponders.

"You are here to give Major Pinchao assistance in hunting down our camps, aren't you?" Conrad was shaking, and crying a little. This only antagonized him. "Stop acting! You are an American spy. Why are you here? Why did you bring this file with you?" He held up the bag. "Why would Major Pinchao be interested in it?"

She looked at me, and I shook my head. She wanted permission to tell him something. The head man noticed Conrad looking at me and spun around. "Why do you look at this man? What is he to you? He is merely a contractor, no?" He walked up to me and backhanded me across the face. Hard. "You will look at the ground and say and do nothing!" He turned back to Conrad.

"Why are you here?"

Conrad shook her head jerkily, closing her eyes, willing the guy to disappear.

"All right, Señorita Conrad. I am sorry to do this. But we will need to resort to 'advanced interrogation techniques' as you Americans refer to them. And unfortunately, we do not care if we leave marks." He turned and looked over my shoulder again. He nodded, and the second man brought a handheld butane canister with a long, narrow spout into view.

"Jesus," I said.

The head guy turned to me. "Yes, good idea, Nicholas. Pray." He turned back to Conrad. "Señorita, we will start at your feet and work our way up to more ... sensitive areas." He fished a lighter from his pocket, held the canister out while the other man turned on the gas flow, and then lit the end. A small, blue flame spurted to life from the tube. He put the lighter back in his pocket, then switched the canister to his right hand. Right-handed. I filed that away, hopefully for use in the near future when I got free and chopped his fucking hand off.

"One more time: Why are you in Bogota? Why are you meeting with Major Pinchao?" He walked toward her, the canister hissing.

"We needed his help," I said. The man stopped and turned to me.

"Help? You need Major Pinchao's help? About what?"

I nodded to the backpack. "What?" he asked. "This? What would Major Pinchao know of this bombing in New York City? I will tell you what he would know. Nothing. Because Major Pinchao is more concerned with killing my brothers and sisters, the freedom fighters in the jungle, than he is with what occurs in America. Just as long as your American money and arms keep flowing. That is what Pinchao cares about. So, Señor Nicholas, I think you are lying to me. Please do not interrupt again." He turned back. He nodded again to his assistant. The helper walked over to Conrad and knelt to remove her shoes, tossing them aside. The lead guy again walked to Conrad.

"The smell of burning human flesh is not pleasant. Trust me, I know personally. I cannot tell you how you will react to the smell of your *own* burning flesh, however. I suspect you will be too busy screaming to notice." He turned once more to his number two, who brought forward a bowl with what appeared to be water, ice, and rags.

"Now, I cannot have you screaming indefinitely, so I will stop periodically and salve your wounds, OK? And if you will tell me why you are here, I will stop altogether. Understand?" Conrad did nothing but shake. He crouched down at her feet, blocking my view, but must have brought the burner to her feet because Conrad screamed.

"She doesn't know anything, motherfucker!" I screamed. The FARC guy stood up and nodded to his assistant, who applied a wet cloth to the wound. The head man turned and approached me.

"I'm sorry, Nicholas. You are quite distracting. I cannot have you yelling while I am working. I don't come to your place of employment and yell at you, do I?" he asked with a smile.

"Fuck you, asshole."

"Charming." He turned to his buddy, who tore a piece of duct tape off a roll and tried to place it over my mouth. I turned my head and bit his hand hard. The assistant howled and hit me about the head and shoulders with his free arm, but I didn't let go. The head man ran over and torched the side of my head. I let go of the assistant's hand, his blood in my mouth.

"Señor Nicholas, you are quite exasperating. Now, I can tape your mouth shut or I can drug you. I will let you choose."

"How about you let me loose and we have a stand-up fight?"

"I am sorry, this is not a tempting offer. You Americans are so big. I am going to inject you with a sedative." He handed the torch to his assistant, who had to let his bloody hand drop in order to grasp it. The lead guy walked behind me, and I heard a clatter of metal. When he returned, he had a large syringe and a small pharmaceutical bottle of clear liquid. He turned the bottle upside down and stuck the needle in the cap, then drew the plunger back and filled the syringe about a quarter of the way.

"Nicholas, I am sorry, but I was unable to obtain a human sedative. This is used for large animals, like bulls at the bull-fights. Appropriate for you, no? So, there is a bit of danger with the dosage, but if you die, it is your own fault." He walked behind me and tore my shirt away from my right shoulder. *And just when it was starting to feel better,* I thought. Then he stopped.

"Señorita Conrad, do you have anything to tell me and my witness?" Conrad shook her head. I admired her for being so tough and holding steady. I also regretted it a little given current events, but I squelched that thought. She was doing the right thing.

"No? OK." He jabbed the needle into me and violently thrust the plunger down with his thumb.

"You're supposed to tell me it will pinch a little," I said.

"Nicholas, we don't have much time before that takes effect, so we'll need to resolve our interrogation with the spy-whore quickly." He lifted up his shirt, revealing a pistol in his waistband. Chrome slide, black body. *Herstal nine mil*, I thought randomly. He removed it with his right hand, then took the torch back with his left. I didn't feel anything from the drug as yet.

"Last chance, Señorita Conrad." He walked up to her. "Why are you here? What were you and Pinchao to discuss?"

Crying, Conrad whispered, "We needed his help."

He thrust the torch into her thighs, and I saw Conrad's body jerk. He removed it quickly. "Stop lying! Why are you here!"

"The deli bombing ..." I said, and noticed my tongue was heavy, the words jagged.

He spun about. "I was not speaking to you, Nicholas!" He turned back, held up the canister and said, "Again?" Conrad shook her head. "Then tell me what I need to know! Why are you here?"

"I already told you ..." she coughed. She looked past him at me, tears streaming down her face. "I'm sorry," she sobbed.

"Ach!" he tossed the canister back to his assistant, who was lucky to catch it with his one good hand without burning himself. The lead man turned back to Conrad. I noticed the room started getting dim, as if the spotlight were going out.

He kicked Conrad's shoulder and her chair fell back onto the plastic. I heard her cry out as he stood over her, pointed the gun down and fired. *POP. POP. POP.* Yep, 9 mm, my wandering mind registered. "Smert spionam!" he screamed as he fired.

He put the gun back in his waistband and walked back to me. My head was dropping down. I was barely conscious. He lifted my head and looked into my eyes. All I could see was his black pupils through the holes in the mask. "Death to spies, Nicholas," he whispered. The last thing I saw were those eyes, withdrawing down a dark tunnel into total blackness.

Chapter 35

Bogota, Colombia; March 2008

"Major Pinchao, we received an anonymous call. The caller claimed he knew the location of the two Americans. He gave us an address in La Calera."

Pinchao was at headquarters, putting what little they knew up on a bulletin board and trying to develop a timeline on an adjacent whiteboard. It had been four hours since the American agents disappeared. They had no real leads, other than they thought some army officers were in on it. In Colombia, that reduced your suspect pool to fifty thousand.

Pinchao held his hand over the phone's mouthpiece and turned to Smith. "They may be in La Calera." Pinchao raised the phone to his ear again. "Give me the address." He nodded. "Warehouse district," he said aloud and hung up. "Raul, Montes. Armin, I presume you'll want to come?"

"Hell yeah I wanna go!" Smith said. They jumped into two black Ford Explorers and sped northeast out of the city to an industrial suburb called La Calera. On the way, Smith called JJ at the bureau and advised him what was happening. JJ put Winkler on the phone, who brought the address up on a real-time satellite map. "OK, I show no significant activity at or in the vicinity of that address," Winkler said. "I also don't see their transponders, but we expected that. Let us know when you get there and we'll give you eyes in the sky."

There was little in the way of zoning laws in Colombia, and the area of the address was a dusty warren of rundown warehouses, wall-less concrete pads with metal awnings over them, and half-finished tilt-ups.

"Slow down here," Pinchao, who was in the lead car, told his driver. The driver slowed to a crawl, and the two trucks eased down a narrow dirt path between several warehouses. "It's the end left," he said, then spoke into his radio. "Jaramillo, back up to the end of the street. This is too good an ambush site." The two cars stopped, rolled back, and blocked off the entrances to the roadway.

Everyone exited and readied weapons. They all wore vests. "OK," Pinchao said, "in groups of two, alternating point, one set of eyes up, the other on either side of the path." The teams leap-frogged down the street, looking into windows where they could, seeing nothing but a desolate industrial area where no economic activity of any significance had taken place in years. Jaramillo and his partner passed the sliding front door of the address they had been given.

The second team took up a position on the near side of the door. Pinchao and Smith stopped. Smith talked into his phone. "You got anyone on the roof, Chris?"

"No one. And no vehicles or bodies on the surrounding street."

"OK, wait one. We're going in."

Smith put the phone in his pocket and attached a Bluetooth headset to his right ear. He checked his weapon, and he and Pinchao stepped away from the door. Jaramillo reached over and slowly pushed the sliding door away from him, an inch at a time. As he did so, he would stop periodically and look up and down for wires, light emitters, or anything out of the ordinary that could be a booby trap. He saw nothing. As the door slid open, light spilled into a warehouse that was dim and empty except for some tall shelving, a chair lying on the ground, and another chair with a large man tied in it. His head was slumped forward on his chest. An uninitiated soldier's immediate reaction would be to run into the building to assist the hostage, but Pinchao, Smith, and Pinchao's men had all been through enough FARC encounters to know they had to take their time and scope out the entire area. The FARC often laid traps for the unwary at suspected kidnap sites.

Smith spoke into his headset. "OK, we are at the entrance. Looks like this guy Sanders may be in here. No sign of the woman. Do you see any movement?"

"Three blocks away you have a slow-moving van, but it came from off the field and doesn't appear to be headed toward you. Doesn't look like there is any street that would easily lead to you. Continuing north. No one on rooftops."

"Thank you. Keep the updates coming."

Back in Manhattan, Winkler had Smith on speaker, and JJ and Borenstein were standing over either shoulder looking at the satellite image on his computer screen. Velasquez was standing behind JJ and Borenstein, trying to get a view of the screen, listening to the play-by-play.

Three rows of warehouses away, Ignacio Guerra pulled the van to a stop in front of a roll-up door. This next part had to be done just right. If he had calculated it correctly, he would be able to remotely open the doors he needed as the van rolled forward. He knew Pinchao was careful, so he had to give them time to get into the building. He couldn't post any lookouts because they might be spotted by Pinchao's team. And moreover, with the American adviser with them, they probably had some kind of air or satellite support.

A top-down view of a battlefield is a valuable thing. But in a city, it becomes difficult to distinguish the mundane from the significant. The FARC was well-aware of this fact, and used it every chance they could to camouflage their activity from "eyes in the sky" that they assumed were watching them all the time. They used nondescript vehicles and the "natural geography," which in a city meant tunnels, large industrial parks, and heavily tree-lined streets, to mask their movement. Enemies wouldn't see them coming until it was far too late.

"Van stopped. Guy's getting out, looks like he's making a delivery three buildings over." Chris and the rest of the New York team watched as the driver of the van got out, walked over at a leisurely pace to a warehouse door, and rolled the door up. He then got back in the van and backed it into the building, out of view.

"Van pulled into a warehouse three buildings away."

"Roger. Proceeding inside the warehouse," came Smith's staticky voice over the phone's speaker. Chris hit the mute button and said to those behind him, "Jesus, why don't they get to Sanders?"

"They gotta make sure it's not a trap. They run in there, there could be a bomb or fifty guys with automatics that open up on them," Velasquez answered. JJ and Borenstein nodded in agreement. But Velasquez shared Winkler's sense of urgency. She was worried for Sanders, too.

What could not be seen from the satellite feed was that the two intervening buildings had roll-away doors on both sides of them. If opened, this left a clear path to the building with Pinchao's team.

Guerra worked quickly. He opened up the back of the van and withdrew two pipes cut to a specific size and a bar with a vise at each end. He had developed the design himself on the fly and was quite proud of his work. He went to the driver's side door of the van, rolled down the window, and then closed the door. He clamped one vise to the door frame and the other to the post jutting from the steering column to the wheel. He checked it to ensure the steering wheel didn't move, then checked the front tires to ensure they were straight and between the chalk marks he had made on the ground. He dropped the two pipes in the front passenger seat and walked to the back of the van. He opened it and set the arming switch.

He had wired one of five bricks of C-4, using a detonator wired to an impact sensor in the front of the van. When the airbags went off, this would send an electrical charge down the wire to the detonator, creating a huge explosion.

Ignacio was only given a single detonator when he picked up the van. He was told not to worry, however, because if the bricks were in proximity when the first brick went off, it would cause the others to detonate. Guerra and the bomb-supplier's understanding of proximity were two different things. C-4 was prized because it was very hard to set off inadvertently. You could fire a gun into a brick and it wouldn't explode. You could light it with a match and it would burn but not detonate. C-4 required a blasting cap to be inserted into the brick. When the cap went off, it detonated a small portion, causing a chain reaction that exploded the rest of the unit. If you wrapped a bunch of bricks together, the chain reaction would be preserved, and all of them would explode. But if you spread them out, there was a chance that only one, or a few of the total collection, would actually detonate. The farther apart they were, the less likely all would detonate, particularly if the C-4 had been stored in less-than-ideal conditions for a long period of time, as was the case here. The texture of the bricks had become crumbly and less cohesive. And Guerra had spread them out across the interior of the van.

He went to the passenger seat and retrieved the two pipes. He set one against the front of the seat and wedged the other end against the brake pedal. He wedged the second to the gas pedal. This next part was tricky. Since no one could be around when the van was released, Ignacio had to develop a method to remove the pipe holding down the brake without actually being near it.

He tied a rope tightly to the middle of the length of pipe on the brake, then ran that rope to the roll-up door on the opposite side of the warehouse, furthest from the planned explosion. He would trigger the door to close with a remote control, thus slowly taking the slack out of the rope and pulling the pipe away. The problem was how to get the pipe out of the van without it dislodging anything vital, such as the pipe holding down the gas pedal. He fully reclined the driver's seat and ran the rope out the back window, giving the pipe a clear path out of the vehicle. He ran the rope through, climbing a double-height ladder to reach the door opener. He knotted the other end to the door, ensuring just enough slack that it would tighten and pull the brake pipe before it reached the end of its cycle. With the van turned off, he tried this twice, and both times the pipe dislodged and came directly out the back window, clear of the van interior and without touching any vital components.

Ignacio's assistant had a second identical van ready. Ignacio and his FARC companion would leave, and as they rolled slowly down the street, he would hit the remote control to close the door, setting off a chain of events that would result in the death of Major Fernando Pinchao. And others.

* * *

Two teams went into the warehouse and spread out. They reported the room was clear. Smith and Pinchao then entered. Pinchao turned to one of his men. "Raul, bring one of the trucks up to the door. Quickly please."

Raul exited, running down the street. Smith was at the chair with the man he presumed was Sanders. The guy was big, maybe six foot one or two, and had thick, wide shoulders. Fearing the worst, Smith gently lifted Sanders' head with his left hand and felt for a pulse on his neck. It was there, but weak. "He's alive," he told Pinchao as he approached. Everyone in New York heard this through Smith's headset and breathed a sigh of relief.

Smith studied Sanders' face, which was slightly bruised and showed a burn mark. He didn't appear to have any significant damage, but there was a jagged cut on his left shoulder and his shirt was torn above his right shoulder. A wallet was in his lap. Smith picked it up and looked at it. All the credit cards appeared to be there, as was a New York driver's license with a picture of the guy in the chair, identifying him as Nicholas Sanders. On the ground between his feet was a bureau business card. Jaramillo was behind the chair, looking it over.

"There do not appear to be any explosives, sir. He's just tied to it," he said.

"Let's cut him loose and get him to a hospital." Jaramillo went to work on the bindings while Smith turned to the other chair. As he walked over, he said into his Bluetooth, "OK, Sanders is alive but unconscious. I am guessing drugged, as it doesn't look as if he's been significantly beaten. The girl, what's her name?"

Borenstein spoke up. "Conrad. Alexandra Conrad." There was a catch in his throat.

"Yeah, well, no sign of her. There's ... oh dear."

Everyone tensed. No one thought to smirk at the thought of a chiseled, experienced, decorated army officer reacting to something he saw with "oh dear." "What is it, Colonel?" Borenstein asked.

"Looks like the FARC used a butane torch on her. It's lying on the ground. The good news is she's not here, which means she's likely a hostage and still alive."

Everyone heard a car start and an engine rev nearby. At first, Pinchao assumed it was Raul, but the Explorer came rolling up to the door relatively quietly, and they still heard the revving engine.

This was the dangerous part. Guerra had no way of moving the shift lever if he wasn't in the vehicle. He had to start the car from the passenger seat and then move the shift lever to drive, hoping the brakes would hold. The fact that all cars were designed to remain stationary so long as the brake pedal was completely depressed—no matter how far down the accelerator was pressed—was of little consolation to the man now shifting the rolling bomb into drive. Guerra had no desire to be a suicide bomber. The van lurched only slightly, but remained in place.

Guerra jumped out quickly. He ran to the second van and opened the passenger door.

"Start it up," he said to his assistant. The soldier did so. Guerra grabbed two of the three remote controls, both wrapped in red tape so he wouldn't get confused. He pressed both and confirmed that the doors to the warehouse next door, and the one next to it, were in fact opening. Then he jumped back in the van and said, "Drive, now!"

✡ ✡ ✡

"Let's get him out of here," Smith said. "You guys show any movement?"

Because he had a straight-down view of the action, Winkler couldn't see the moving doors of the two adjacent warehouses. "No … wait. Yeah, that van three buildings over is leaving out the opposite side, proceeding south."

"OK." He turned to Pinchao. "That other van is leaving. We need to look around for the girl, or evidence of who's been here."

Jaramillo and his teammate were carrying Sanders outside to the Explorer.

"I agree, let me get …" Something was bothering him. The pitch of the revving engine hadn't changed at all. "Has that van left yet?"

Chris overheard this and said, "Well, he's moving south, slowly, but moving."

"Out now! Everyone out now!" Pinchao ran, Smith ran, but the soldier charged with searching the shelving was confused and hesitated before joining them.

"Close that door!"

One team member ran to the sliding door and began pushing it closed. The revving engine was getting louder.

✡ ✡ ✡

About one building away from the back door of the warehouse, Guerra leaned out the window and hit the remote wrapped in blue tape. The roll-up door to the warehouse containing the bomb van began to close.

When the door reached its halfway point, the rope went taut, then popped the pipe holding down the brake. Guerra had tested it with the van standing still. But the moment the brake was released in motion, the van lurched forward. The end of the pipe against the brake rotated upward and was momentarily caught between the seat and the steering wheel. As the van shot forward even more, the pressure on the rope increased. The bottom end of the pipe tore through the upholstery and cushioning of the seat, then flew through the cargo area and out the rear window. The tear in the seat reduced the resistance of the accelerator pipe, so that the van that would have been traveling at forty when it reached full speed would only achieve twenty-five miles per hour. This would not affect the operation of the bomb, but it would allow Pinchao's team more time for a potential escape.

✡ ✡ ✡

Just as the soldier was getting the door closed, the one who had hesitated jumped through the last bit of opening. The van engine sound was growing louder, and Pinchao yelled at Jaramillo: "Get that truck out of here!"

Smith grabbed Pinchao by the sleeve and yelled, "Come on!" They both ran south to the remaining truck, and the Explorer with Sanders shot forward north, leaving the last two soldiers to decide where to run. They both ran south after their leader, Pinchao, a mistake since the door they had come through was at the north end of the building. Their run would expose them to the lion's share of the blast.

The van moved perfectly through the two empty warehouses. From the view of those in New York, it looked to be controlled by a driver. The bomb van broke through the wall of the target warehouse at twenty-five miles per hour. It kept moving until the electrical signal set off the airbags and reached the detonator of the first brick of C-4. Of the five bricks, only two detonated. To the team in New York, it appeared to be a two-part explosion. The first took out the east side of the building, but the van continued its forward momentum despite the fact that two of the wheels on the passenger side were demolished by the initial blast. This caused the vehicle to tilt right, then fall over as the second brick exploded in the middle of the warehouse. The roof lifted up and out, corrugated sheet metal and debris flying in all directions.

"Shit!" those crowded around the computer said at once as several pieces of steel flew down the pathway and cut down the two soldiers running south. Two others, ahead of them, fell to the ground and covered up, but were far enough away that no debris hit them. The Explorer had reached the end of the dirt road and turned west, getting away at a high speed.

"Smith, this is Jordan. Are you injured?"

Silence.

JJ remained very calm. "Smith, this is Jordan. Are you reading us?"

Coughing. "Son of a bitch!" Everyone in New York exhaled. "Yeah, we're still here. The major and I, I mean. Where's that other van?" On screen, the New York contingent watched Smith getting up and helping Pinchao to his feet as well. Pinchao and Smith turned around to see two of their men literally cut in half.

"My God" was all Pinchao could say.

JJ leaned over Chris, who was momentarily stunned by all the action. "Chris," he said gently as he put his hand on the kid's shoulder, "the other van."

"Oh, oh, shit," Chris said as he regrouped and moved the cursor about. He expanded the view, but the second vehicle could not be seen. Further east, just past the industrial center where the explosion took place, was a busy highway. "Gone. A nondescript white van. I see four in just this view. No way to know if it went north or south."

"We lost it, Colonel," JJ said.

"Dammit!" came through the speaker loud and clear.

Pinchao ran to the other truck and grabbed the radio microphone. "Jaramillo, this is ..." He stopped. He waved Smith over and whispered in his ear. Smith nodded.

"New York, our communications may be compromised," said Smith. "We'll have to get to a hard line before we speak further." He turned off his Bluetooth and shut down his phone. Smith took the CB handset from Pinchao and, speaking fluent Spanish, had Jaramillo regroup with them. He then called in to the base in Bogota and had a bomb investigation team, paramedic, fire, and coroner all report to the scene. Pinchao jumped into the driver's seat of the truck containing Sanders, pulled his cap down and drove off to a hospital that served only his anti-FARC team. He had Jaramillo stay and coordinate rescue and investigation operations, with strict instructions to let everyone know that Major Fernando Pinchao was gravely injured and it was unclear if he would survive the wounds he received in the FARC trap, which was clearly set for him.

Borenstein and JJ retired to JJ's office. The moment the door was closed, Borenstein began speaking. "We need them all back here, and I mean Sanders, that Smith guy, and Pinchao. Conrad's disappearance has really fucked things up." Borenstein was visibly agitated. He seemed nervous and angry at the same time. And it was the first time JJ had ever heard him use foul language.

JJ looked at him a moment. "You want me to have a major in the Colombian Army come to New York? For what?"

"Look, JJ, your communications are compromised. And now I think DHS's might be too. We need to talk to everyone. And we have to do it in a secure location face-to-face. Until we get this figured out, we're back in the Stone Age."

"I don't understand. We wanted to see if Pinchao could help us with the deli bombing. All we have to do is deliver a file to him and have him look it over—"

"That was just a pretense! Conrad was there for something else."

JJ stared at Borenstein for a good ten seconds. Borenstein looked away. JJ spoke. "Al, are you telling me you're running an operation directly out of DHS?"

"JJ, I'll tell you what I can when you need to know. And that won't be until all these folks are safe and in the same room, here in New York. Now I have to go make a very uncomfortable call to the president."

Back in his office, Al Borenstein took a deep breath and let it out. If he were given to cursing, every nasty word in the English language, and in German, would have spewed in a flood from his lips. He picked up his phone and dialed. When one is going to call the president of the United States, there is a protocol to follow, in which an underling calls a secretary, who calls another secretary, who calls the chief of staff, who tries to fit you in, but only if he likes you. Some cabinet heads have direct access, but not many. Al Borenstein was such a cabinet head. He had a direct line to Susan Riccardi, the president's personal secretary, who sat outside the Oval Office.

"The president's office," the very professional voice said, clearly and distinctly.

"Ms. Riccardi, this is Al Borenstein at DHS. I have some news for the president of some importance, and I was hoping he was available."

"I'll see, Mr. Borenstein. Please hold."

Two minutes passed. "Mr. Borenstein, I am putting you through to the president."

"Al?" the president's voice came through almost immediately.
"Sir."

"Whaddya got?"

"Nothing good, I'm afraid, sir. My agent, Alexandra Conrad, apparently was captured by the FARC and tortured. We think she is being held hostage. In addition, the FARC took the opportunity to use Conrad and an FBI contractor, Nick Sanders, as bait to lure Major Pinchao into a trap in Bogota. The major escaped injury, but if I analyze the situation correctly, that's not what is going public. I think the major will be in hiding, letting his staff indicate he is on his deathbed, even dead. This will give him a chance to plan a counterattack and let the FARC believe he is out of the picture."

"Well, at least the major is all right. We need to find your girl, obviously. What does this do to our plans regarding the FARC?"

"Mr. President, without Ms. Conrad, there is no way to replicate the program."

Silence. The president was thinking it through, and Borenstein knew exactly where this was going to go. There was no way around it.

"Al, I'm going to call the Director of Intelligence. We need to get the CIA's Operations Department involved right now. I am ordering you to get all the relevant parties together and debrief them securely. However, I am also ordering you to limit the sharing of information to only those parties who need to know."

"I've already begun that process, sir. In my estimation, we'll need to include Jordan, an agent named Nicholas Sanders, the DDO, and Major Pinchao and his adviser, Colonel Smith."

"Agreed. I am going to call the director and have him contact you directly. I want morning and evening updates, Al. We need to get your girl back."

"Yes, sir."

✦ ✦ ✦

The moment he got back to Bogota, Lt. Colonel Armin Smith used his landline to call a personal contact at the CIA.

"Paul Blattman," the weary voice grumbled into the phone.

"Paul, it's Armin Smith."

The voice brightened. "Armin! How are you, son?" The fact that Smith was in his early fifties didn't prevent Blattman from referring to him as son. He was, after all, one of Blattman's first trainees. Despite the fact that Smith had taken his career route in reverse, from CIA to the military, they still had great affection for each other.

"Not well, I'm afraid. Paul, look, I'm down here in Bogota. The FARC set a trap for Pinchao, tried to off him. He smelled it out before I did. The guy's good. Anyway, they used some guy named Nicholas Sanders, an FBI contractor, as bait. But they took a girl, Alex Conrad, as a hostage."

Blattman was bolt upright in his seat. "She's with Borenstein's group," he blurted out.

"Homeland Security?"

"Yeah."

"What the hell were they doing in Colombia?"

"I don't know."

"And there's another thing. I was going to call you anyway. The FARC has gotten their hands on some super encryption software. Pinchao hasn't been able to intercept anything from them for over a year. Thought they had gone old school on us, but looks like it's the reverse. We were hoping you could provide some help."

"Well, I don't run tech or listening, so I really don't know what they've got on that side, but I'll look into it for you. Not sure how far I'll get, they don't like us Humint guys much." "Humint" was shorthand in the agency for "human intelligence."

"I know what you mean—"

"Hey, Armin, hold on. My other line's going." Blattman put Smith on hold and picked up the call from the DDO. "Sir?"

No greeting. No how do you do. Just a straight blast: "I think that motherfucker Borenstein's running his own operation!"

Blattman said nothing but noted that his boss wasn't as naïve as he thought. "The president called the director. They want me at DHS in New York for a briefing Borenstein's going to give us on a bombing in Bogota. How he would know about it before us is beyond me. Anyway, I need someone who knows him. So you're elected. Get a bag, we're going tonight. Meeting's tomorrow." The DDO hung up.

Blattman shifted over to the other line. "Armin, looks like the shit's hitting the fan up here regarding your bombing. I'm going to New York tonight with the DDO to hear from Borenstein."

"What the hell ... Hey, Paul, hold on." He clicked off and a minute later clicked back on. "Looks like I'll be seeing you there with Major Pinchao in tow. That was the director calling me personally. Order came directly from the president."

"Well, this is going to be interesting. See you tomorrow."

Chapter 36

Bogota, Colombia; March 2008

"You're dead. So's he."

I was on a C-130 to New York with a guy named Armin Smith and Major Pinchao, whom I had met for the first time after I got out of the military vehicle on the tarmac of a U.S. airbase outside of Bogota and climbed the steps of the transport plane. Pinchao was seated, and Smith greeted me at the door, introducing himself as an American military adviser to the Colombian Army. He then introduced Pinchao. Until I got to this point, no one had told me a thing about what had happened in the time since I had been drugged and then woke up in a Colombian military hospital. Once I awoke, things started happening fast.

On the hospital gurney, I was handed a cell phone. It was JJ. "Listen, I don't have time to explain. Things are developing fast around here. Don't use names on this phone. You're coming home. An American is going to escort you. Some army guys are going to take you to an airbase, and you'll be on a plane home in about two hours. Don't talk to anyone down there about what happened. We'll debrief you here. We think most of our communications are compromised, especially cell phones, so don't say anything over the phone. You should get here late tonight. You can talk to your escort about what happened after he got there, but under no circumstances are you to discuss what happened to you before. You can do that here when everyone's in the same room, got it? Sorry about all this. I can't imagine what you've been through. You're lucky to be alive."

My mouth and throat were dry, like I had a bad hangover, I presumed a result of the drug I was given. I kept going over what had happened in my head. It didn't make any sense to kill Alex. There was no percentage in it. And if you were going to kill her, why keep me alive?

When I got to the plane and met Smith, I told him what my orders were. He nodded in understanding.

"You guys pulled me out of the warehouse?"

"Yes, barely."

"What do you mean?"

"You're dead. So's he," he said, turning to Pinchao.

Pinchao smiled and said: "Señor Sanders, you are lucky to be alive, as are we all. For purposes of public and FARC consumption, you and I never made it out of that warehouse. It was blown up. You were being used as bait to draw me into a trap."

"I don't know whether to be relieved or insulted I wasn't worth holding as a hostage." Smith smirked. Pinchao looked confused. He didn't get my humor. "Well, gentlemen, thank you for saving me. I would love to talk about this more, but I think if I do I won't want to stop and I'll end up violating JJ's orders in about five minutes. He says you can tell me what you found after you got there."

Smith gave me the rundown. He mentioned that they were operating under the assumption that Conrad was a hostage, but because of JJ's orders, I didn't correct him. They'd find out soon enough.

I took JJ's advice and tried to get some sleep on the plane, which was not easy. I dozed on and off but was restless and couldn't stop my mind from working overtime on what had occurred. One thing I kept trying to puzzle out: "You're meeting was at 8:30. You're a half hour late." It was 8:00 a.m. when JJ called me. What the hell? I looked at my watch. 7:45 p.m.

"Colonel Smith?" I asked. He looked over at me. "What time do you have?"

"2045," he said after looking at his watch. He smiled when he realized he was talking to a civilian and corrected himself. "Sorry, 8:45 p.m., for now. Have to move that back when we get to the States. Thanks for the reminder."

I was confused. "Aren't Bogota and New York in the same time zone?"

"They're on daylight savings all year-round down here. Like Arizona. They never fall back. So even though we're in the same time zone, New York is still an hour behind half the year. Lotta newcomers make that mistake."

Son of a bitch. But that only lead to another question. If Conrad and I were an hour behind, why were the terrorists behind too? By all accounts, they should have been picking us up at 8:00 a.m. local time, not 9:00. I needed to talk this out with someone and work out a timeline on a piece of paper. It would have to wait until I got to New York.

Midtown Manhattan

"What the hell's he doing here?" Borenstein asked, quite put out by the sight of an unkempt, sixtyish man sitting at the conference table at DHS's New York office. I noted that the budget for décor at DHS must have been significantly more than the bureau's. The table was mahogany with inlays of burled wood.

The chairs were all leather, with quite a bit of padding. The artwork looked original. (It was probably seized from some high-end criminals, though, so I gave them props for looking out for the taxpayer.)

It was just after one in the morning, and I had already been in a separate meeting with JJ, Borenstein, and the Director of Operations of the CIA, Alfred Lopez, whom I had never met before. Lopez was impeccably dressed, especially for a post-midnight meeting. He even had a kerchief in his coat pocket that matched his tie.

Since there were two Als in the room, I had to call Lopez *Director Lopez*. Of course I was tempted to just call Borenstein *Adolph*. I should have been tired, but given all that had happened, I was wide awake.

Normally, Borenstein was a pretty cool customer, and he could afford to be: he sat at the apex of all domestic and foreign intelligence information received by the United States. He knew what was going on all over the world every day. Now, he was agitated. I assumed his present nervous state was caused by two things quite foreign to him: he had never lost an employee under his direct command, and he lacked any information as to the whereabouts of that employee.

"Please state your name for the record." JJ began the questioning as he switched on the recorder.

"Nicholas Sanders."

"Date of birth?"

"17 November 1964."

JJ established preliminaries: the investigation of five apparently related deaths, the questioning of Lazeris and Winfield, the contact by Lazeris, the bombing, and the results of forensic analysis of the bomb, leading us to believe the bombing of the deli was an act of the FARC.

"You were assigned to travel to Bogota, Colombia, to make contact with Major Fernando Pinchao of the Colombian Army, correct?"

"Yes."

"For what purpose?"

"Agent Conrad believed that the major would be able to assist us in locating the bomb maker or deliverer," I said. JJ glanced briefly at Borenstein, who continued to look at me. Something was going on between them, but I didn't know what.

"Please detail all of your actions from the moment you arrived in Bogota until you were found."

I related almost all of the information, leaving out the fact that Conrad and I had spent the night together before the abduction. They didn't need to know, nor would they find out from any other source. I was particularly careful when explaining exactly what Conrad told me regarding her communications with Pinchao's office. I did this for two reasons: it was apparent those communications were compromised, but I was also trying to work out the time element in my own head.

"Agent Conrad advised me the night before the intended rendezvous that she had spoken to Major Pinchao and that he was sending a car for us in the morning."

"She said specifically that Major Pinchao and she had spoken?"

I thought about it. She told me that they had called while I was getting ready. "No," I responded. "I got the impression she spoke to someone in his office since she told me 'they' had called her, not that the major had called her."

We went over the morning timeline very carefully. Since all I could do in this venue was answer questions posed to me, only my memory and impressions were being recorded. No one else offered any information they might have had about the events.

"Had it not been for our watches being off by an hour, we would not have been late to the meeting and wouldn't have been alerted by you, SAIC James Jordan, that we were overdue and that Major Pinchao did not know where we were."

"Why did you conclude that the people transporting you meant you harm based on my call?"

"Since the individuals who picked us up had allegedly been sent at the direction of Major Pinchao, I would have expected the major would know exactly where we were and what time we had been collected. Since he did not know that, I concluded these individuals were imposters."

I related being tased. I pointed out that our captors were aware of the tracking devices implanted in our shoulders and had specifically tased us in that spot. Then we got down to the nitty-gritty. I discussed the questioning by the head honcho in the warehouse, up to the point of drugging me.

"What did this man do next?"

"When Agent Conrad would not answer his questions to his satisfaction, he drew what appeared to me to be a nine millimeter Herstal pistol from his waistband. He pushed the bottom of his right foot against her shoulder. Her chair fell over backwards. The man then straddled Agent Conrad's torso and shot her three times in the chest."

"Oh God!" gasped Borenstein. His forehead went down into his right hand. Lopez did not seem to react but was holding his left hand over his mouth, so his facial expression was difficult to make out.

JJ did not lose his composure, even though this was the first time he had heard that Conrad was dead. "Mr. Sanders, I want to be certain of something. You had been injected with some kind of sleep agent, correct?"

"Yes, that's correct."

"But you were still conscious at this time?"

"Yes."

"You saw this man fire the weapon into Agent Conrad's chest?"

"Yes, sir."

"Wasn't this man's body blocking your view?"

"Conrad was on the ground, and when he kicked the chair, it angled sideways to me. He had to straddle her. While the view was somewhat obstructed by the chair seat and his left leg, I clearly saw that muzzle flash and her body react to the three shots between this man's legs. The man then walked over to me, said death to spies, and I passed out. When I awoke, I was in a Colombian Army hospital."

After some more questioning on the timeline and several other minor points, the tape was shut off. Everyone sat back and breathed out.

"Shit" was all Borenstein said.

"Al, do you want to share with us what Conrad was really doing down there?" JJ asked. I looked sharply over at JJ, then at Borenstein.

"Let's get everyone in the conference room, and I'll fill you all in. Doesn't matter now, anyway," he mumbled as he got up.

When we walked into the conference room, the unkempt man in a suit, no tie, thick glasses, was sitting patiently in one of the chairs. He was the polar opposite of Lopez in appearance. Next to him sat Armin Smith, and next to Smith, Major Pinchao. Lisa Velasquez was also present, since she now headed up JJ's tactical squad.

"What the hell's he doing here?" Bornstein asked, pointing at the guy in the bad suit but looking over at Lopez.

"Mr. Blattman is here at my request. His operational experience may help us analyze the information we hear."

"I don't want him here," Borenstein said.

"Come on, Adolph," the man Lopez referred to as Blattman said. "I've spent taxpayer money to take the shuttle up from Washington. You don't want to waste more resources, do you?" he asked, looking around the ostentatious room.

"This wasn't your operation, and you have no experience with information systems," Borenstein insisted.

"Last time I checked, human intelligence was an 'information system,'" he said, making air quotes. "And I've got loads of experience with terrorist groups and human intelligence." I liked this guy already. He had no fear of authority. Moreover, I gathered from what was said that Lopez thought Blattman would help him watch Lopez's back.

"Gentlemen, may I suggest we get started, it's quite late," JJ interrupted. "If Director Lopez wants one of his operations team here, and the man has the appropriate security clearance, then let's move on."

JJ's voice-of-reason bit worked, but it didn't go over well with Borenstein. His face contorted like he had just bitten into a peanut butter sandwich that had liquid soap mixed in with it. Still, he nodded and everyone sat down.

"First," Borenstein began, "I need to bring those of you who were not at the debriefing up to speed. Agent Alexandra Conrad has been murdered." There were some gasps, not the least of which was from Velasquez, who looked over at me. I kept looking down at the burled wood inlay. "Agent Sanders saw her shot point-blank in the chest three times."

"You sure of what you saw, son?" It was Blattman asking. Did he just call me son?

I nodded, then looked up at Smith. "You did not see her body anywhere?"

Smith shook his head. Pinchao offered: "It is not unusual for them to kill a hostage and take the body into the jungle. One of their tactics is to cut the body up and mail it piece by piece back to loved ones. Sometimes they will follow this practice up with a letter asking if the recipients had gotten their message."

"This actually creates a much greater prob—," Borenstein began to say before the conference room telephone rang. JJ, closest to the phone, reached over and hit the speaker button. "Yes?" Borenstein asked.

"Sir, we have an urgent call for you from Ambassador Moody from Bogota."

Borenstein looked around in surprise, then said, "Put him through."

The operator advised that they were connected, and Borenstein said, "Bill?"

"Yeah, Al, Bill Moody here. Listen, we have—"

"Hold on, Bill. I just want you to be aware I am in a conference room with representatives from the agency and the bureau, as well as Major Pinchao and Lieutenant Colonel Smith. Everyone here has top secret or better clearance."

"OK, thanks for that. We received a message from the FARC. Well, more like a film." My gut tightened. I knew where this was going, and it was nowhere good. "I have it downloaded and can send it to you. You all in a conference room?"

"Yes, Bill, we are."

"Al, you may have to get a tech guy in there, but if you've got a computer, PowerPoint projector and wall screen, you all can see this right now. I have to warn you, it ain't pretty. Looks like some torture and murder, figure it's of the event we heard about today."

Surprisingly, Al Borenstein was quite adept at the tech stuff. A panel in the table slid back and a keyboard rose up. Borenstein tapped away at that and a side controller. An overhead projector, quite subtly installed such that I hadn't noticed it before, turned on. A wall screen appeared from what I mistook for a long, thin ceiling air vent at the front of the room behind Borenstein at the head of the table. Within five minutes, Borenstein had the file on the wide screen. He clicked on it. "OK, Bill, we got it. If we need anything else, we'll call you."

"Wait a minute," I said. "Ambassador Moody, how did you get the video?"

"Who's speaking please?"

"Sorry, this is Agent Sanders." OK, I wasn't really Agent Sanders; I was Contractor Sanders. But he didn't know that, and Borenstein had addressed me that way earlier. "With the Financial Crimes Unit. I work for James Jordan."

"Thanks. The DVD was delivered by a messenger who was both paid and threatened by someone he didn't know to deliver it to us."

"Thank you, sir."

"Anyone else?" Borenstein asked. Everyone shook their heads, apparently eager to see Alexander Conrad get killed. I was not.

Borenstein hung up and clicked on the "Play" icon.

The video was quite clear given that it was shot in the dimly lit warehouse. It showed the entire scene from the point of view of someone standing behind me to my left. I was only partially in frame on the right side of the screen. Conrad took up the middle and left of the screen. The whole thing played out again. The burning, the slapping, the chair being kicked over and the shots. Before the screen went black, you could see the guy lean into me and barely overhear him whisper "Death to spies, Nicholas."

I tried not to react at all, to be a stone, but most stones don't sweat from the palms and forehead like I was doing. I got up and grabbed a couple of tissues from the credenza and water from the pitcher that was on it, then sat back down.

"I'd say that supports Sanders' testimony," JJ said.

Blattman was staring at me across the table. Then he turned to Borenstein and said, "I wish she were one of mine. She didn't give them anything. They were burning her skin and she said nothing. She had field training?"

"Yes" was all Borenstein said.

JJ, Velasquez, and I looked at Borenstein. This was news to us. I needed to get to the bottom of what was going on right now, so I spoke up.

"It doesn't make any sense to kill her. They got no information from her, and no ransom for her. All we were doing was trying to liaise with the major."

"They accomplished quite a bit by killing Alexandra and taking the bag," Borenstein replied. "As I was saying before Bill called, her death has caused a much bigger problem. Alex's death means we may never be able to break the FARC's encrypted communications, and therefore never stop the supply of arms running to them, or the hedge fund money funding the arms supply."

These statements sat in the air a little while as everyone considered them. I felt like a college freshman who thought he was pretty smart until he walked into the Advanced Particle Physics class.

"The FARC have encrypted communications too?" I said, stupidly. If I'd considered this for even a moment, I would never have asked it. A well-funded terrorist organization would have some kind of protected communications.

"What do you mean 'too'?" Borenstein asked.

"We asked Conrad to help us try to break the encryption we recovered from a Ponzi schemer named Jonathan Huntington a few months ago."

Borenstein looked at me quizzically. "I don't know who that is. Conrad never told me she was helping you on another case."

"It was the side project we mentioned the other day, and we hoped her talent in cryptology would be useful," JJ put in to head off what might have become a little bureaucratic pissing match.

Borenstein shrugged. "She already had the FARC's cipher key."

At this, both Smith and Pinchao leapt forward in their seats. "What?" they said at once.

"She was going to Colombia to give Major Pinchao the cipher key," Borenstein said. "The bombing investigation gave her a good excuse to make the trip."

Numerous people started talking at once, and I took the opportunity to lean across the table to Smith. "Colonel, what kind of encryption software was the FARC using?"

"Some fancy military grade stuff. I don't know the name. Ten twenty polymotal or some shit. The PhD down in Bogota identified it but couldn't break it. Said it really couldn't be broken."

I thought about this for a moment, and then said, "Son of a bitch!"

The room quieted and everyone looked at me. "Mr. Borenstein, are you telling us Alex Conrad broke the FARC's encryption?" I asked.

"No."

Everyone looked confused, except Borenstein and me, who were staring at each other. I saw the slight curve of a smile at the corner of his lips like he was playing "I've got a secret and someone else just figured it out."

"Fuck me," I said. "She wrote it."

Blattman closed his eyes and leaned back in his chair, like he was the last guy to catch up and hated it. "Shit," he said.

JJ turned to Borenstein. "Explain."

"Alex Conrad was recruited out of MIT for her ability to encrypt and decrypt. It was difficult to intercept FARC communications, however, because they had stopped using cell phones, radios, email, and other airwave communications soon after 9/11, when it became apparent we could locate the persons communicating. In fact, the FARC were living in the seventeenth century, practically speaking. Every message was passed on via human being. While it made it difficult for them to do business efficiently, it made it impossible for us to locate the sources of the communications—the group's leadership. What the FARC needed was a better, quicker method of communication. What we needed was for them to start using a modern form of communication so we could track them. We came up with a plan to accommodate both parties' objectives."

"You gave it to them," Blattman said, leaning forward, crossing his arms on the table.

"Oh, hell no, Paul. You should know better. You're the operations expert. You think we'd just give them 1024-bit polymorphic encryption?" At this, Smith looked at me, pointed to Borenstein and mouthed "what he said" motion. I nodded. "You think the FARC would just take it, no questions asked? 'Here, the Department of Homeland Security of the United States of America would like you to have this software so you can communicate with each other and we can hear what you're saying and see where you're saying it from.' No. We *sold* it to them. Through an intermediary, of course."

At this the entire room erupted. Lopez looked over at Blattman, who was just smiling to himself, almost like he admired the gambit. Various forms of cursing flew through the air. "Shit." "Jesus Christ." "Holy shit!" I had to remind myself to do a study at some point on the merging of religious and vulgar terminology.

"You sold it to them so you could break it?" I asked.

Borenstein nodded. "Elegant, don't you think?"

"How'd you sell it to them?" Velasquez asked, speaking for the first time.

"We had Conrad pose as a security consultant to a Cayman Bank which was purchasing and installing the software. One of the largest depositors of the bank was a hedge fund we connected to the FARC. Conrad made an approach to the owner of the fund, asking if he would purchase the software from her as well. The not-too-subtle undertone of this was that Conrad, a corrupt security consultant, would sell it to him at a significant discount, and all of his communications and banking transactions would be untraceable and unreadable to anyone without the correct cipher key."

"How much?" I asked.

"Excuse me?" Borenstein asked.

"How much did she charge? It had to be enough to make it worth the while of someone who risked losing their livelihood if they got caught—which Conrad was pretending to be—but not so much that it would scare off the individual you were selling it to, right?"

Blattman looked at me, nodded as if to say "good point" and waited for Borenstein to reply. "Ten million dollars, wire transferred to a DHS front company in Bermuda. The bank in Cayman, which thought they were buying software from a reputable manufacturer, paid substantially more—twenty-five million, plus ongoing consulting fees."

"So the U.S. government sold encryption software to a bank and a terrorist and made thirty-five million dollars?" JJ asked.

Borenstein nodded, adding, "To be accurate, we sold it to an arms dealer, who in turn sold it to the FARC."

"DP Partners?" I asked.

Borenstein nodded. "Yes. By all appearances a legitimate hedge fund. Run by a gentleman named Alejandro de Plata, who it took Conrad nearly two years to see once she started making overtures and working her way through the organization. Quite a secretive fellow. Then it was another six months for him to dip his toe in the water and try out the software. Once he was convinced the code was unbreakable, he went full bore. He in turn sold it to the FARC so that they could communicate with each other and schedule shipments and payments. Since then, not a single arms shipment has been intercepted, presumably because their communications were secure. Conrad had been working on this case for nearly five years."

My mind was working overtime now. Conrad didn't have a C.I. in the Cayman bank; she *was* the C.I. And I thought I knew how Huntington got the software too. "He also sold it to Jonathan Huntington. Jesus, Alex could have broken the Huntington code anytime she wanted to. Who knows who else this de Plata guy sold it to? We could have a whole network of Ponzi schemers we can't prosecute because the evidence is unobtainable but for the cipher key."

"Yes, well, that's actually the problem," Borenstein began to say.

Major Pinchao was listening intently to everything that had been said. He leaned forward and put up his hand. "Yes, Major?" Borenstein asked. The room went silent and all eyes turned to the major.

"If I understand what you are telling us, Director Borenstein, you could monitor the FARC communications with this de Plata from the start?" Borenstein nodded. "Therefore, we could have been intercepting the FARC gun shipments, disrupting their operations, and preventing hundreds of deaths if you had simply given us the proper passwords? But you chose not to?"

"Yes," Borenstein said simply. "For operational security, it was imperative very few people knew about the software. As we clearly have a leak somewhere in our communications, I must assert we chose correctly. Moreover, we had to convince the FARC that their communications were secure. The only way to do that was to allow them to operate unmolested. If we did not, they would not have distributed the encryption to their entire network. Even though we knew what was happening, and what they were doing, we couldn't let anyone else know. However, now that they are quite comfortable and have apparently, as proven by your recent raid on the jungle camp, passed the software out to their village network, we would now be in a position to take their entire network down at once."

"Who's we?" Blattman asked.

"Myself, Conrad, and the president, of course."

"The president authorized this operation personally?" Lopez asked.

"Indeed." Borenstein's revelation seemed to cut off any argument the agency would have had that Borenstein was stepping outside his authority.

"So what's the worse part?" I asked.

"For security purposes, Conrad was the only one with the cipher key." Silence. It was like a vacuum had sucked out all evidence that humans occupied the room—no warmth, no breath. Then a low rumbling, which developed into a chuckle issued forth from the man across the table from me. Paul Blattman was shaking. His glasses slipped down on his nose a bit. Everyone looked at him as if he had broken out of Bellevue.

"Ha!" He slapped his hand down on the table. Everyone jumped. "Well, you certainly screwed the pooch on this one, didn't you, Adolph? I admit it was a great idea, from which I conclude it wasn't yours. Brilliant, actually. It's just in the execution that things got cocked up. You just handed the FARC and their allies an unbreakable code that we can no longer break! This is classic. This is like the Bay of Pigs, only it's not on us anymore. Jesus, you really aren't an operations man, are you? When do you resign?"

"Are you through?" Borenstein asked, exasperated but defensive.

"Who's idea was it?" I asked. Borenstein looked over at me.

"Excuse me?"

"The original idea. For selling the code to the FARC. Who's idea was it?"

"Conrad's. When I brought her in to review communications, and she found the money passing back and forth between accounts we suspected belonged to FARC and DP Partners, she noted that it would be nice if we could verify it with communications between the parties. But as far as we knew, there were none. She suggested that if they felt certain their communications could not be intercepted, they would use electronic communications often. That was the genesis of the plan."

"So all that stuff in our office about there not being a connection, that was just bluster to keep us in the dark."

"Operational security. Echelon referred the murder cases to your unit, but we had to slow it down and control it, or risk the entire operation. That's why Conrad was attached to your case. There's a leak somewhere. We had to keep the information to as few people as possible."

Keeping a key piece of information limited to one person is risky, since if the person gets hit by a bus, or murdered by South American terrorists, that effectively ends the operation. "She really was field personnel, wasn't she?" I asked.

"Damn good too," Blattman said before Borenstein could respond. "Never gave those guys anything. The FARC still don't know DHS supplied their communications software. I wish she were one of mine."

"And we have no way of breaking the code?" JJ asked.

"Not without the encryption keys," Borenstein explained.

That's when I realized we still had the keys. "Shit. Wait a minute." I turned to Lopez. "Does the agency have some supersecret software that would help break the 1024 poly— really freakin' insane encryption?"

Lopez looked at me as if I were nuts. "First, if such software existed, it would be eyes-only clearance I presume you don't have. What I can tell you is we have a lot of code-breaking tools at our disposal, but my understanding is that there is not a single, all-powerful program that would magically break that encryption. And I'm pretty sure you'd have to have a quantum computer for that, which doesn't exist— yet, anyway. Why?"

"Before we left for Colombia, Conrad said she downloaded such a program directly from CIA servers to her laptop." At this the room broke up in gasps. Blattman said, "Bullshit." And Borenstein gave me a "you're insane" look. I gazed at Borenstein. "You don't have a direct line into CIA secure servers, do you?"

"What? Hell no! I have to go through the director if I need material like that. The analyzed intelligence is the only thing my office is regularly copied on." He could have been lying to protect a secret, but I didn't think so. The more I thought about it, the more far-fetched it seemed that Conrad could simply plug into CIA servers remotely. And now I thought I knew why.

Blattman spoke. "Look, far be it from me to defend Adolph here, but I've never heard of such a program, and while I'm not much of a tech guy, I should know. We read intercepted communications all the time. And this business of downloading a program like that remotely? No way. Something like that would be on a stand-alone, I think." He looked over at Director Lopez, who nodded in agreement.

"Good."

JJ turned to me. "Sorry, Sanders, you lost me. Just why is that good?"

"I think Alex left us the cipher keys. Before she left, she made a point to tell me that this supersecret agency software was chugging away on her laptop, and that she was leaving it in her apartment while we went to Colombia, that hopefully there would be results when we returned. What she was really telling me was that if anything happened to her, the encryption codes were in her apartment."

"Don't you think she would have told someone else? I mean, if she was in danger there, so were you," Blattman said.

"She did. Winkler was there when she was claiming to download this stuff."

"She just left it sitting in her apartment?" Borenstein said.

"Hide in plain sight. It was her MO. She carried the murder investigation files around in a backpack, for Christ's sake," I explained.

"OK, let's get over there," JJ said, turning to me. "Take Winkler with you, secure the laptop, take it back to our office. Al, you have her address, right?" JJ asked blandly. Blattman snickered. JJ suggesting Al might not know where his employee lived was ballsy.

"Of course I do." He leaned forward to hit the intercom.

"Can you share the file on the de Plata guy as well?" I asked. "Since we're all part of this investigation now, seems we should know who we're dealing with."

"Good idea." Borenstein buzzed his assistant, still in the office at 2:00 a.m. because her boss was still in the office at 2:00 a.m. She brought in Conrad's personnel file and a three-inch-thick folder labeled "DE PLATA".

Borenstein fished Conrad's address out of the file and I wrote it down. I was about to walk out, when I noticed the edge of a black-and-white photo sticking out of the top margin of the de Plata file. "That a picture of the arms dealer?"

Borenstein followed my eyes to the file, opened it, and retrieved the photo. "Yes, not a very good one, I'm afraid. It was taken from a camera hidden in a button on Conrad's blouse when she had her one and only meeting with him." He flicked the photo down the table like a playing card.

I picked it up and looked at it. It was grainy. It was slightly blurred, particularly at the edges. But Alejandro de Plata was in relative focus. "You gotta be kidding me," I said.

"What?" Borenstein asked.

I held up the picture. "You don't know who this is?"

"Yes, I just told you. That's Alejandro de Plata."

"Bad phrasing. You don't know his real name?"

Borenstein looked at me inquiringly "What are you talking about? De Plata has been a businessman in Latin America for decades. As far as I know, he has no aliases."

"JJ," I said, handing the photo to him.

JJ looked at it. His face registered curiosity at first, then minor shock. He shook his head. "No. No way, Sanders. Ain't him. He's dead."

"I never said who I thought it was, JJ, but you came to the same conclusion. You ever see his body? No one has."

"He'd have to be in his nineties by now."

"Nope, just over 88." Blattman leaned over, trying to get a look at the photo. He didn't recognize the guy and shook his head. "Agent Velasquez, what does Plata mean in Spanish?" I asked.

"What?" she asked, confused.

I turned to her. "Plata, what's it mean?"

Before she could answer, Major Pinchao spoke. "Silver."

I nodded. I held the photo up to Borenstein. "You want to know the biggest problem with operational security, Al? You don't have enough professionals analyzing information. Only you and Conrad saw this photo, right?" He nodded. "Well, this guy who's been selling arms to the FARC in exchange for drugs? This guy is Alan Sterling."

Chapter 37

Butterfield Bank Building, Grand Cayman, Cayman Islands; March 2008

Alan Sterling / Alejandro de Plata patted the edge of his computer screen. "Still rich," he thought. Actually, he was richer. He chuckled to himself in his Cayman offices, looking out over the port at Grand Cayman. Grand Cayman was an unplanned mix of business and residential buildings, with ultra-luxury resorts thrown in here and there to break up the landscape. Mickey Mouse smiled at him from the stack of a cruise ship docked at the port. That was an annoying ship, because every so often it played "When You Wish Upon a Star" quite loudly. He would be glad when the tourists boarded and departed. That said, it was slightly less annoying than the rooster that crowed every afternoon from the house behind his building.

De Plata (as he now thought of himself) was preparing to receive his best client, Jeremy Winfield, in two days. John Lester would be arriving the day before to set up security. In the meantime, de Plata had ledgers to doctor, client statements to produce, and investment policy statements to prep for the meeting. He also had to spend a tidy sum on a send-off dinner. He hated the expense and saw it as a worthless ceremonial exercise. The fact was, the real meeting and exchange of information would only take a few hours. But Winfield would be coming in the night before the meeting and would not depart until the morning after. This meant cocktails at the hotel, followed by dinner, all at the expense of DP Partners, even though Winfield was the one who asked for the meeting.

De Plata reflected on his priorities. He was eighty-eight years old and didn't mind spending his money on a comfortable existence. But money was primarily a *security* measure. Money ensured no one could fuck with him, because he simply had too much of it and could go anywhere he wanted. Consequently, de Plata didn't mind that he spent millions for John Lester's services. He didn't mind that his encryption software had cost him ten million dollars (this was, after all, a significant discount from the sticker price). And he didn't mind the legal fees he paid to draft documents establishing labyrinthine corporate entities all over the world. All of these expenses ensured that de Plata could continue to do what he did best—make more wealth anonymously, the growth of which ensured his continued security. Consequently, the large expenses he approved allowed him to sleep at night, knowing that he and his wealth were well-protected. He was rich and would stay rich until the day he died, which he still felt was somewhat far off. The fact that he had no one to leave his money to, and that logically he should spend it all before he died, was of no import. He *had* to have the wealth. If he had it, he was secure. If he did not, he was vulnerable. He was nervous. He could be thrown out on the street at any time. The money needed to remain in existence until his very last breath.

He minimized the screen giving him up-to-the-minute summaries of his various accounts and the investments in them, and maximized a ledger for DP Partners V. It detailed the mythical emerging markets commodity arbitrage strategy that the fund employed. Well, not completely mythical. DP Partners had such a strategy. It involved only two commodities: arms and drugs. De Plata's added touches of detail gave the ledgers and reports a ring of truth for any analyst, attorney, or forensic accountant who cared to look. Every fifteen minutes or so, he would flip back to his investments screen and watch the numbers tick ever upward.

JFK Airport

While professionals of every law enforcement stripe were converging on New York City, John Lester was on his way out of town, and he wasn't sure if he'd ever be back. He had made arrangements for his money to be transferred among his many offshore shell corporations in several jurisdictions. Not trusting anyone, he had set up these accounts in person, using account and routing numbers and passcodes that only he knew and that he never wrote down. God forbid he ever hit his head or developed Alzheimer's.

Lester arranged to fly a roundabout route through Miami to Mexico City, then to Grand Cayman. When he arrived in Mexico City, he mailed all documents referencing his U.S. alias to his mailbox service in Hoboken, where it would be held indefinitely. If he never returned, it would likely be disposed of. But as long as he continued to pay the box fee (wired automatically every month from a local bank account), he always had the option to return. He began using a Canadian passport under the name Andrew MacAdams. He only bought the ticket to Grand Cayman when he arrived at the airport in Mexico City. Unlike the United States, this was not an infrequent occurrence elsewhere, nor was the fact that Lester/MacAdams paid cash.

The job was simple. All he had to do was provide surveillance of de Plata's office in a building in Grand Cayman and be present at all the meetings between de Plata and Jeremy Winfield as a "security adviser." It would be unlikely that he would say a word the entire time. When the meeting was over, he would drive Winfield back to the airport, ensure he got on the plane and that the plane took off. Afterward, John Lester's career as hit man, security adviser, fixer, enforcer, all of it would be over. He didn't share his future plans with de Plata. Clients got twitchy when their hit man said he was throwing in the towel.

Valle del Cauca, Colombia

The next morning, Reyes and Marulanda recovered from their hangovers after celebrating the planned demise of Major Fernando Pinchao. When they got to work, emails were flying back and forth between them, Ignacio Guerra, and various jungle camps from which supplies would be shipped to the capital.

"We can't miss, Tirofijo," Reyes said. "This will be the final push that gets us out of the jungles and into the capital. So, we have to be ready to move within days of the president being killed. Two days, and we must be in the capital."

Marulanda nodded. They had studied the art of the coup over and over. Coups fell apart when the current leader was not killed. Gorbachev and Chavez had proved that. But even if the leader could be killed, the army had to be in disarray. It was through such power vacuums that successful revolutionaries were able to seize power. Consequently, not only would Uribe have to die, so too would his military staff. The FARC had sympathizers in the Colombian Army, but they were not near the top. If the top ranks could be removed, then their contacts in the army could seize control, order the troops to remain in their barracks, and the FARC could stroll into the Presidential Palace.

Luckily for the FARC, the president would be present at a Victory Day parade in the presidential box with his top military leaders. So, the first impediment was solved. Next was method.

Since it was a parade, a large vehicle could simply pull up and detonate a bomb. The problem with this approach was that bombs were random, lacked control, and couldn't guarantee the desired result. Numerous things could go wrong. Many leaders had escaped injury or death from bombs because of improper placement (Margaret Thatcher), premature detonation (Charles de Gaulle), and shielding/angle of the blast (Adolf Hitler).

A sniper, on the other hand, was far more reliable. But when multiple targets needed to be hit, the first shot served as a warning to the remaining victims, who would quickly cover, so that wouldn't do either. The only answer to ensure the deaths of all necessary victims was to have a platoon-sized force jump from the parade a la the Muslim Brotherhood attack against Anwar Sadat. If properly coordinated—and so long as the element of surprise was preserved—the gunfire and grenades would ensure the required deaths.

Reyes and Tirofijo were students of history: the history of capitalism, of socialism (both agrarian and urban), of dialectic materialism, and of terror. Useful lessons could be learned from many people of diverse backgrounds, including, and in some cases most importantly, your enemies. The FARC was no friend to the Muslim Brotherhood, but that terrorist group had shown Reyes and his followers the way forward.

✣ ✣ ✣

Mexico City, Mexico

There was just one last thing for John Lester to do before getting out of Mexico City for Grand Cayman, and it required making a phone call. That he made it from his hotel room and the call could be traced there was of no importance. He was registered under a false name and had changed his appearance. So, assuming they sent a couple of field agents around to take a look, he would be long gone and the description of the room's occupant would throw them off. They would assume the years had not been kind to John Lester. Or that he was wearing a disguise, which wouldn't help them in any event. By the time he got anywhere a camera could film him, his appearance, name, and documents would have changed yet again.

He dialed the number he had written down a year before. The paper had been carefully folded and placed in his wallet, and moved subsequently to two wallets since. The crease had caused the number in the center to fade, but it could still be made out. His single-use cell phone was plugged into his laptop, but not so that he could encrypt the call. He really didn't care. Rather, it would allow him from the moment the recipient's phone rang to trace the call using the GPS system. All CIA agents' phones had such tracking devices. Those not in the agency weren't supposed to be able to access them, however.

The phone rang and Lester saw the dot on the map flash. He was a bit surprised. Instead of Virginia, or Washington, it was pinging in New York City. He had waited until 3:00 a.m., because disorientation would be useful in delaying any attempt to trace. It would take Paul a minute to figure out what was going on. He would attempt, while appearing nonchalant, to notify someone at the agency using another device that the call he was currently on needed to be traced.

Lester knew he shouldn't make the call, which really only exposed him to danger. But he had made a decision that was in his best interests. He had decided to relinquish his hold on the hate and vengeance he felt, since he would likely never again step foot in the United States. There was no point, anymore. And he wanted Paul Blattman to know how lucky he had been. Because while Lester had (because it was expedient) decided not to severely injure Blattman, he had not forgiven him.

"Hello?" The voice did not sound sleepy, tired, disoriented, or even a touch drowsy. Blattman was wide awake at 3:00 a.m. Lester had no way to know that Blattman had been up at the Borenstein meeting until 2:30 and had arrived in his hotel room only a few minutes before, knowing he would be going back to regroup with everyone at eight in the morning.

"How's the Big Apple treating you, Paul?"

Silence. A long bit of silence. "Who is this, please?" Blattman asked.

"You know who it is, Paul."

"John? Jesus Christ. John?"

"Yes, Paul. You didn't think I would rot away in Southeast Asia, did you?"

"No, John, but you just disappeared. What the hell? Why didn't you come home?"

"You're kidding, right? To do what? Be brought back into the fold and sent to some other exotic location where I could be betrayed again and left in another prison where inmates tried to buttfuck me?"

"John, I'm not going to justify what they did—"

"What you did, Paul! What *you* did!"

"John, listen to me very carefully. I'm not tracing this call, and we can talk all night if you want. I was not allowed to mount an operation to get you out. A craven administration and a spineless director wouldn't let me acknowledge that you were one of ours. I wasn't allowed to trade for you, or to break you out. I told them you'd escape. And I was right! I was right, son!" Blattman sounded happy, almost joyous that his prodigal son had contacted him. This wasn't the reaction John Lester had expected at all. He didn't know what to say. He sat there, trying to process what he was hearing, thinking it all an act.

Blattman could tell he had an opening. "Look, John, I can meet you. Anywhere. Anywhere you want. I'd love to see you again."

"Talk over old times, something like that?"

"No, John, to debrief you, to bring you in."

"I don't think so, Paul. If you debriefed me, you'd have to arrest me."

Blattman knew what Lester was getting at. "You remember when we first met, John? That coffee shop where I stuck you with the bill? You were a bright-eyed kid who wanted to help your country. But sometimes, when you see the business side of doing your duty, it all seems to deteriorate, right? It's all the same. Them and us? Hell, you start to think they are us and we are them, but we're not. You start to think that your talents are being misused, that you might as well sell them to the highest bidder. You wouldn't be the first field agent in history to go native, John. It happens. And if you live long enough, you make a bundle. Jesus, it's been, what." Blattman did the math in his head, but was too slow.

"Eleven years, three months," Lester said.

"If you're doing what I think you've been doing, you're a rich man. But it's empty, isn't it? Working for the highest bidder. When you were here, you understood why you were doing what you did. Money's a wonderful motivator if your goal is to make money and nothing else. But it also makes you do things that if we suggested them, you'd tell us to fuck off, am I right?"

Silence.

"What did I tell you in the coffee shop? The hours suck, the pay's shitty, but you'd being doing something you loved for a good reason. Well, I was right then and I'm right now. People think money solves all their problems, that it liberates them. Bullshit. All the money does is make you a slave to the money.

You have to protect it, preserve it. But if you don't need it, no one can make you do something you don't want to do. If we told you to drop a bomb in a mosque where women and children were praying, what would you say? You'd ask us why, right? You'd want to know what they'd done. And if we said fuck you, we're paying you enough not to ask questions, you'd tell us to blow you and walk out, because the fact was money wasn't the reason you were working for us. You were doing it for patriotism, a sense of duty, honor. All the things that people make fun of, that some in this country claim corrupts our actions. Bullshit, John. It's when we forget why we're doing it that we get corrupted."

Lester sat there in silence, knowing he should break off the call. "Have a good life, Paul. You won't hear from me—"

"Wait! Wait, John, please. Look, all those years ago, I made the same mistake that you're making. Instead of telling the president and director to fuck off, I looked at how many years I had to retirement, made a calculation, and followed their orders. I shouldn't have, and I've regretted it ever since. I was wrong, John. I could have broken you out on the sly, used an offshore slush account to fund it, used mercs to do it, complete deniability, the works. I should have, but I was nervous that if it got back to me I'd lose my job. Let me bring you in, son. Please. Don't make the mistake I made."

"Too late for that I'm afraid, Paul. But it was good to talk to you." He was about to click off, but his curiosity got the better of him. "Paul, what the hell are you doing in New York? Are you recruiting? Or is it that deli thing I've been reading about?"

"John, I'd love to tell you what I'm doing, get your take on it, but I can't do that until you come in." Yup, deli bombing. If Blattman was on it, a domestic terrorist attack, they were pulling out all the stops.

"Good luck with the investigation, Paul. I hope you catch the party responsible." Lester did not mean himself, of course.

He hoped the agency would trace the bombing back to its real source, de Plata.

The line went dead. Blattman looked at his cell phone. He didn't bother to ask himself how Lester had gotten the number, or how he knew where Blattman was. Hell, Lester was probably across the street, eye behind the scope of a sniper rifle. "Damn." That was all he thought as he dropped the phone down, smiled slightly, and tried to get some sleep.

Chapter 38

Eastside Manhattan; March 2008

Winkler, Velasquez, and I took one of the Suburbans over to an address on the East Side. It was a nice building. Somewhat small, but most were. It had an elevator, which set it apart from many of the older rail houses in the area. The building even had a doorman, which made getting into the apartment easy once we showed our credentials. The man was familiar with Conrad, even though she had only been there a couple of weeks. I understood why. He was a man, and presumably heterosexual.

The doorman woke up the super, who fished out the key and escorted us up. I said to him: "The apartment will be sealed and not opened unless someone from our office, or other law enforcement agency with a court order, comes by. Do you understand?" He nodded, then opened the door and stepped away.

Velasquez pulled her service pistol. We really didn't think anyone was in the apartment or that anyone else had been there since Conrad was killed. But we weren't taking any chances. Velasquez did a quick sweep of the small studio and came back. "Clear."

"Thanks for your help," I said, turning to the super. "We'll call you if we need anything else." I closed the door. The layout of the apartment was simple: couch in the center, facing a wall with an entertainment unit. Kitchen beyond that to the right. Bedroom area to the left, and straight on, against the outer wall between two windows, was a desk with a laptop on it. There were a couple of shelves above it, set into the wall. On them were various knickknacks: a flashy red and pink ball cap with sequins, the kind I had seen a woman poker pro wear during the World Series of Poker; a DHS mug with pens and pencils in it; some books on programming with titles I couldn't pronounce; an MIT graduation photo (only three PhDs that year, at least in Conrad's department); and a box of Rosetta Stone software for learning Spanish. I laughed. It was just like an overachiever like Conrad to learn as much Spanish as possible because part of her most recent case had a Latin American connection.

We all approached the desk. "Pretty bling for Snow White," Velasquez said, pointing to the hat.

"Yeah," I grunted. "Damn, look." I pointed to the laptop, which was on but the screen blank. There was a Post-it note stuck to it: "Sanders, get this to Chris."

"She knew something might happen to her," Velasquez said.

"Mm" was all I said. Chris stepped forward and removed the Post-it. He tapped the spacebar and the screen came up. It was a usual Windows start-up display, with the Start toolbar along the bottom of the screen. Unlike most other computers, however, the screen had only a single icon above the toolbar. It was a movie reel titled "Click Me".

Chris looked over at me. "Should we get it back to the office?"

Unplugging the computer and taking it back to the office was the safe move. However, we didn't know what would happen if we shut the computer down and then tried to start it back up. We weren't sure if the information Conrad had provided would disappear or not. "Hold on," I said. I picked up my phone and dialed JJ. I explained the situation. He gave us permission to proceed. I hung up.

Chris sat down and Velasquez and I leaned over each shoulder. He clicked the icon. The movie player opened up, taking up the entire screen. It showed Conrad sitting at her computer in exactly the position Chris was sitting now. I looked above Chris's head for a camera and noticed that the laptop came equipped with one set into its lid.

"Hi, Sanders," Conrad started. The picture was a little jerky, not smooth like film, but it was certainly clear enough for me to see her somewhat-worried face. I closed my eyes and turned away from the other two for a second as Conrad's voice continued. "If you're watching this, something has gone wrong, and Borenstein's shitting a brick. Don't worry, he does that a lot." We all chuckled, and I took the opportunity to wipe my eyes. "It's extremely important you get this laptop to Winkler and he follows my instructions. It's OK if you want to stop the message now and shut down to get it to the office. It will restart just the same." She paused to let us do it, but since we could re-watch this at the office, we let it go.

"I'm sorry I had to lie to you, Sanders, but we couldn't let anyone know what we were doing. If Borenstein hasn't told you by now, I will, since you have to know to understand the importance of what Chris has to do. The 1024 polymorphic encryption program,"—here she paused a smirked—"you know, the really fucking hard encryption, well, I wrote it. I have instructions for Chris to access a subfile, and in there he'll find the master cipher key, the back door into the program. You have to get this to Major Fernando Pinchao as soon as possible. It will allow him to monitor all FARC communications and triangulate their positions. Whatever Major Pinchao does has to be coordinated with the CIA and the bureau, though, because they're going to have to go after the arms dealer, a guy named Alejandro de Plata, who runs the hedge fund DP Partners.

"Have Chris open up the My Documents folder and click on a Word doc titled 1024. It will give him the backdoor password and instructions for using it. There's going to be a lot of info all at once and not in any semblance of order, so you guys will need to take your time and put it in sequence, otherwise none of it will make sense.

"I'm sorry things couldn't have turned out differently, Sanders. I told you I had issues." She smiled into the screen. "Anyway, take care." Then she leaned close to the camera and whispered, "I still think Velasquez is jealous." She leaned back, smiled, and the screen went blank.

Velasquez smiled and laughed quietly, shaking her head. "Damn. Bitch was good. Sorry, Sanders."

"Yeah" was all I said.

We shut down the laptop and packed it up. We looked around the apartment one more time but didn't see anything of significance and left for the office. It was 5:00 a.m., and the sky was just starting to turn from black to powder blue.

Back at the office, Winkler followed Conrad's instructions, but it was slow going. The fact that none of us had slept in twenty-four hours (well, except for me) didn't help. Conrad was right: once Chris entered the code into the database for DP Partner's electronic funds transfers, a bunch of code came up that, if you looked close, you thought you could make out dates, but that was about it. Transaction amounts got lost between routing numbers and account numbers. Chris would have to isolate the sequences that repeated. These would be the account and routing numbers. Then he could match them with amounts and dates. Conrad provided instructions for writing some code to unwind and match transactions among multiple institutions, but what was surprisingly difficult was determining sender and recipient. Looking at the raw data, you couldn't tell which way the money was flowing.

By three in the afternoon, Chris was able to print out a year's worth of transactions spanning 2005 to 2006. The very cool thing was that not only did we have account numbers, we had account *names*. The money coming from ASBT, as well as other domestic banks, was easy to determine because it was flowing from American institutions to banks in Cayman, Bermuda, Antigua, BVI, and other jurisdictions. Plus, the numbers tended to be big compared to the other transactions. It was once the money came out of DP Partners that things got a little tough to discern. You couldn't tell what was a legitimate company and what was a front company. DP had a $10 million payment early in the year going to a Bermudan company named Gold Star Trading, which we presumed was the DHS front company. Borenstein confirmed this for us later. Cash deposits were made into DP Partners V account all over the Caribbean and Latin America, in various amounts and in numerous currencies. We were pretty sure these represented the drug trafficking profits.

However, DP Partners, while maintaining a couple of billion in their account, also appeared to be spreading their cash among many other accounts. For while it seemed in this single year that $2 billion flowed in from the U.S., then $1.5 billion flowed out, $3 billion more was deposited in cash transactions all over the region. So DP's account balance after deposits should have been $3.5 billion. It wasn't. It was about $2 billion, which meant $1.5 billion had been "invested" elsewhere, either legitimately or illegitimately. We didn't know which.

"This is going to be harder than we thought," I said. "We need to see the corresponding FARC front companies too, and the other recipients. Can we do that?"

"Eventually," Winkler said. "But first I have to organize the data, match transactions, then put it in a form someone other than Neo can read." Chris was making a little geek joke—Neo was the main character from *The Matrix* who could see the world he lived in as pure code.

"Well, Chris, shitty deal, but you're the only one who can do it. Let's regroup at, say, 9:00 p.m., then we'll knock off for the night and you can try to get some sleep. Velasquez and I will stop standing over your shoulder."

"Sounds good."

I presumed Velasquez was going to want to go home and get some sleep in the interim, but she didn't. "I don't feel much like sleeping, Sanders. Let's you and me go out and get shitfaced. It ain't fun losing a partner."

"All right."

We ended up at Mel's Corner Tap. I was having a Guinness, Velasquez was drinking a Stella with a side shot of vodka.

"Fuck that! The MP5? It's a kid's toy! You can drop an AK in mud, pick it up and it'll still fire. Way more stopping power than an H&K too!" I wasn't exactly shouting, but we had been drinking awhile and our voices were raised. Velasquez loved to talk guns, and we had an ongoing debate about the best handgun, the best sniper rifle, the best assault weapon. She was a fan of the MP5. I, obviously, was not. But really I was just trying to get her riled because it was funny to watch. Since your choice of weapon depended on how it would be used, I offered a stealth, nighttime assault scenario: Mafia don is holding an agent hostage in a well-guarded seaside dockyard. How do you assault, and what is your choice of weapon?

"Jesus, Sanders, you don't know shit about guns, do you? Go back to practicing law. The AK's too fuckin' big for a surprise assault, and you'd have to spend time taping it up with electrical tape or rubbing it down on the barrel guard and the butt with black shoe polish. The MP's all black. It can be modified to fire more rounds, and easily silenced. You ever seen the silencer for the AK? First, you'd still hear that *clack clack* the bolt and chamber make—no way to silence that. Then the barrel silencer? Fuckin' thing's about ten inches long. Makes it too big and bulky. Try whippin' that out at a moment's notice. Guy like you, you'd catch the barrel on your leg, end up shootin' yourself in the foot."

"Oh, that's such bullshit." I laughed. "MP5 doesn't have enough power. What if the guards are wearing vests? You can try Teflon bullets, but that's like putting them in a pistol. You'd have to go for a head shot to make sure. Why do you think the AK's so popular? Versatile, foolproof, a lot of stopping power. Freakin' Russians know how to make a gun, that's for sure."

Lisa raised her vodka. "I'll drink to that," she said and downed the shot. After she put the glass down and her face recovered from its contortion, she said, "Hey, Sanders, look, I wanted to let you know something." She was slurring just a touch. "Friggin' Conrad. That girl was solid. I know you liked her. I didn't at first. Hell, I thought she was the leak. But she proved herself, man. I know you liked her. I'm really sorry, Sanders."

I nodded. "Friggin' A she was solid. More than we knew. She was more field ops than any of us." I took another drink. "She couldn't have been the leak, though."

Lisa looked at me, squinting. "Why not?"

"Huntington. She wasn't around until after the Huntington thing. And if the leaks are related, then it couldn't have been her. I think they're related. Doesn't make sense they'd be independent, especially since Huntington had the same encryption software."

"So what? Why tip the guy?"

"Whaaddya talkin' about, Lisa?" I noticed I was slurring too.

"You been lookin' at *how* the tipoff happened, not why. Why would someone in the bureau tip off a Ponzi schemer? What do they gain?"

I was about to drink but put my glass down. "That's—a—good point," I said between burps. This was getting ugly. I tried to cover my mouth after the fact. "Gotta be on his payroll, right? So, once we're done with de Plata and the FARC, we're gonna find payments going to an account belonging to someone inside the bureau, aren't we? That's it, right? Huntington was paying someone to keep him up to speed on whether he was the target of an investigation?"

She nodded. "Thass what I think, Sanders." I ordered us a couple of waters.

"Naw, wait. That doesn't work," I said. "If he's paying someone off inside, how do they not know about the raid until the morning of? Right? I mean, if it was someone in the raid party, or even in JJ's unit, they're gonna know days in advance that we're gonna raid him." I shook my head. "Gotta be someone outside the unit who had access to communications, otherwise it doesn't make sense. And that same person either monitored the Lazeris call or one of the calls we made right after to set up the meet. Gotta be someone outside, but who had broken in on our communications."

"Wait. You saying that the same person somehow found out about your meet with Pinchao in Colombia? How? Who knew that? All the phones had been changed by then. None of it went over email, did it?"

"Not that I know of," I said, sucking down the whole glass of water. "I gotta think about it more."

"Hey, Sanders?" I looked up at her. "You're a friggin' great agent."

I was shocked. That was the biggest compliment I had ever gotten from Velasquez, and the biggest compliment I ever heard her give anyone. "Thanks, Lisa" was all I could say.

"And Snow White was right. I was jealous. A little." She was looking down into her glass as she mumbled this. She downed the rest of her beer, then said quickly, "Let's go check on Winkler."

We weren't in any condition to check on anyone and needed to go get some sleep. Nevertheless, we stumbled back to the office. Chris was still occupying a conference room, paper strewn about the entire table, but organized somewhat in piles.

"At the far end is 2005, and we get closer to the present as you work your way toward me. I could use some help on this."

He looked at both of us. I didn't realize the office was on rollers until then, as the room swayed like the deck of a ship. "You know what?" he said, apparently noticing our condition. "Why don't you guys go home? I'll go home. We'll come back in the morning and do this."

"Great idea," we said in unison and walked back out.

Back on the street, Velasquez gave me a quick hug and said, "See you in the morning." She turned and walked down the street, relatively steady. Certainly steadier than I felt. I turned around and walked to my subway stop. When I finally stumbled into my apartment, I collapsed on the couch, instantly asleep.

Chapter 39

In flight over the Gulf of Mexico; March 2008

John Lester slept fitfully on the plane to Grand Cayman, despite his fully reclining first-class seat. His conversation with Blattman was a bad idea. All it did was create doubt, and the last thing a man like Lester needed was doubt. Many security professionals (as Lester liked to call himself) or mercenaries (a slightly more accurate but less-kind term) or hit men (just rude) tried to justify their actions. There were plenty of things you could say to explain why you killed people in exchange for money, most of which blamed the victim. And, truth be told, most marks were unsavory themselves. At the very least they were thieves or bribe takers; at worst they were murderers themselves.

But Lester knew this was all bullshit. It was about the money, pure and simple. You did it because you could make a huge amount of money in a short time. And you got to do something you were good at. And, God forbid, you enjoyed it. Most people enjoyed what they were good at. He liked the money and he liked the work. He was good at it. Somehow, Paul Blattman had seen that nearly twenty years ago, before Lester had even so much as stepped on an ant.

"I'm rich, I'm done. What the hell? Stop squirming about it, you pussy," he thought to himself. Try as he might, he couldn't sleep. He could only think. And he didn't like what he thought.

Jungles of Eastern Ecuador

The key was choosing enough men you could trust, who wouldn't back out at the last minute or run to someone in authority. This was no problem because Reyes and Tirofijo had been nurturing relationships with key soldiers in the army for many years. They knew who the loyal ones were (loyal to the FARC, of course). Then there was planning the details, something Reyes knew was not his strong suit. He and Marulanda were strategic thinkers, big picture planners, CEO-types. The details of a particular operation would be left to men like Guerra, who were excellent at that sort of thing, as he had proven in killing Pinchao and the American agent. Reyes emailed Guerra the time, place, and method. Guerra would take care of the rest.

Hamilton, Bermuda

Jeremy Winfield landed in Bermuda and went straight to three meetings in a row at hedge funds in downtown Hamilton.

Bermuda is a wonderful place and would be a wonderful island on which to retire, if you could purchase property there. But recent laws made that difficult for noncitizens. The fish-hook shaped island is twenty miles long and two miles wide. The government wasn't eager to extend rights of citizenship to many non-islanders, or at least not beyond the immediate family of non-islanders. Not that Winfield really thought about pursuing it. Truth be told, he knew he would never retire. He'd rather die first.

Bogota, Colombia

In Bogota, Ignacio Guerra received and acknowledged the email from Reyes. He was being given a big job, the biggest of his relatively young revolutionary career. Guerra knew that if this operation succeeded, he would have a high place in the new government, a governorship or vice presidency. The fact that Guerra had no experience in government or management did not occur to him. He knew how to organize equipment and people to kill other people. Such skills were transferable.

Chapter 40

Midtown Manhattan; March 2008

"Hey, Sanders," she said. "How ya feeling? You look like shit, ya know?"

Velasquez was in her cubicle, bright-eyed and refreshed. I was hungover. Damn, why do I let my coworkers do this shit to me?

"I can get that from my ex. Let's go see Winkler." I walked down to the conference room with Velasquez in tow, and there was Chris Winkler hammering away at the keys on Conrad's computer. He had inserted a flash drive into the side to save material. Borenstein and JJ weren't there, and I presumed they were talking to Al Lopez, and maybe that Blattman character.

"You guys want to start down there at 2005?" Chris asked. We went to the end of the table, and I split the 2005 transactions with Velasquez. What had been decrypted were transactions between DP Partners' accounts in the Cayman bank and its clients around the world. Since we didn't have access to DP Partners' computers or hard drives, the only material we were looking at were records of transactions where the bank had been used as the clearinghouse or intermediary.

It was difficult to decipher, but there were clues based on dates and transaction sizes that allowed us to guess which were DP Partners' shell corporations, which were FARC front companies, and, if our analysis was accurate, what the money was for. We could see payments to shippers operating out of Venezuela and Colombia. What we didn't have was any email between these parties, which would have been helpful. Even with the hard drive Pinchao had recovered, it was slow going. We had transactions but no context. That's when I had an idea.

"Anyone seen Blattman? Seems like he's a guy that would be able to help." Everyone shook their heads. I went to JJ's office suite and talked to Barry, who let me know Blattman was at breakfast in the executive dining room with Borenstein and JJ.

"We have an executive dining room?" I asked.

"Yes, Mr. Sanders, reserved for VIP meetings. I presume that's why you've never been there." Everyone's a comedian.

"Where is it?"

"Twenty-one, but your card will not get you access to that floor. Why don't I interrupt them?"

Barry picked up the phone and called, and after some discussion Blattman came down. When I explained our predicament, he nodded. "Sorry I didn't think of it myself. Not sure how much help that's going to be, though. If Echelon monitors an encrypted communication, it creates a file and stores it indefinitely. Problem with this is each communication is going to have a distinct file, and since this software masks not just content but location source …" He was thinking out loud now and turned away from me, his head tilting to the side. "Hmmmm. See, kid, here's the thing." Did he just call me kid? "Echelon is gonna organize those files with whatever information it has. So, if it's encrypted and there's no content to identify source or subject matter, it'll rely on source of transmission and file it that way, essentially geographically. So, for instance, let's say a drug dealer in Mexico City gets on an encrypted satellite phone and schedules a pickup at an airport.

The call's encrypted, so we don't know what's being said or who is saying it. The only reason Echelon makes a record is *because* the call's encrypted. Now, in typical encryption, Echelon can still identify location based on triangulating the transmission source. So, Echelon would create a file that says something like 'Encrypted phone transmission, Mexico City' and might even have an address or cross street, or longitude and latitude, and the date of intercept.

"Conrad's program prevents triangulation too. So all you'd have is a file labeled 'Encrypted' and a date. So you have to narrow your search to those files, between date X and date Y. Son, there could be a million of them in a single year."

"For a guy who doesn't know tech, you seem to know a hell of a lot about Echelon."

"Do me a favor. Don't tell anyone, OK? I got Borenstein and Lopez thinkin' I don't understand what they do. I wanna keep it that way." He winked. "Anyway," he continued, "my suggestion is that you give me the date parameters and we'll look for unsourced encrypted communications. Probably want to keep the file small, too, so that whatever you decipher will be short and we can go through a lot of them. If we seem like we're on the right track, we can pick larger and larger files."

"Let's start around dates that we know money transferred from DP Partners to what we think is a FARC arms supplier." I gave him a date. "Let's do one week on either side of that and see what we get."

"OK, I gotta make some calls and then it'll be a while. This has to come from a secure server to a secure server, or so they tell me." Yeah, like he didn't already know. "So we'll need Lopez to sign off, JJ to get us a secure server, and then a guy I know at army intelligence to give us the data."

"Why army intelligence?"

"They run the listening devices and satellites that make up Echelon. This could be a few hours, but I'll let them know it's a pressing matter."

"If they want, Borenstein could probably have the president call them."

"You only wanna pull rank in this business if you absolutely have to. Otherwise, you just piss people off, get a bad rep, and no one wants to work with you." From what I could tell, everyone wanted to work with Paul Blattman. Except Adolph Borenstein. I'd have to ask about that sometime.

Between Blattman working the email/phone intercepts side and us working the organization of transactions side, we had a pretty good picture by the end of the day of how money was flowing between DP Partners and numerous front entities. What we could tell was that DP was making about five-to-one on its money. For every dollar that went out, within a year DP was bringing in five dollars. One billion gets you five billion. But what was flowing back to investors in DP, like ASBT's clients, was about a 15 percent return. So DP Partners was making a lot more than it was telling its investors.

It wasn't until Blattman came through with the emails that we saw the full scale of the operation. In the time period I had identified, a Mr. P sent an email regarding payment to a Mr. R, who replied with a date and time for payment receipt. After payment for "products" following this exchange, a Mr. R sent Mr. P an email confirming receipt of a shipment. After expanding our search out, we noted that DP Partners' contact with FARC members was almost exclusively between Mr. P, who we presumed was Alejandro de Plata / Alan Sterling based on the context of the messages, and Mr. R, who we thought was Raul Reyes.

The beauty of Conrad's program came through here. Not only were we able to see what was being said between the parties, but the GPS coordinates of the sources of the transmissions were saved in a subprogram within the messages themselves. The senders had no idea this information was being recorded. By the end of the day, we knew de Plata was based in Costa Rica and the man we thought was Reyes was moving about on the borders of western Colombia, eastern Ecuador, and Venezuela.

I would have thought that the job would get easier, since we knew what we were looking for, but in some ways it was harder. First, with the proliferation of encryption software in recent years, there were more encrypted messages to search, even unsourced ones. And even though we found messages between Mr. R and a Mr. L about action on the eve of the deli bombing, the actual text was so cryptic that proving it in court would be another matter.

"Mr. L, huh?" I heard Blattman mumble at one point as he reviewed the email.

"What?" I asked.

"Huh? Oh, nothing. Could be anyone. Mr. P, Mr. R, no way to actually prove who is sending the messages, and they seem to have codes within codes. These guys don't trust anyone."

"Would you? You know it's encrypted, but you might as well keep whatever messaging convention you had before, right?"

"Yeah, I guess," Blattman said, looking down at the table, considering something. I left him to his thoughts and went to Winkler, Velasquez, and Pinchao.

"Anything from the days before our Colombia trip?"

"We got something from a Mr. R to a guy in Bogota, but that's it," Velasquez said.

"Weird. No one sent anyone an email message from the U.S. about it," Chris added.

"We're missing something. It had to be coordinated, and it had to be connected to everything else, doesn't make sense otherwise," I said.

"We haven't touched cell communications yet. There could be voice or text messages."

Later that evening, as pizza was delivered, we all regrouped in the conference room.

JJ, Borenstein, and Lopez were present. JJ summed it up: "Looks like Mr. P is in Cayman, and Mr. L will be meeting him there. Looks like L lives or works in Hoboken, by the way, so he's a good suspect for the deli bombing. Reyes is still in the jungle as of his last message, but the FARC have got some operation that they're planning. He keeps texting a guy in Bogota but never uses a name. Messages are going three ways: Reyes to Bogota, back to Reyes, and then from Reyes to Marulanda and a couple of other camps." By now we were all quite familiar with the command structure of the FARC and the names of the players. "Question is, how do we use this information?"

"Gotta take them all down at once. Otherwise, they'll figure out communication is no longer secure and stop sending and move," Velasquez said.

Pinchao spoke up. "I agree with Señora Velasquez—"

"It's señorita," Velasquez threw in.

"*Pardóname*, señorita. We need to take as many camps down at once as we can *and* head off their planned operation."

"And that'll make the news and tip off Sterling, not that it matters much," I said. "We can't get an executable warrant against Sterling in Costa Rica or Cayman. This might put Winfield in danger."

"We've found nothing connecting him to this?" Borenstein asked. I'd almost forgotten he was in the room.

"No encrypted communications from ASBT to any of these people, at least that's decipherable with Conrad's key," Chris said. "In fact, not much of anything to anyone in the States, except for what we think is the deli thing."

"Only from Mr. P to this guy in Hoboken, and he looks more like a hitter than anything, judging by the messages," I added. "I never really thought there was much in it for Winfield anyway. I don't think he's involved."

"Well, he's a U.S. citizen about to meet a drug and arms dealer," JJ said, "and it doesn't look like he knows who he's dealing with. Do we know when they meet?"

"No, Velasquez and I were supposed to go over to ASBT and talk to his assistant, but we got sidetracked."

"OK, Sanders, go wake up the secretary if you have to. Let's find out when the meeting is. Al, I'd like you to deputize Ms. Velasquez and Mr. Sanders. We're going off U.S. soil, and the Cayman government can't know about it." I was surprised. JJ was pretty by the book when it came to what we could do, and leaving U.S. soil for anything if we weren't invited by a foreign government was pretty out there.

Borenstein looked at JJ and said, "I'm not sure I have the authority—"

"Sorry, not you, Al. The other Al, Director Lopez." JJ turned to Al Lopez and said, "Other than Mr. Blattman, there's no one in the agency familiar with the players and with what's going on. We need to get Winfield out of there and see what we can do about Sterling, if anything." JJ was right about the lack of personnel on the agency side. Borenstein's need for secrecy had assured that the agency was kept out of the entire investigation until the last minute. But it was a stretch to think we could arrest Sterling. He'd have a habeas writ to the Supreme Court faster than you could say "rendition."

Lopez looked at JJ, then Blattman. Blattman's head nodded slightly, and he shrugged a little. "Look, JJ, I'd feel better if I had someone at least nominally heading up whatever you're considering, and we need to talk to justice about Sterling, if that's who he is. There may not be much we can do."

JJ looked at Blattman. "What about it, Paul? You want to lead this team of misfits for a couple of days?"

"I haven't been in the field for years," Blattman objected, then smiled. "I'd love to." He looked at Lopez, who nodded. It was the only choice that made sense.

Resigned, Borenstein looked down the conference table at everyone. Events had overtaken his carefully planned operation.

A course of action was being dictated to him instead of by him. "Well, Major, you and Colonel Smith better get back to Colombia. Chris will liaise with your tech support down there so that you will be able to monitor FARC communications in the field. Mr. Sanders, we need to know when and where Winfield is meeting de Plata. Ms. Velasquez, you will lead tactical, with Mr. Blattman close at your side. Al, JJ and I will contact justice and work on what, if anything, can be done with de Plata. Let's get moving."

Chapter 41

In flight over the Gulf of Mexico; March 2008

"We don't have enough troops to take down all the camps at once." Smith stated the obvious to Pinchao on the unmarked C-130 back to Bogota.

Pinchao nodded. "Not enough we can trust. Jaramillo will need to lead one team. I can't show my face in public, so will need to lead a jungle camp raid. Colonel, I would like you to lead a third team. I might be able to put Montes in charge of a fourth. That's all, plus protection of El Presidente."

"So how do we choose? Leader camps first?"

"I have been thinking about this. From what we have been able to see from the decoded traffic, there are two camps that have high-profile hostages. I think we must free them. Otherwise, they could be in danger if those camps become cut off from the leaders. There may be standing kill orders if Reyes or Marulanda are captured. That leaves two more camps with leadership to choose from."

Smith nodded. The only thing left to be decided was which teams would take which camps, and how. This was the hardest part. How?

✵ ✵ ✵

Bogota, Colombia

For Ignacio Guerra, the how was the easy part, at least the how at the end. It had already been decided for him how the president and his general staff were to be assassinated. But he had to arrange for all of those soldiers loyal to the FARC to be on the same vehicle in the parade. This would require the intervention of the logistics officer.

Unfortunately, the parade planner was not a FARC sympathizer. That would have been too good to be true, Ignacio realized. Well, the man did have a family. And since the FARC had the practice of kidnapping down to a science, it would be a simple matter of blackmailing the man into getting what they wanted. It would simply take a few more resources, which was no problem for Guerra.

Chapter 42

George Town Harbor, Grand Cayman; March 2008

S o you may have asked yourself how U.S. agents smuggle all the arms they need into another country without its government knowing it is happening. Or maybe you don't dwell on such things. If they're on official business, there is an established, if lengthy, procedure to allow certain individuals (such as secret service agents) to carry firearms. But what if they aren't on official business?

In most countries, save Iceland or Tonga, the weapons are already there, in the underground market. The CIA (and local law enforcement, usually) knows who the arms traders are. And, since the agency doesn't want to arrest these people, but rather deal with them when needed, the CIA operates through a trusted intermediary. So, you could say that the U.S. is partially supporting the illegal arms trade of other countries. Of course, you could say the same about many other countries vis-à-vis the U.S.

The Cayman Islands, it turned out, had large caches of illegal weapons. Such weapons are rarely used on the islands themselves. Much like real police officers, Cayman criminals rarely fire their weapons in the course of a crime. Most shoot them off while they're drunk on some random Independence Day (Caribbean countries have a lot of those). And in Cayman, the criminals know better than to kill someone who really matters, like a tourist. Tourists, after all, are most of their drug business in the islands, so that would be biting the hand that feeds you. No, criminals are at least bright enough to know to be selective, take their quarry offshore in a boat, do the deed there, and dump the body in the ocean.

Blattman had many contacts in the islands, and within a few hours of our arrival, Blattman, Velasquez, and I found ourselves on a boat in Grand Cayman Harbor, looking at a false bottom panel, beneath which a hidden compartment was full of assault rifles, firearms, and ammunition. Velasquez was like a kid in a candy store.

"She'll take the MP5," I said. The Rastafarian fishing-boat captain and drug and arms dealer leaned down and pulled one out. "I was kidding," I said.

"You're a dork, Sanders," Velasquez muttered. "Holy shit, is that a Barrett 107?" she asked, titling her head at a particularly long rifle toward the back of the compartment. He handed it to her. She held it at arm's length at first, studying it. Then she quickly brought it in close and opened the breach. She took a long smell, like testing the bouquet of a particularly cherished Bordeaux. "You keep 'em well oiled," she said.

"'Course I do, missus," the smuggler/fisherman answered.

Velasquez worked the breach several times, studied the stock and the balance, then looked down the barrel from the trigger to the end. She slowly worked her hand across the barrel, feeling for imperfections in the workmanship. It looked like she was starting a relationship with it. "This'll do," she said, turning to Blattman. Blattman had been giving me a "where'd you find this chick?" look, but covered it well when she turned toward him.

"Sanders?" Blattman said.

"H&K's fine," I said.

"I'll take the Smith," Blattman said. He turned to Velasquez. "You want a backup piece?"

"I don't plan on getting in close, but … you gotta shoulder holster to go with that Sig sidearm?"

Mr. Weed 'n' Gun smiled. "Lady knows her guns. No, I don't have a holster for that. But I got one for the CZ."

"That's a winner, I'll take it."

"We'll need a duffel bag," Blattman started to say and looked at the Barrett sniper rifle, "a long one, for transportation."

"Sure, Paul, no problem," the guy said, moving past us to the back of the cabin.

I turned to him. "Paul?"

"Gerald and I go back a long way, to the Carter administration, right Gerald?" he answered.

"Yeah. Those were dark times for my country," Gerald said as he went to the back of the boat and retrieved a duffel bag.

"He doesn't look that old," I said.

"He was twelve when I met him. Selling reefer to tourists. I got him started in the gun trade. Find 'em young, support 'em, they'll be loyal for life," he explained. After a pause he said, "Most of the time."

So not only were we supporting the local gun smugglers, we started the industry. "Some day we're gonna have to have a beer and talk over your life, Blattman."

"Call me Paul. I'll let you buy me a beer, but the last thing I'll do is talk about my life. I'll tell you some wild stories about Stansfield Turner. Hell of a drinker, that one. Hated human intel, though." He turned back to Gerald. "Gerald, we're supposed to be meeting a guy named Alejandro de Plata, you know him?"

"Of him. He owns the Grand Cayman Golf Club & Resort. The casino is the biggest on the islands."

"That's where Winfield is staying. Narrows it down, sort of. But they could be meeting anywhere," I said. Then I got an idea. I pulled out my cell phone. "You got a phone book?" Gerald didn't have a phone book, but his fishing boat bridge had a display with various resort and activity vendor pamphlets in it. One was for the Grand Cayman Golf Club, with an address and number on the front. After a couple of false starts learning how to correctly dial using a U.S. cell phone, I got the front desk.

"Hello, this is Jeremy Winfield. I am to meet Mr. de Plata this evening at the hotel, and I'm ashamed to say I've forgotten the room we were to meet in. Could you—"

"Certainly, Mr. Winfield," a cheery English-accented woman's voice interrupted. "Mr. de Plata has arranged the Presidential Suite for you tonight, top floor of the west wing. Best views of the ocean. Mr. de Plata has arranged for a private dinner. We look forward to seeing you."

"Thank you so very much," I said in my most eastern blue-blood accent. Wow, that was easy. Pretty sure Sterling would want to know his staff so easily revealed his location to others. I looked at the front cover of the brochure. The hotel was set back from a wide white-sand beach. It was a twenty-five story half-circle affair, the concave side facing the ocean. So top floor, west wing. Helpful, but we still had to do some ...

"Reconnaissance time," Velasquez said as she broke down the sniper rifle and packed it into the duffel. We dropped all our handguns in it too.

"Paul, we're gonna need rooms at the hotel," I said. We needed them for two reasons. First, we needed an excuse to be there. Second, we needed a place to stay that night if nothing happened.

Reconnaissance from the exterior was no problem, but once we stepped into the hotel we would be on camera and, if we had only standard or deluxe rooms, our movement would be restricted to the lower floors. The upper floors, with high-end rooms and suites, were accessed by sliding the room key into a slot in the elevator, allowing the key holder to then press the button of the selected upper floor. Luckily for Blattman, CIA maintained a cover travel service which allegedly specialized in luxury travel. Its representatives had contacts at all the major resorts around the world and were able to get available rooms at a moment's notice for "VIPs." One call and Blattman got himself a suite two floors below the top floor, but in the east wing. Velasquez and I were each relegated to a room on the lower floors. We went straight to Blattman's room.

The accommodations were ridiculous. A living room, full dining room, butler's pantry, two bedrooms, and three baths. We stepped out onto a balcony that was nearly as big as my studio apartment in New York. Velasquez went back to the bed, opened the duffel and pulled the scope off the rifle. She looked across to the top floor in the west wing.

"Eh. Not great. Balcony wall blocks my line of sight. I need to be up on the same level. Hey, someone's moving around in there."

I took the scope from her and looked through. There was a guy who appeared to be in his thirties, tall, well-built, walking through the expansive suite. He was looking behind chairs and couches, giving it the once over. "Let me see that," Blattman said. I handed him the scope.

He looked through it. He pulled the scope down immediately and said, "Back inside, slowly. Very casual, no sudden movements, just turn around." We did as we were told. Blattman closed the slider, then the curtains. He created a small opening and looked through. "I'll be goddamned."

"What?" I asked.

"That's de Plata's head of security. I don't think he saw us."

"You know him?"

"I used to."

"That's it? 'I used to?'"

"Yep. That's all you get. Classified and all. You understand." He pulled away from the window and threw the scope to Velasquez. "This guy, he's one of the best. I doubt we're getting into the room. We're gonna have to stop Winfield before he goes in there. Do we know where Winfield is now?"

"Yeah." I looked at my watch. Noon, local time (I had learned my lesson with the Colombian fiasco). "I know where he'll be at 3:00 p.m. I have an address on Church Street in George Town."

Blattman thought some more. "Agent Velasquez, you're not gonna like this, but I think I want you to stay here and cover the suite. If we miss Winfield, or something goes wrong, you need to be able to see if de Plata and Winfield show up here and report."

"You're right, I don't like it, it's stupid," Lisa responded. "If something goes wrong, no one's gonna show up here. De Plata and his enforcer are gonna run for Costa Rica, and the only guy who might show up could be Winfield, if he's not dead. Besides, if anyone should stay, it's you. The muscle knows you. He sees you, it's all over."

Blattman considered this for a moment. Velasquez was absolutely right. We had no idea where Sterling was, but we did know where he would be, and that meant both Winfield and Sterling's security would be there too. "Well, you can't very well carry a sniper rifle around the banking district in daylight," Blattman objected.

"We're gonna need wheels," I said. "Lisa and I go to the building, I go in, and Velasquez stays in the car for surveillance and support. The rifle stays in the duffel in the trunk. She's got the pistol in the shoulder holster."

Blattman looked between the two of us. He finally relented. "OK. I'll have the concierge arrange a car."

Velasquez looked at her watch. "We got four hours. I'm gonna take a nap."

"Three hours. Change your watch," I said to Velasquez.

"Same time zone, Sanders," Velasquez responded.

"They're always on daylight savings," I said, like I'd known it forever. And something occurred to me then, scratching at the back of my brain.

Chapter 43

Bogota, Colombia; March 2008

The problem with trying to locate someone transmitting coded messages, and confirming your belief about the code they're using, is that they have to actually send a message you can intercept. And the problem was the FARC didn't send messages all that often, even with their "unbreakable" system. Smith and Pinchao thought at first that they could try to coax a communication by using Conrad's system to send their own false email to a FARC camp. But the risk of attempting to send false messages using your enemy's code was that the alleged sender, the person you were posing as, might actually see it. Consequently, convincing the purported sender of the message to *actually send* the message with the content you wanted would be much better. American codebreakers did this successfully before to the Battle of Midway: they tricked the Japanese into sending a coded message relating to Midway Island that confirmed the code word the Japanese were using for the island, which in turn revealed it as their intended target.

In Pinchao's case, sending a message to the camp he *thought* was holding the high-value targets and telling them to release the hostages would never work. Such a message would certainly be confirmed prior to it being acted upon, and Reyes would immediately deny he had sent it and realize his encryption system had been compromised. There would be no way to locate Reyes, Marulanda, or anyone else after that discovery. Smith offered the Midway solution. Pinchao's office would send a message in the clear that a camp had been located at the coordinates they *thought* corresponded to the hostage camp. Reyes would, through one of his numerous spies in the army, intercept it and then likely send an encrypted message to that camp, allowing Pinchao to triangulate Reyes's position. After the message was sent, Pinchao and Smith moved to the next meeting, this one with the president of Colombia.

Jungles of western Colombia

Felix Corrivas reviewed the email from Reyes. *Damn.* The army had found their location.

C: Competitor may have located your factory. I am sending a chopper to retrieve your guests. One of my assistants, Sr. Larayeva, will lead the retrieval team. Please show him all cooperation, then prepare camp for movement. Sr. Larayeva should be there by late afternoon.

Bogota, Colombia

Ignacio Guerra put his arm around Staff Sergeant Rojas. "Look, we have no interest in harming them. Your daughter is beautiful, as is your wife. Your son, he is your image, no?" Guerra held up a picture of a woman and two children. The young girl, who looked to be about nine, held up the newspaper from that morning showing the day's headline. A masked man with an AK-47 stood behind them in the photo. Guerra wore a uniform he had been given from a contact in the army, a lieutenant's uniform. He had had to shave and cut his scraggily hair, which he had not wanted to do, but sacrifices had to be made for the revolution. He was asking Rojas to make one now.

For Rojas's part, had this man not held his family's lives in his hands, he would have knocked his arm away, stood up, pulled his sidearm and shot him point blank. As it was, he could only sit there and let this man touch him. He hated the weakness, the utter emasculation he felt. The man's arm burned as it touched him. This guy had simply walked into his office, unchallenged by anyone on the base (clearly he had assistance from sympathizers in the military), and sat before him. He threw the picture on the desk, and explained what he wanted.

Staff Sergeant Rojas was a master of organization. For every major event to take place at the capital involving the military, Rojas was called upon to plan the logistics. And he was a smart man. But he could not organize any way out of this situation other than to cooperate. He understood the FARC's reputation: they did not kill hostages needlessly, and returned many once they got what they wanted. They would get what they wanted here.

✲ ✲ ✲

Bogota, Colombia

"I was afraid of that," Smith said. The triangulation came back with the location from which Reyes had sent his message. Raul Reyes was in a camp five miles over the border in Ecuador.

Pinchao picked up the phone. After a few minutes, he was able to get through to the party he wanted. "Mr. President? We have had another development and will need your approval to proceed."

Chapter 44

George Town, Grand Cayman; March 2008

Velasquez pulled up a couple of blocks from the building where the meeting was to take place. I was betting Winfield would hole up somewhere down the street where there were numerous coffeehouses and bars, walking distance to this building. He should stride just past our car.

Twenty minutes before the scheduled meeting, an SUV (an unusual sight in Cayman) with blacked-out windows pulled up to the curb in front of the bank building. The guy who had been looking around the hotel suite got out of the driver's side, then opened the curbside door. An elderly man exited the car. His scalp was completely bald, the tan skin only slightly sagging at the back of the neck. He wore an open-collared dress shirt and cotton pants, leather shoes, no socks. He moved with surprising verve.

"Sterling."

Velasquez squinted. "What? That guy? He isn't eighty-eight. He ain't even eighty."

"Must be all that clean living. Looks like him."

The two men entered the building.

"You're going in there, right?" asked Velasquez.

"Yeah," I replied.

"You can't be wired. Guy like that will sweep you."

"Agreed."

"OK, look." She reached into her pocket and pulled out a tiny button-shaped object. "Drop this in your ear canal. It's a wireless ear-bud speaker." I did as instructed, and she had me turn my head several times to confirm it could not be seen, even looking straight at the ear. Velasquez then pulled out her cell phone and a headset.

"You can't talk to me with that. They can monitor it," I said.

"It's secure. B set it up before we left. It's not really a cell phone, just looks like it. It's a transmitter. B put it in a cell body so it would look like I'm talking on the phone. I need to test the level. I don't want to blow your eardrum out." She turned on the phone/transmitter and spoke a few times. After a few adjustments, I could hear her clearly. And even though she was right next to me, Velasquez could not hear the ear bud make any noise.

"Next thing—gun. You can't bring it. They'll check."

"Yeah. Here." I reached back and pulled the gun and holster off my belt, handing it to Velasquez. And beginning to feel very naked. "If things start to go bad, try to hide it in a place I can get to. See that planter next to the building walkway?" She nodded. "Say, between the first and second shrubs from the door on the left as you face the building."

Ten minutes later, in the side mirror, I saw Jeremy Winfield approaching us. I stepped out of the car, keeping my back to him, leaning into the car until he was almost just on us. I turned on him quickly and blocked his path.

He looked startled at first, then confused. "Agent Sanders?" He recovered quickly. "I didn't know the FBI had jurisdiction outside U.S. borders. I think the media will want to know you're interfering with legitimate business offshore." It was a good gambit, and predictable. I had one of my own.

"The man you're about to meet with is an internationally wanted fugitive. If you're knowingly doing business with him, that makes you an accessory. And it makes your bank a money laundering operation, since you are funding drugs and arms deals with U.S. dollars. How do you think the media will like that?"

"What are you talking about?"

"The man you are meeting is Alan Sterling."

He seemed surprised, but not very.

"You need to get your facts straight, Mr. Sanders. Alan Sterling has been dead for nearly twenty years."

"I would be too if I could pay a Costa Rican doctor for a death certificate."

"What do you want, Mr. Sanders?"

"Simple. Cancel your meeting, feign illness, whatever, and pull your clients' money back as soon as possible."

"Agent Sanders, do you have any idea how impossible what you're asking is? I have a fiduciary responsibility to my clients to perform due diligence. You're preventing me from doing that. Moreover, if the man is who you say he is, do you really think he'll honor my redemption requests? I presume given your presence here, your agency will be arresting him, and then it will be quite impossible for any money to be returned."

He was right, of course. If I could get in there, verify Sterling's identity, and fill out a declaration to that effect, the Cayman government might be obligated to apprehend him. "Take me into the meeting."

"You are out of your—"

"Yeah, yeah, my ex says the same thing. Take me into the meeting or I'll arrest you right here and we'll work out the legalities later. Just introduce me as an analyst that you've hired recently and you're bringing me along, showing me the ropes."

"You're a bit old for that, aren't you?"

"Just do it, Winfield, or this thing is over before it starts."

He looked at me, thought, and said, "You use your real name so I don't have to remember a lie. You introduce yourself and then keep your mouth shut. You say nothing, understood?"

"Understood. I just need to verify his identity, that's all."

"You're a tad underdressed for one of my associates, so I'll tell them your baggage was misplaced."

"Fine." I turned to the car and leaned in to talk to Velasquez. "Stay here. Watch the front. Something happens, call Blattman. And if something bad happens and you have a chance to take out the enforcer, do it. OK? Call Blattman, let him know what's going on." She nodded.

"OK, let's go," I said, and Winfield and I walked the remaining block and a half to the bank.

"Some guy just jumped out of a car and talked to Winfield. They're walking together to the building," Lester heard in his earpiece.

He spoke into his wristband microphone. "Description?"

"Late thirties, brown hair, six-two, athletic. Light coat, probably hiding a weapon, khaki pants, golf shirt, leather shoes."

"Thank you."

"One other thing. The car the guy got out of, driven by a woman, she's staying. What do you want me to do?"

"Hold until I call you back. Need to know more."

"Copy."

The man Lester was speaking to was an off-duty Cayman police officer and an on-duty de Plata employee in a moving van parked across the street from the bank. He had a full view of the street in both directions and the front of the building. Lester never took chances, and he was already glad he had not in this case.

Winfield led the way into the building not bothering to hold the door open for me. I was a little surprised that his upper class manners had deserted him, but he was pissed. I would have been too.

We took the elevator to the fifth floor and found DP Partners' office in the corner. Judging by the other tenant names I saw on the wall next to the doors along the way, I figured DP had only a small portion of the floor. This surprised me, especially considering they had billions under management. Old habits die hard— Sterling wasn't managing anything, and was spending as little as possible to maintain a façade of a real business. I am sure if I asked him about it, he'd tell me they just ran a lean operation, no point in spending money on fancy offices, put the money to work for the client, yada yada.

Just before he turned the door handle, Winfield turned to me and reiterated: "You don't speak unless spoken to. I will lead the discussion. And if everything goes well, I prove to you Mr. de Plata is a real money manager and all of our clients' money is safe. You may even get a nice dinner out of it." He smiled wryly, then turned back and opened the door.

While the offices were small, the décor and furniture was top drawer. All mahogany and oil paintings. Winfield would feel right at home. A brunette in her late thirties sat behind a desk with a headset on, speaking into it. Her phone was ringing. "I'm sorry, may I put you on a brief hold?" she asked the caller in a proper British accent. After a short pause, she hit the hold button and then another button. "DP Partners, may I place you on a brief hold? Thank you." The phone rang again and she repeated the greeting. Then she looked up at us.

"Mr. Winfield? And ... guest?" she asked, looking at me.

"Yes, my associate, Nicholas Sanders."

"I'll let Mr. de Plata know you are here." She dialed. "Mr. de Plata, Mr. Winfield and his associate, Mr. Sanders, are here. Yes, sir." She looked back up. "Mr. de Plata's assistant will be up to collect you momentarily." De Plata's head of security came out a door to our right seconds later. Now that I could see him clearly, I thought I might have seen him before. When he looked at me, I saw the briefest flicker of curious recognition, as if he couldn't place where he had seen me before. He was a bit taller than me, and despite the fact that he wore a business suit, he was obviously quite fit.

John Lester did recognize Nicholas Sanders, immediately. He had seen him the day of the deli bombing, getting out of the sedan, walking toward the deli, then being called back. FBI? Off U.S. soil? Doubtful. This was going to be interesting.

"Mr. Winfield?" Less a question than a statement, but with a little rise in the voice for courtesy's sake, not to be presumptuous. Lester stuck out his hand. "John Lester, Mr. de Plata's personal assistant." They shook hands all around, all gave a short, firm shake. "Gentlemen, I don't mean to insult you. However, Mr. de Plata is quite meticulous about security. I'm going to have to pat both of you down, as well as run a wand over you."

"Seems a bit much for a due diligence meeting," Sanders said, and Winfield turned and glared at him. He looked down sheepishly.

"Well," Lester responded, "let's just call it DP Partners' due diligence. I'm also going to have to hold on to cell phones and Blackberries until the meeting is over." The two visitors looked at each other, and the Sanders guy looked like he was going to protest. "Gentlemen, we cannot have the threat of transmission or recording of the meeting, since the fund's strategy will be discussed. I'm sure you understand." Both men reluctantly handed over their phones. Winfield and Sanders were lead into a secondary office, and Winfield was patted down thoroughly and a metal-detecting wand was run across all sides of his body. Then Lester did the same for Sanders.

It could have just been me, but it seemed that the "personal assistant" spent quite a bit more time checking me over, going so far as to run his fingers through my hair, which I found a bit disturbing. If he had whipped out an ear scope, I could have been in trouble. The earpiece, made mostly of plastic, didn't set off the wand. We were finally lead to a conference room. At the far end of the table sat Alan Sterling. Tan. Liver-spotted skin pulled tight across a bald head. Splotched, wrinkled hands resting lightly on the table. It's the hands. Always the hands. No one ever has work done on them. Women get their faces and breasts done. Men with a certain vanity have targeted work done about the eyes, jowls, sometimes the cheekbones. But the hands are always the giveaway because there's really nothing you can do about them. These were the hands of a near-ninety-year-old. The ironic thing was that de Plata's efforts to stay young gave away his identity. He looked like Alan Sterling looked in newspaper file photos before he absconded with his loot those many years ago.

Despite his age, he certainly did have energy and enthusiasm. De Plata nearly jumped out of his chair and met us halfway across the room. "Mr. Winfield," he said. "I'm so pleased to finally meet you."

"As am I," Winfield responded. "Please, call me Jeremy."

"Excellent, excellent. Call me Alejandro." The accent was decent. A tinge of Latino accent with formal English, the sign of a Latin American businessman who was used to dealing with Americans and Europeans and was at great pains to speak like a native English speaker. Sterling had no doubt spent quite a bit of time perfecting it.

Winfield turned slightly and introduced me as his associate. Sterling shook my hand and then ushered us to the table. There were some thick files on the desktop, to which Sterling motioned.

"These are the files reviewing the investments for the past twenty-four months, as well as the algorithmic trading strategy the firm uses in choosing its buying or selling position, both from a timing and quantity standpoint. For obvious reasons, I can't allow you to copy the files or take anything with you. It all stays in this room. Also, ASBT's agreement with the firm has a lengthy nondisclosure clause, which I'm sure you'll be mindful of."

It was a good show. The entire time, Lester stood in the corner to Sterling's right, out of the way but never out of reach. At one point early on, he leaned in and whispered something into Sterling's ear. Sterling said nothing, just nodded. After that, it seemed like Sterling's mind was in two places at once. Answering questions and at the same time making calculations. A bit later, he motioned to Lester and whispered in his ear. Lester nodded and went back to his spot in the corner.

Winfield wasn't exactly Sam Donaldson to Sterling's Ronald Reagan. His questions were softballs, designed more to gauge Sterling's character and philosophy than anything else. After about an hour, Lester stepped out of the room, and twenty seconds later, stepped back in. Sterling looked up at him, nodded, then said, "Well, I was going to suggest dinner in my suite at the hotel, but I must admit I'm getting tired of the place. So, I've arranged for us to have dinner on my yacht in the harbor."

Shit.

When Lester leaned in and spoke to de Plata, he had whispered he believed the Sanders guy was a government agent. De Plata had only nodded, then waved him back and told him to move dinner to the boat. Lester then stepped out to take care of Sanders' backup.

"OK, moving dinner to the boat instead of the hotel," Lester said into his wrist mic as he stepped out of the conference room and closed the door. "Delay the girl, but don't harm her. Just make sure she can't follow."

"Copy that," Lester's cop-on-the-take responded.

The off-duty cop then called his on-duty partner, who pulled up on a motorcycle behind Velasquez, still sitting in the car, two minutes later.

I heard Velasquez's voice low in my ear. "Crap. Sanders, I've got the local cops on me. I'll see what he wants but I won't be able to transmit for a while."

"Miss, you can't be parked here." The man was dark and tall. He wore uniform shorts and a short-sleeve shirt but carried no weapon other than a club on his belt. "I noticed also that your registration is out of date."

"Sorry, it's a rental." Velasquez handed him the paper-work. He looked at it, then walked to the back of the car and leaned down, apparently comparing the plate with the papers in his hand. He then stood up and walked back to her window.

"They gave you the wrong papers for this car. Not unusual, it happens often. Many of the employees do not read well. In any event, you should contact the rental agency as soon as possible, and please move around the block where there is a formal parking spot." He handed the papers back, pointed to the next street past the building Sanders was in, and walked back to his motorcycle.

"Sanders, gotta move the car. I'll be north of your position when you come out." Velasquez turned on the car, not noticing that she drove over some small spikes near the rear tire.

The whole thing was becoming a shit show, and fast. I had no weapon, no phone, and was dubious of my ability to overpower John Lester. Velasquez was on the move, and we weren't going back to the hotel, where Blattman was sitting on his ass waiting for us. I saw Lester put his hand to his ear, then excuse himself and step out of the room again.

✻ ✻ ✻

"OK, she's down around the corner," Lester heard in his earpiece. He stepped out of the room and put the mic to his mouth.

"Disabled?"

"Copy that."

"OK, we're heading to the boat. Can you follow?"

"Negative, my shift started a half hour ago. I gotta get to the station."

"OK, thanks for your help. I can handle it from here." Lester turned and went back in. He saw Sanders finishing up a call on the conference room phone and wondered how the fuck that had happened in the thirty seconds he was gone.

✻ ✻ ✻

I decided to take Lester's absence as an opportunity. "Pardon the interruption, Mr. Winfield, but I have to check in with your assistant, Rebecca, regarding our next meeting. We're on a tight schedule," I said, by way of explanation.

Winfield was about to say something when Sterling interrupted. "I have a phone on the boat which you can use. We might
as well get going." He stood.

"Why not now?" I asked.

"You're on a tight schedule," Sterling responded.

"Mr. de Plata, it's almost closing time," I said, looking at
my watch. "In fact, she may have left already, and if she has to
make changes to our schedule, she'll need to be in the office to do
so. I can use this phone," I said, reaching for the handset on the
conference room table. I had the phone in my hand and was dial-
ing. Sterling looked like he wanted to say something but stopped
himself. I quickly dialed Velasquez's cell, remembering to punch
in the country code first.

Velasquez picked up and answered merely with "Hello" in a
curious manner, probably because she didn't recognize the number on her phone.

"Rebecca, hi, it's Nick Sanders with Mr. Winfield. Yes, well, I
just wanted to make sure you confirmed our meetings for tomorrow. We may be out of touch for a while on Mr. de Plata's yacht
... Yes, he's apparently got a fine dinner ready for us ... Could
you call Paul and let him know our flight times? Just send the
confirmations to our email and we'll get them later tonight. OK?
Great, thanks." I hung up. Velasquez hadn't said a single word.

Once I hung up, I heard Velasquez's voice low in my ear
again: "Copy, calling Blattman, going down to the docks."

The moment I hung up, a restless Sterling said gruffly, "OK,
let's go."

As we were walking down the hall, I heard Velasquez again in
my ear. "Sanders, we might get separated. I'm going to put your
gun and holster in the flower bed next to the walkway. If you can
get to it without being seen, get it." God love her.

✳ ✳ ✳

While Lester's rent-a-cop was walking away from the scene, he missed seeing Velasquez exit her car and walk quickly back to the main drag. She took a left and headed up the walkway to the building. She looked down at her shoe and pretended to tie it, planting the gun in the planter about five feet from the door. She stood, turned, and walked back to her car, hearing the door to the building open and several men speaking as she did so. Just in time, she thought, resisting the instinct to look back over her shoulder at who was coming out. As she rounded the corner at the end of the block, she saw the left rear tire of her car. Dead flat. Goddammit, she thought, scurrying forward and leaning down to look at it. She felt around the tire and nearly cut her hand on several embedded spikes. She put her phone to her ear and hit the transmit button. "FYI, Sterling's security has local help." Then she called Blattman.

I hung back as we exited the building. I saw the edge of my holster just a few feet from the steps descending from the front door. I kneeled, pretending to tie my shoe, and the three men kept walking. Lester could feel I had dropped behind. He stopped and began to turn. Before he did so, I grabbed the holster and clipped it to the back of my belt in one swift movement, standing as I did so. By the time Lester's eyes were on me, I was standing up and walking slowly toward him, appearing to have simply dropped back. I picked up my stride to catch up to the group.

Chapter 45

In flight over western Colombia;
March 2008

Armin Smith was on a helicopter with just one of Pinchao's trusted soldiers. The rainforest zipped by beneath them, a fast moving strip of green that, if you tried to look at one piece of it, tried to make out a single tree, would make you dizzy and nauseous.

The "team" had done its weapons checks. The team consisted of two men, Smith and Manuel Vaya, as well as a pilot and copilot. Rather than the normal American-supplied materiel, the group's guns consisted entirely of weapons seized from the FARC. The team's uniforms were a mix of worn army camo and urban street wear. Vaya wore a bandana. Smith wore a Chicago Bulls cap to hide his gray hair. While he spoke perfect Spanish without a trace of American accent and was well-tanned, he still did not look Colombian; therefore, he would not take the lead in this operation. Caution was the better part of valor. He thought about Pinchao, probably also on his helicopter, worrying not about his own upcoming raid, but the three others he could not see or control.

✵ ✵ ✵

In flight over the Colombia-Ecuador border

Indeed, even while his team was checking their American-supplied weapons, Pinchao's mind was wandering. Had Smith's team landed? What about Jaramillo? Was the president protected? How was Montes coming with the rescue? Damn. Too many things had to happen at once. If one operation failed, it would still be a successful day. But it was the lack of control that bothered Pinchao. And the not knowing.

"Five minutes to LZ, Major." The pilot's statement registered in Pinchao's earphones. Pinchao nodded and turned to the five men, the lead team, on his chopper. Two other helicopters followed close behind with ten men each. They had no way of knowing how well-protected Reyes's camp was. Was this enough men? Who knew? It had been enough on prior attacks. But this was Raul Reyes.

Pinchao's mind snapped back to the moment, and he forced himself to concentrate. He recalled what he always trained his men: focus on the job. There was no such thing as multitasking. All that meant was you did many jobs poorly. One job at a time, with all your concentration.

✵ ✵ ✵

Bogota, Colombia

"Looks like two kids sitting on the floor watching TV. Can't see the wife. TV sounds are loud, so can't make out any other noises."

That wasn't a bad thing. That meant the bad guys wouldn't hear them coming either, Montes thought.

"Got two guys with rifles out at ready in the TV room, sitting behind the kids at our three o'clock. Pistols in waistbands. No others in the room," said Montes's number two, Mario, as he pulled his face away from the lens of the thread camera they had fed through a tiny hole drilled silently into the wall of the apartment next door.

"Well, she's in there, and someone's watching her, so minimum of three bad guys. Assume as many as five, but that seems like a lot."

"Agreed. Position isn't good. Can't blow through the wall. Kids will be in danger, maybe even hurt by the explosion," Mario pointed out.

It had all looked so good on paper. When they looked at the plans as laid out by Staff Sergeant Rojas, the next door apartment seemed the best option for a quick entry. The walls were thin, made of wood and cheap drywall. Most of the square footage of the second floor apartment, save the kitchen and the master bedroom, could be seen from there. Rojas had taken a huge risk in contacting Jaramillo, who he assumed was in command since Pinchao had been "severely injured, close to death." For security purposes, they did not dissuade Rojas of this widely held belief. And Montes had promised he would retrieve the family safely. He hadn't even bothered with the "I can't make promises" or "These things can go bad" or "You can't predict what a desperate man with a gun will do" protestations. "I'll get them back" was all he said to Jaramillo. *Fuck, what an idiot I am*, he now thought.

So far, the most dangerous part of the operation was gaining entry to the next-door apartment. It shared a hallway with the Rojas residence, so quietly advising the owner that the army needed to occupy his apartment was dangerous. Then the team drilled through the common wall and their plan had gone by the boards. They could not blow the wall out, followed by flash-bangs, when the children were right there.

And that's when an incredible thing happened. A stroke of luck so random, so unlikely, that it surely meant three things: the terrorists were unprepared for the operation; they didn't suspect they were being watched; and they had never seen any movie in which hostages were rescued. One of the FARC gunmen turned to the opening of the kitchen and said: "Laurente, can we get something to eat? We've been here over ten hours. I'm starving." Montes and his four companions looked at each other and smiled: Time for the Latin American variant of the cop posing as a pizza delivery man.

Bogota, Colombia

"Lieutenant, you are going to have to do the best you can with what you have. I will not change my plans."

Jaramillo knew this would be the president's response, but he had to at least try. "I understand, Señor Presidente. You understand what we think the FARC is planning? It is quite a difficult position to defend if they get close."

"Yes, Lieutenant, I understand. I also understand that Major Pinchao believes you are his best man from both a strategic and tactical planning standpoint. I have seen the after-action reports and am inclined to agree. So, other than me not attending the parade, what can we do?"

"I have several ideas in that regard, sir. First, we have to fill the presidential box with many of my men. This will mean displacing some guests, but that can't be avoided. Next, I would suggest moving your chair back one row. You will still be able to see the parade quite well, but it will put us between you and the FARC. Also, I need some dress uniforms for my men."

"Don't they have their own?"

"Yes, sir, but none that will make them appear to be senior staff. If it looks as if you have increased security, the FARC agents will wonder why and may call off their attempt."

President Uribe looked at him curiously. "Forgive me, Lieutenant, but wouldn't that be a good thing?"

"Sir, we have an opportunity to capture urban FARC operatives and gather intelligence on their chain of command in Bogota, something we have been unable to do to date. This is why I would urge you to not be in the presidential box. We could use a double, lure them into their attack, and capture or kill many of them."

"Absolutely not. Use me as bait if you wish, but I will not show weakness to these terrorists."

"Yes, sir."

✫ ✫ ✫

Bogota, Colombia

While Pinchao's teams were checking their weapons and plans, Ignacio Guerra's men were doing the same in the privacy of a warehouse near the parade grounds. Guerra was able to secure an officer's dress uniform for himself, including a "scrambled egg" shoulder loop and a forged grounds pass clipped to his sharply starched pocket. All of his men, also in dress uniforms, would be riding on the outside of the troop transport carrying well-oiled and loaded M-16 rifles set to fully automatic.

"Everyone ready?" All ten men nodded. "Good. No hesitation. The moment you are parallel to the presidential box, you begin firing, jump off the transport, continuing firing, and move forward deliberately, but not running. Once you see the president is down, you run back to the transport. It is very important none of you run while firing. It makes you less accurate, and you might hit one another as you cross fields of fire. Everyone understand?" Nods and sí's all around. Ignacio smiled and gave a quiet, confident nod. Everyone jumped on the vehicle, and it drove out to take its place in the parade ground.

✵ ✵ ✵

Jungles of western Colombia

Smith felt a light bump as the helicopter settled down. He stayed in the chopper as Vaya jumped out. Vaya carried a rifle, but looped on his back, and looked generally disheveled and unorganized. They had seen the camp from the air as they approached, but the LZ was several hundred yards from it. Consequently, they expected to wait a few minutes until a messenger from the camp leader summoned them. As it turned out, they did not wait long.

Two men walked through the heavy foliage, emerging as if from a green envelope that parted. Behind them came three people in dirty, tattered urban garb: a woman who looked to be about fifty but who they knew was in her late thirties; a man about forty, and a small boy who could have been five or ten (hard to tell with the bad diet that he was subjected to).

"Subcommander Larayeva?" the lead man called.

Vaya nodded. He stood his ground—not approaching, arms at his side—while simultaneously exuding both caution and a definite air of control, exactly as one would expect of a soldier given the important task of retrieving hostages from a camp he had never been to.

The leader smiled. "I am Felix Corrivas, camp commander. These are the hostages Señor Reyes has requested for you." Vaya nodded and waved the hostages forward and past him into the chopper cargo area, where Smith assisted them aboard. Smith saw Vaya's head tilt slightly, as if he was considering something, and then Vaya spoke. "Señor Reyes requests you accompany them to his camp for a debriefing. We will return you here tomorrow. Do you have a second-in-command who you trust to leave to dismantle the camp?" It was pretty bold. Vaya was trying to retrieve the hostages *and* a high-value terrorist at the same time. As the three hostages were settled in, Smith could see the face of Corrivas register pride, which then gave way to fear. Corrivas apparently wasn't sure if he would truly be coming back from Reyes's camp. Vaya saw this also. "He is concerned only with the health of the hostages, particularly the boy, and wishes to thank you personally for taking care of them."

Vaya was really shooting in the dark. Intelligence reports had suggested that Reyes might be the father of a hostage's child, and the female hostage and son fit the parameters of what they thought they knew. But this was far from certain. Nevertheless, Corrivas nodded his head in understanding, saying, "I followed Señor Reyes's instructions regarding the boy to the letter."

"He knows," Vaya answered. "Please, get on board and we will have you back in the morning. We need to get moving." Corrivas began to move forward, then stopped. He now heard what Vaya had heard, the reason he was speeding Corrivas along: the distinct, low, rhythmic *thumpthumpthump* of another helicopter in the air.

Shit, Smith thought.

✳ ✳ ✳

Jungles of eastern Ecuador

Big camp, thought Pinchao as he gazed down the slope of the Ecuadorian jungle hill he sat atop, camouflaged by the trees and leaves. Bigger than they had expected based on past experience. Still, it could be done. As long as the Ecuadorian Army didn't unexpectedly drop by in the next few hours. They had to be in and out. President Uribe knew what was at stake. This would without doubt cause an international incident. If successful, most countries would side with the Colombians. But unsuccessful? A military raid in a neighboring country's territory? And a daytime raid at that. Not ideal. Much risk. Failure was not an option.

"Generator to the south," Edgar Montevideo said, handing the field glasses to Pinchao.

"Hmmm," Pinchao responded, looking through the lenses. "And they've learned the lesson about putting the fuel near any buildings." He shifted the glasses north, to his right. The preponderance of buildings lay immediately below them, flowing down the slope to the valley floor. It was at least fifty yards from the building to the generator.

This was more than a camp. Given the reassuring haven of Ecuadorian territory, Reyes had built a small town. Hence, numbers could be a problem. But it also meant surprise would be that much more of an advantage. No one believed that Colombia would violate the territorial sovereignty of its neighbor to pursue the rebel army.

Pinchao scanned the airspace above the buildings. Despite the fact that they were well-supplied, the fact remained that this was a camp in the middle of the jungle and required everything to be brought in on horseback. Resources were meted out sparingly, and only some of the buildings had power going to them.

To the west, many people, including children and women, were engaged in a late morning soccer match on a makeshift field that had been cleared of jungle and the land scrubbed. Nevertheless, one could make out, even through the binoculars, errant roots poking through, even a bush here and there. The participants were obviously experienced at this, as they dodged not only opposing players but also these natural obstacles.

The camp itself had comparatively little activity, and there appeared to be no guards posted. Why bother? They weren't even in Colombia, after all. Pinchao's field glasses kept shifting from the football field to the camp. No one to the west of the camp had a visible weapon. If not carried, they were therefore stored, either in individual buildings or, more likely, in one storehouse.

"Inside out," Pinchao said aloud.

"Sir?" asked Montevideo.

"We have an opportunity to seize their weapons before they ever get to them. We need to take the camp from the inside out."

"Sir, in order to get among the buildings, we would be exposed for"—Montevideo gazed about the camp, looked north where the jungle line ran closest to the buildings, then continued—"fifty yards, at least."

"But shielded by the buildings to most of the population, and they have set no lookouts. I agree it is dangerous, and it concentrates all our force in one area, but if they cannot get to their weapons, then their envelopment of us is irrelevant. It is the quickest way to take the camp, and this operation is based on speed. We have to be out of here soon.

"We move to our right, well inside the tree line, then come into that group of buildings closest to the jungle. Most of them have power lines going to them, so we would want to take them first in any event. Let's move."

Bogota, Colombia

Pizza delivery was uncommon in Bogota but was becoming more prevalent as American culture continued its dominant march around the globe. Nevertheless, the terrorists were unfamiliar with the neighborhood, so asked Rojas's wife for suggestions, "generously" offering to pay for a meal for everyone. Montes was concerned that they still couldn't see into the kitchen and had no idea how many total gunmen there were or the condition of Mrs. Rojas. On the other hand, the fact that they might be able to go in the front door, and thus take potential danger to the children out of the picture, was certainly an advantage. The group heard a muffled voice from the kitchen, some movement, then Mrs. Rojas named a local Colombian restaurant that offered meat, rice, and beans, all staples of the Colombian diet.

Montes set a lookout down the street at the corner. If this wasn't done right, then the FARC would see the delivery guy intercepted and taken to the apartment down the hall. Most delivery personnel didn't wear uniforms identifying them with the restaurant, but they would have bags of food (and the odor of freshly cooked cuisine). Montes had a corporal change into street clothes and take the equivalent of twenty U.S. dollars down to the corner. About thirty minutes after the terrorists made their call, a twenty-something man in jeans and a T-shirt rounded the corner and approached the front door of the building carrying a couple of bags. The bottoms had grease stains. The corporal caught up to him, said he had called, named the correct apartment number and paid the guy off.

The soldier brought the food back up, tiptoeing past the Rojas apartment and knocking softly on the adjoining one. He was let back in. By far, the corporal's job would now be the most dangerous. He would wear no body armor, and the only weapon he would have would be stuck in the waistband at the back of his pants as he stood in the Rojas's doorway offering the food. His job was to get the door open and get the hell out of the way as soon as possible, allowing the rest of the team to breach.

Montes would leave one man on the radio looking through the rat tail camera and advising what he saw. So, down two men, four would actively breach and the corporal would back up if necessary. With two men crouching five feet away on either side of the Rojas's apartment door, guns at the ready, the corporal again tiptoed past the door, then approached from the other end of the hall in a normal gait. He stopped in front and knocked without hesitation.

"Delivery," he called.

"Yeah, hold on," came the reply, a man's voice.

The voice in the corporal's Bluetooth earpiece was low, whispered, and rushed. It all came out as one sentence. "OK, the guy who just spoke is taking his rifle off shoulder, setting it behind door left of the hinges. Door hinges to your right, so door opening left to right. Other gunman being waved over toward kids, probably so door will block view. He's not pointing it at the kids. They're still on the floor watching TV."

The door began to open in front of the corporal. "Your order?" he asked.

The gunman said nothing, just nodded and opened the door about a third of the way, smoothly moving in to occupy the space and cut off the delivery man's view. The guy was big, maybe six feet, and broad shouldered. He also had quite the beer gut on him. Wrestling him to the ground would have been a hassle, if they had any intention of hand-to-hand combat, which they did not. The man looked at the corporal, waiting.

"Seventy-seven pesos," he said, startled as if he had forgotten, which he had. Beer Belly handed him a 100-peso note and told him to keep the change. Here's where it got dicey. A lot of soldiers would, from nervousness, breach immediately, pushing the door-opener back, hoping to access the room as soon as possible. This was not ideal, however. If the terrorist was holding bags of food, by definition he was *not* holding a gun, and there was one less armed terrorist. So, the goal was to hand the food off and, just as the hostage-taker was closing the door and turning away, slam the door open into his back.

This is exactly what occurred. As the FARC member turned away, closing the door with his heel since his hands were full, Montes's corporal stepped back quickly and reached into his waistband for his gun. Montes jumped in front of his ersatz delivery man and slammed his shoulder into the door, sending the fat guy and the food flying. As the man was falling, Montes entered with Mario on his heels. Before the Beer Belly hit the ground, Montes had leveled his silenced MP5 and pumped three rounds into the man's upper back and head while he continued moving at a brisk clip to the kitchen, just as a woman was walking out.

Behind him, Mario had turned around the open door and come face-to-face with the second terrorist. The man's brain had only processed the fact that his fat friend had apparently tripped or fallen and the food was flying when a man in military garb appeared before him. He was just raising his weapon when Mario's rifle coughed two rounds into his face and he went down between the children and the TV. Mario immediately jumped in front of the kids, letting his gun fall to his side on the shoulder strap, and enveloped them in his arms. He pushed them back against the wall so they were slightly shielded by the open door. To Mario's right, two more soldiers were following Montes in.

The woman exiting the kitchen wore a threadbare camo jacket and held a metal stick in her hand. There was a plunger button at the top near her thumb. She had just cleared the jamb of the opening when Montes fired. One round splintered the jamb and sent the woman back with a cry. A second round caught her arm as she fell back and dropped the stick on the kitchen floor. Montes continued two more steps and saw the legs of a woman sitting in a chair at a circa 1950s metal dining table. *POP POP THUMP THUMP.* Montes was thrown against the wall and went down in front of the table as he rounded the kitchen opening. His vest protected him, but it hurt like hell. He had a full view of the kitchen. Rojas's wife was sitting at the table, strapped to a chair with a bomb vest on her torso. The shots had come from the woman he hit. She was sitting on the floor, back up against the kitchen cabinets, right arm dangling useless and bleeding but left hand holding up a Smith & Wesson .45 Autoslide. Montes realized that at this range he was lucky the vest actually protected him.

"She's wired!" he yelled. *POP.* The female terrorist shot him in his left cheek. The round was not a hollow point, so didn't mushroom. Normally, that wouldn't have mattered. The .45 round would create enough havoc sending bone shard into the neck and brain that a face shot would be just as effective as a head shot and kill the recipient. The round, however, hit just under the crest of Montes's cheek and glanced off his jaw, breaking it and exiting into the wall behind him. This happened so quickly that Montes only registered burning pain in his face. He saw the detonator on the floor between him and the woman. Mrs. Rojas, gagged, was trying to scream but was muffled. As the terrorist readied another shot, the first man in the backup team entered. The woman shifted her aim and fired. Montes couldn't tell if he was hit or not, but the soldier fell back out of the doorway. Montes tried to one-hand the grip of the MP5 as the FARC woman lunged for the detonator.

Bogota, Colombia

The band struck up the Colombian National Anthem as President Uribe entered the viewing stand. "Viewing stand" was a euphemism for bleachers that had been carpeted, decorated with bunting in the national colors, and had a few padded chairs added. All the occupants stood. The president climbed up three steps at the back center of the stand. As he came into view of those in the stand, applause broke out. Still accompanied by his handlers, Uribe went around the box and shook the hands of the occupants, who were members of his cabinet and the military. He didn't know all of the officers or their guests, but this was not unusual, since tickets to the presidential viewing stand were handed out as perks or rewards for the latest deed well done. Many times, a general would send his chief of staff in his place, feigning a pressing schedule when in fact he was off on vacation in the Bahamas.

After the round of glad-handing, Uribe took his seat in the presidential chair, now set back one row behind the first, but one step up. Consequently, the additional protection was somewhat minimal, since a head shot would be quite effective in killing the president. On the other hand, the placement also allowed him to drop down behind other chairs in the event of an attack. A shot from behind, a la John Wilkes Booth at Ford Theater, would be somewhat difficult as there were three rows of attendees behind the president. Jaramillo understood this also made difficult a quick exit from the stands, but he felt the shielding provided by so many intervening objects and bodies was worth the risk of a slow escape.

The parade began with the ceremonial horseman in dress garb wielding a saber. The band played continuously, fluidly transitioning from the national anthem to several popular marches. First the cavalry, then tanks, foot soldiers, and then various motorized vehicles carrying all manner of personnel. One personnel carrier rounded the corner at the edge of the grounds and took its place in line two hundred yards from the viewing stands. It was draped with ten men all holding weapons in the appropriate, saluting manner.

"That's them," the voice of Staff Sergeant Rojas sounded in Jaramillo's ear. Ignacio Guerra had been forced to let Rojas go about his normal duties since forcing him to feign illness or keeping him confined might tip off the president's protection staff that something was wrong. Guerra felt since he had Rojas's family, Rojas would be no threat.

Jaramillo spoke into his hand microphone, acknowledging. At the parade march rate, the truck would be level with the viewing stand in about one minute. Jaramillo looked left at the body of military officers in the bleachers. One, wearing the uniform of a general, looked over at him and nodded. Jaramillo gave a quick nod in return.

Quite nonchalantly, several of the officers in the viewing stand slipped their hands down to their sides and slowly worked the slides of their MP5s. The security personnel on either side of the president, including Jaramillo, did the same. Jaramillo had sprinkled his men throughout the dais, but with a preponderance of five officers at the south end to intercept the aggressors as they approached.

Jaramillo leaned forward in his seat to garner a better view of the threat. He identified the personnel carrier and tried to count bodies, but his view was obstructed by the audience and intervening vehicles approaching in the parade. As vehicles and marching platoons passed by the box, the soldiers would turn sharply, face the president, and snap a salute.

"Thirty seconds," Jaramillo whispered into his mic. He looked left and saw brief nods from the men he had planted. He saw several lean slightly forward in their seats, ready to jump up if the threat were real.

Jaramillo looked back at the carrier. One, two, three ... ten. He counted ten men total, although there could have been a couple more on the far side of the carrier. He saw them turn sharply, but instead of saluting, the ones on the edge of the vehicle jumped down, and all ten leveled their weapons. Jaramillo, to the right of

Uribe, jumped up in unison with his second-in-command, Juan Agalpa, on the president's left. They pushed Uribe to the ground and fired their weapons. From the corner of his vision, he saw his five planted men jump from their chairs, weapons firing. None of their fields of fire crossed, despite the fact that the three in the front row jumped over the railing, firing continuously, and rounded the back end of the personnel carrier.

Several of the audience members in the front row fell forward, but Jaramillo couldn't tell if this was because they were hit or diving for cover. He fought the instinct to move forward, leaving that to his team. He saw and felt several of them move past him on either side. The FARC members were pinned down, unable to move forward. They fired continuously now only to provide cover for a retreat. However, because of his men rounding the truck to the south, the only avenue of escape was to the north. Jaramillo's team cut that off too.

Jaramillo could hear screaming in his earpiece but could not make out what was being said over the gunfire and screams around him. He ceased fire, knelt, and put his hand over his ear. He could hear Roas' voice: "Not him! . . . not there!" Jaramillo squinted and crouched down, as if that would help him hear better, then saw blood spray across his field of vision. As he looked up, he saw Agalpa fall forward. An officer with a pistol stepped on his body and lowered the weapon toward the president, firing into his back.

Jungles of western Colombia

"It is the army!" Vaya screamed. "We must go now!" He grabbed Corrivas by the collar and practically threw him into the cargo hold of the chopper after the three hostages. Vaya jumped on top of him as if protecting him.

"*Vamanos*!" Smith yelled. The copter jerked up—not the smoothest takeoff ever, and dangerous considering the tight LZ.

Vaya looked up at Smith. "It's them, right?" Smith looked up and back. The sorriest looking excuse for a helicopter approached. It had primer on it, a rusted bottom, and one of the skids was bent, probably from numerous hard landings. However, the tail section did carry the crest of the FARC. Smith nodded. The chopper he and Vaya were using had none of the usual weaponry associated with an army helicopter, so there could be no gun or missile fire to take out the FARC copter. Smith motioned to the hostages to stay where they were and strap in, which they did on the bench opposite him. Vaya was on top of Corrivas on the floor between the two benches.

"Grenade launcher!" Vaya yelled in Spanish, pointing under Smith's seat. Smith reached down to release the Velcro straps securing it.

By now the chopper was up and pulling away to the left. Vaya looked over his shoulder and could see the face of the FARC pilot in the other helicopter. There was a mix of surprise and anger. "We can't let him call it in!" Corrivas also tried to look up, but Vaya said, "Stay down, amigo. You are too valuable to lose." Vaya and Smith would laugh about that later. If they lived.

Smith knew what he meant. If the pilot radioed someone on the ground that the army was at the LZ, they would figure out pretty quickly that their communications were not secure, and all the other operations could be blown.

"I need a clear shot," Smith said in Spanish as he extended the launch tube. "Pull up and spin it left." The pilot did, almost sending Smith falling backward out the opposite open doorway. He grabbed the webbing above his seat and attempted to aim. "Fuck, too close!" he yelled in English. The FARC aircraft was practically a boat length away. At this distance, any secondary explosion might take them out, too.

At Smith's exclamation, Corrivas looked up. He looked about the cabin wildly and suddenly realized he had been duped. He twisted up and left, smashing his elbow into Vaya's face and side repeatedly. Vaya was looking back, not expecting it, and fell off Corrivas and against the front bulkhead. Smith let go of the bench webbing and smashed his left hand into Corrivas' face. It did not have the desired effect. Corrivas was stunned by the punch, but its force rolled him on top of Vaya, pinning him under the FARC camp commander. Corrivas shook it off, trying to get up in the churning cargo hold.

"Pull up, get above them," Smith yelled. As Corrivas got to his knees, Smith moved the grenade tube to his left hand, then reversed motion and swung it in a wide arc at Corrivas' face. Vaya had regained some composure, only again to be forced down by Corrivas' weight after Smith's baseball-like swing of the launcher. Smith saw the FARC copter begin to pass beneath them as the pilot of his chopper pulled up. "Push him over!" Smith yelled at Vaya. Vaya hesitated just a moment, then pushed with his legs and arms, throwing Corrivas out the open cargo door. The tilt of the chopper assisted him, and Corrivas went flying over the door's edge. They both heard a deep, sickening *thunk thunk thunk* as Corrivas hit the rotor blades of the FARC helicopter passing below them.

Corrivas' gruesome death was just a catalyst. What Smith was hoping for was that the FARC chopper would be disabled, and he was not disappointed. He heard the rotors wind down, and turned to look out the opposite door as the FARC aircraft had now passed completely underneath them. It began losing altitude immediately, and the body of the craft spun as the pilot autorotated to try to restart the engine. He worked furiously at the controls, but to no avail. The aircraft continued to plummet and fell through the forest canopy, a huge fireball erupting from the trees.

Vaya was up and had turned to the hostages. "We are members of the Colombian Army here to rescue you. You are free." The woman looked incredulous, then began to cry and hugged the boy. The man leaned forward and put his head in his hands, his body shaking convulsively.

"Back to Bogota," Smith told the pilot.

Eastern Ecuador

Pinchao's team had taken its time getting into position, but that was to be expected since silence and invisibility was desired. They came across no lookouts or booby traps along the way, which was also as expected. Pinchao surveyed the scene. Numerous cabins. Three with power and what looked to be phone lines, although they could have been networked computer cables. Minimal activity—a man here or there going in or out of one of the shacks. They waited.

"Sir?" Montevideo whispered.

"Wait a bit. We might get lucky and find someone coming out of one of the shacks with a weapon."

"Why would that be lucky, sir?"

"Because that would be a good indication ..." A man approached a cabin without power or phone lines. The door was locked from the outside. The man withdrew a key from his pocket and opened the door. He went inside. There was some banging about and the man exited with a Kalshnikov. He turned and locked the door. "... that it might be the weapons storehouse," he said, smiling. "OK, we go. We take that storehouse first. If we set up a perimeter at either end of the row of cabins, we should be able to hold it indefinitely and resupply from the arms cache."

"But, sir, *we* could get surrounded."

"That's no threat, Montevideo. Only a few have guns. What are they going to do, throw rocks?" Montevideo mulled this over and then did the only thing he could do anyway, capitulate. "So, storehouse first, then the powered shacks. Let's go."

It has been said that every battle plan is excellent until the battle starts. The problem, of course, is you either made a mistake in estimating the skill or strength of the enemy, or you failed to predict how the enemy would react, or both. The risk was that there were many more guns outstanding than the team thought. Nevertheless, they could not sit in the forest forever. It was already beginning to get late in the afternoon. Montevideo took a crew of three to the end of the "street" and maintained an outpost. Another crew set explosives on the door, Pinchao approached the door of the first cabin they came to that appeared to be wired, and the last part of the team set up a defense at the jungle line.

The weapons team indicated they were ready. Pinchao nodded, then kicked at the door of the cabin he faced. He heard the explosion behind him from the charges on the storehouse door. The cabin he entered was empty, but had lighting, a landline telephone, and a computer. He turned, weapon ready, and walked across the lane to another wired cabin. At the end of the street, Montevideo's team established a defensive perimeter, but most of the camp's population was still at the soccer field.

As Pinchao approached the door of the opposing shack, it was flung open. A tall man in his fifties with a mustache and beard, dressed in camo wear, exited, pistol in hand. He froze. It was Raul Reyes.

"Pinchao!" He looked astonished.

"You are under—," Pinchao began.

Reyes fired, hitting Pinchao in the chest. The bullet struck his body armor. Quite painful, but not debilitating. Pinchao fired back, and Reyes fell backward into the cabin floor, kicking the door shut. Pinchao wasted no time, racing to the door and kicking it open, his adrenaline getting the better of his training.

Reyes, bleeding from the stomach, was sitting on the ground holding his pistol in one hand and a grenade in the other. As Pinchao entered, Reyes pulled the pin off the grenade with his teeth and spit it out. "Look around, Major Pinchao. I drop this, this whole half of the camp goes up." Pinchao's eyes darted about, and he saw boxes of plastic explosive stacked along either wall.

Pinchao fired a round into Reyes's forehead, running toward him as he did. Reyes's grip on the grenade began to relax as his body fell to the side.

A man can do a lot in three seconds. Football games can be won in three seconds. The score at the end of a basketball game can change four times in three seconds. A dropped grenade can be retrieved and thrown before it blows up in three seconds. Pinchao had done it before, but that was in training camps when trainees dropped live grenades by accident and he had been standing right there, so that was not very reassuring. He preferred not to have to throw it at all if possible.

Letting the rifle drop by his side, he grabbed Reyes's hand with both of his, hoping to keep pressure on the grenade's safety clip. Instead, the grenade squirted up and out of Reyes's grip like an oiled lemon. It was lathered in Reyes's blood. Pinchao saw it jump up and the clip fly free. He caught it as it fell back, put it on the ground and rolled Reyes's body over it, throwing himself on top. He clamped his hands over his ears and buried his face into Reyes's back. *FUMP!* The grenade exploded in Reyes's torso with a muffled bang, the blast force lifting Reyes, and by extension, Pinchao, up off the ground. Pinchao separated momentarily from Reyes, then fell back down on top of him, feeling searing pain in his lower legs and feet. While Reyes's body had shielded him from much of the blast and shrapnel, his legs were askew and exposed to the grenade's flying metal shards. He would live, and considering the circumstances, it wasn't a bad outcome.

He rolled off of Reyes and looked down at his shins and feet. His boots protected his feet fairly well, but he could see that his pant legs were shredded and dark with blood speckles. Montevideo burst through the door. "They're coming! A few armed," he said, then looked down. "Can you walk, sir?"

"I think so," Pinchao answered. He reached out for assistance, and Montevideo helped him up. As he took a few steps, it didn't feel as bad as it looked. He was bleeding, but none of the shrapnel had cut deeply, and he could walk unassisted after his initial paces. Running was another story.

Pinchao walked back down the lane, trying to appear as nonchalant as he could despite the pain, and took a look. They had not cleared the other cabins, so he ordered the demo team that secured the weapons store to do it. As he came up behind Montevideo, he could see the rag-tag population approach, not understanding what was happening, dumbfounded that Colombian Army personnel were even here. Pinchao figured he had one chance of avoiding a bloodbath, so he took the risky move of actually telling the crowd the truth.

"Raul Reyes is dead ..." he began.

Bogota, Colombia

Since he was on his butt, back up against the kitchen wall, legs out in front of him, Montes had no chance of grabbing the detonator first. He shoved his back against the wall, trying to slide his feet closer to it in the hopes of knocking it away. Instantly he realized how stupid that was, as this knocked the stick slightly closer to the FARC woman. Montes, focused on the gleam of the chrome stick, saw the woman's hand close around the base of the detonator and a flash of movement up to his left. Mrs. Rojas and her chair crashed down on the woman's elbow and lower arm. There was a loud *crack* as the arm broke. The woman screamed and Mrs. Rojas grunted in pain.

Montes's backup man reentered the kitchen, kicked away the detonator, and leaning over Mrs. Rojas, saw the terrorist looking up at him, hate gleaming proudly in her eyes. He shifted his aim and fired two rounds into her forehead. He looked about and yelled, "Clear!" Montes realized that—other than his bark that Mrs. Rojas was wired—these were the only words spoken in the entire time since they entered the apartment. He also realized that what seemed like minutes was less than fifteen seconds.

His backup helped Mrs. Rojas up and a second man came to assist. Montes tried to get up, but one of the men told him he was hit and to wait for a medic. Montes looked down and realized his face wound was pumping blood down his left side. He wanted to tell Mrs. Rojas she was incredibly brave, but as his jaw was broken and his face burning, he couldn't speak. He watched as his men carefully picked up the detonator stick and laid it upon the table. It took them about thirty minutes to defuse the bomb strapped to Rojas's wife. He hoped the other teams had been as successful.

Bogota, Colombia

Jaramillo snapped left and fired five rounds into the impostor army officer. The man, hit only once in the torso but several times in the legs and arm, went down on top of Agalpa next to the president.

"The president has been shot!" Jaramillo said into his microphone as he kneeled over the him. He could see three shots in Uribe's back, but no blood. This was not unusual even without the protection of body armor, since layers of clothes and their dark color could obscure bleeding wounds. Moreover, since bullets tended to cauterize the area from their own heat as they entered the body, many bullet wounds didn't bleed at all unless the bullet exited the body.

Jaramillo ran his fingertips carefully over the president's back. He could feel him panting in short, staccato breaths. He identified three closely grouped wounds at the center of the back, normally a terrible thing. At the very least, the president would have had spine damage, and at worst, a mortal heart wound. "Stay still, Mr. President. Remain calm."

Jaramillo called some men over. They took the terrorist, still alive but likely bleeding internally from the stomach wound, off of Agalpa. Agalpa had been thrashing underneath the man and, once he was removed, attempted to jump up. Agalpa's vest had protected him, but he had taken a hit in the shoulder. He got about halfway up and sank to his knees from dizziness. He was able to focus and looked at Jaramillo, then the president, in horror.

"I have killed him," Ignacio Guerra said gasping from behind Agalpa. "I have killed the American puppet. The FARC are victorious."

Jaramillo's face turned into a wry grin, and Agalpa looked at him like he was insane. "Help me turn him over, Agalpa." They carefully turned Uribe over, and Agalpa noticed that the president had some strength, as he appeared to be trying to assist them. Once on his back, Uribe picked his head up, but Jaramillo told him to lie back. A medic arrived as all the audience members were running away. The medic pushed them roughly to the side.

Only a few generals and one legislator remained in the box, more concerned with the president than their own safety. Jaramillo heard shots to his right on the parade ground. He looked up and saw that the rest of the military who had been participating in the day's event realized what was happening and had effectively and immediately surrounded the FARC terrorists. Some were dead, others were lined up on their stomachs with men over them securing their hands behind their backs with flex-cuffs.

Jaramillo turned his attention back to the president and carefully unbuttoned Uribe's dress jacket as the medic opened his kit near the president's head. Jaramillo removed Uribe's tie, then unbuttoned his shirt.

"Brave, but not stupid," Jaramillo said to Agalpa. Beneath the shirt was a Kevlar vest. A few inches north and Uribe's head would have been blown to pieces. As it was, he would have significant soft tissue damage to his back, but would fully recover. On his stomach, bleeding out, Ignacio Guerra saw the body armor. He closed his eyes, crying. "No" was all he gasped before he died.

Chapter 46

George Town, Grand Cayman; March 2008

A s we exited the car at the dock, Winfield's cell phone rang in the security guy's pocket. Lester reached in and looked at the screen. He looked up at de Plata, who only nodded slightly. Lester handed the phone to Winfield. "Pardon me a moment," Winfield said as he took the phone and turned away. I could hear some of the beginnings of a business conversation as the rest of us walked down the slip plank to the side of a large yacht. I counted four decks. A ship's crewman lowered a skid-resistant plank down to the slip. As we waited for him to finish, Winfield was walking toward us and finishing up the call. "Yes, let's go ahead and close that issue out right away. Thanks. I'll call you back when we're finished here."

We walked up to the main deck, then to the back of the boat. Lester went ahead of us and opened a sliding glass door to a den area, ushering everyone in. Once the slider on the expansive cabin shut, we made our way toward the other end, where there was a couch, some sitting chairs, and a leather inlaid cherry wood desk with a laptop computer on it. The desk was nicely furnished with a cup with pens in it, a notepad, a fancy letter opener with a handle that looked like a peacock tail, and a blotter on which the computer sat. I wondered how all that stuff stayed in place when the boat was moving. De Plata took a seat in the chair. Before any of us could sit down, Winfield spoke. "I probably should have told you a while ago, but Mr. Sanders here doesn't really work for me. He's an FBI agent."

Lester had his gun out faster than I had ever seen anyone pull a gun. A blur of movement. By the time it was out and pointed at me, my hand was still at my waistband pulling my piece. I saw Winfield's hand go up at Lester in a "stop" motion. Winfield's movement momentarily drew Lester's attention. That allowed me to get my gun out and point it at Lester. Two guns, four men.

If I had taken the initiative to shoot Lester first, I was pretty sure the rest of us would live. Pretty sure. But my hesitation broke a cardinal rule of such situations. You have to take the initiative immediately and be the first to act to survive. Now that the first few tense seconds had ticked past, the ability to take charge had passed as well.

"Well, this certainly is exciting, isn't it?" Sterling was almost giggling, clapping his hands together and rubbing them.

"Speak for yourself. I notice you don't have a gun pointed at you," I said, never taking my eyes off Lester. I didn't really worry myself about Winfield since he had no weapon. His eyes were jumping back and forth between me and Lester. Lester and I were staring at each other, and neither of our arms were wavering.

"Put it down, Sanders," Lester said. "I don't want to shoot you."

"How 'bout you put yours away first," I suggested. He shook his head slowly, almost sadly. That was a bad sign. It told me that despite all appearances, the guy was in control of the entire situation, knew it, and was confident about the outcome because he'd already seen it fifty different ways. And in all of them, he lived.

Sterling stopped laughing long enough to speak. "You know, John, you're going about this all wrong. Mr. Sanders is only a threat when he has a gun. If you would threaten to kill our client, Mr. Sanders would give up his gun." Winfield glanced over at Sterling, concern on his face. "Don't worry, Jeremy, I'll only have him wing you." He began to giggle to himself again, certain that he was bringing the house down with his humor.

Winfield apparently had a better idea. "Agent Sanders, please put your gun down."

"Not gonna happen," I said.

"Actually, it will happen, one way or another," Lester said in his low tone. Damn, this guy was so calm. His eyes were moving all over. You could see the calculations he was making, both strategically and tactically. "Your girlfriend from the car isn't covering you. She's probably still waiting for triple A. You've got no support. And the one thing you got going for you is I have no reason to hurt you, except for the fact that you're pointing that gun at me."

Winfield spoke. "He's right, Mr. Sanders. No one wants to kill a federal agent. Even if you tied any of us to a crime, you can't extradite us. We have nothing to fear from you. Except the gun. Also, if you shoot someone on Cayman territory, you'll have a huge international incident on your hands. The U.S. will almost certainly disavow you, calling you a rogue agent, or contractor, I should say. You'll spend a good portion of your life in jail in the Caymans."

The thing I hate the most is when criminals know the law better than law enforcement officers. And make more sense. Both of them were right. I pointed the barrel down, flipped the switch to "safe," and dropped it on the carpet in the middle of the cabin. Lester stepped out slowly and pulled it back toward him with his heel, never taking his eyes off me. Winfield sighed and his body noticeably relaxed. Lester crouched down and picked up the pistol, looking at it. "Nice. Made a stop at Gerald's Gun Shop and Fishing Service, I see. You're not FBI. You must be one of Paul's boys."

I looked at him curiously. I almost said that Blattman had told me he knew him, but realized how stupid that would be. If I said that, Lester would know Blattman was on the island and that we had a third person backing us up. Instead, I said, "How do you know Blattman?" Lester was about to speak when he was cut off.

"Enough. Can we get down to business? Mr. Lester, handcuff this gentleman and sit him on the couch. We'll drop you back on the dock when we're done, Agent Sanders," said Sterling.

Lester pulled a pair of handcuffs from his coat pocket after putting his gun in his holster and my gun in his waistband behind his back. He sat me on the couch, telling me to lean all the way back. That would make it more difficult for me to pop up at a moment's notice.

So there I was, Sterling at the desk on my left, Winfield across the room, and Lester to my right. And both Sterling and Lester looking at me as I sat. And I looking at Winfield. Sterling turned to a phone on the desk. "Billy? Move us out of the slip and into the harbor." He hung up the phone and said, "We don't need any extra participants in our meeting."

It was getting dark, and Sterling turned the lights on in the cabin. Lester saw this and began close the curtains. Fuck. This guy was as good as Blattman said. He recognized that despite us being on a boat that probably no one knew we were on, and that the boat was moving away from shore, the internally lit cabin would be like a bull's-eye to a sniper. He didn't even know Velasquez had a sniper rifle. He just wasn't willing to take the chance. Still, even with the curtains drawn, Velasquez might be able to see silhouettes. Problem was, even if she was on the shore and looking through her scope, she couldn't distinguish the good guys from the bad guys.

✧ ✧ ✧

Velasquez was at that moment two hundred yards away at the entrance to the boat slips. She had hailed a cab in the financial district and was able to arrive at the dock only minutes after Sanders. When the cab driver offered to take the duffel bag she was carrying from her and put it in the trunk, she demurred quickly. He didn't question her. She had called Blattman and told him to meet her at the dock. She arrived to see the yacht backing out of its slip. If they left the harbor and went to sea, she couldn't cover Sanders. A cab pulled up next to her and Blattman got out.

Velasquez dropped to a knee, opened her duffel and had the weapon assembled in under one minute. Blattman's right eyebrow tilted up in admiration. "I coulda used her," he thought.

"Sanders, if you can hear me, I'm at the dock with Blattman and weapon. If the boat leaves the harbor, we'll try to commandeer a chase vehicle. If we can't, you're on your own."

✧ ✧ ✧

"So, Mr. Sanders, why would the FBI be investigating me?"

"You can't guess? You think it's the drug dealing or arms sales that raise the first red flag, Sterling?"

He didn't physically react much to me using his real name. "Sterling? You mean Alan Sterling? Oh, I'm afraid he's dead, Mr. Sanders." He smiled a little, but that seemed more a result of nervousness than his wit. He picked up the peacock tail letter opener and worked it end over end in his liver-spotted hands, thinking.

"I would have thought someone who tried to fake their death would at least try to change their appearance. Anyway, we're more interested in why you're killing ASBT's clients."

He didn't seem surprised by this statement. Instead, he studied me a bit, and then his head went sideways, as if something had just occurred to him. "How would the FBI even know the deaths were related?" He was wondering aloud, but seemed to be speaking mostly to himself.

"So you were killing them?" Winfield asked, not nearly as shocked as he should have been. I was thinking back to the second conversation we had had in his office, and I figured that's when he began to suspect that DP Partners, or one of ASBT's other money managers, was doing it.

Sterling's head jerked up as if he'd forgotten Winfield was in the room. He said, "What? Oh, well, not me really. Lester here did the heavy lifting, but at my direction, of course."

"In God's name, why?"

Sterling chuckled. "You're kidding, right? Money, of course!"

"But—"

"Oh, stop blathering, Jeremy. You should understand what's at stake. If I waited for all those big clients to die, I'd be in the ground long before I could hope that you and the other banks I do business with would invest their money with me. I just sped the process along, that's all. You should appreciate that more than anyone. I turned your boutique little bank into a powerhouse far faster than your skills as a banker could have."

"But you already had millions—"

"Billions. But it's never enough. You should know that." He turned back to me. "Well, that still doesn't explain how you traced the money back to me, unless you served Jeremy here with a search warrant, and I would have known about that. And I'd know about a warrant on the banks too." I said nothing, wondering if his paranoia would get the better of him. It did. "You couldn't have broken my security program ..." His voice trailed off.

Winfield tried to speak, but Sterling told him sharply, "Shut up, Jeremy!" Lester stood there, his gun now holstered, my gun in his waistband at his back. He looked back and forth between the three of us and seemed mildly amused. "You couldn't have been tracing the money ..." He turned quickly to his computer, dropping the letter opener in front of the keyboard. He punched the keys madly, and his screen brightened. I could just see the screen over his shoulder. He opened a window, and a screen popped up showing nothing but random numbers. I wish Winkler had been there to translate. I assumed this was the portal into the encryption program. Sterling punched what seemed like a hundred keys, and the code screen dissolved. Another window sprang open. This screen looked like a trading window on the desktop of a brokerage house. Some words, a lot of symbols, and four or five columns. Normally, such screens show red and green, listing stocks that are up in green and those that are down in red. If the market as a whole is tanking, the entire screen is red. Sterling's entire laptop screen was red. There was a small gasp, then he hammered away at the keys again. Windows cascaded on top of each other, all red. He spun around in his chair and faced me.

"Where," he said slowly, "is it?"

"Where's what?" He spun back, grabbed something off the desk, and before anyone could react, he had whipped the chair back around and jammed the peacock letter opener deep into my left leg.

"FUCK!" I screamed.

"Where—is my—GOD—DAMN—MONEY!" he screamed at me. The man was eighty-eight years old, but was strong, fast, and had a clear, strong voice. Veins in his skull were pulsing and his skin was turning red. He yanked the opener out of my leg, which spouted blood as the blade was withdrawn, then began to ooze.

"Fuck you! I have no idea where your fucking money is!" I yelled at him. He lifted the opener again, but Winfield reached out and caught his wrist. Lester stepped closer, hand on his gun.

"He's telling the truth. He doesn't know where your money is." Winfield's voice was calm, yet forceful. He held Sterling's wrist firmly, and the arm didn't budge. Sterling looked confused, looked back and forth between me and Winfield, then relaxed. Winfield let go of the wrist, and Sterling turned toward him. Lester visibly relaxed.

"How would you know what he knows, unless you're working with him?"

"I'm most certainly *not* working with him. I'm working for me."

Now I was thoroughly confused, as was Lester. His hand slowly moved into his coat, but Winfield didn't notice. Lester began to step back, increasing his target angle so that everyone in the room was in the potential shooting cone in front of him.

Velasquez looked through the scope. She had a clear view of the main deck cabin, lit from the inside but with the drapes closed.

"OK, I got four shadows, two sitting, two standing. Tall guy to the right, probably the enforcer. Shorter guy standing middle, partially blocked by seated guy with his back to me, and then the fourth seated left. Wait. Tall guy's backing up a bit. Slowly. The remaining guys, I can't tell who's who. Sanders, I need some sign from you if you can hear me. I need to know which one is you."

✳ ✳ ✳

Listening to two conversations at once is exceedingly difficult. Velasquez's voice in my ear was reassuring and annoying at the same time. I was glad she was there, but it interfered with me trying to figure out Winfield's angle, which was difficult enough without her voice in the ear, judging from the reaction of the other men in the cabin.

"Jeremy, what the hell's going on?" Sterling asked.

"I have your money. Or better said, I have my money. And everyone else you stole from your whole life."

Lester pulled his gun. "I wouldn't do that," Winfield said matter-of-factly. "You kill me, he never sees a dime." Sterling put his hand up toward Lester, waving him off. Lester kept the gun in both hands but dropped the barrel so it pointed at Winfield's shins. The advantage of all current events was that both Sterling and Lester seemed to have forgotten I existed.

"OK," Sterling said. "John, do me a favor and shoot Mr. Sanders in the leg. The uninjured one." Damn, that was short-lived. Sterling looked Winfield in the eyes. "I'm going to ask you again, where is my money?"

Winfield ignored Sterling and looked at Lester. "Mr. Lester, you're a contractor for hire, aren't you?"

Lester, who was walking toward me, stopped. "What?" he asked. It wasn't that he hadn't heard, just that he couldn't believe the surreal nature of what was occurring, like a twenty-five-year-old construction worker forced to watch a Fellini movie.

"You're a mercenary, a gun for hire?"

"Security consultant."

"You typically work for free?" Winfield asked him.

"Of course I don't work for free," Lester said.

"Well, if you shoot Mr. Sanders there, that would be working for free, because this gentleman you've been working for doesn't have any money."

Lester looked at Sterling. "Oh, for God's sake, John, it's a bluff. Shoot him."

Lester waited, then spoke. "First, sir, you're breaking your own rule about not harming government agents. Second, it's obviously not a bluff, because you appear to believe your money's gone. Three, he's right, I don't work for free."

"Christ, John. I've got ten million in cash in the safe in the captain's cabin. It's yours, now shoot Winfield."

Winfield cleared his throat. "Shoot me and he never sees any of his money again."

Lester pointed the gun back at Winfield. "Cut the crap. What do you *want*, Winfield?"

"He wants the money. Same as Sterling. It's always about the money with these guys," I said.

"It's not about the money, Agent Sanders. It's about justice," Winfield said. "That's what I want, Mr. Lester, justice."

"Not my department. And I'm not sure I see how stealing Mr. de Plata's billions results in justice. Only moves numbers around a ledger."

"Mr. de Plata is really Alan Sterling, as Mr. Sanders has guessed. Back in the mid-1980s, Mr. Sterling stole billions from his clients, everything they had. People that trusted him. People like my father, who gave him every dime he ever earned at a chain of gas stations along the eastern seaboard that he spent his entire life building. He ruined my father, and thousands just like him. Now I'm going to ruin him. Justice, Mr. Lester."

Well, I have to admit I never saw that coming. But I should have. History matters, and while I was busy looking at the history of every bad guy, I never looked at the past history of the one guy I thought *wasn't* involved. But then my mind started working overtime, and I realized that I passed over a connection that a thorough search of Winfield's background might have revealed, and it wasn't his father.

I couldn't tell what was going on in Lester's head, but his face showed a tug-of-war. His gun dropped slightly.

Sterling leapt at Winfield. He jabbed the letter opener into Winfield's side, and blood gushed forth. His right hand grabbed Winfield's throat as Winfield went down, and Sterling throttled him, yelling, "Give me my MONEY!" *Bang!* Sterling took a round in the left shoulder and fell back into the corner between the desk and a credenza on the adjoining wall, howling. I took the opportunity to stand, slowly as it hurt like hell, but Lester's gun was on me.

"Stop," he said.

"Shit, Sanders!" I heard Lisa's voice in my ear. "I need a sign. We heard the shot. Saw two guys go down, one get up. Two now standing. If one is you, move now." I stepped left, my injured leg searing, and turned to give her my profile, hoping I would be able to nod yes or no and she could make it out. From Lester's point of view, it looked like I was backing away from his gun, so he did nothing. "I'm going to shoot the guy to my right if that was you that just moved left." I shook my head. "Did you just shake your head no, you don't want me to shoot?" I nodded slowly. Lester was looking over at Winfield and Sterling, both bleeding on the cabin floor, so he didn't see this. "OK, holding for now. Weapons ready."

The letter opener was still in Winfield's side. Winfield got to his knees and moved to take it out.

"Don't touch it!" Lester and I both said in unison. His eyes snapped up to us, now both standing, he kneeling. Lester explained: "You pull it out, it could open the wound more, you could bleed out. Sanders, go get him a towel from downstairs." I turned, motioning to my hands. "No way," he shook his head. "You're a big boy. Go." He opened a door that I thought was a closet. In fact, it was an interior stairway down to the deck cabins below. Getting down them was difficult. Every time I lifted and then planted it, my left leg seared. There was a handrail, so I turned my back to it and held onto it with my hands, side-stepping down the stairs.

When I got to the bottom, I was in a short hallway that ended into a longer one running the length of the boat. All the doors onto it were closed, but I was able to back up to them and push the latches down to open them. I tried just the doors on the land-facing side of the boat. I found a cabin with a porthole and looked out. It was too dark to see the shore, and I couldn't open it with my hands cuffed. I was hoping Velasquez was scanning the whole boat. "Sanders, you just disappeared. Where'd you go?" I waited. Apparently her scope found me. "Ah! They lock you below decks?" I shook my head. "Should I shoot the tall guy?" I hesitated, then shook my head. I wasn't sure what John Lester was all about, but I also didn't think he wanted to harm me. I mouthed, "Gotta go," and left the cabin for the hallway. On my second try, I found a head with a towel rack holding hand towels. Quite luxurious ones, actually. I backed into the head and grabbed a towel. Going up proved easier than down, and I noticed the more I walked on the leg the better it felt. My pants had acted as a makeshift bandage, staunching the blood flow.

"Just relax, Sterling. You'll live. Don't try to get up," Lester was saying to Sterling, who was moaning and trying to grab the handrail that was set at chair height along the wall of the cabin. At Lester's words, he gave up and sank back down, sitting on the floor with his back against the cabin wall. Lester had moved Winfield to the couch and laid him on his right side. The bouquet-like handle of the letter opener was sticking straight up. I walked up to Lester and he turned around. He grabbed the towel and motioned to the desk. I kicked the chair over close to him. Lester re-holstered his gun and wrapped the towel carefully around the hilt of the knife. "Put your hand here, keep pressure on it. Now, sit up." Winfield sat up. Lester motioned for me to retake my seat on the couch, which I did, turning slightly to my left so Velasquez could see my shadow profile. My movement had to be exaggerated so she could make it out, but no one was looking at me now. Lester helped Winfield move to the desk chair.

"That you sitting down again?" I heard her ask. I nodded. "Copy," I heard in my ear.

"I'd pay you to kill him, but I assume your answer would be no?" Winfield asked Lester.

"Correct," Lester said. "Bad for business if word got out that I killed former clients." I rolled my eyes. Everyone had ethics, even killers for hire.

"I understand. I'll settle for a gun. How much for Mr. Sanders'?"

Lester smirked, then stood up. "You have all his money?" he asked Winfield, nodding at Sterling.

"Yes."

"And you can access it from here?"

"Certainly." Lester's eyes moved to Sterling, then back to Winfield. He reached into his pocket and withdrew a wallet and fished out a card, handing it to Winfield.

"Wire sixty million to this account and routing number. When I confirm it's there, I'll leave the gun on the credenza. Then I'm gone. Understand?"

"Yes."

"I'll sell it to you for half that," I said, as I thought what a weird number $60 million was.

"If you had one, Mr. Sanders," Winfield said, "I would pay you for it, but you don't. Same reason popcorn is so expensive at the movies—you can't get it anywhere else."

Winfield turned to the computer. He was pretty good with one hand but was looking sweaty and pallid. I saw the encryption screen come back up, and Winfield typed in his code. "You have his encryption key?" I asked, astounded.

"Yes," Winfield said simply, not explaining.

Sterling groaned in the corner. "That bitch double-crossed me," he said, more to himself than anyone else.

While Winfield was typing away, I turned to Lester. "You always have your account number and routing code with you?"

"Never leave home without it," he said. "Never know when you're going to have to make a quick deal. Pays to be prepared in my business. Literally." He smiled. Then he turned fully to me. "If you make it out of here alive, do me a favor. Tell Blattman I forgive him."

"You can tell him yourself after I arrest you."

He cracked a little grin at me. "Not gonna happen, Sanders. I like your spirit, though."

Winfield turned. "OK, done." He pointed to the screen, and to several lines of code.

"Hold on a second," Lester said. "Don't get up," he reminded me. He stepped through the slider and into a foyer, which opened onto an outdoor seating area. The space he stood in was not visible to Velasquez. Had he stepped just a bit further to the open dining area, Lisa could have taken him out with one shot. He dialed his cell phone.

"You said your father owned a gas station, not a chain of them," I said to Winfield.

"He started with one. You never dug any further. But I doubt even if I had told you that for the greater portion of my childhood we were quite wealthy it would have made any difference. You would have had to do some significant digging to figure out my dad was ruined by that piece of garbage in the corner," Winfield replied, pointing to Sterling.

"You knew he was Sterling the whole time?"

"Yes."

"And you knew he was killing your clients?"

"Not really. Not until you brought it up. After three of them had died in strange circumstances, I entertained the thought they were somehow connected, but it seemed so far-fetched I disregarded it." He shifted in his chair, and it obviously hurt. He breathed in deeply, exhaled, and then slowly leaned back. He was looking more pale and sweaty, and despite the towel and pressure on the wound, I thought he might bleed out. "But then you and Ms. Conrad showed up making the same allegation. Using Ed's murder and what's been going on in the markets, I was able to get a face-to-face meeting with Sterling."

"All these years the only thing you were trying to do was kill him?"

"That was my original plan. It ... evolved."

In the foyer, Lester called his offshore bank to confirm the receipt of funds. He then immediately ordered the funds wired to a second bank and advised the order could only be rescinded by him appearing in person at the second bank. He then called the second bank in the Cook Islands and confirmed *their* receipt of the wired funds.

Once confirmed, he told the cheery English girl on the phone who was answering at what was probably the early morning hours there, "Also, could you confirm you received the distribution instructions I sent a few days ago?" There was some tapping of computer keys and she happily confirmed receipt of the instructions. He reiterated an in-person rescission order, and then authorized the bank to execute his instructions the next business day. He turned back and stepped into the cabin.

✵ ✵ ✵

"Evolved?"

"When I realized I might be able to actually steal his money back. Listen, Sanders," he looked up. Lester looked like he was finishing up his call. Winfield's breathing was labored. "I'm in pretty bad shape here." He fished around in his coat pocket with his free hand and withdrew a small cartridge. It was a flash drive. He held it up. "Everything you need to get it back. Account numbers, routing codes, passwords. Sterling can repay the people he ruined, with interest." He leaned forward and slid it into my windbreaker pocket. "Oh," he groaned. As he sat back, the slider opened again and Lester walked in.

"Mr. Winfield," Lester said, "the funds are confirmed. Here's how this is going down. I'll place Sanders' gun and the clip on the end of the credenza closest to the door. No one moves until I step out. Then I'm gone, and you can do ... whatever it is you plan on doing."

"Fair enough," he wheezed.

"You better get yourself to a hospital, Winfield," Lester said as he retrieved my gun, withdrew the clip, cleared the breech, and placed them both on the credenza. "Oh, one other thing." He reached into his jacket pocket and pulled out the handcuff keys. He walked to me, and placing a hand on my shoulder to hold me down, dropped them into my hands behind my back. "Good luck." He turned and left without another word.

☼ ☼ ☼

Through her night scope, Velasquez saw the big shadow move back and forth across the cabin, then out of view. She matched the pace and followed it through the foyer space she couldn't see into until Sterling's enforcer came into view, perfectly framed in the reticle of her scope. "Got a shot at your boy, Blattman, taking it."

"Hold fire!" Blattman's bark of a whisper came in her ear.

"What?"

"Hold fire! Do not shoot him."

"Goddammit, that guy probably built the deli bomb!"

"We don't know that. If he did, we'll track him down and take care of it. But right now I owe him. He walks. That's an order, and last time I checked, I'm in charge."

"Fuck!"

She continued to watch Lester as he came down the ladder to the lower deck, went to the swim step at the back of the boat and, fully clothed, dove into the bay. "What the hell? He gonna swim back to shore?"

"He's had it worse," Blattman said.

I wanted to be the first to the gun, but I had to have my hands free. With surprising speed, Winfield was up and across the room, I assume propelled by a mixture of his hate for Sterling and a desire to see his life's mission fulfilled. With some dexterity, he was able to work the clip into the hand grip with his one free hand.

Unlocking hands that are cuffed behind your back is not as easy as you might think. If the chain between the cuffs is short, you have limited mobility, so just getting the key in the right position to match up with the lock can be difficult. Then there's the problem of the lock being on the wrong side of the cuff—facing away from you. In my case, the chain gave me enough slack, but I had to take time to feel which side the lock was on, switch the key to the opposite hand, and then try to match it up. By the time I actually got the key in the lock, Winfield had the gun and was standing over a moaning Sterling.

"You're going to die poor and alone, old man." He raised the gun to Sterling's head and pulled the trigger. Nothing happened. He had forgotten to place a round in the breech by working the slide. He raised the gun, looked at it, and realized what was happening. I got one cuff off, and while Winfield was busy figuring out the gun, I reached up and slid the curtain back. Neither Winfield nor Sterling noticed.

Winfield apparently realized he'd have to remove his hand from the towel/knife to work the slide. I could have told him to turn the gun over, put the slide between his knees and push the grip down, but I was busy making sure Velasquez had a view of the cabin. The moment Winfield's hand came away from the knife, Sterling's torso jumped forward. His arm shot out, grabbed the knife, and yanked it out. Blood spurted out of Winfield's side in a shower. Winfield madly worked the slide, but just as he got it pulled back, his knees buckled and he fainted. He'd be dead in eight seconds.

Sterling had other ideas. The pistol dropped right in front of him. I tried to jump up too fast from the couch and my left leg seared with pain. Sterling fell forward onto the gun. He clicked the slide release, and it snapped back over the barrel. Then he made a huge miscalculation, the kind men used to having power make a lot: He wanted to be standing when he fired, so he reached for the handrail with his free hand and stood. The pain must have been incredible, but he withstood it and righted himself. I was only halfway to him when the gun came up to face me. "I'm glad Mr. Winfield was thoughtful enough to give you the map to my money. Should come in handy. Goodbye, Mr. Sanders."

"Nick, get down," I heard Velasquez say softly in my ear. I fell backward onto the floor, a horrible position normally, except for one thing: Sterling had just begun to adjust his aim when I heard the telltale *tink* of a bullet breaking glass. A black navel appeared in Sterling's tanned forehead. Blood sprayed the wall behind him in the shape of a fan. His eyes registered confusion, then glazed as he fell forward at me. I rolled to my right, and Alan Sterling hit the floor with a thud, well and truly dead.

I crawled over to Winfield and grabbed the towel, trying to staunch the blood flow, a useless effort at this point. But he was still alive, and amazingly, still conscious. "Who was working with you, Winfield? Who was on the other end of the phone? Who moved the money?"

Winfield looked at me, closed his eyes, and exhaled.. "It was never about the money."

Chapter 47

George Town, Grand Cayman; March 2008

I trudged slowly up the stairs to the bridge, showed my FBI identification and gun, and told the captain to re-slip the boat. I finally got a guy who didn't study my creds too closely. He did as he was told. His boss lying in the main cabin oozing blood and brain tissue from his head might have had something to do with it. Before the boat was even secure, I hopped to the dock, where Velasquez and Blattman were both waiting. It hurt, and it took a lot of strength to remain standing.

"Shit, Sanders, you're hit."

"Knife wound, can't worry about it right now." I turned to Blattman. "You have a field office here?"

"Yeah, of course."

"We gotta get to a computer. What happened to Lester?"

"Got away. Dove off the boat and swam. He's probably to shore already," Velasquez explained.

"Got away?" I said, incredulous.

Before Velasquez could blame him, Blattman offered, "I ordered her not to fire. I'll explain later."

We took a cab to the U.S. consulate, where the CIA maintained a field office. All communications were as secure as they could be. I called JJ and filled him in. Someone was going to have to explain two dead bodies on Sterling's boat, but I was going to leave that to the captain. Borenstein was going to have to smooth it over. I also asked him to get Winkler into the office right away. About a half hour later, we had a video link between the conference room in the consulate and our office in New York.

"Sanders, dude, you can't keep doing this. I was moving in on not one but two of the hottest—"

"Chris, focus, OK? I have a flash drive that Winfield gave me with account numbers and routing codes. With the encryption key, we might be able to retrieve all of Sterling's money."

"What? Holy shit, really?"

"Yeah, really. You need to walk me through how to download this to you." After about ten minutes, Chris had the info in New York.

"OK. I'll start tracing funds."

"Not yet. Something's more important right now," I said.

I heard JJ speak and then step before the camera. "More important than billions in ill-gotten drug and arms money? I'd love to hear this."

"Huntington."

"What? Bullshit. Huntington is small time compared to this. He can wait."

"It's not about Huntington per se, it's about who tipped him off. You know how we thought Sterling sold Huntington and a bunch of other guys the encryption software?"

"Yeah."

"We were wrong. Winfield had outside help to move Sterling's money. Sterling couldn't have tipped Huntington off about the raid—he wouldn't have known about it. The same person who sold Huntington the software wanted to tip him off to keep his or her identity from being learned. Winfield had Conrad's cipher key, but he didn't get it from Sterling. Which means neither did Huntington."

"OK, so who?" JJ asked.

"Alex Conrad." I turned to Velasquez. "You were right. I should have listened."

"Well, that doesn't do us much good since she's dead," JJ's voice came through the phone speaker.

"Yeah. About that," I said. "Winkler, can you cue up the video of the Internet café the morning of the Huntington raid? The one in Chevy Chase."

"Hold on. It'll take a sec." I saw him punch keys and a picture window opened in the upper right corner of our screen, cutting off Chris's head. The box was black, then the video came up. Two dudes in gangster garb, a short woman, maybe Asian, and then the girl with the smokin' body and trendy sequined hat.

"Freeze that. Can you zoom in on the hat?" I saw his headless arms punch the keys and the picture zoomed in.

"I'll be damned," Velasquez said. "Same friggin' hat in Conrad's apartment."

"Yup. I didn't remember at the time. Chris, pan down to the left wrist." The picture moved down to a gold watch on the left wrist, identical to the one I made Conrad take off in Bogota. "Same watch, too."

"Let's say that's her. So what? She's dead," said JJ.

"You find her body? She's not dead. Winfield had someone on the outside moving the money. He got off the phone with them just before we got on the boat and told them to take care of something immediately. Winfield and Conrad were working together. Winfield got to kill Sterling, Conrad got the money, but she knew she couldn't keep it unless we already thought she was dead."

"No way. Sanders, you—we all—saw her get shot three times in the chest," JJ protested, but sounding less sure of himself.

"We saw what she wanted us to see. The fact that the FARC guys posing as Colombian Army were late proves they were working on her timeline. She screwed up, and forgot to set her watch ahead."

JJ asked quietly, "How would she even know we were raiding Huntington's place?"

"We told her, indirectly," I answered. "We had the U.S. attorney begin freezing Huntington's accounts the morning of the raid. She had his name and anything to do with his business flagged to report to DHS. She saw our request when DHS was copied on it—"

JJ interrupted. "She could have sent Huntington an encrypted message. Why risk sending one in the clear?"

I answered: "Winkler, check me on this. If I receive an encrypted message, the only way to read it is if I have the software on my computer, right?"

"Yeah. You probably wouldn't even know you got an email unless the software notified you."

"So both the sender's computer and the recipient's computer have to have the program. Huntington didn't have it at home, only at work. She could have sent him encrypted emails all day, but he never would have gotten them until it was too late. She had to make sure he got it at home to give him a chance to get away. When we interviewed him, she passed him a message that told him to keep his mouth shut and he would be OK. I thought she was trying to bluff him." We—I—had been played the entire time. And while it may not have been about the money for Winfield, it was only about the money for Conrad. And now she had it. All of it. "We gotta face it, JJ. The chick faked her death."

Chapter 48

Midtown Manhattan; March 2008

At that point, it simply became a race to see who could snatch the money in the various accounts all over the world faster, us or Conrad. I wasn't pinning too much hope on us, but Winkler was able to quickly locate and retrieve billions into a blocked FBI account typically used for receipt of fines and penalties from financial firms. In fact, using the Winfield-supplied account maps, Chris pulled over $5 billion from various accounts within a few hours.

Maybe I was wrong: maybe Conrad really was dead and Winfield had someone else doing his bidding. We'd have to analyze the data and the accounts, which meant we all had to return to New York, have a meeting with Borenstein, and decide on next steps for identifying and returning money to victims. But before that, I had one additional meeting that could prove my theory about Conrad. And that was one meeting I was looking forward to.

✵ ✵ ✵

FHU, Downtown Manhattan

Jonathan Huntington III sat across from me in the conference room in the federal holding facility in downtown Manhattan. He did not seem surprised to see me. His nonentity of a lawyer sat next to him.

"So, you got a deal for me or what?"

"Or what, Jonnie," I replied.

He looked at me quizzically and said, "I got nothin' to say unless I get a deal."

"OK, I got a deal for you. You do twenty years, and we get all your money back." I pulled out an Excel spreadsheet of banks, account numbers, and balances maintained all over the Caribbean in various shell companies, including the BVI corporation that owned his fractional share in the jet he tried to escape on. I laid it on the table. He and his attorney leaned forward and looked at it. From what we could tell, he had spent about half of his clients' money, but there was a good $300 million left. He didn't move for a second or two, then swallowed. His face reddened.

"That bitch!" he screamed, slamming his manacled fists on the table. "That fuckin' bitch! She gave you the passwords!" A statement, not a question.

"Sort of," I said. "The woman you're describing, the one you bought the encryption software from, did you ever see her, I mean, meet in person?"

"No, at least I don't think so. She mighta been that broad you brought with you the last time. At least I got that impression from what she said to me." Yeah, so did I, only too late, I wanted to say.

"Tell you what, Jon. You tell me everything about how you were first contacted about the software, how you paid for it, who you paid, and what contact you had, and I'll see what we can do about lying to the judge and telling him you've been very cooperative with us."

His attorney leaned over and talked in his ear, and this time Jonathan Huntington III listened. When the attorney leaned back, Huntington took a breath, then began:

"I got a phone call from a gal describing herself as a security consultant for a Cayman bank. She said she was updating the bank's system with some new, unbreakable software that would make sure no one, not even the U.S. government, could ever get a peek at the accounts on the bank's books. Said she worked for a company called Cooper Cyber Security, CCS. Because of what she did, she had access to all of the bank's records, and she was able to identify private parties she thought might also be interested in using the software in their own business, and would I like to buy it. At first, it sounded like a bullshit sales call, but when I told her I wasn't interested, she gave me a couple of dates and amounts of transfers I made to the bank for client investments."

"Yeah, 'investments'," I said.

"Hey, you wanna hear it or what?" I nodded. "Then she says that she thinks the U.S. authorities would be interested in seeing this information, which she noticed wasn't reported to the IRS. So I says, 'How the hell do you know that?' and she says she's got someone over at the service who she checked with. And she also tells me that for an extra fee, she can notify me if I'm being investigated by the SEC, FINRA, the FBI, whatever."

In fact, Conrad probably didn't have a friend over at the IRS or anywhere else. What she did have was a view of everything Borenstein's office was copied on from many of these agencies, including reported offshore accounts.

"I told her I didn't believe her—it was bullshit, too good to be true, yada yada. She said she would let me try it out for three months free, and if I wanted to continue, after that I would pay or it would be shut down."

"How would you know whether it worked or not?"

"I got a buddy of mine who's an Internet security consultant,"—he meant a hacker—"and I had him try to hack my system. He could see anything not covered by the software. You know, Outlook contacts, non-secure email, shit like that. But he couldn't hack my banking transactions. I had him try it four times over a few months, and each time he couldn't get into it. So I bought it."

"How did it get onto your system?"

"She overnighted me the disc. When I bought the full program, she overnighted me a replacement. I just dropped it in and it loaded by itself. I created my own password."

"How much?"

"What, for the program? Ten mil. Wire transferred to a CCS account in Antigua."

"And the extras? The ongoing monitoring?"

"$100,000 a month. And that almost paid off in spades if you hadn't been handy with the wrench."

"How'd you pay that? CCS as well?"

"Nah, that went to some other LLC, like in BVI or something. I think the name was TCP. I never learned what that stood for."

I stood up. "OK, we'll probably have more questions for you. By the way, the remaining clients' funds are being held in an FBI account until after your trial. Might go better for you if you saved everyone the time and pled out and relinquished your claims to the money."

"What, you a lawyer now too?" he sneered.

"Yes, I am. See you, Jon."

"You gonna tell the judge, right?"

"Yeah, I'll tell the judge. Just like I promised." I turned again to the door, stopped, and looked back at Jonathan Huntington III. "You know what surprises me a little, Jon?"

"No, agent-man. What surprises you?"

"Not once did you think about trying to make a deal for your wife and kid. You know, make sure they get to keep a little to live on, send the boy to college. It never even occurred to you, did it?"

Huntington said nothing, just grunted derisively. I turned and walked out. Actually, it didn't surprise me at all.

☆ ☆ ☆

Midtown Manhattan

"So whadda we got?" I asked Winkler as I walked back into the conference room. Chris was at the laptop, punching keys. Velasquez was huddled at the other end of the table with JJ and Engler, going over reams of paper.

"Over five billion from DP accounts all over the world, mostly in cash, securities, and commodities like gold and silver," Chris responded.

A new voice from behind me said, "The Costa Rican government wants to know what the hell's going on, why a bunch of money has left a couple of their banks, and why the U.S. government is laying claim to luxury properties in their country." It was Borenstein, walking into the room.

JJ stood. "Al," he said. Borenstein nodded.

"Nice job, all of you. This is actually going to create quite a diplomatic headache for many years. We have to sort out who has claims to what. And then there's the problem of actually proving de Plata is Alan Sterling." That was ironic, since it was some corrupt official in the Costa Rican government who supplied Sterling with a (false) death certificate so that he could become Alejandro de Plata. They knew damn well who he was. "But the Caymanis are cooperating with the retrieval and autopsy. They've decided to send the body to our medical examiners for the autopsy."

"Decided?" I asked, while simultaneously wondering if the term "Caymanis" was correct.

Borenstein smiled. "We didn't give them much choice. But great job. We have much more than we expected to retrieve. We've shut down the arms network, and Pinchao has been able to seriously hobble the FARC while rescuing high-value hostages. On top of that, drug flow from Colombia should slow significantly. The president is very pleased. How's the leg?" Borenstein asked me.

Aw, I didn't know you cared, Al. "Doc says I'll be all right. Thanks for asking."

"Of course, Agent Sanders. Well, I know you'll update me on the retrieval process, and I appreciate you doing the heavy lifting on the analysis." He turned to leave.

"Aren't you forgetting something?" I asked.

"Am I?" he turned back.

"Conrad. She's still out there. She's got an unbreakable encryption code and she can probably hack any bank she wants. Don't we have to do something about her?"

"First, while I appreciate your efforts, I have to say I find your theory far-fetched. There's no proof she's alive."

"No proof she's dead, either. Pinchao's forensic team said there's no physical evidence she was killed."

"Yes, just a video showing her death and your sworn testimony, Agent Sanders."

I shook my head. It was in Borenstein's best interest to assert Conrad died in the line of duty. He wouldn't take any blame for a rogue agent, and the operation was successful, so he would get all the credit for coming up with a plan that was originally Conrad's. This guy was going to turn lemons into lemonade, but that was how operators like Borenstein survived: they took no blame and got all the credit.

He continued, "Second, assuming you're right, what can we do? Where is she? Can we extradite her?"

He was right about that. It was time to dig in, locate her, give her jacket to every friendly law enforcement agency around the world, and hope she so much as breathed the air of an extradition treaty country.

We were in the office for weeks before we could account for most of the Sterling and Huntington money. More important was what we couldn't account for.

"I count about forty million missing, and not spent by these guys," Chris concluded.

"Ten each for the software, a few more million for the ongoing monitoring of our activities. Some lost to bank fees, transfer fees, bribery, you can get to forty mil pretty quick," I responded.

"You really think she only kept forty million for herself, when she could have siphoned off billions?" Velasquez asked.

"No, I guess not," I considered. "But what we're not seeing is money from other criminals she might have sold it to. There are guys out there right now using the software."

"Maybe," Chris said. "But here's what I don't get. She's gotta be communicating with them, right? So where are those emails and phone calls. They'd be encrypted and flagged. Why can't we see them?"

I thought about it. "Different users get different access rights," I said. Conrad said something similar. "There isn't just one backdoor key. We have *a* key, one that lets us see what Conrad's willing to let us see. The ones we can't decrypt are still sitting on Echelon servers. Doesn't change the fact a bunch of felons have this software."

"And no way to trace them," Chris said.

"Let's think about that. Conrad found Huntington by identifying U.S. sourced accounts and cross-referencing them with the FBAR index. Huntington's account was large, and no FBAR had been filed for years. So she assumed he was a swindler and contacted him to sell him the software. We can use that same system to identify who she *might* have sold it to, right?"

"Yeah, but we'd need to have access to the banks' records, and the FBAR index," Chris said.

"We can get the index. And the banks should be extremely cooperative once we explain that they've been assisting in the laundering of drug and arms money."

"OK," JJ said, "I'll get the index. And I'll call State to see if they can help with the bank. Regroup tomorrow."

Velasquez and I found ourselves in Mel's Corner Tap again. We took it easier, sticking with beer, no shots. "So how 'bout you tell me what a great agent I am, Lisa?"

"Did you just call me Lisa?"

"That's your name, isn't it?"

"Yeah, you just don't use it unless a bomb exploded or something."

"I'm trying to expand the use of first names in the unit."

"Yeah? Well, don't. I like last names, keeps it impersonal."

"Maybe I want to get personal."

"Maybe I'm married."

"Shit, really?"

"No," she said, laughing, "just screwing with you. You shoulda seen the look on your face. A boy who lost his puppy. How about we figure out how to handle your girlfriend—"

"Ex-girlfriend."

"Your ex-girlfriend before we go thinking about other things, OK?"

"I got that one figured out," I told her.

"Well, since you want to get personal, how about you share it with me?"

"Probably better you don't know. Gotta go, gotta meet a guy."

"What? We just got here! I thought you wanted to talk about ... stuff."

"I did," I said, throwing twenty bucks on the table. "I wanted to thank you for saving my life. Thanks. I'd thank you more but I gotta meet this guy. Let's do it again tomorrow."

"Can't, I got my kid tomorrow."

"You got a kid?"

"No, just screwing with you."

☆ ☆ ☆

"I don't know, Sanders. You sure you want to go down this road?" Paul Blattman asked me.

"She can hack any bank, anytime she wants. She can sell her software to a hundred con men," I answered.

"You sure that's what this is about?" I didn't respond, just looked at my beer. He continued, "You got played. It happens. Shit, in my business it happens all the time." I remained silent. "We don't even know if we can locate either of them."

"I'll find her. You find your guy. Can you arrange it?"

"Shit, kid, I can 'arrange' almost anything. You better be sure this is what you want."

"I'm sure."

"I'll let you know if I contact him."

"Good." I got up. "Thanks for coming up from Washington. And the beer."

"Hey! You sticking me with the bill?" I heard him call back.

☆ ☆ ☆

Paul Blattman looked at Sanders' barely touched beer across the table, picked it up, and poured it into his. He hadn't paid a tab in twenty years. If he was going to shell out for this one, he wasn't going to waste anything.

☆ ☆ ☆

By midday the next day, we had a list of twelve other Cayman accounts, all from fly-by-night U.S. brokers or money managers, all employing the Conrad encryption software. JJ's unit would be working overtime for months investigating these guys. For the time being, our goal was to determine how much money Conrad had been paid, and where that money had subsequently gone. The first part was easy; the second, not so much.

Conrad had funneled about $150 million from all the brokers, including Huntington and Sterling. But the payments were all to different entities. And the entities, all BVI LLCs, were initials only: CCS, TCP, RSC, SCS, and so on.

"JJ, can we access BVI records to see the articles of incorporation for these entities?"

"I'll talk to State."

A few hours later, we received a call from a very helpful individual in the British Virgin Islands who had apparently been told to help us in any way she could. This was the inherent problem with Americans doing business offshore: if you stayed below the radar, you could be assured of privacy; but if your case was elevated and enough political pressure was brought to bear, all the much-touted banking secrecy went out the window. The offshore government would simply deny they ever assisted in the investigation, and there was no record that they did. But in the end, they gave us the information we wanted if we wanted it badly enough.

"OK, let's start with CCS, Limited."

Some keys tapped in the background, and the young lady's British-accented voice came back. "That is Cooper Cyber Security Limited. A local trust company is listed as the director." I was afraid of that. That meant we'd have to dig further.

"RSC, Limited?"

"That is the acronym of Rich Security Consultants, with the same trust company listed as the director."

"SCS?"

"That is an abbreviation for Sterling Consulting Services, Limited."

"I'm beginning to see a pattern here. Is TCP something like Tomasi Cyber Protection?"

More key tapping. "That's correct, same trust company as director."

I muted the phone and shook my head. "Damn this chick likes to rub it in."

"I don't get it," Velasquez said.

"They're all criminals who got away with it," JJ explained. "DB Cooper, Marc Rich, Alan Sterling. The last one, Rollo Tomasi, is fictional, from *LA Confidential*, Conrad's favorite movie."

"She knew we'd find out, right? She's just rubbing salt in the wounds?" Velasquez asked.

"Yeah. A lot of salt."

Chapter 49

St. John's, Aruba; August 2008.

"Daylight savings is a bitch, isn't it?"

The girl in the chaise lounge on the beach looked up, and I couldn't tell if there was any surprise in her eyes, since she had a pair of gigantic fashion sunglasses on. There was a table next to the lounge on which sat some fruity drink with an umbrella in it. It was only missing the little plastic monkey hanging off the edge. The woman wore a two-piece bathing suit that accentuated perfectly shaped and muscled thighs, arms, and shoulders, and revealed a flat stomach. I noted her legs and feet showed no signs of burn injury.

"Hi, Sanders. How are you?" Alexandra Conrad slid her sunglasses to the top of her head, closed her book after dog-earing the page and looked me up and down. "You're a little overdressed, aren't you?" I was wearing jeans, flip-flops, and a T-shirt that read "My ex-girlfriend is dead". OK, I made that last part up. It said "Antigua, the beach is just the beginning." It was the cheapest thing in the hotel gift shop at the last island I had visited.

"Us feds always overdress for this shit." A waiter, wearing a Hawaiian shirt, shorts, and no shoes, came by to ask if she wanted another drink.

"None for me. You want one, Sanders?"

"I never turn down a free beer. I assume you're buying."

"Please get him the local brew," she said, waving him away. He scurried back to the edge of the sand where a beachside bar sat. "How'd you find me?"

"Gotta say, you're pretty good about staying away from extradition treaty countries. Your BVI trust company was helpful. It wasn't easy, but eventually following the money yields results, no matter how many fake identities you use."

"You definitely were one of the smarter ones."

"Not that smart. I never would have known you faked your death if the FARC guys hadn't been late. But they were operating on your schedule, right? You forgot to turn your watch forward when we got to Colombia? Pinchao said 8:30, and you called them the next morning and told them, 'Pick us up in an hour.' They were just carrying out your orders?"

"Yeah. I couldn't figure out how you knew that the guys in the van were fake. It wasn't until later that day that I realized my watch was off. Pretty stupid for a math genius, huh?"

"It's always the little things. You tipped off Huntington?"

"Had to," she said after taking a sip of her drink. "Couldn't risk you guys getting the encryption software early. Borenstein would have known the leak was in his office, not yours. When he didn't escape, I was pretty worried, but I followed up and heard he was angling for a deal he was never gonna get. I just reemphasized his need to keep quiet in our meeting. Seemed to work. You had to get it at some point. Otherwise, you couldn't get the money back once Winfield killed Sterling."

"That's what I don't get. How'd you hook up with Winfield?"

"We sort of ... found each other. I interviewed him when we first made this connection between de Plata and the FARC, since we knew a lot of the money was coming from ASBT. I wanted to know why so much money was invested with DP Partners. We met several times, and I told him I had an idea of how to find where DP Partners was really investing the money. Eventually, he confided in me and I in him, and our plans just … merged. He was the one who suggested I should get paid for my work on the side. I don't know how he knew I'd go for it. He was good at reading people, I guess."

"And why not, right? It was your program, your software, right?" I asked.

"My *idea*, Sanders, as much as Borenstein will take credit for it. My idea to trap the FARC. I was just going to siphon a few bucks off the top of their accounts. No one would know. But my conversation with Winfield gave me the idea of actually selling the program on the side. That's the money I'd keep, and you guys got to take back everything else. I'm not greedy, Sanders."

"You sure a hundred and fifty million is enough to live on? You know, keep you in the style to which you are accustomed? Wash away the guilt of getting five innocent people at the deli killed?"

"That's bullshit!" she hissed, spit coming off her bottom lip, then lowered her voice when others looked over. "I had no idea they were going to kill Lazeris like that. All I did was tell them Lazeris was going to talk. For God's sake, I thought they'd just shoot him or something. One less corrupt lawyer in the world. Who'd care?"

"I don't get it. Why tip them off to the meeting? It could only help you to let them know after the fact that Lazeris had spilled the beans, right?"

"How does that help? Lazeris didn't know who he was dealing with. It would have taken you months to follow that money trail while Lazeris lawyered up and cut himself a deal. We needed a catalyst. Something to happen right then to get de Plata nervous and off the dime. And for de Plata to do something that would get Borenstein to push our timeline forward. You FBI guys might have found me out before Winfield and I got the chance to do our thing."

"Your beer, sir." The waiter walked up and handed it to me. I tipped him a buck. "Thanks," I said and took a drink as he walked away.

"You should thank me, Sanders. I made sure you survived the warehouse in Bogota. It was part of the deal I made with the FARC, even if they did think it was de Plata asking for it."

"Bad deal. I almost didn't make it. And you got two Colombian soldiers killed there."

"They didn't tell me what they were going to do. They violated the instructions I gave them. You're also forgetting my software allowed Pinchao to shut down the FARC and probably saved thousands of Colombian lives."

"You weren't doing me any favors, though, right? You needed me. I was your messenger. You needed me to sell the fact that you were dead." She said nothing. "I'd ask you why, but I already know."

"Yeah, you do, don't you, Nick? You always know, right?" She put her glasses back on and turned her attention to her book. "I did like you, Sanders. It was fun. But, like you say, it's always about the money." The meeting was over.

"Thanks for the beer." I turned and walked away. As I passed through the lobby of the hotel, I retrieved a single-use cell phone from my pocket. I had received it via private messenger with a note to hit the redial button one time, and one time only, when I had located Conrad. I debated whether to press the button. I debated for about three seconds. I heard the phone ring two times and someone picked up.

"You got her?"

"Grand Hotel of St. John under the name Nicole Leeson. Don't know how long she'll be here."

"Doesn't she know Nick Leeson got caught?" Lester's voice said. "You can dispose of the phone. It won't work anymore."

"How soon—" *CLICK.*

I dropped the phone in a trash can on the street outside the hotel.

The hotel Conrad had chosen was the nicest in Aruba, of course. Despite the fact that my business was booming, I couldn't afford it. It was about a twenty-minute walk from my hotel. I finished my beer about five minutes in and soaked up the sun the rest of the way. I strode up to my room and looked at the hammock on the deck.

"H&K nine mil or Sig .40?" I asked.

Velasquez put her book down and looked up at me. She looked great in a bikini. "What, this distance? .40 all the way."

"You don't know shit about handguns, do you?" I said. "You shoot that, the gun would kick up, the bullet would miss, pass through the wall and kill the two honeymooners next door."

"You're so full of crap, Sanders."

"You know, since we're on vacation together, you think you can call me Nick?"

"I dunno, I'll try it out. Later. You see your girlfriend?"

"Ex. Ex-girlfriend. Yeah. She's untouchable and knows it."

"I thought you had that figured out?"

"I do." She stared at me. I said nothing. She didn't ask. "You got room in there for two?"

Velasquez slid over an inch or two and I eased into the hammock.

"Push us off, will ya?" she asked. I reached down and gently pushed against the ground. The hammock swayed right, then left. When it swung back right again, Velasquez's hand came up from the edge, holding a beer bottle by its long neck between her graceful fingers. She passed it to me. I thought as I took a sip: this could get complicated.

Epilogue

St. John's, Aruba; August 2008

"Your drink, Ms. Leeson."

"Thank you," Alex said to the waiter.

"Yes, ma'am. This one is compliments of the gentleman at the bar."

Conrad looked over her shoulder. She saw a man with wavy, sandy brown hair, well-built, wearing board shorts, flip-flops and a tank top that revealed a muscle-rippled physique. His age was tough to determine, but she thought he could have been thirty. He lifted his drink to her and winked. She took the fruity beverage with the sugared rim, gave him a toast back, mouthed "thank you" and took a sip. Mmmm. That was good. She took several more sips.

John Lester turned his stool back toward the bar and rolled up the empty baggie of "sugar" he had brought. He had been getting to know the bartender all morning, and when he suggested he wanted to make the drink for the pretty girl himself, the guy let him have the run of the bar. Lester left a hundred-dollar tip and walked back to the hotel.

✳ ✳ ✳

Tri-State Area

About a month after the death of Alejandro de Plata, six families, including Ed Lazeris's parents, received letters explaining that a charitable fund had been established in the Cook Islands by anonymous donors who had heard of the loss of their loved ones in the Fifty-fourth Street deli bombing. The letters explained that each family was to receive ten million dollars, but that the money would be held in trust and paid in quarterly installments of $50,000, until the funds ran out. If funds remained after the immediate family passed away, payments would continue for their heirs.

✳ ✳ ✳

Bern, Switzerland

John Lester sat in a cybercafe, checking on the payments to the Fifty-fourth Street victims' families. He didn't really believe that he could buy off Blattman, the agency, the FBI, or even these people with his payments, especially considering he was using the $60 million payment of de Plata's stolen money to do it. Blattman was obligated to come after him, despite the fact that Paul had asked him for the favor for Sanders.

There was no absolution to be had, absent turning himself in and facing the death penalty. Since his former affiliation with the CIA would obviously come out in a public venue, there would be no trial, just a bullet in the back of the head in a cornfield somewhere. So turning himself in was something John Lester would not do. He would run. He would change identities. He would keep moving. Blattman had given him a head start in exchange for the Conrad thing. He understood that. But it was only a head start. Eventually, they would find him. They always did.

Washington, D.C.

The materials used in a CIA or NSA briefing of the president, even the daily ones, were required to be copied to DHS. Paul Blattman had prepared the paperwork for Deputy Director of Operations Al Lopez's briefing with the president. Blattman assured him the materials would be routed "as appropriate." The deputy director smiled, shut the folder, and placed it in his safe to be retrieved for the briefing.

The briefing detailed the espionage of Alexandra Conrad, and the fact that it was believed she had been assassinated by FARC operatives in the Caribbean in retaliation for her betrayal. Exactly how the FARC rebels would know Alexandra Conrad even existed, much less locate her, was never explained, and the president didn't ask.

Adolph Borenstein was asked to retire from his post as Director of Homeland Security. He was, however, later awarded the Presidential Medal of Freedom in recognition of his long history of service to his country.

New York, New York

Two weeks after the events in Cayman, Nick Sanders received an email from a cybercafe in Bermuda. The missive suggested he check out an address in Harlem, and also asked how his leg was doing. Sanders forwarded it to JJ, who sent a team to the address. The agents discovered the largest illegal arms cache on U.S. soil in the bureau's history.

✡ ✡ ✡

Grand Cayman

The body of Jeremy Winfield was flown back to the United States at the expense of ASBT, and a funeral was held attended by hundreds, including the mayor of New York, both U.S. senators from the state of New York, and several well-dressed but tired (and in one case, injured) individuals whom some employees recognized as FBI agents who had been to the bank a couple of times.

The body of Alejandro de Plata was returned to Costa Rica after the FBI's lab had finished its autopsy and confirmed by DNA that de Plata was in fact Sterling. No one claimed the body. Sterling's corpse languished in the San Jose coroner's storage facility for months until the government relented and paid for the burial in a municipal cemetery. No service was held.

Afterword

In the spring of 2008, the Colombian Armed Forces raided a FARC camp in Ecuador, killing leader Raul Reyes and revealing a treasure trove of intelligence that suggested both tacit and active support of the terrorist group from the governments of Venezuela and Ecuador. Also that spring, numerous hostages were freed, including long-time French-Colombian hostage Ingrid Betancourt (freed in a raid by Colombian forces and U.S. military advisers) and Clara Rojas (who had given birth to a son while imprisoned by the FARC). Manuel Marulanda Velez died of a heart attack in March 2008. This novel was a result of the author's imagination running rampant over how the sudden successes against this terrorist group occurred. The truth is (as usual) more mundane than the resulting tale, but uplifting: While they were assisted by U.S. military aid and advisers, the Colombian people, leadership, and military deserve all the credit for their courage and perseverance in fighting back against the terror into which their country had been plunged for over twenty years.

About the Author

Paul Stam is an attorney and tax consultant. He works for a large Wall Street financial services firm. *The Trust Company* draws on his experience in law and banking. He lives in Southern California with his wife and three children.

Made in the USA
San Bernardino, CA
20 February 2014